**Geri Krotow** ... vy veteran. She ... ces abroad, inclu... Her family has fi... nia but Geri sti... en. An award-winning author, Geri writes ... lver Valley PD for Mills & Boon Heroes. Visit her website: gerikrotow.com

**Nicole Helm** writes down-to-earth contemporary romance and fast-paced romantic suspense. She lives with her husband and two sons in Missouri. Visit her website: nicolehelm.com

**Danica Winters** is a bestselling author who has won multiple awards for writing books that grip readers with their ability to drive emotion through suspense and occasionally a touch of magic. When she's not working, she can be found in the wilds of Montana testing her patience while she tries to hone her skills at various crafts (quilting, pottery, and painting are not her areas of expertise). She always believes the cup is neither half full nor half empty, but it better be filled with wine.

# One Night...

June 2022
**to Forever**

December 2022
**to Seduction**

July 2022
**to Scandal**

January 2023
**for Business**

August 2022
**to Marriage**

February 2023
**of Convenience**

September 2022
**for Revenge**

March 2023
**to Safety**

# One Night...
# to Safety

**GERI KROTOW**

**NICOLE HELM**

**DANICA WINTERS**

**MILLS & BOON**

First Published in Great Britain 2023
By Mills & Boon, an imprint of HarperCollins*Publishers,* Ltd
1 London Bridge Street, London, SE1 9GF

www.harpercollins.co.uk

HarperCollins*Publishers*
Macken House, 39/40 Mayor Street Upper,
Dublin 1, D01 C9W8, Ireland

ONE NIGHT...TO SAFETY © 2023 Harlequin Enterprises ULC.

*The Pregnant Colton Witness* © 2018 Harlequin Enterprises ULC.
*Wyoming Cowboy Sniper* © 2019 Nicole Helm
*Protective Operation* © 2020 Danica Winters

Special thanks and acknowledgement are given to Geri Krotow for her contribution to *The Coltons of Red Ridge* series.

ISBN: 978-0-263-31872-2

Printed and Bound in Spain using 100% Renewable electricity at CPI Black Print, Barcelona

# THE PREGNANT
# COLTON WITNESS

## GERI KROTOW

For Ellen – it's been a joy watching you turn into the beautiful young woman you are.

# *Chapter 1*

The Red Ridge, South Dakota, autumn morning sky streaked pink and violet across Black Hills Lake. Dr. Patience Colton, DVM, took a moment to soak it all in. Nestled in the northwestern part of the state, Red Ridge—and more specifically, the town's K9 clinic—were home to her. The only place her heart ever found peace. She committed the view of the mountains to memory, knowing there stood a good chance she'd never look at it, or anything, the same way again. It all depended upon the results of the simple test kit in the Red Ridge Drugstore bag that she clutched in her left hand.

No one had seen her yet; none of the staff knew she was already at the K9 clinic, ready for another day of veterinary medicine. She could run—but to where? Her townhome? Her cabin in the mountains? Another state, where her veterinary license wouldn't be valid? If the test proved positive, running wasn't going to change it or the overwhelming implications. Running away might be an option for another person, but not her. Patience never backed down from a challenge, and what might be her toughest yet was no exception.

She sucked in the crisp mountain air before she entered the building, hoping for a few minutes to herself to figure out if the signals from her body weren't random.

Fifteen minutes later, she wondered if maybe running away wasn't such a bad idea.

"No. Freaking. Way." Patience's hands shook as she spoke under her breath, staring at the test strip she'd used only minutes earlier to determine if she had skipped a period again for any reason other than stress. She stood in the restroom of the Red Ridge County K9 Clinic, *her* clinic, and struggled to get a grip. Locked in the staff bathroom, the weight of how her life was changing triggered a gush of tears. It had been a mistake to do this at work.

She couldn't be caught like this—crying over a pregnancy test result. "Calm down." She gave herself the same advice she wished she could give her K9 patients when they were stressed.

It hadn't been uncommon for her to miss one or two cycles while in veterinary school and also working extra hours at a part-time job to help pay for her expenses. And the last few months had been incredibly stressful, not just for her but for all of Red Ridge. The modestly sized town was in the midst of a criminal crisis. Patience worked closely with the Red Ridge Police Department, as well as the K9 training center, the latter of which housed the clinic. So it was impossible to not be aware of the stress placed on the RRPD over the local serial killer, dubbed the Groom Killer. Red Ridge had erupted into all-out panic after the fifth and most recent groom-to-be had been murdered. With a population of thirty-five thousand, it made for a lot of fear in the air.

She grabbed ahold of the sink counter, her fingers crushing the cardboard box that she'd pulled the test kit from. It had felt odd sneaking into the local drugstore and purchasing three magazines, a candy bar and a ginger ale along with the test, as if the cashier wouldn't notice the box. As if she probably hadn't told all of Red Ridge by now that Dr. Patience Colton, DVM, could be knocked up. That was the problem with being an heiress to the richest family in a small town in South Dakota. Everyone knew your business.

As a K9 veterinarian, she prided herself on her steady hands and the ability to remain calm and focused under pressure. But her cool demeanor, practiced almost since birth, had shattered. All for one night of incredible sex with the sexiest bachelor in town.

Nash Maddox. They'd seen each other plenty since their sexual healing rendezvous three months ago. Nash was a K9 police handler on the RRPD and they often trained the dogs together. The heat that had passed between them a few months ago was still there whenever their eyes met, and she'd been tempted to ask him if he'd consider breaking their promise that their night together be a one-time-only event. But just as she'd get her nerve up, another crisis would hit the community and they had to save lives. Nash and his K9 partner, Greta, saved humans, while Patience saved dogs and other animals.

Maybe assigning blame for her predicament would help her anxiety. She tried to stir up some animosity toward the man who'd unwittingly gotten her pregnant, but couldn't. They'd used protection, but it obviously wasn't 100 percent. Nash wasn't only the sexiest man she'd met in forever, but he was the consummate gentleman. He'd even agreed with her that their affair would be short-lived, with no emotional strings attached.

A sharp rap on the restroom door snapped her out of her misery.

"Dr. Colton? Are you there? We have an emergency surgery en route. Gunshot wound. Canine, civilian." As though through her favorite jar of apple jelly, Patience heard her veterinary assistant's voice, but couldn't shake off the shock of finding out she was pregnant.

Pregnant with Nash Maddox's baby. Would it look like him? The tall, muscular blond officer had the most beautiful hazel eyes. They'd be perfect whether the baby was a boy or girl. Whether they had Nash's sandy hair or her own brunette.

More rapping, this time louder. "Patience?"

"I'll be right out, Grace."

As much as it was a total shock, she felt she needed to mark the occasion somehow. Patience quickly washed her hands and then pulled her phone out of her pocket. She made a note of the date and time, and was startled by the sudden flash of her future that her mind conjured up. Telling her child exactly when she'd found out he or she was on the way into the world, and how she'd felt about it.

It was at this moment that she knew she was keeping the baby. Nash had a lot of his own family issues and she was certain having another child on top of raising his four orphaned half siblings wasn't part of his plan. No matter. This was her life, and now it was going to have to revolve around a baby.

Could she do this?

The sound of doors slamming open, shouts of the arrival team, forced her back to the present. She sought her eyes in the mirror, used to saying a positive affirmation before jumping into a tough case. All she saw reflected back at her was the unanswerable question. Would she be able to be a better parent than either of hers had?

Nash Maddox groaned at the sight of the large kitchen that was the heart of the home he'd inherited when his parents had been tragically killed in an auto accident five years ago. Drips of maple syrup dotted the table and floor, pancake mix powdered the countertops, and four dirty, sticky dishes were piled in the sink. He'd been so busy getting the kids out of the house in time to catch the school bus that he'd neglected to make sure they each picked up after themselves. He had to be at work in fifteen minutes, which gave him eight minutes to straighten up. Usually Paige, the oldest at seventeen and a busy high school senior, corralled her siblings into cleaning up. Her studies and social schedule were preoccupying her again.

"Why didn't you tell me they'd made such a mess?" He spoke to his K9 partner, Greta, a Newfoundland. Nash knelt to meet her eyes and scratched under her chin, ignoring the profuse drool that spilled out of her wobbly cheeks and pooled onto the already sticky floor. "You are such a good girl, Greta. We'll be at work soon, I promise." He patted her head and she flopped her tail on the ground, her wags loud and slow. Greta was the epitome of a family dog at home, but a fierce K9 on the job. In so many ways, she'd been his anchor these last challenging years.

Until a spectacular night with the K9 clinic veterinarian, Patience Colton. He'd not thought it possible for a woman to soak into his psyche after only one evening, but Patience had. Whenever he found his anxiety rising due to something as simple as the kids messing up the kitchen, or more serious reasons, like trying to find and apprehend the Groom Killer, his mind went back to that night like a homing pigeon.

He closed the sink drain and added liquid soap to the running water, reminding himself for the fifth time in as many days that he had to call the repairman. He didn't have time to be hand-washing his half siblings' endless dishes. They had a chore list that they were actually pretty good at following, but his rule was "academics first," and with the heavy backpacks that came home, the dishes seemed to pile on. Nash was accomplished at many things, but fixing a cranky dishwasher wasn't one of them.

As the bubbles grew into a frothy mound, his mind flashed to the soft, very sexy rounds of Patience's breasts. It hadn't been the smartest thing he'd done, giving in to his needs, but he had no regrets over their one-night stand almost three months ago. A surge of protectiveness toward that night—no, toward Patience— blindsided him. It wasn't fair to call it a one-night stand. It had been more. Or maybe he'd misinterpreted the obvious pleasure she'd enjoyed at his hands as more than the sexual release they'd shared.

He wasn't dating anyone regularly, how could he with four half siblings to take care of? But that night with Patience had reminded him that he needed some caretaking himself. And while both he and Patience had agreed that one night was all their lives allowed, both for time and family reasons, maybe they shouldn't have been so hasty in their agreement. He sure wouldn't mind seeing her again.

A beautiful woman like Patience was probably already involved with someone else. Although she'd said she wasn't, and that she had no plans to date anyone. She needed her personal life to remain simple, she'd said, because of the heavy demands being the K9 vet and community vet in general made on her. Didn't they all have demanding jobs, though, in Red Ridge? The small mining town was incredibly productive for its size, and required nearly every citizen to do their part to make the municipality thrive. Besides, if Patience was anything like him, no matter how busy life got there were those moments of realizing you were missing something… Yeah, maybe he'd ask her out again. Of course, that could lead to more than he was able to handle, but he wanted to handle Patience—

The house phone rang and he answered, cradling the receiver between his jaw and shoulder. "Maddox."

"Nash, it's dispatch." He recognized Shelly Langston's voice. She worked dispatch for Red Ridge County since he'd been on the force, and probably ten years before that. Shelly filled in whenever Frank Lanelli, the senior dispatcher, was off.

"What do you have, Shelly?"

"We've got a child who fell off a bike on the way to school, over the highway shoulder on Route 10. They want Greta on the scene."

"We're on our way."

He hung up and motioned for Greta, but she was one step ahead of him, at the door with her leash in her mouth.

"Good girl. We've got today's first job."

They worked as one, leaving the house, getting into the police K9 vehicle, arriving on scene and helping to determine if the child had fallen by accident or if a vehicle had forced them off the road. Greta used her expert sniffer to relay information and Nash translated to the officers and first responders. Immediately after they'd wrapped it up, they were called to a home burglary downtown, and then later, to the site of an arson. Before their shift finished, Nash and Greta had participated in no fewer than eight cases, from shoplifting to drug dealing to escorting a lost memory-care patient back to his care facility.

No matter how long the day grew, as tiring as the work was, thoughts of a brilliant evening with the lovely

Patience Colton never left him. Maybe he'd scrape up the nerve to call her. In an unofficial capacity, of course.

Patience looked at her staff, all gathered in the break room. Reception was closed after normal clinic hours, and they'd endured an especially long day of surgeries and urgent calls.

"That's it for today, folks. Unless we have another emergency call, I want everyone going home and getting a good meal and rest. This weekend could end up being just as taxing." She referred not just to the fact that the K9 unit was often busiest on weekends due to a surge in criminal activity, but the fact that weekends were when weddings happened. Most couples had quietly postponed their weddings once it was a clear a killer was targeting grooms, but everyone was on edge, worried that the Groom Killer could strike again at any moment. There were always couples who wouldn't let anything stop them from their big day.

"Do you think that the animals are trying to tell us something, Doc?" Pauline, the newest vet tech, didn't ask the question with cynicism. She was new and trying to absorb all she could about how the facility worked. The staff had discussed more than once the apparent connection between animal distress and human anxiety. Animals were empathic, and Red Ridge's pets had to be feeling the edginess of their owners these last months. It'd be abnormal to not be worried about the serial killer.

"It doesn't matter what I believe. It's fact that they seem to have an edge on us when it comes to predicting bad behavior, and to a T each patient has demonstrated the signs of stress brought on by a perceived threat. Our resident parrot has been squawking twice as much, the cats have been mewling no matter their pain level, and the dogs have whimpered at random times. While any of that could be coincidence, as we've had a high number of surgeries this week, I'm inclined to trust experience. Go home and get some rest—you could be called back within hours. Let's all pitch in and get Surgery cleaned up. I don't want anyone tackling that alone—we've made a mess!" Her staff laughed and she used the energy to buoy her through the next thirty minutes of a thorough scrubbing down of their operating room.

It was a mess from the day's routine spaying and neutering surgeries, and the unexpected gunshot wound. She'd spent two hours picking out birdshot pellets from a sweet labradoodle's right haunch. These were all in addition to the regular duties she had as the K9 veterinarian. The RRPD encouraged her clinic to help the community whenever possible. But her first duty was always K9.

Not to mention the personal connection. The Red Ridge K9 unit, training center and clinic were dedicated to the memory of Patience's mother, who'd died in childbirth. Her father, Fenwick Colton, lived up to his reputation as a wealthy, self-serving ass most of the time. But when it came to her mom's legacy and the K9 facility, Fenwick didn't waver. Until recently, when he'd threatened to shut down funding because of Colton Energy's dwindling bankroll.

Her father had put his family through its paces, fathering five children by three different wives. Her older half sister, Layla, was the only one from Fenwick's first marriage, while Patience and her older sister, Beatrix, were from his second trip down the aisle. After their mother died birthing Patience, Fenwick remarried again and had her younger half brother, Blake, and then half sister Gemma. While Patience enjoyed a pretty good relationship with all of her siblings, she'd always felt closest to Layla. She'd taken her cue from hardworking Layla, too, dedicating herself to veterinary work as diligently as Layla did to Colton Energy.

Which made Patience furious with her father for mismanaging his funds and putting the K9 program at risk. She was convinced that it was by no fault of Layla's that Colton Energy was struggling. If anything, Layla's contributions kept the company from going belly-up much sooner. Patience wanted to ask Layla more detailed questions about it but her caseload prevented her from digging too deep into the financial records. She trusted her corporate tycoon half sister to fill her in on the details. Not that Layla was thrilled to share anything with her. Not since Patience had blown up at her for agreeing to an engagement to that old geezer Hamlin Harrington. His son, Devlin, was Layla's age, for heaven's sake. But all Fenwick saw was that Hamlin's money would save Colton Energy and the Red Ridge K9 facility, and so that was what Layla focused on. As much as Patience loved her job, nothing was worth her sister's happiness. She'd begged Layla to call of the wedding.

Layla disagreed. Their epic fight had occurred hours before Patience had found blessed escape in Nash Maddox's arms.

Once the cleanup was done, she dismissed her remaining staff. Patience relished the alone time, a chance to pick through her thoughts over her family's conflicts.

She stopped at the sink and ran the hot water, hoping she'd still be able to convince Layla to come up with another way to make bank. While she was grateful that Layla's fiancé had postponed their wedding until the Groom Killer was caught, Patience still couldn't contain the revulsion she had toward her sister's fiancé. Naturally, their father wanted the killer behind bars so that the wedding could happen as soon as possible. Fenwick Colton was always about himself and his company and he'd stop at nothing to get the money out of Hamlin. Worse, Fenwick threatened to cut off his K9 endowment if the Groom Killer wasn't apprehended ASAP. Patience shuddered at what she'd heard her father tell the police chief. *Do your job or you won't have one.* Even as the mayor of Red Ridge, Fenwick was clueless as to the man-hours and emotional dedication required to nail down a hardened criminal, and it took that much more effort to corner someone as wily as the Groom Killer. But even her father's intimidation hadn't produced the killer, not yet.

"What are you going to do for dinner, Doc?" Ted Jones, the college student who volunteered as he waited to apply for vet school, spoke up as she washed her hands. Normally she didn't mind having a meal with him and answering his myriad questions on the application process, but she was spent.

"I've got a lot of food in the staff refrigerator, and it's

my turn to pull night duty. You go ahead and get out of here. Don't you have midterms to study for?"

"Yeah, I do. Thanks, Doc." He grinned and sauntered off. Patience enjoyed the camaraderie her staff shared, paid and volunteer alike. It was what had made her want to be the K9 vet for the RRPD. The sense of belonging and being part of a bigger picture had wrapped its arms around her the minute she'd walked in here three years ago.

Patience waited until everyone had left the building before she went back into her office and sat at her desk. She needed some time to ground herself before eating dinner and then starting the care rounds for the dogs and cats, and the one parrot they were boarding for an elderly woman who'd broken her hip and was in ortho rehabilitation for the next month. Patience opened her top desk drawer and gazed at the pregnancy test result from this morning.

"Well, look at that. Still pregnant." She giggled at her own joke, but her laughter turned to sobs as the enormity of her circumstances hit her. She was going to have a child and had no clue how to handle a baby. A puppy or kitten, sure, she could do that blindfolded. But a human child, her child?

Her father had been absent at best, throwing himself into his work and accumulation of wealth her entire life. Patience had never known anything but the selfish man Fenwick Colton was. Yet she'd never given up on him, or broken contact with her full and half siblings. Family was important to her.

A baby.

She was going to have a baby. Her profuse tears had to be from the hormones, since she usually prided herself on her self-control.

Loud guffaws sounded from the boarding area and she sniffed, unable to keep the grin from breaking through her tears. Mrs. Bellamy's scarlet macaw was hungry. Patience's stomach grumbled in response, and she wiped her cheeks with a tissue.

"Coming, Gabby!"

The brilliantly hued bird tilted her head in welcome and made kissing noises with her smooth white beak as Patience walked into the huge room and opened the birdcage door.

"How are you doing, sweetie?"

Gabby climbed out of her cage and onto the playpen atop her dwelling as Patience gathered some mixed veggies from the freezer and heated them in the microwave. The parrot let out a loud shriek that was half laugh, half scream.

"Stop it, silly. You still have plenty of pellets and nuts in your bowl, beautiful bird."

After Gabby was busy with her warm supper, Patience checked on her other charges. Most of the post-op animals were resting, the effects of anesthesia and their bodies' ordeals exhausting them. But Fred, the labradoodle gunshot victim, had his big brown eyes open and managed to wag his tail the tiniest bit when she approached.

"It's okay, Fred. You're doing great." The poor dog had done nothing to deserve the hit from a bird hunter's gun. It had been a legitimate mistake, as Fred had escaped his owner's yard via a broken fence post, and the hunter wasn't in a residential area. With his caramel coat, Fred had blended in perfectly with the South Dakota hills and underbrush. Fred and the hunter had been after the same duck. Fred had inadvertently saved the duck's life.

"What am I going to tell Nash, Fred? How will I tell him? He needs to know, so there's no sense trying to be all trauma drama and play 'I've got a secret' about this."

The dog's eyebrows moved as if he understood her dilemma. A part of her brain knew that Fred was a dog, and he was in the midst of serious recuperation, but as she looked around the room full of animals, he was her best bet.

She leaned in closer and opened the kennel door to stroke his sweet, fluffy head. "Let's pretend you're Nash and I go up to you. Should I go over to the RRPD? Or call him? No, can't do this over the phone. This is a serious matter. I'm having his puppy! I mean, his baby. My baby. Our child."

Gabby's shriek of laughter rent the room and Patience jumped. "Jeez Louise, Gabby, you scared me! But you're right." She gently closed Fred's crate door and went back to the macaw, who'd polished off her veggies and was scraping her beak clean on the cage bars. "Come here, sweet birdie."

Gabby promptly got on Patience's forearm and leaned close to her face. "Give me a kissy." Gabby's voice perfectly mimicked his elderly owner's and Patience laughed. As shocking and emotional as her day had started, this was the best therapy anywhere. Being with her animals. Of course, they belonged to their various owners, the K9s to their handlers at the RRPD, but while they were under her care, they were her responsibility. It was a sacred commitment.

Right now, Gabby needed some human touch and affection. And Patience needed to calm down before she faced Nash again, most likely in the morning, to tell him the news. They were having a baby. Well, she was. She in no way expected anything from him.

"Okay, Gabby girl, come here and I'll have you and Fred help me practice telling Nash."

The parrot stepped daintily onto the T-stick Patience used to handle the exotic bird to prevent a bite. She'd learned the method during her avian course in vet school. As much as Gabby wanted to be on her shoulder, Patience never allowed it. Just as she exuded an alpha energy around the K9s and other dogs, she kept birds from thinking she was a tree and her shoulder a branch by using the perching tool.

She walked with Gabby the few steps to Fred's kennel, which was at eye level.

"Now, you two tell me what sounds better. First choice—Nash, I'm pregnant and keeping your baby. I don't need you to do anything. You've done quite enough already." She looked from Fred to Gabby, surprised to find that they were both staring intently at her. Gabby was used to touring the dog kennel with other members of the staff for a break in the monotony of her cage. Fred wasn't reacting to the parrot as he had to the duck earlier. Of course, he was heavily sedated.

Since both animals didn't react, she tried again.

"Too serious? Well, having any man's baby is serious business, but I get your point. How about this... Hey,

Nash, how have you been since we hooked up after the K9 training session? In case you were wondering, your sperm is viable. I'm pregnant! Congratulations!"

Fred's tail gave a firmer thump than earlier and Gabby nuzzled her huge white beak into her brightly feathered chest, inviting touch. Patience gently scratched the back of the bird's nape, marveling at the silky soft skin under her feathers. Gabby made lovey-dovey noises, indicating her enjoyment of the contact.

"Okay, you both seem to like option two. I think it's going to need more work, though. I'll think about it and we'll practice again after dinner." She walked Gabby back to her cage and put her inside. The bird went obligingly but Patience had to coax one claw off the T-stick. "Sorry, hon. I know you'd rather be out, but your cage is the safest bet until I come back."

Back in the staff area, she heated up the leftovers from last night's dinner—or was it two nights ago?—and streamed two episodes of her favorite sitcom on her laptop as she ate. She had to make a concerted effort to eat as nutritiously as possible, especially now.

She was going to be a mother. Have her own family. Thinking of it, the prospect was at once terrifying and thrilling. She had shared a bumpy relationship with her father since she'd gone to college and vet school on her own, scraping and saving to pay back every cent of her loans. Fenwick had watched in exasperation, trying to convince her that she didn't have to make things so hard on herself. She had her own trust fund.

But Patience had to know that her degree and career

were hers. It wasn't another freebie from being born into a rich family.

Her phone lit up with a call from Layla. Patience considered ignoring it; she wasn't about to tell anyone she was pregnant until she told Nash. And even then she wanted to keep this to herself for a bit. As the phone vibrated, she put it on speaker.

"Hi, Layla. What's up?"

"Where are you? I need a drink. I want you to meet me downtown." Layla sounded just like their father. Her harsh countenance grated at times, same as Fenwick's. But unlike him, she was soft and kind underneath her hard corporate exterior.

"I'm on duty." Thank goodness. Patience wasn't ready to face her half sister yet. Layla always seemed to sense what was going on with her, as different as they were. "I'm tied to the clinic all night." Not completely true, as she could call on a volunteer to watch the patients at any time. She was still miffed at Layla for getting engaged to Hamlin Harrington. No business, even Colton Energy, was worth a marriage of convenience. Screw the millions Hamlin promised Fenwick he'd pour into the utilities company.

"We had a labradoodle come in with birdshot and I need to make sure he stays comfortable through the night."

"Oh, that's awful! Who would do such a cruel thing?" More proof that Layla had a kind heart. She loved animals as much as Patience did.

"It was an accident, truly. Trust me, if I thought it was foul play I'd have called the RRPD." Animal welfare was a safe topic with Layla, who was otherwise too preoccupied with her corporate role as Colton Energy VP for Patience's liking.

"Make sure you report it if you change your mind." Layla never seemed to realize that Patience had her DVM and was fully capable of deciding when and why on the calls into the RRPD. Not to mention her K9 certification.

"What are you up to now, Layla?" She heard the hard edge in her voice but it couldn't be helped. It rarely could with Layla.

"Since my sister can't meet me for a drink at the only decent bar in town, I think I'll spend more time here in the office. There's always more to do, and I'll need to have things in order for when we have our cash flow back in the black."

Patience gritted her teeth. Layla was goading her. When it came to the subject of Layla's secret engagement with the smarmy Hamlin, silence was the best approach.

"Patience?"

"I'm here." She rolled her eyes and popped a grape into her mouth. Good thing they were on speakerphone and not doing their usual video call.

"You know your judgment is stinking over the line, don't you?" Layla's tone was pure corporate executive with a dollop of big sister.

"I haven't said a thing!" Either the grape had been sour or she was reacting to Layla's tone, for her stomach began to roil. She'd felt fine for the most part, until she realized she was pregnant. And thought back to how shaky her stomach had been the last couple months. Another reason to put off meeting Layla. Her sister would connect the dots in an instant if Patience turned her nose up at food and, of course, alcohol. Gourmet meals paired with fine wine were the one luxury Patience indulged in, and only with Layla, on occasion.

"You don't have to say anything, dear sister. I do think Hamlin cares about me, by the way. Dad's putting pressure on us to make it legal ASAP, but with the Groom Killer around, Hamlin's rightfully nervous. I know you don't approve of us or how we're handling our engagement. But it is what it is, little sis. I'm doing what you always say you believe in and putting family first."

"By keeping it secret?" Stung by Layla's accurate assessment, she couldn't help but to strike back.

"From the public. There's a serial killer on the loose, or have you forgotten?"

Patience remembered she was alone in the K9 clinic, and saw the darkening October sky through her office window. The early sunset was a sign of the winter to come, not a harbinger of more killings. Her body thought otherwise as shivers ran down her spine.

"Of course I haven't forgotten. But Hamlin's just like our father. His priority is always business and that means Colton Energy. Above all else, Layla, even your marriage." She almost choked on the word *marriage*, and yet guilt tugged at her. How could she judge anyone, even Hamlin, for postponing the nuptials? A psycho intent on killing grooms remained at large. Even if Hamlin had the resources to provide himself with the best security on the planet. And she had to admit, if only to herself, that she was a hypocrite. She'd been relieved that the wedding was called off for now. The thought of Layla on Hamlin's arm made her sick, and it had nothing to do with baby hormones.

"Tell that to Bo Gage, Michael Hayden, Jack Parkowski, Joey McBurn or Thad Randall." Layla's sharp reply sounded as if she was a woman sure of her place in life, but Patience saw through her sister's smoke screen. Red Ridge wasn't a tiny town, but it was small enough that they'd both known all five victims, at least as acquaintances. "And the RRPD still hasn't caught our cousin Demi—if she's the killer, of course."

Layla referred to Demi Colton, a bounty hunter whose relation to the murders was circumstantial at best. Patience didn't know Demi well as they hadn't spent a lot of time together growing up, or now as adults. But she didn't believe the gossip one bit, not since Demi brought in an injured dog to the clinic shortly before she'd fled. Demi *cared*. Killers didn't.

"She's not. She's only a suspect."

Demi had left town right after Bo Gage, the first victim, had been found. Because Demi and Bo Gage had been engaged for a week, until he'd dumped her for Haley Patton, there was circumstantial evidence, as well as motive, for Demi's guilt. It made no sense to Patience, though, because Demi had zero relationship to the other victims. But community opinion named Demi as the killer. Fortunately, the RRPD worked with facts, as did Patience.

Patience had to stand up for the truth, even if they flew in direct opposition to popular opinion. She put her trust in the RRPD's investigative capabilities over fear-fueled town scuttlebutt.

Layla's silence grew long and Patience wondered for the umpteenth time if her sister needed her to talk her out of the Hamlin Harrington agreement.

"Layla, you know I admire your loyalty to Colton Energy and our father, even though he doesn't deserve it. And we haven't talked about it since the fund-raiser, for obvious reasons, but are you sure you still want to marry Hamlin?"

"Of course I do." Her prompt reply was too quick, too reactionary. "Look, I'm not the one who went off the Colton straight and narrow. I'm holding up my part of the family business." Nice dig at Patience, who'd eschewed accepting the family legacy of becoming a financial wizard, like her father and sister. Finances had never appealed to her; serving others had.

"That doesn't mean you have to marry a man you don't love."

"Who says I don't love him?" Didn't Layla hear the lack of conviction in her own reply?

"Please. We can agree to disagree about your engagement, but we need to drop the pretense that you care for Hamlin if we're going to remain sisters." Patience would never have been so direct even a day ago. Was the baby giving her some kind of relationship superpower? Where she was realizing the preciousness of life and wanted to protect her bond with her sister?

"I wish I could tell you more, Patience, but you're going to have to trust me. I know what I'm doing."

"I'm here if you need me, Layla. Let's meet sometime next week, after I get through this weekend."

Layla's sigh sounded over the phone's speaker, and Patience felt sorry for her sister—almost. It was her decision to become involved with Hamlin, a man their father's age and just as disagreeable and greedy when it came to business. They weren't wealthy by accident. Although Fenwick's recent investment blunders were bleeding the company funds to near bankruptcy. From a pure economic standpoint, Colton Energy was desperate for what Hamlin Harrington offered.

Gabby's screech reached through the walls. Layla gasped. "What was *that*?"

"Our resident parrot. She's ready to come out of her cage again and stretch her wings. I'll give you a call later tomorrow, when I'm off duty, okay?"

"Maybe we can meet for a meal, then? With a nice bottle of red. My treat." Layla's infectious optimism made Patience laugh. It'd be soda water for her from here on out, but Layla didn't need to know that yet.

"We'll see."

# Chapter 2

Patience managed to get all the animals taken care of by eleven o'clock that night. Her legs thanked her as she lay down and stretched out on the folding bed assigned specifically to the overnight watch. She rotated the duty with another local veterinarian, who worked for the clinic on a contract basis, and the vet assistants. She'd thought that finding out she wasn't just bloated or had gained a few pounds, but was in fact pregnant, would keep her up all night. What did she know about being a mother? And what was she going to say to Nash? How was she going to tell him? How could she make sure he completely understood that she wanted nothing from him, needed nothing?

Snuggling into the rose-printed down comforter she'd brought from home, she promised herself she'd worry about it later. She had a few hours before the next rounds. She fell into a sound slumber that lasted until the alarm on her watch pinged at 2:00 a.m.

She blinked in the stillness, her mind blank for a brief second until reality seeped back in. Her entire life had changed only hours earlier with the positive sign on the pregnancy test's pee stick. Stretching her arms and legs, she chuckled in the inky dark. Who was she kidding? Her life had changed almost three months ago after the K9 training seminar with Nash. They'd made this baby while the summer sun was still shining, before autumn was more than a thought. And now the fall was passing quickly, the cold arctic winds beginning to dip down into the mountains.

Anxiety mounted at the task ahead of her and she sat up. Her job at the moment remained to care for her animals—the clinic's caseload.

Patience mentally ran through the patients that needed to be checked and, in particular, walked. Fred was the only canine needing a walk, unless some of the other dogs asked to go. Moving through the familiar steps she'd done countless times when she'd had night duty gave her comfort in the midst of the chaotic change a baby added to her life. But it didn't erase her exhaustion. No wonder she'd been dragging the last month or so. It wasn't the change of season or heavy workload—she was pregnant!

As an extra bribe to herself to get up and get going, she planned to take a look at the trees surrounding Black Hills Lake in hopes of spotting a great horned owl. There was a family of the majestic birds that roosted in the nearby fir trees, but the nocturnal animals were difficult to spot most nights and impossible in daylight hours. Tonight, with the full moon and predicted clear skies, she hoped to see one of the creatures' unique silhouettes.

Patience loved the squeaks her sneakered feet made on the floors when the clinic was closed and she had it all to herself. It was just her, the animals she loved so much and the sense of purpose being a K9 veterinarian gave her.

The motion-detector lights came on as she walked through the corridor that ran along the back of the building. No sounds came out of the kennel. A good sign. This time of night it was usually silent, but if an animal were really ill, this could be the worst time for them, too. She let out a breath of gratitude as she saw that all the animals were quiet and resting peacefully in their respective kennels. The usually feisty Gabby had her head tucked firmly under a wing, one eye peering at Patience as if to say "Don't bug me."

"Hi, sweetie girl," she whispered to the parrot as she walked by.

Fred was her main concern. The labradoodle needed to get an easy walk in, not so much to relieve himself as to help with the healing and to prevent his muscles from freezing up. He acknowledged her with half-open eyes, a tiny wag of his fluffy, untrimmed tail. She smiled at his sweet face. "Come on, boy. Let's go for a little stroll."

She braced her core muscles as she gently half lifted the eighty-pound dog onto a portable ramp and onto the clinic floor. How had she not noticed the way her stomach was beginning to bulge out? She'd had strong abs all through vet school, as it was essential to being able to do her job well. And while the strength was still there, she was going to have to start modifying her routine soon. Heat crawled up her neck. Had her coworkers noticed her changing shape and simply remained quiet out of pure professionalism?

No, her sister would have noticed if she looked heavier or larger in her belly area. Layla was all about keeping up appearances. If it wasn't such an ungodly hour Patience might be tempted to call Layla and share her situation. But then their father would find out, since Layla worked so closely with him and it'd be almost impossible for her to keep her mouth shut. Patience loved her sister and they shared a close bond, but it was probably best to keep this news to herself for the time being. She'd tell all her siblings—Layla, Bea, Blake and Gemma—when she was ready. She ignored the obvious: Nash Maddox needed to be told first.

Snapping a collar and leash onto Fred, she waited for him to steady his legs before they walked to the exit. "Here you go." She wrapped a dog jacket made from space blanket material around him, being careful not to touch his suture area. Normally a large dog like Fred wouldn't need a coat, but right after surgery it was her clinic's protocol, and the night temperatures were dropping precipitously as autumn faded and winter hustled in. She'd had what—three, four winters in her clinic so far?

*Her* clinic. She'd worked so hard through vet school,

hoping to work with K9s, never dreaming she'd land such a plum job. It was a plus to be able to live and work near her family, even when they demonstrated a multitude of reasons she might want to consider a job elsewhere.

And now she was expanding the Colton family by one.

Yes, the everyday physicality of her job was going to need some modification as her pregnancy progressed. Lifting heavy dogs was going to have to take a back seat to her baby's safety. That was what the other staff members and volunteers were for. She'd get through it.

She shoved gloves on and zipped up her ski jacket, bracing for the cold mountain air. South Dakota in October was not only desolate but could be bone-chilling. Thank goodness it hadn't stormed today, and there was bare, dry ground for Fred to relieve himself on. Having to take care of his needs on sticky mud or frozen snow would have been tough on her patient.

"Here we go, buddy. Get ready for some cold." She draped the binoculars they kept on a hook near the door around her neck. Still no sign of clouds, so she might see a great horned owl, after all. Ever since she'd been a little girl she'd loved searching trees for birds. Identifying them played second fiddle to enjoying their unself-conscious way of living. And who didn't want to watch a feathered creature fly?

The air didn't disappoint—it was freezing—as she and Fred stepped into the fenced yard area where the dogs could run free, whether they were boarders or healing from treatment. It was atop a hill, on the way to the mountains, and overlooked Black Hills Lake. The yard sloped down to where the RRPD had installed a small concrete pier for training purposes. The insides of Patience's nose stung from the harsh temperature, but the beauty of the view was worth it.

"How are you doing, Fred?"

Fred didn't respond to her verbal inquiry, but sniffed the ground and in short order lifted his leg against a small bush. A burst of relief filled her, warming her from the inside out. Nothing was more satisfying than to see a patient recover quickly and return to normal. As Fred resumed sniffing the frosty ground, she looked up at the stars that speckled the dark sky, the full moon their only competition. She and her canine companion could stay out a few minutes more before the cold became a concern for Fred's healing body.

A creaking sound floated through the air and she turned her attention to the lake. It was beginning to freeze over with a thin crust of sparkling ice, but was too deep to solidify in just one cold night. A movement caught her eye and she noticed a small boat in the middle of the lake, approximately two hundred yards from shore, dead center from where she and Fred stood. Patience blinked, hoping she was imagining the warning signals from her tightening gut. It was too early for ice fishing and too late, as well as too cold, for anything else recreational.

Something very wrong was happening on Black Hills Lake.

She raised the binoculars with shaky hands and focused on the boat. What she saw seemed out of a nightmare. A tall figure, masculine in stature, was holding the limp body of a woman in his arms, her slim limbs hanging lifeless. At least Patience believed it to be a woman, as the figure had long hair. The pale gold strands hung over the man's arms and reflected the moonlight. Her gut tightened painfully and Patience held her breath, waiting for the woman to wake up. *Wake up!*

Before she could yell to let them know they were being watched and should cease whatever they were doing, the man dropped the woman over the side of the boat. There was no struggle, nothing but the soft splash as the body disappeared from sight. As if it'd never been there.

Patience couldn't stop the gasping cry that escaped her lips. Her exclamation, while not at top volume, carried across the eerie stillness. Frozen in place, she kept the binoculars focused, noting whatever details she could.

Icy shock crept over her as the man turned toward the clinic, searching for the source of the sound. She saw the moment he spotted her on the shore, his ice-blue eyes clear and sinister in the moonlight, through the binocular lenses. She didn't recognize him, but knew that he saw her, and his frown was the only warning she had before he leaned over and started a high-power motor she hadn't noticed before. Patience dropped the binoculars to her chest and scooped up Fred, adrenaline lending her strength. She'd lifted heavier dogs before, but she never had to move this quickly with them.

"Hang in there with me, Fred." She ran back into the clinic and quickly put him in his kennel. Her phone was on her desk where she'd left it, but she had to lock the back door before running for it. When she turned the standard lock, she looked through the window and noted that the boat had carved through the thin layer of lake ice and the hulking man was close to the shore behind the clinic. He was clearly aiming for the small pier that the RRPD used for its launches and when training the K9 divers.

Patience went into alert mode, following the protocol practiced in drills with the RRPD. She locked herself in her office, grabbed her phone and went to the gun safe as she called the dispatcher.

"Nine-one-one. What's your emergency?" Frank Lanelli's familiar, confident voice eased her nerves as she rattled off her circumstances. All the while she unlocked her gun safe, took possession of her weapon, ensured it was loaded and then climbed under her desk, her designated safe spot.

A shot rang out and she couldn't keep from flinching. She knew the killer must have gotten through the outside security fence by now, which she told Frank.

"The shot I heard had to be him breaking through the outer gate."

"Good action, Patience. You locked the back door up tight. That will slow him down, too." Frank had known her since she was a kid and had five children of his own, whom she'd gone to school with. He was an anchor for the Red Ridge County emergency dispatch system. "Where are you now?"

"I'm in my office—the room closest to the kennel, farthest from the clinic's back entrance. I'm under my desk with my .45." She heard a crash and instinctively tightened her hold on her weapon. "I think he just broke a window." She couldn't help gasping for breath.

"Where are you, you bitch?" The man's roar reverberated through the walls.

"Oh, no. He's coming for me, Frank." Frantic, she tried to focus, figure out what to do next.

"Hang on, Patience. Was that the intruder yelling?"

She clung to Frank's voice. "Yes. That was him. He's angry and calling me a b-b-bitch." She could barely breathe as fear's noose tightened the muscles around her chest, where her heart raced. She felt its beats on her thighs, pressed up against her as she was folded under the desk. And against her baby bump. Her *baby*. Please, please let her make it through this. For the baby if nothing else.

"You're good, Patience. You locked your office door?"

"Yes."

"And turned off the lights?"

"Yes, but he has a weapon—"

"Tell me what you hear, Patience." Frank's voice remained steady and clear.

"He's calling for me. He's going to kill me, Frank." And the baby. The baby no one but she knew about.

"No one's going to hurt you, Patience. You're doing great. You have your weapon ready to go. Keep me on the line. Keep talking if you can. If you have to put your phone down, keep it on, okay? Two units are en route. You're certain you saw a body go into the lake?"

"Yes, positive." She repeated the details of what she'd seen. "Even if she was alive, there's little chance she still is. She looked unconscious, or dead, and the water is too cold."

"Okay, we're dispatching one K9 team now. That will be Sergeant Maddox with Greta. They'll go straight to the lake. You stay put until the other RRPD units arrive."

All she heard was Nash's name. Nash would make it okay. He was an accomplished, practiced, proficient K9 officer.

Frank continued with the running commentary, but even his professional expertise, his years of calming traumatized citizens, couldn't soothe her. There was an intruder in her clinic, most likely a murderer. The doom that shrouded Red Ridge over the Groom Killer had nothing on the dread that choked her. Had she found out she was going to have a baby today only to lose everything at the hands of some evil stranger?

A loud crash, followed by the sound of splintering glass hitting the clinic's floor, sharpened her senses. He was breaking the kennel windows that lined the corridor. The dogs started barking and Gabby shrieked in outrage. *Please don't let him hurt the patients.*

"Where are you? Come out now or I'll take out your precious animals!" And he had a weapon to make good on his promise.

He was closer, too close. Patience tightly hugged her knees, weapon ready in her right hand. She'd do whatever she had to do to stay alive and protect her baby.

"One minute out, Frank." Nash spoke to dispatch, his siren blaring as he raced through town in his RRPD K9

SUV, Greta secured on the back seat. His entire shift had been routine until Patience's call came in from the clinic. He had to help her, to reach her before the suspect did. He kicked himself for not calling her, asking her out again. And then immediately shoved that thought aside. There'd be time for self-reflection later, after Patience and the clinic were secure.

"Go ahead to the lake, Nash. We've got two units approaching the clinic."

"How far out?"

"Three and four minutes." Frank's concern was audible. "Repeat, K9 officer is to go to the lake. Victim in the water."

"I hear you. But I'm going into the clinic first if no other unit is there yet." Nash was only a minute out, and seconds could mean the difference between life and death. He'd be damned if he let anyone harm Patience. He strained to see up the road, willing the clinic to appear.

"You're right, Nash—we need you to go to the clinic first. We've now got a crazy man in the kennels, threatening Dr. Colton. She's armed."

"Copy that. Clinic first." Like it was going to be anything else. A victim in the cold depths of the lake, even with his and Greta's expert abilities, stood a slim chance of making it, if any. There was still hope for Patience.

Damn it. Why hadn't he called her, reached out to her after their night together? If he got them through this, he'd make it up to her.

Greta whined in the back seat.

"It's okay, gal. We're going to get there." Greta never

made a sound unless reacting to her instinct that something was wrong. That made two of them. It was constant these days in Red Ridge, from the Groom Killer case to the incessant pace of drug crime.

The clinic buildings came into sight, and as they appeared on the horizon Nash expelled a harsh breath. He willed the vehicle to go faster, faster as he navigated the familiar road. The security lights were blazing, but no inside lights were visible. He also noted no sign of RRPD units, confirming Frank's reported ETA for them, so Nash pulled around to the back, next to the fenced area for the dogs and K9 training.

Wasting no time, he got Greta out of the vehicle. With his weapon drawn, they ran for the building. Greta needed no orders, for they'd practiced and served together thousands of times. They were more than K9 partners; they were a team.

Nash went to let himself in through the secured fence, ready to punch in the code known only to himself as the lead K9 officer and Patience. His gut sank when he saw the broken gate, proof of forced entry. Together he and Greta ran to the clinic's rear entrance, where he found shattered glass on the concrete doorstep, the door ajar. He signaled for Greta to jump over the sharp shards.

"Come on, Greta!" Employing the moves that were second nature to them, Nash and Greta went through a coordinated series of tactics that allowed him to ensure the way was clear, while she remained on alert for any unusual sounds or scents. Several of the windows that looked out onto the lake and lined the corridor had been smashed, but Nash noted that none of the animals in the kennels appeared to have been injured, and only a few were yipping or meowing in distress. The loudest of the bunch was Gabby, the bird Patience boarded so often she was becoming a familiar sight. What wasn't usual was the huge red parrot's screams that threatened to split his eardrums.

"Help, help!"

The parrot's cries were downright spooky as he and Greta moved forward through the dark corridor. *Patience.* He had to get to Patience.

# Chapter 3

Patience grasped her .45 and aimed it at the office door. The thug continued to pound on it after firing once, and it was beginning to splinter around the handle. She stayed steady behind her desk, resting her arms atop it, ready to shoot. Mentally, she recalled all she'd learned at the firing range, and in various training scenarios the RRPD had put her through in the rare event she'd ever need to protect herself or the K9s. She'd never expected someone to break into the clinic to come after her, though. To steal the valuable K9 dogs, sure, or to score prescription painkillers for street sales—specific crimes the clinic was at risk for. But to have a murderer break in and come after her? Not expected.

Adrenaline surged as she prepared to shoot, but she

maintained her steady focus on the door, visualizing the shape of the man she'd take down.

And then…nothing. Footsteps running away. Sharp barks, more footsteps.

"Patience, Nash Maddox is on scene with Greta." Her phone, on speaker, barked into the quiet office.

"You mean at the lake." Despite the silence she remained ready to shoot. Her mind heard Frank's calm explanation, but her nerves weren't ready to stand down.

"No, he's come to ensure your safety and apprehend the assailant." Sirens reached her ears. "Stay put as he clears the front reception area."

"Okay." She heard Nash's deep voice echo through the halls, heard Greta's bark as the K9 team secured the clinic.

"RRPD is on-site, Patience." Frank's relief was evident. "Nash and Greta chased off the suspect, turned over security to the other RRPD units and are headed to your office now."

"Thanks, Frank." She let out a shaky breath, but still couldn't let go of her weapon. What if the man had circled around back?

A knock sounded on the damaged door, followed by a deep bark—Greta's.

"Patience, are you there? It's Nash." Greta's second bark let her know the huge Newfoundland wanted to declare she was there, too.

Slowly, Patience unfolded from behind the desk. "Nash is at the door, Frank."

"Affirmative. You can let him in, Patience. Repeat, he's chased off the intruder and our units are on-site."

"Patience?" Nash's voice reflected concern, even muffled by the door.

"I'm here." She unlocked the door and opened it, and was immediately engulfed by Nash in a bear hug. His arms pressed her to him, his solid, hard body the most comfortable thing she'd ever felt. Patience melted against him and let herself receive his warmth.

"Thank God you're okay." He placed his free hand, the one not holding his Glock, on her shoulder, and his eyes blazed with intent as he looked at her. "Are you? Okay?"

"I am. It was…" In a totally uncharacteristic move, tears fell from her burning eyes and she fought to speak. "I'm sorry. This isn't like me."

"It's just the shock. I've had to fight tears on ops before, too." He wiped one cheek with his thumb, then the other. She relished the rough, calloused slide of his skin against hers. It grounded her, allowed her to stop gulping for air.

"Thanks, Nash. You're right. It's shock, I guess."

"And some adrenaline." He dropped his arm and looked her over. "Did you hit anything while you were diving under the desk?"

"No, really, I'm fine." She rubbed both eyes with the heel of her hand, and realized that she, too, still gripped her weapon. "Except I didn't know I was still holding this." She engaged the safety and placed it on her desk. "I think I used everything I ever learned in our practice drills over the last twenty minutes."

"You probably did. And you handled it perfectly, from what I can see." As she looked into his eyes she saw his conviction, and it chased away the dark cloud of anxiety that the killer had left in his wake.

"Where is he now?" Quakes of relief started to move through her. She'd done it. Nash had helped. The killer was gone.

"Hopefully, in custody. He took off toward the mountains. The RRPD will get him." Nash sounded certain, but she wasn't so sure.

"A man who's so cold-blooded as to…to dump a body in the lake like that?" She shook her head. "He's not going to get caught. Not this easily. I'll bet he has a getaway car stashed nearby."

Nash put his hand on her shoulder again. "That's not your problem anymore. You're safe. The clinic is secure. Get some water or coffee." He nodded at the teakettle behind her desk.

"Okay." Her stomach heaved at the thought of ingesting anything, but tea might be good. *Her stomach*—had Nash noticed her midsection was thicker?

"Stay put until the other officers show up. They're here now, I think. Greta and I have to run to the lake."

His attention was focused on the case at hand, not her burgeoning baby bump. She had to tell him. But not now, in the middle of a crisis.

She tried to offer him a wobbly smile. "The man came up in his boat—it's on the shore at the bottom of the clinic property. You could take that out to where I saw him dump the body." Shivers raced up and down her spine. "Nash, be careful. He's—he's going to kill you if he can."

"He's not going to hurt anyone else, Patience. You're

safe now." He repeated that, as if he understood just how shook up the entire circumstance made her. "I'll be back for you." He paused, and for a moment that hung between them like eternity she thought he was going to kiss her. His eyes glittered with promise, one not solely related to the dark happenings of tonight. Dare she read anything into his heated stare? But instead of placing his lips on hers, he offered a wink instead. "Be right back."

Nash and Greta disappeared into the corridor, and as she watched through the broken windows, they raced out the door and across the training area toward the lake, their movements in perfect unison. Her instincts told her to go into the kennel and calm her patients, but Nash was right—she needed to wait until she knew the entire property was safe again, that the killer hadn't come back.

"Dr. Colton!" Officer Maria Ruiz caught her attention, waving from the other end of the corridor. Relief swamped Patience. If Maria was here, then what Nash said was true. The building was secure. For now. She'd feel better when he was behind bars, when the mental image of him sneaking back to kill her didn't seem an inevitable outcome to her hyped-up brain.

"Maria. Thanks for clearing the place."

"It's my job." Maria looked at her, then peered out a window toward the lake. The K9 team was in the boat after the evidence team quickly dusted it for prints and searched for evidence. The launch made its way toward where Patience had seen the woman's body being dropped. "That Officer Maddox and Greta in the launch?"

"Yes. They're headed for the center of the lake, by the dive platform." Patience had a hard time reconciling the spot with where they trained the diving K9s and sometimes sunbathed during the summer. "It's where the suspect was when I saw him with the woman."

Maria nodded. "Yeah—the other K9 unit is already there. See the other launch? They just said Greta's going to be diving." She looked around Patience's office, checking every cranny and under the desk before she was satisfied. "You should be safe in here for now. How did the man get into the clinic to begin with?"

"I heard a gunshot when he was still outside. I think he must have broken through the security gate and then smashed a window to unlock the back door."

As she replied Patience realized how slim the chances were that the thug was able to not only expertly break through the eight-foot security fence, but also enter the clinic so quickly. "He had to be trained to do this. Or knew the codes." But then that would mean someone they trusted was a criminal. Or maybe one of her staff had unwittingly given information to the wrong person.

Maria watched her with a gravity reserved for their toughest cases, reflecting Patience's concerns. "That he knew the codes seems unlikely—we'll check to see if he actually shot the outer gate, and determine exactly how he got in. At the very least he has a good understanding of the clinic's layout, judging by how quickly this escalated. The fact that he came right to your door…"

She assessed Patience with a compassionate gaze. "Do you want to come out back with me?"

"Sure." There was nothing she'd like more than to see the assailant caught, or better, the woman he'd dumped into the lake still alive and okay. And staying in her office alone right now wasn't high on her list of fun things. Patience needed to be with people, and Maria's grounding presence fitted the bill.

They walked past the kennel and Patience noted that most of the patients were amazingly calm, even with the wide-paned windows shattered. "We'll be back, everyone."

"Do you think they understand they're okay now?" Maria spoke as they reached the back door, which had clearly been broken through, its window also smashed.

"Absolutely. Gabby, the parrot, is being quiet—that's telling. When she gets riled up, she can incite a puppy and kitty riot in there, let me tell you."

Maria laughed. "At least your sense of humor hasn't left the building. That's a good sign."

"Probably." She wasn't feeling particularly jovial, but more like punch-drunk. The adrenaline comedown affected everyone differently. The baby's welfare gnawed at her. Adrenaline flooding her system was bad enough; it couldn't be great for the baby. She had to make an appointment with her doctor soon, and get a referral to an ob-gyn if necessary.

Thoughts of the baby's needs took a back seat as they approached the open gate. Patience saw bullet holes in the area surrounding the keypad.

"I've got to take photos and gather evidence." Maria pulled out a plastic evidence bag.

"Of course. I'm going to see if I can watch the dive ops from the deck." Patience jerked her thumb over her shoulder, indicating the clinic's small pier. There were a half-dozen launches used for K9 and police diving exercises and ops. Three were out in the center of the lake. "Thank you, Maria. I wouldn't have left my office if you hadn't shown up."

"No problem."

Once she was on the deck, looking across the icy water, it hit Patience how close the killer had come to reaching her. The fact she'd made it back to the clinic and managed to lock the door was incredible, seeing how easily he'd broken through the fence. It had felt as if she'd run miles with the recuperating labradoodle in her arms, but it had been less than a hundred yards. Too close.

Her heartbeat raced and she closed her eyes. The baby needed her to be calm. Patience reminded herself what Nash had emphasized: she was safe. But the woman the man had dumped in the water—probably not. Patience quickly refocused on the dive operation.

With the binoculars still around her neck, she used them to watch the divers from the shore, ignoring the cold as she shivered in her jacket. It was clear that Greta wasn't having the luck she was expected to, as Nash and the other K9 officers repeatedly encouraged her to go back under, to find what they knew was there. The woman with the long pale hair. Finally, Greta's large head surfaced and Nash's arm signaled for the other officers to help. Patience made out something in Greta's mouth as several shouts from the assembled RRPD officers echoed across the water.

"We have something!"

"Positive contact!"

"Pull her up!"

The rescuers got the body on board a slightly larger RRPD vessel normally used in the warmer months when boaters and swimmers got into trouble. EMTs who'd joined the op worked over the woman, valiantly attempting to ascertain if she'd survived, or had a chance of life once at the hospital and warmed back up. But the pit in Patience's stomach confirmed what she already knew—there was no way the victim had survived her chilling plunge.

"Good dog." Nash gave the hand command for Greta to shake herself off, and she did so, her huge bulk moving with unexpected grace aboard the small launch. The woman Greta had found was unresponsive and already being transported to the Red Ridge Medical Center, on the off chance she could be miraculously brought back to life. Nash wasn't expecting good news, though, as she'd been in the water for too long. There was a gash on her forehead that appeared lethal. He suspected she'd been dead already when the killer dumped her.

Frustration that the killer had gone free chased away the relief he felt over Patience's survival. Someone cold-blooded enough to kill and dump a woman in the chilly lake waters wouldn't have hesitated to kill a possible witness. Thank God Nash and Greta had made it there in time.

"You're a good girl, Greta." He petted her, wet fur and all.

"They both are good dogs." Officer Mike Georges stood next to him, his Belgian Malinois, Rocky, under a space blanket. Mike had been first on the scene and Rocky had dived for the woman with no luck. It was common knowledge that Greta was their best water dog, but Rocky was well trained, too, as were the several Belgian Malinois on the K9 team. Still, Nash couldn't help the surge of pride at Greta's job well-done.

"I'm sorry I didn't get out here sooner." Nash knew that it didn't matter—they'd all been too late to save the woman. Still, he'd had an option and he'd chosen to rescue Patience from the intruder over heading for the lake. He'd do it again, even if dispatch hadn't agreed.

"We both know it wouldn't have made a difference, unfortunately. And we were here at least five minutes ahead of you, with no luck." Mike's face was grim, softening only when he looked at his K9. "Is Dr. Colton okay?"

"Yeah. She was armed for bear and ready to take out the jerk."

Mike nodded. "She was a great study when we did our training last time. And her shot is perfect—as good as any officer's."

"I know." And he did. Nash knew a lot about Patience Colton that would cause Mike to raise his bushy eyebrows. More than he should, in fact, for a woman he'd known only one night, no matter how incredible.

He couldn't help noticing her whenever she was in the vicinity, or listening extra carefully when one of the other police officers mentioned her name in passing.

"I'm going back to check on her. She can give Greta a quick look over, too." He knew Greta was okay; the dog was bred for cold water activity. Newfoundlands excelled at pulling half-ton nets full of fish, as well as soaked men, aboard ships in the northern Atlantic. A quick dip into the bone-chilling lake in the middle of autumn was all in a day's work for Greta. In fact, judging from the dog's smile as she panted, she wouldn't hesitate to jump back into the water. It was in her DNA.

Still, Patience insisted on looking over all the K9s after they'd performed any particularly demanding task, or had worked for an extended length of time. Another reason she was so respected by the RRPD. Dr. Patience Colton cared for her charges.

"You look like you need a rest, too, Nash."

"I'm good." He'd be better once he was with Patience again, saw that she was doing all right. She'd set off his internal warning radar as quick as any one of the kids. More so, in some respects.

"Okay, then, I'll see you in there in a bit. Rocky's going to do a sniff check around the clinic and then we'll go see if we can figure out what direction our man in question headed. I'll take Rocky into the clinic for his check after that."

"Juliette and Sasha will be in on that, won't they?" RRPD Officer Juliette Walsh was dating Patience's brother, Blake, and was the K9 partner to their strongest sniffer, a beagle named Sasha.

"For sure, but we can help, too." Mike nodded at the streaks in the eastern sky that heralded sunrise. "We may as well finish out the morning. See you back at the station." They'd reached shore and Nash was relieved to see at least six patrol cars, lights blazing, parked alongside the clinic. He knew Patience was safe, but he still felt the tight band around his chest loosen as he drew closer. As if he was the one person who could keep her safe.

It was purely his concern for a colleague. And okay, he felt a sense of responsibility because they'd had that night together. Which underscored why he wasn't in a place to get involved with anyone. If he was this connected to Patience after only one night of sex, along with working together, he'd be doomed if he seriously dated anyone.

*Patience isn't just anyone.*

He shrugged off his annoying conscience and nodded at the RRPD officer guarding the clinic entrance, who let him pass.

Greta followed alongside him, down the long corridor to Patience's office. But they didn't have to go that far; he saw her in the kennel, through the portion of the glass wall that was still intact. She was talking to another officer, but when she saw Nash her expression softened and she gave him a half smile. Before he could acknowledge her silent greeting, however, the smile faded and creases appeared on her forehead. He remembered them in a different context, when she'd broken apart in his arms, her orgasm shaking both of them. But she wasn't in his arms now, and this expression wasn't that of a woman in the throes of passion. Patience looked worried. As if something about him made her anxious.

Patience stopped Maria midsentence.

"I'm sorry, but will you please excuse me? I've got to examine Greta."

She walked up to Nash and Greta, waiting in the main corridor.

"Nash, wait."

He turned around and she couldn't read his expression.

"I—I should take a look at Greta. Please bring her into the exam room."

She didn't wait for him to answer, but shoved open the door to the large space. Within seconds she'd lowered the stainless steel table in the middle, and Nash led Greta to stand on it. He held her by the harness while Patience grasped the dog's collar, then used the foot pedal to raise the examination table. Nash removed Greta's harness and stepped back to allow Patience the space to care for the dog.

"She's fine. Just wet," he stated.

Nash's bond with Greta gave Patience the first sense of normalcy since she'd seen the woman's lifeless body slip into the lake. She mentally shook the image away.

"How long was Greta in the water?"

"Not more than twenty minutes tops. She dived four, five times before she found the victim."

"It was a woman." Patience wasn't asking. She knew what she'd seen.

"Yes. And she was deceased. They tried to revive her, but…" He grew quiet. Hypothermia and longevity in cold water weren't something he had to explain.

"But they couldn't. To be honest, I thought she was dead as he held her. Nothing I can prove, of course, but that's what my gut told me."

"Gut instinct is there for a reason." Their gazes met and it was as if Nash tried to communicate something else. Did he regret they'd only had one night together, too? Patience broke the eye contact and turned back to her examination.

"You did good work, Greta." She spoke softly to the canine, pausing to shoot him a quick glance. "Has she shown any signs of distress?"

Patience felt along Greta's abdomen, her flank. As she pressed her stethoscope to the dog's rib cage, she was acutely aware of Nash being so near.

"No, she's good. Another day of work for a Newfie, right, Greta?" He spoke with ease to his K9 partner, underscoring the tangible bond between them.

"She's fine. Good to go. We can get her dried off in the grooming area." Patience lowered the table and Greta promptly walked over to Nash, then plopped down. "And she'll need to rest for the remainder of the day. It's normal for her to be a little more tired—that water is frigid."

"Yeah, I was worried when she had to dive down more than a few times. I'll keep her harness off until she's completely dry." At the concern etched in his face, Patience realized with a start why she'd been attracted to him in the first place. The reason she'd given in to her desire and agreed to their night of passion. His dedication to duty, his ability to put others before himself. This was a man raising his four half siblings. How many men in their twenties would do that? Warm, tingling awareness lit up her insides.

"What?" He looked at her as if he'd heard her thoughts.

The result of her attraction and their shared night was so obvious to her as she stood in front of him, her belly on full view under her scrubs. While she knew no one else might notice yet, it would be a matter of days or maybe a week or two before her weight gain became obvious. Heat spread over her chest, up her neck. *Now or never.*

"Nash, we need to talk." Could she sound any more commanding? This was not something to break to him in a rough way. "Can I make you a cup of tea, coffee? There's hot chocolate in the break room, too, if you'd prefer."

His face went blank before his steely determination returned. "Uh, no, thanks. Yes, we do need to talk. Not here, though. I have to escort you to the police station so that you can file a report."

Her heart sank at how professional he sounded. And for good reason. The sooner she gave her report, the more accurate it would be. The better chance of providing a tidbit of information that might aid in apprehending the suspect. She needed to tell Nash she was having his baby, but it would have to wait. Again.

"I anticipated that. My standby is on duty now, for the duration. I'm free to give a statement." And go home after and sleep in her bed, which sounded divine. "As soon as we get Greta dried off, we can go."

Nash nodded, and she sensed a tension in his body. It could be the adrenaline from such a demanding op. But when he looked up at her, she saw vulnerability.

"Patience, I'm so sorry. I've been an ass. I should have contacted you before work put us together again. I've thought about you often since our night together." His eyes shone with what could be longing, attraction. Nonsense—he was tired from the recovery op.

"No worries, Nash. Why don't you take Greta to the grooming station and use the power driers? The sooner she's dry, the sooner we'll all get to bed."

Her face immediately heated. If Nash noticed her self-consciousness over the unintended reminder of their night together, he didn't reveal it. He had Greta by her leash and his hand on the door. "I just wanted to say that I'm really glad I got here when I did. Tonight."

Of course, that was what he was going to say. Patience swallowed, knowing in that instant that telling him he was tied to her forever as her baby daddy was something she had to do pronto. But not here, not in the midst of trying to find a murderer.

"Thanks. Me, too. If you hadn't shown up when you did, I know I'd have had to fire my weapon." She couldn't stop the shudder that ran through her. And she wasn't the shaky type. Digging deep, she tried to find the woman she'd been just yesterday. The uncompromising K9 veterinarian who knew what she wanted. Instead of the emotional wreck she felt like, wondering how on earth she was going to raise a baby.

Nash's hand dropped from the door handle and he closed the few feet between them. His touch was firm, warm, reassuring as he squeezed her shoulder. It was meant as a collegial reassurance, so why did it send lightning bolts of awareness through her?

"You didn't have to use your firearm. And if you had, you'd have protected yourself. You're a brilliant veterinarian, Patience, but you're also a great shot. I was there on the firing range with you during our last weapons refresher, remember?"

She nodded. "I do. Thanks, Nash."

He flashed his trademark sexy smile at her before he led Greta out of the room. Patience listened to their footsteps, walking in sync as they always did. Nash and Greta made a great team.

And now they were going to have a baby to fit into their routine. *If* Nash wanted to participate as a father. She'd thought for certain he wouldn't, but the man who'd protected her tonight wasn't the kind who balked at a challenge. And helping to raise a baby while still the guardian for his four half siblings would be the challenge of a lifetime.

Of course, he didn't know about it yet. She wished she still had the clinic all to herself, because she needed to talk to labradoodle Fred and scarlet macaw Gabby most desperately now.

She needed the words to tell Nash Maddox she was pregnant with his child. Yet the image of the woman going into the water, the terror that had sliced through Patience when she'd thought the killer would harm her and the baby, put a dreadful pall over such happy news. Now she understood how the would-be brides and grooms all over Red Ridge felt. The threat of being murdered trumped the desire to host even the most joyous occasion.

Patience squared her shoulders. No one would harm her child or erase the thrill of anticipation at his or her existence. But even as she made the silent vow to herself, a shiver of knowing rushed over her.

The Lake Killer wanted her dead.

# *Chapter 4*

Nash ached from being out in the cold on that boat for so long and directing Greta during the recovery dive, so he knew her bones had to still feel the chill, no matter how thick her coat. He turned the doggy blow-dryer on High and maneuvered the corrugated plastic tubing in a methodical motion over her fur.

"You've got a lot of hair here, girl." She stood in patient compliance as he worked his fingers through her long black curls, taking care to lift all the way to her undercoat and get her thoroughly dry. He swore Greta loved it when he had to act as her hairdresser.

He chuckled. "It's okay, Greta. You've earned this tonight."

He wished he could have put Patience more at ease. She was the cool and collected veterinarian he knew as she'd examined Greta, with no remnants of the panicked woman he'd held an hour earlier. Except for the lines at the edges of her mouth; they let him know she was still wrung out over the night's events.

And she'd said they needed to talk. Had she been thinking about their time together, too?

Greta let out a happy croon and he laughed. "Are you reading my mind, girl?"

"Great work out there tonight, Nash." Maria walked into the grooming room.

"Thanks."

"I thought I'd let you know that we're wrapping things up in the clinic. It's secure for now, but we can't guarantee the suspect won't come back." She spoke loudly enough for him to hear over the drier.

"Yeah, I'm going to bring Dr. Colton to the station with me to give her report. As soon as this beast is dry."

"Patience agreed to that? To you driving her in?" Maria's brow rose. They all knew how independent Patience was. She ran the clinic single-handedly and never missed a beat. This was the first time she'd been threatened by the crime that had come to Red Ridge, though.

He nodded and shot his colleague a grin. "Yeah, she did, for now."

"She handled it better than I might have." Maria was a rookie but a tough one.

"Don't sell yourself short, Maria. All you're lacking is time in service. You're as well trained as any of us, and a better shot." And she knew it. Nash knew what was going on here—he'd mentored countless rookies as they entered RRPD service. It was a tough life but rewarding. A calling.

"Thanks, Officer Maddox." She ruffled the dog's damp fur. "And you, too, Greta."

"I've got it here. Thanks for finding us."

"How long is it going to take you to dry her?" Maria's glance took in Greta's bulky form, her huge paws, her long black, shaggy coat.

"Until she's dry." He rubbed Greta's chest as he focused the drier there. "Seriously, though? Another half hour or so."

"Better you than me." Maria's eyes followed the fluffs of black hair that floated through the air.

"No way you'd consider joining K9?"

"I love dogs and all, but what you and the other handlers have is a connection with your partner that I don't see myself having. Unless the right dog comes along, I'm a better fit for street patrol."

"That's fair. See you back at the station, Maria. Good job tonight."

"See you."

He wanted Greta dried yesterday. It was time to get Patience to the station and her report filed. And he'd have to approach the thought that had formed in his head.

Patience had no business being alone without police protection until the assailant was caught.

The RRPD station was bright inside, voices loud, drawers slamming as Nash and Patience walked to his desk. It was as if it were noon on a weekday instead of nearly five in the morning after a long night of unexpected operations. The aroma of fresh roasted coffee hit his nose, and while his stomach balked at the thought of it at this hour, his brain needed the clarity. He stopped by the coffeepot and looked at Patience. "Coffee?"

She blanched. "Um, no. Water is fine."

"Sometimes a case can take my appetite away, too." He poured himself a large, steaming cup, then reached into the small fridge for a bottle of water and handed it to Patience. Away from the clinic, she appeared a bit out of sorts.

"Thanks." Her fingers wrapped around the bottle, and his brain, the sex-starved part of him, flashed back to their night together, and all the delicious things she'd done with her hands on him. And her mouth. He had to stifle a groan.

"Hey, Nash!" Juliette Walsh slapped him on the back, crashing through his distraction. "Did you hear? Sasha got a good track on the suspect." Her pride in her beagle partner beamed from her face.

"Hey, Juliette. No, I hadn't—that's great. Any idea where he is now?"

She shook her head and looked at Patience, then back to Nash. "No, it seems he had a getaway car. It was gone by the time we tracked it."

"That sucks, but I'm glad you got that far." His gut sank at the revelation. He'd hoped they would luck out and catch the loser by now. If he was as much of a professional criminal as it looked, he might never get caught. Nash turned back to Patience. "Let's find a place to get your statement."

"Lead the way." She waved at Juliette. "Give Pandora a hug from me." Pandora was Juliette and Blake Colton's three-year-old daughter. Nash wondered if Patience was close to her business-investor brother, Juliette's boyfriend. He knew so little about Patience's personal life. It was best, of course, to keep things uncomplicated. Although if he were to get to know a woman more than as a one-night stand, Patience was the woman he'd pick.

Nash greeted each officer they passed as he and Patience headed for the conference room. It took a bit of time, as everyone wanted to greet their favorite veterinarian and also say hello to Greta, who thrived on the attention. Patience looked more weary with each step and he was anxious to get her seated.

He opened the door to the conference room, only to find it crammed with officers debriefing the case.

"Of course it's full," he said.

The anxious look stamped on her beautiful features tugged at him, deep in his chest. She'd been quiet in the SUV on the way here, and her obvious distress at being nearly attacked by a murderer had kept him from trying to draw her out. "We can go back to my desk."

She bit her lip as she glanced into the conference room. "I was hoping we could be alone for a bit. I have to talk to you, Nash."

"Do you mean you want to speak to the police counselor? It'd be totally natural after the night you've been through." He listened to his siblings' issues day in and day out, but he was far from a professional.

"No, I'm fine with all that. Tired, a little shaken up,

but that's not what I want to discuss with you." Impatience edged her tone.

Great. She was going to put the kibosh on any chance they'd repeat their one night of escape from their staid Red Ridge lives. Well, he didn't have to end his fantasy about being with her again. Not yet.

"We'll talk later. Right now, let's get your statement. Then I'm going home with you."

"Okay. Wait—what?"

He noticed there were flecks of amber in the dark brown depths of her widened eyes. Eyes that had glowed with pleasure that one night.

"You can drive me back to the clinic after we're done here," she said. "Please. I'll take my personal vehicle home."

He shook his head. "Not a great idea, Patience. The killer's on the loose and he visually ID'd you, remember?"

"It's not something I'm ever going to forget." White teeth tugged on her full bottom lip again, making Nash hard, not something proper in uniform. He couldn't look away from her sensuous mouth if he wanted to, and his awareness of her reached a supernatural degree. In the midst of a huge murder investigation, in the wee hours of the morning, in a boisterous police station, he wanted her.

"Let's get your statement."

As he turned, he almost ran into Red Ridge Police Chief Finn Colton, Patience's cousin.

"Nash—and Patience. Glad you're both here. You did great work on the lake, Nash. Greta." Finn nodded at the dog before focusing entirely on Patience. "How are you doing, Patience?"

"I'm fine, Finn." Her pale skin and tired stance didn't match her reply.

The chief remained silent, studying her. Nash wondered if she was going to break down again. To his surprise and unexpected relief she smiled and stood up straighter. "I made it through due to the training you and the department have always made sure to include me in. I can't thank you enough, Finn."

"Glad to hear it. You're giving Nash your statement?" To his credit, Finn kept it brief and businesslike. Exactly what Nash knew Patience needed in this moment. Heck, he needed it, too, about now. The less emotional any of them were, the quicker they'd get the work done and capture the murderer.

"Yes, right now." Patience's grit impressed him.

"Well, I'll let you two get to it. Nash, I need a quick word with you."

"Yes, sir." He looked at Patience. "Go ahead and wait for me at my desk."

"No problem."

Nash walked to Chief Colton's office, but his mind remained on the woman he left alone. Patience did that to him, made him unable to focus on anything, anyone but her. It should concern him, as his job required his full attention. But it didn't. Patience, and the feelings she stoked in him, felt damned good.

When Nash came back to his desk Patience saw the strain in his face.

"What did Finn want?"

"We lost the victim. As you suspected, she was dead before she hit the water."

"Do we know how he did it?"

"Yes. He gave her a lethal injection of fentanyl."

She didn't have a reply as she stared at his chiseled features and berated herself for noticing the shadow of his beard, wondering how the scruff would feel against the skin of her thighs. Either the pregnancy hormones were kicking her libido into overdrive or sex was a way to escape the gravity of their situation.

*Or you have feelings for Nash.* Nope. She wasn't going there.

He sat in his chair and they worked on getting her report filed.

Patience saw the tightness in Nash's jaw as she gave him her description of the suspect. She knew she was the reason he clenched his teeth. The sexual tension between them should seem ridiculous in the midst of their work. He'd just told her the woman at the lake had been murdered before Patience saw her body being dumped. And yet the sexual awareness only intensified the longer she and Nash were together. She wondered if he was afraid she was going to try to get him to meet up with her again.

If she weren't pregnant, facing such a life-changing event, she'd do it. She'd meet him again and let him work her body into a frenzy with those magic hands of his. Hands whose fingers now flew over a laptop keyboard as he entered the pertinent details of what she'd witnessed, up until he and Greta had shown up.

"You said you thought his hair was blond?"

"Or gray—it was hard to tell in the moonlight. Don't forget his eyes. They were a very particular shade of icy blue." She had the shivers again. Nash's fingers paused, his gorgeous eyes focused on her.

"Take my jacket—over there, on the back of the door."

"Thanks." She stood and retrieved the navy blue RRPD cold-weather jacket from the hook, not caring that it swamped her. It was warm, cozy and—damn it—smelled of Nash. As if being in the same room with him wasn't enough to remind her of how completely open she'd been to him that night, the night they'd conceived the baby. Her child. *Their* child.

No, *her* baby. She was going to raise him or her on her own. It would only prove disappointing later if she started to think Nash would want to be a fully invested father. He'd already had four kids to care for before he was thirty years old.

"What exactly did he say to you in the clinic?"

Nash's question brought her back, and she spent the next hour going over every painstaking detail of the night. Finally, Nash pushed back from his desk. "You look exhausted, Patience. Let's go to your place and get you settled for some rest." She noted he was careful not to mention getting her into bed. Smart man.

"I'm perfectly capable of driving myself home, Nash. I'll need a ride back to the clinic to get my car."

"Sorry, no can do. Greta and I are taking you home and, well…" He scratched the back of his head and his sandy hair reflected the overhead light.

"What are you saying, Nash?"

"I'm going to stay with you."

"That is absolutely not necessary. I have a weapon." She'd locked it back in its safe in her office, but she could get it and take it home.

"On you? All the time?" She damned his inscrutable professional bearing.

"Well, no, but I'm not usually worried about running into a murderer. Look, I'll pick up my weapon when you take me back to the clinic to get my car. And don't you have four brothers and sisters to take care of?"

"Four, ages twelve to seventeen. And they're fine. Our neighbor Mrs. Schaefer stayed with them last night. I phone her whenever I have a middle-of-the-night call." His emotional investment in his family impressed her. "They can be on their own as needed, since the oldest, Paige, can watch the younger ones. It's her schedule as a high school senior that is the deal breaker. She's off to marching band practice by six, three mornings a week. And while the rest can get themselves dressed and fed, it can get a little chaotic with all those teenagers under one roof."

Patience couldn't help but laugh. "I can't imagine. I know I think I'm busy at the vet clinic when we get a spike in patients, but I have a team helping me. And they're animals, not teens with the ability to get away with whatever they pretty much want."

"They're all good kids. I'm lucky. So far." He stood. "What I was starting to tell you is that I'd originally planned to take you to my place until we catch the killer. It'd be easier, for sure. But we have to assume you're being followed by the suspect until we know you're not. We can't lead the murderer to a house full of innocent kids. It's best for me to stay with you. Before you argue, the chief has ordered it. Think of it as not me being your bodyguard—you know cops don't do that. I'm hanging with you in the hopes of catching the bad guy."

"I love being mouse bait."

"You're not bait as far as the RRPD is concerned. You know that, though." He looked frustrated. "We have to keep you safe, Patience. Greta and I get the job."

She thought of trying to get him to change his mind, but Finn had ordered it. And truth be told, if she needed protection, there was no one else she trusted more. She'd heard the thug calling for her, knew his intent. Her life was on the line. What Nash didn't know yet was that along with her life, so was the baby's. She could use the backup, at least for the next few hours while she tried to get some rest.

But how was she supposed to sleep with the sexy Nash Maddox in the vicinity?

"I'm so sorry for the inconvenience to you and your family, Nash. Your brothers and sisters must hate your job at times."

"Like I said, it's all taken care of on my part. I have an aunt and uncle on their way into town, to help out for as long as I need. Aunt Clara was my mother's sister, and she asks to see the kids whenever it's convenient. She and Uncle Jim live in Sioux Falls and regularly make the trip. They'll stay for the duration of the case."

"What do you mean by 'duration'?"

"As long as it takes to ensure you're no longer a target."

He stood in front of her, but left a respectable distance between them. She was grateful because the combination of the long night, being with him in such close proximity for the better part of the last hour, and his overwhelming masculinity were making her feel as though she'd do whatever he asked her to. He wanted to move into her house? No problem. She could have the guest room ready in minutes. Or even better—her room. *Shoot.* She needed room to breathe before she did something stupid in her hyped-up-by-pregnancy hormonal state.

*Your attraction to Nash has nothing to do with the baby.*

"Nash, I appreciate the concern, but really, I'm okay. I'll sleep better knowing I'm not a burden to anyone." As he kept looking at her, the heat of desire unfurled low in her belly and she glanced away. "I suppose you're right. Just for the rest of today, though. After that I'll manage on my own."

"We'll worry about tomorrow later. And as for being a burden? You've got that wrong. It's my job, Patience."

Nash's dedication to duty, one of many things that attracted her to him, suddenly took on a different facet, as she was painfully aware of wanting to be more than just another case. Maybe it was finding out she was pregnant with his child, or the resulting hormones, but whatever it was, Patience couldn't deny it.

She wanted to be more than a case detail to Nash.

"I'm surprised you don't have any pets of your own." Nash sat on her sofa, where she'd laid out sheets, a blanket and pillow. He'd forgone the guest room, as it was too far removed from the rest of her house. He needed to be right near the front door and kitchen entrance, both within twenty feet of one another. Patience hadn't argued, which clued him in as to how exhausted she was.

She sipped at a spicy-smelling tea she'd made for herself, and assessed him from the kitchen island. Her open-concept house made it welcoming and easy to converse, but he wasn't thrilled with the lack of walls. Fewer obstructions for the murderer to break through, less resistance to a bullet.

"I get my fill of animals at the clinic. I'd love to have my own dog and a few cats, but for now, this is easier. I spend the majority of my time at work these days, so it's like having my own pets."

"Yeah, it's been a busy year for Red Ridge." He was too tired to mentally review all the criminal activity, but there had been plenty. Record breaking, in fact. The Groom Killer was still out there, and now the Lake Killer.

"You sure you'll be comfortable out here? I promise, the guest room bed is practically brand-new. Only one of my sisters slept there."

"Layla, Gemma or Bea?"

"Layla." She didn't elaborate. In a place like Red Ridge, with Fenwick Colton as the energy mogul, everyone knew the entire Colton clan. Nash had had to revisit his prejudices against the wealthy family when he'd first started working with Patience. She was the exact opposite of having a sense of entitlement.

"Answer me one thing, Patience."

"Okay."

"Why did a rich girl like you want to be a veterinarian? Have you always like animals?"

"I'm going to ignore your 'rich' comment. Why should my family's financial history have anything to do with my vocation? Or with me choosing what I want to do?"

"Jeez, I'm sorry. I was honestly curious. It seems to me you could have become whatever you wanted to. I'm impressed that you went through vet school and were hired to run the K9 clinic."

The wall she'd erected over her expression fell, revealing the Patience he'd made love to for several hours just a little under three months ago. She made her way to the sofa, where she sat on the end opposite him. He tried like heck to not mentally revisit that night, at least not while she was so close.

"I've never been interested in finances or being an entrepreneur. Science and math were my mainstays through school. My counselors suggested med school, dental school, even joining the military to become a physician. But I knew how much I loved horses and dogs, and it was natural for me to pick vet school."

"Your parents supported it?"

"I'm sure my mother would have. She's been gone a long while, as I'm sure you know. My father, he's a tough bastard. I love him unconditionally, but he's always made it clear what matters to him."

"Money."

"Right. The bottom line. That's just not who I am."

Nash watched, incredulously, as tears filled her eyes,

making their normally brown hue a rich, dark amber. They matched the highlights in her hair. Holy hell in a handbasket, what was he doing, noticing her hair color? He was reacting like his twelve-year-old brother. Jeez.

"Patience—"

She held up her hand. "I know a lot of people probably think I got the clinic position because of my father's endowment in my mother's name. But I competed fairly against applicants from all over the country, and even some overseas. I won my job fair and square."

"Of course you did. It's obvious in how well you do it. I'm sorry, Patience, I didn't mean to come across so tough."

The air between them shifted and he felt the intimacy of that special night return, at about the same time he noticed trepidation in her eyes.

"Nash, I have to tell you something." He'd heard that tone before—when a woman meant business. Usually the breaking-up kind, not that he'd had anyone to break up with these last several years.

"Save it, Patience. I know what you're going to say. And I get it. Please don't mistake my professional concern for personal interest. Don't worry, I'm not going to ask you to go out again. We made a deal that night—and I understand you don't want to break it."

Her eyes not only filled with tears, but he saw one, two, *three* spill over her long dark lashes and track down her creamy cheek. "Aw, Patience, I didn't mean for that to come out so rough."

"You don't get it, Nash. This isn't about us getting together again, but it is about that night."

He felt a kind of tingly awareness in his gut that had nothing to do with his attraction to her. His inner prescient warning system, the talent that helped him as he and Greta sought out evidence or conducted rescues, was going full-bore. What was she trying to tell him?

"What is, Patience?"

"I didn't want to tell you like this." She wiped at her cheeks.

"Tell me what, like how?" Was she going through an adrenaline comedown? He felt low after a hard call, but never wept.

"Like this—at eight o'clock in the morning after we've been up all night, after I saw a murder, or at least the last part of it, and Greta had to dive to find the body—"

"Spit it out, Patience." He heard the growl in his voice and it was like when frigid lake water hit his face. He stood up and paced away from the sofa, giving them both needed space.

Greta remained unruffled, lying on her side and only thumping her tail when Nash walked by. She'd also had a long night.

"I'm trying to." Patience wiped at her eyes with the sleeves of the fuzzy sweater she'd donned over her pajamas the minute they'd arrived.

"I hate this, Patience. It's as if you're afraid of telling me because of my reaction. As long as we've worked together, have you ever known me to overreact to anything?"

Clear brown eyes met his. "I'm pregnant, Nash. The baby's yours. I mean, you fathered the baby. But it's my baby. I'm going to raise it on my own. I completely understand that you have four siblings to raise and your kid calendar is booked for the next half-dozen years. But you should know it's your baby, and again, you're free to not worry about it."

Nash heard nothing more after Patience said, "I'm pregnant." Of course, he knew in his gut it was his kid. Unless Patience was more social than she'd let on, she'd been on her own and single for quite some time. If he could trust her, he'd been her first in a long while, and he doubted she'd been with anyone since. Not just because he hadn't, but because he knew how busy the K9 unit had been, which spelled extra hours for the clinic.

Looking around her great room, he decided her sparse furnishings and stacks of magazines and unopened mail on the kitchen counter validated her assertions and his assumptions. She was a loner in every sense of the word, except for their foray into unbridled passion three months ago.

"I believe you. I know it's my baby." Only then did it hit him, really register. He was about to become father to a child.

# *Chapter 5*

**P**atience wanted to grab the words and shove them back down her throat the second she'd said them, right before Nash's features froze and his eyes glazed over. Relief soothed her upset stomach, though, indicating she'd done the right thing. Of course, she had—she and Nash were adults, and they'd both made the decisions that led to now. To a baby.

"This was a terrible time to tell you. I'm so sorry." She wasn't sure if he felt the constant pressure she had since she'd witnessed the murder, if he felt like someone was continually watching them.

"There's never a great time to drop news, is there? How long have you known?" He stood there, hands on hips, clearly processing.

"Since this morning. I mean, yesterday." Had it been

only twenty-four hours ago? "I thought I'd skipped my period from stress, like I used to during college and vet school. I should have known better. I'm a vet, for heaven's sake. But I never thought to do a pregnancy test until the last few days. The stomach bug I thought I couldn't get rid of, the exhaustion, the bloating—it's been the baby all along."

"I'm not blaming you for not telling me sooner." He sounded sincere, looked...calm. Too calm.

"I didn't know sooner! Look, I told you, you don't have to worry about me coming after you for support of any kind—financial or otherwise. You know I'm able to support this child with my job." She refused to mention her trust fund—that wasn't on the table. Patience prided herself on being able to fully support her life, and now the life of her future child. Without any of her family money, other than her reserve for an extreme emergency, or to maybe pay for her child's college.

"Of course, you can support a child." He looked stymied, speaking in the most general terms. "This isn't about finances, though, is it? We both have good jobs. And security, more than if we were running our own businesses."

"And I'm planning to work right up until the baby comes, take some maternity leave, then go right back to working at the clinic." She realized that while she hadn't consciously thought it all out, some part of her had been sifting through her options since yesterday morning.

"You're keeping the baby? For sure?" He looked at Greta as he spoke. The dog had perked up, her ears alert. As if she expected them to have a fight about it.

"Yes. Yes, I am. Have you heard anything I've said?" Hadn't he listened? Anger flooded her as she watched him, finding his attention was clearly not on her words. He was totally focused on Greta now, and the dog was issuing a long, low growl.

A loud rattling at her door, followed by a gunshot, was Patience's only warning before she was thrown by Nash onto the carpeted floor beside the sofa, then covered by Greta's body. The dog lay alongside her, shoving her up against the couch and placing herself between her and any bullet. Patience shoved her head under the upholstery skirt, the one place she could breathe freely without Greta's coat in her face.

She heard Nash shout, heard him fire his weapon, then a return shot and the sound of glass hitting the tiled foyer. *Not again.*

Nash had fired at an intruder.

"Stay down!" He gave the order to Patience. Greta knew to keep Patience covered until he released her; they trained for this all the time.

He caught a glimpse of a tall male figure with a knit watch cap running from the front door. The dark hat contrasted sharply with silver hair, matching Patience's description of the Lake Killer. Nash quickly approached the door, weapon in front of him, constantly sweeping the foyer, the doorway and then the front porch. There could be more than one shooter.

A dark beat-up sedan was peeling off onto the suburban street, too far away for Nash to make out the license number. He watched as it turned the corner out of the subdivision, and memorized its profile. He stepped back through the front door, and he pulled the SUV keys out of his pocket.

"Greta, release." He paused to make sure the dog stood up and that Patience followed. Their eyes locked across the great room. "You okay?"

"I'm good. You?"

"Same. I'm going to call this in—stay in here with Greta, away from that back sliding door." He knew that as much as he'd spooked the intruder, if it was the murderer, he'd be likely to circle back and come at the house from the rear. "Do you have a weapon in the house?"

"No, only the one at the clinic."

"Fine. I'll be right back." He was going to have to talk to her about keeping a weapon close by. At least as long as she was targeted by this nutcase.

"Of course." Patience laid her hand on Greta's head. "Want to come help me make some tea, girl?"

Satisfied that they were okay for now, he went out to the K9 vehicle and called in to dispatch. He kept the SUV running in case the assailant returned.

Frank's voice sounded over the hands-free system. Normally cool as a cuke through all kinds of situations, the dispatcher sounded shaken. Everyone at the RRPD adored Patience, and he was no exception. "We'll have a forensic team out there ASAP, Nash."

"I doubt they'll find anything." If there'd been snow or ice on the ground, tire tracks would have been a great lead. But with the streets still dry after the unexpected cold snap, there was little likelihood of any kind of imprint.

"Give me a description of the vehicle again," Frank said.

"Black sedan, late model but a little beat-up, not something you see around here a lot." In this part of South Dakota, folks opted for four-wheel drive, or at least all-wheel drive, especially at this time of year, when a sudden snow squall could leave you stranded without the extra traction power.

"Copy. And, Nash—is our favorite K9 veterinarian okay?"

Nash smiled at Frank's fatherly concern. Everyone at the police department and training center seemed to get that while Patience had a biological family in town, they weren't very loving or close. Fenwick Colton, mayor of Red Ridge and billionaire energy tycoon, had a reputation for treating his children like stock assets. The RRPD knew this and wrapped its arms around their prized veterinarian. The department was its own family.

"She's fine, Frank." As he replied, the reality of what Patience had blurted out just before the gunshot hit him. He could have lost both her and his unborn child with either of those bullets. *It's okay.* Patience and the baby were fine. But Nash's stomach felt as if he'd swallowed a lead weight. He'd just found out he was going to be a father, *was* a father, and it all could have been irrevocably shattered in the blink of an eye.

"Good to hear. You staying with her for now?"

For *now*? Heck, he was in it with Patience for at least the next eighteen years. No, scratch that. He was learning with his half siblings that being a parent wasn't something that would end once they left the house. He'd always care, no matter their ages or places in life.

And now he had a biological child—his son or daughter—to care about. And Patience to work through it with.

"Nash, you there?"

"Yeah, copy that, Frank. I can be reached on my cell phone." He shut the SUV down and stared at the dash. He hated cutting Frank off, but he had to think.

Nothing was going to be the same again. He knew he needed time, but no matter how long it took him to process the news of a baby, and his now permanent attachment to Patience as its father, life went on. The baby was going to be born, and it would need parenting.

He'd been here before, right after his parents had died in that awful car accident. That had been tragic, unexpected, the sorrow reverberating still through him and his siblings with each holiday and school benchmark that passed. Another opportunity to remember his parents would never be there to see the kids graduate, date for the first time, get into college.

Patience being pregnant wasn't tragic. A surprise, sure. A major life change, definitely. But Nash would be damned if he'd let anyone, including a cold-blooded murderer, take from him the joy that the baby would undoubtedly bring.

He wasn't sure how Patience felt about it, but there was no time like the present to ask.

Patience's hands finally stopped trembling as she stroked Greta's thick fur. "You've been through a lot in less than twelve hours, girl."

Greta leaned into her as they sat on the kitchen floor

between the island counter and the sink. They'd gotten up from the living room floor and the dog had sniffed around the entire house until, satisfied they were alone, she'd resumed her protective stance.

Nash didn't have to tell Patience that it had been the murderer who had found her, and wouldn't hesitate to break in via her patio and garden area. She was safest here, behind the kitchen island, away from the line of sight of the sliding door and yard.

Greta's ears perked up and her body stiffened, indicating that Nash was coming back in. Sure enough, Patience heard the front door open and close, his footsteps thudding as he walked over to them. He stood in front of them for a full minute before he spoke to Greta. "Move over, girl."

Greta complied, lying down in the narrow space left, and Nash sank down next to Patience. It would have been too close even five minutes ago, but right now the solid, warm length of his body alongside hers felt good.

"The front door's going to need to be replaced." His voice was low and comforting.

"Is it functional for now?"

"Not really. But I'll get it boarded up. And we need to move you out of here. I know we're both exhausted, but we can't stay here. You won't be able to until we catch the murderer."

"Did you see him? You're sure it was the same guy?"

"He matched your description, at least his height and the color of his hair." Nash's hands were hanging between his bent knees. He lowered one to hers, on the floor, and squeezed. "You're not alone in this, Patience. I'm not going to let anything happen to you or our baby."

She couldn't speak right away. What they'd been through, this latest attack, the enormity of figuring out they were going to be parents—it was all overwhelming.

They sat with his hand over hers, Greta's soft pants filling the silence, for several moments. Patience was beginning to realize that when she was with Nash, time seemed to stand still. When they were together, whatever connection they shared beyond parenthood was uniquely soothing. As if nothing else mattered and she had all the time in the world to get to the next task. Just being with Nash was enough. This wasn't a place she'd been before. Seeking the next career goal, striving to hit the next benchmark were traits she'd gained from her father. With Nash, they didn't seem as urgent.

Finally, her voice returned.

"That was quick—you calling the baby 'ours.'" She shifted her hand out from under his and immediately missed the warmth.

"It—I mean, he or she—*is* ours. I'm in this with you. We need to hash it out, but this isn't the time to talk about it." As if on cue, the siren from the RRPD unit reached them.

She stood up. "I think we're safe for now. That man I saw on the lake is too calculating to come back when he knows the police are here." Yet her hands still shook, and the weight of knowing she was a target zapped her energy.

"We're not done with the baby conversation. First, we have to get you to a place where you'll be safe. Somehow this jerk figured out where you live, so he knows your name. Going to your father's isn't an option, either. He'll find you there."

Which was a relief as far as Patience was concerned. Her dad's autocratic attitude was the last thing she needed. "My father lives in a very secure compound, but you're right, I don't want to put him at risk. Or any of my siblings."

"I'll figure something out."

"You don't have to—I have a place up in the mountains. No one knows about it." She didn't even tell the clinic staff about it. It was her private escape, the one nod to her healthy bank account that she didn't feel bad about. "It's a two-bedroom cabin."

Nash's eyes lit up. "How far away?"

"Twenty miles. A forty-five minute drive on a clear day. It's really up there, with lots of twisty turns." The thought of the drive to her mountain hideaway made her queasy, but that was her pregnancy talking. Mentally, the respite was irresistible. As long as Nash would be there; she didn't want to be alone. "To be honest, I forgot about the length of the drive, or how twisting it is. I'm not so sure I'll enjoy it right now, but we don't have a choice, do we?"

"You're having morning sickness?" Compassion smoothed the rough edges of his voice and his expression was one she wanted to drown in.

"What does a single dude like you know about morning sickness?"

"I remember when my stepmother was pregnant with the kids. I was already thirteen or fourteen when she had the oldest. She'd throw up for, like, the first three months with each baby." He shook his head. "I decided then and there I'd never get a woman pregnant."

"Well, that's a resolution you've busted. And I'm okay. I feel nauseous here and there, but it's not been as bad as I've seen my friends struggle with. Plus, now I'm pretty sure I'm at least twelve if not as much as fourteen weeks pregnant. The worst time for morning sickness has passed."

"I'm so sorry, Patience. I haven't been here for you for any of it."

"I haven't been here for myself! I ignored the symptoms until the last few days." When they'd become impossible to overlook. "If anyone's failed in responsibility to the baby so far, it's me."

"I am an equal partner in this pregnancy." He spoke as though he were taking his oath to be a police officer.

"You didn't mean to get me pregnant. It happens. We were careful." She tried not to think about how careful they'd been, how huge he'd been as she'd rolled the condom over him, begging him to take her again. *Do not look at his crotch.* It would be the ultimate humiliation—trying to console him that this wasn't entirely his fault, as he was taking it, yet coming on to him in such a blatant way.

"But not careful enough." His mouth was a straight line and he stood with his hands on his hips, looking out the kitchen window. She'd expected him to regret that night; he hadn't signed up to be a new father. He had enough with his siblings. No doubt the reality of her pregnancy was hitting him. She decided to let it go for now. Meanwhile, no matter what he said, she wasn't going to have any expectations that he'd be a fully participating father. It was better for her heart to not go there. Nash Maddox was a heart-stopper of the highest caliber.

She nodded at the window, where they could see the patrol unit pulling up in front of her house. "That was quick. I'll make them a pot of coffee."

Nash went out to greet the officers and Patience immediately felt the loss of warmth from his nearness. If her hyperawareness of him affected her this much after only a very long night and part of a day together, how was it going to be when they were holed up at her cabin?

There was no use squelching the thrills that fluttered in her gut, sending heat over her breasts and between her legs. Her desire for Nash was undeniable. And welcome.

# *Chapter 6*

Nash drove to Patience's cabin, and while he had to focus on the treacherous road, he couldn't ignore how much he enjoyed being in her company. They'd both been awake for over twenty-four hours and yet her nearness buoyed him. Why hadn't he followed up with her after their one-nighter? It shouldn't have taken a murder investigation and danger to Patience to bring them together again.

"You weren't kidding when you said your place is way up here. I don't think I've ever ventured to this part of the mountain before." Which was saying a lot, since he'd camped and hunted and ran roughshod with the best of them while he was growing up. As an only child for almost fourteen years, Nash had had his father indulging his every whim. Even after his parents divorced and his dad remarried and had four kids in his new family, he'd always made time for Nash.

"I picked it on purpose." Her voice was stretched thin, but he couldn't look at her to see why as he made a hairpin turn around the mountain. The shoulder was nonexistent and he'd guess the drop-off was at least two hundred feet.

"This might be fate, you know. We need to get to know one another better if we're raising a kid together. It's clear neither of us wanted to make the first move toward a relationship after our night together." *Crap.* His thoughts had turned to words before he engaged his mental filter. He was going to tick her off before they even got to the cabin.

"You don't need to stay with me, Nash. Leave me an extra weapon if you want to, but no one else knows about this place, save for my family. I'm safe here."

Back on a straight stretch of road, he risked a glance at her. Her eyes were closed, her hand hanging on to the overhead handle of his personal Jeep for dear life. "If you think you're going to throw up, I can pull over." He couldn't look at her for as long as he wanted—the road was taking them around another particularly tricky switchback. He heard Greta shift in the back and silently thanked the dog for her steadfastness.

"Just. Keep. Going." Spoken through gritted teeth, yet with steel. He couldn't help but smile. Patience was nothing if she wasn't tough as nails. One of her many qualities that attracted him to her.

"I'll bet the views here are spectacular when it's not so overcast." They'd entered some low-lying clouds, making the trip seem all the more mysterious. Clandestine. The highway evened out, but he still drove with care, as there was barely a shoulder on either side of the road. He knew it was deceptive—the woods made it look like there was level ground right off the paved road, but a sheer cliff was just beyond the trees.

"They are spectacular." Her eyes opened and a bit of color came back into her cheeks. "We're almost there. Take the next left and pull up to the gate. I'll give you the code."

"I'm impressed that you have security up here."

"It was a compromise with my father. I needed to use a portion of my trust fund as collateral to buy and upgrade this place, and he agreed only after I promised to put in top-notch security. Not many people know about it—my family is all."

"I like your father's thinking on this one." Although he wasn't a fan of Fenwick Colton, the pompous ass who basically controlled the county's—and therefore the RRPD's—purse strings, Nash appreciated that the man cared enough about his daughter to insist on the security measures.

"I'm not so sure it was about my safety as much as his pride. He's never gotten over me paying my way through college and vet school, and I've since paid back every penny of what I borrowed from him for this cabin."

"I had no idea you'd done that—paid for your schooling." He'd assumed her father took care of it.

"Most people believe I didn't, but that's okay. I didn't do it for anyone but me."

Within minutes he pulled up to a large gate, blanketed on either side by dense forest and a lethal rock outcropping that rose to high cliffs. They were in a valley of sorts, which made it feel like a fortress. "I don't see the keypad."

"Because there isn't one." She had her phone out and was tapping on it. "It's app-driven. I control it all with my phone."

"Any chance I can have that code, or whatever I need?"

"We'll set your phone up once we're in the cabin."

The deceptively rustic gate swung open and he drove them onto the graveled road, which after about another mile led to what appeared to be a modest, almost run-down cabin.

"And we're here." Patience was out of the passenger seat in a blink, her long legs practically loping up to the quaint porch. Chairs, a rocker and a couple tables made it appear well used.

"You spend a lot of time on this porch, don't you?"

She cast him a shy smile. "I do. Layla comes up with me sometimes, but other than that, it's all mine."

"So the phone unlocks your door, too?"

"Yes." An audible click sounded from the front door and he followed her into the cabin. Greta entered in turn and immediately plopped herself on the largest area of open floor, in front of the fireplace. Greta always sought out the coolest place in any dwelling, as her bulk kept her body temperature high. Patience laughed and he liked the sound of it. She visibly relaxed, the tension in her face easing as they walked around the cozy space.

"Patience, please know I'm here to protect you. You're safe."

She shot him a sharp look. "I know. Why are you saying that?"

"You've been wound tight since you saw the murder. That's understandable, but you don't have to carry that worry. Let me do it for you."

"You're not the one with the target on your back." Her sharp reply communicated her fear.

"True. But if you can't totally let it go, at least let me shoulder some of it with you." It was tricky convincing her to trust him. So far he'd failed at keeping the murderer from coming after her. And then there was the pregnancy; she hadn't wound up pregnant on her own. He owed her at least a sense of personal safety.

"Fair enough." She turned toward the kitchen area and he followed.

The cabin was rustic in all the right places—the log walls, river-stone fireplace and chimney, a cast-iron teakettle on the six-burner gas stove. But it was a fully modernized home, too. Granite counters and a solid butcher block–covered island, stainless steel kitchen appliances. Even the fireplace, as authentic as it was, had a gas insert.

"Go ahead and flick on the fire if you want. It'll take the chill out of the room. The top switch is for the flames and the bottom for the fan, to circulate it through the great room."

Nash hit the switches and watched the fire ignite.

"Not what you expected?" She spoke from the kitchen, but she must have been watching his reaction, his smile when, with a touch of his finger, the old-fashioned country fireplace lit up as if he'd stoked it all night.

"When you said *cabin*, I envisioned something more plain, quite frankly."

"Trust me, this was all that when I purchased it. The kitchen and back bedrooms are the only original parts of the building. I had the front wall knocked out to create the great room area, and added on the porch. Before, it served as no more than a hunter's hideaway."

"How did you find it?"

"While I was in vet school in California, I used to keep an eye on rural homes in this area. I always intended to return to Red Ridge, even though my father never believed me. He thought that once I lived in California long enough I'd never want to come back here."

"Why did you come back?"

She regarded him. The midday sun reflected in her eyes and brought out the amber sparks. The rich color belied the shadows under her eyes, and a sharp pang of guilt hit him. The mother of his future child needed to rest.

"My calling is to heal animals. I've known it since I was a very young child. For a while I wasn't sure if I could do it." As he stared at her, silent, she went on, "Animals have been my solace throughout my life. My parents had a volatile relationship, and after my mother died, my father had a slew of women he dated, some more seriously than others. As I'm sure you know, he married and divorced several times. It made life unpleasant, depending upon the wife. Our dogs and horses kept me going. I knew I'd only be happy if I could work with animals as an adult."

It was easy to imagine her as a young girl, with the same big brown eyes and flame-touched caramel hair. "Before I had to take care of my brothers and sisters, I wouldn't have appreciated what you're telling me as much. I understand now how much kids value security, routine." He swallowed around the perplexing lump that had formed in his throat. "I'm glad you had your pets to help you through it." The thought of any of his siblings having to search for love from an animal instead of their parents or him made him ache. And feel angry for Patience's sake at the same time.

"It wasn't just my pets. They were wonderful, and pets are great companions. But I love them all—farm, domestic, wild. All animals fill my soul."

"Even the bears?"

She grinned. "Yeah. Even the bears. Although I don't have any desire to run into one out here. I keep a bullhorn by the front door for that reason."

"To scare them off." He thought it was ingenious, but would feel better if she had a weapon. "You know, a rifle—"

She held up both hands. "Hold it. I get that you're law enforcement and used to being around firearms. I'm not antigun, in that way. Around these parts, we all learn to use rifles early on for good reason. And it's not that I'm against having a rifle out here to protect myself from bears and the occasional mountain lion. I just don't need one. I haven't ever come close to being targeted by an animal on this mountain. The bears pass through every spring, and I'm always extra careful to make a lot of noise so that I never surprise a mama or her cubs. And you know as well as I do that there's enough wildlife and plants to support them. They don't have to come after me or try to break into the cabin for a meal."

"It's just that…you have more than yourself to consider now."

She wiped her eyes with her hands and her shoulders sagged in exhaustion. Guilt gut punched him.

"I'm sorry, Patience. You need rest." As did he, but he wasn't carrying their child. "Mind if I look around the rest of the place? Why don't you go get a hot shower, then settle in to sleep?"

"I don't mind at all. Go ahead, make yourself at home. A shower sounds good. There's actually two showers, so don't hesitate to take one yourself if you'd like. I've installed a flash heater so the hot water never runs out."

"Thanks. I'll take you up on that." Later, after he was certain she was asleep. He'd post Greta on guard at the front door.

While Patience showered, he poked around inside and outside the cabin. Built on a solid rock-and-concrete foundation, it was impenetrable except through the front door and the bedroom windows. There was a loft above the great room where she'd set up a technically up-to-date office. It also had a sleeper sofa, and provided an eagle's-eye view of the front door. It would be the perfect place for him to bunk, with Greta taking the ground floor.

Getting to Red Ridge each morning was going to be

trickier and, in all truth, a pain. They'd have to budget their time and coordinate shifts. Because no way was he going to let Patience commute on her own. He was going to stick to her like pine tar in June until they caught the killer.

He pulled his phone out to call the kids and see how his aunt and uncle were managing. The thing was, he hadn't thought much at all about his siblings until now. He knew they were safe and well taken care of. He was more worried about Patience and what all this stress was doing to the baby.

And if he were really being honest with himself, he wasn't convinced he'd be able to stay under the same roof as her without touching her again. Being around her roused his desire, and it wasn't something he could boil down to basic horniness or physical need. He was hot for one woman, and she happened to be naked under the shower just one flight of stairs down from the loft he stood in.

This was going to be a challenging mission.

Patience had never felt more tired than she did as the hot water massaged her neck and shoulders. She'd wanted a long hot bath and had a soaking tub to do it in, but was too worn-out to contemplate filling it. And she couldn't risk falling asleep in the water. Not that the constant nagging sensation of being stalked would allow it. Nash had taken evasive measures to ensure they weren't followed, and it made sense that the killer would lie low for a while, until the hunt for him wasn't so intense. Maybe she could catch a few hours of sleep.

If she wasn't so tired she would have giggled at Nash's expression when he saw the cabin, especially the interior. Layla had reacted the same way when she'd first seen the transformation Patience made. As much as she'd paid for every single cent of her education, including vet school, she'd not felt an iota of guilt for taking the loan out and making the cabin exactly how she wanted it. Her pay was excellent and it wasn't as though she needed it to feed a family. So she'd sunk her first earnings into the cabin.

Thinking about her paycheck reminded her that her father had mentioned that future funding for the K9 clinic wasn't a guarantee. It had been a huge part of the family blowup they'd had right before her fateful night with Nash. Layla had assured her that the clinic remained a top priority of Colton Energy, and that Layla's fiancé would solve everything.

Patience shut off the shower and reached for a towel. How she and Layla had both come from the same DNA was beyond her. They were close and loved one another, but her sister put money and business ahead of all else in her life. Layla's agreement to remain engaged to smarmy Hamlin Harrington was a clue that she cared more about Colton Energy than herself.

Patience dried off and put on the long johns she kept at the cabin. Her stomach, which she hadn't even thought twice about before she took the pregnancy test yesterday, was definitely more pronounced, but not so much that it affected her stretchy clothes. Yet. Her scrubs and workout clothes were more forgiving, but no way could she squeeze into her favorite jeans. She ran her hand over her belly, musing over the fact that an entire human being grew in there.

She sat on her bed, thinking about getting a cup of hot tea before she turned in. But fighting her comfy surroundings was too much.

The wrought iron bed frame that she'd found in an antiques store in Sioux Falls and painted white offset the fluffy comforter and pillows with her favorite floral pattern. She knew she needed to talk to Nash more, reassure him that it was totally okay with her that he wasn't interested in being a father, but sleep beckoned.

As she slid between her flannel sheets, the last thing she thought about was phoning the clinic when she woke up, to check on her patients. Especially Fred. That made her mind flash to the cold, heartless eyes of the killer, and his voice calling out, "Where are you, you bitch?" as he stormed the building. But even that didn't keep her awake.

Nash heard the complete silence settle on the cabin like a down blanket not long after the water stopped. He shoved aside any sense of politeness or healthy boundaries as he went and checked to make sure Patience was okay. Her form was still under a mound of covers in the decidedly feminine master bedroom. It was a grown-up version of the room Maeve and Paige shared, which they'd decorated before their parents died.

Patience was down for the count, or at least for several hours, so he put a cup of decaf coffee on to brew, thanks to the ultramodern machine in the kitchen, and took Greta for a quick walk on the property. They'd missed dinner, but sleep was more important at this point. The surrounding woods were dense and definitely a deterrent to a casual trespasser, hunting or hiking. Nothing was impenetrable to a professional criminal, however, and Nash's instinct told him the murderer was definitely experienced. He hadn't handled many murder cases in his decade-long career, but the Groom Killer had changed that. Nash had seen enough lately to know that the lake murder was no random event. Nor was the way the bad guy had tried to dispose of the victim.

Nash's phone buzzed as he came back to the house and he took the call from Finn.

"Sir. Maddox speaking."

"Nash, I want to thank you and Greta for your hard work last night and this morning. How's our favorite K9 veterinarian doing?" Chief Colton had ordered Nash to stay with Patience until they caught the Lake Killer.

"She's doing better, sound asleep at the moment. We're at her private cabin, about forty minutes out from Red Ridge. I'll be commuting in with her until the coast is clear."

"Sounds like a plan. We're going to need you and Greta when we comb the lake for any other unknown victims. It's already getting too late to go in and do it properly today, and I'm not sure about tomorrow, as we have to wait on the state unit to back us up, but we'll be set within forty-eight hours. Get some rest and we'll see you by daybreak."

"Yes, sir." He made a mental note to check out his dive gear, which he kept in a locker at the RRPD.

They disconnected. Nash retrieved his coffee from

the kitchen, noting that the house was still peacefully silent. Good. Patience needed the sleep.

Greta raised her head from her front paws to look at him when he stepped back out onto the porch. She'd taken up almost half the space, obviously needing her rest, too. But she'd never be fully asleep, he knew. Greta always had at least one ear listening for trouble.

"You're a good girl, Greta. Chief says good job for yesterday." He rubbed the top of her head and behind her ears as she languidly thumped her tail against the wooden floor.

He sighed as he sat and put his feet up on the porch railing, settling into the rocking chair with the cup of coffee he'd made. Seeing Patience's flowery room reminded him of the girls, and then the boys. All four were fine and had made it to school, according his aunt and uncle. He wished he could let any worry for them go, but it was impossible.

The girls were seventeen and fifteen. Paige would be out of the house and in college this time next year. It was early in her senior year, but all indications were that she'd be getting into her first choice—Pennsylvania State. She wanted to go away, and while he supported all the kids in going to whatever schools they could get into, he wished she'd picked a place like Sioux Falls. As hard as the past few years had been, he'd grown attached to his siblings more than he'd ever dreamed. He was going to miss her. And it wouldn't be long before Maeve would follow on her heels. She'd already begun to apply to the US Naval Academy in Annapolis, Maryland. She wanted to be a navy fighter pilot.

At least the younger two—Troy and Jon, twelve and thirteen—were going to keep him busy as they grew from boys to young men. With them being complete opposites, he often had to juggle taking them to either Jon's soccer team practices or Troy's card games at the local game store. Both wanted to go to college someday, but for different reasons. Jon wanted to earn a full-ride athletic scholarship and become a sports journalist. Troy wanted to develop video games. If Nash could harness their combined energy and abilities, it'd pay for all four kids' college and graduate school expenses. He smiled as he looked out on the dozens of tall fir trees that guarded the cabin.

The serenity lulled him and he actually felt the tension drain out of his frame for the first time in days. But the chill in the air wasn't conducive to napping, and besides, he needed solid downtime. He stood and stretched.

"Come on, Greta. You can keep watch from inside."

He'd have to ignore the constant pull of Patience's presence from her bedroom, the hum of awareness in the air whenever she was around. Otherwise he'd never get to sleep.

# Chapter 7

Patience woke up in a darkened room, and from her smart watch saw that it was almost morning. She'd slept straight through the night. The October days were getting shorter and shorter, and under the canopy of the mountain forest it was more pronounced.

She slipped out of the bed and donned sweatpants and a hoodie over her long underwear, needing the extra layers. It was time to light up the heater.

Only after she pulled socks on did she remember everything. The shock of finding out she was pregnant. The murderer dumping his victim into a frigid lake as if he were throwing garbage over the side. Her frantic call to dispatch. Nash.

*Nash.*

She leaned on the door frame before she left her

room, forcing herself to take several deep breaths. It was a calming technique they all learned during stress-management training at the RRPD or at the K9 clinic. And usually it worked. The slight tremble she felt, no matter how calm the moment, was caused by something she couldn't help. The worry of being killed, of course. That wasn't going to ease up until the Lake Killer was apprehended.

Her attraction to Nash wasn't letting up anytime soon, either. And he was here with her.

"Let it go." She forcefully expelled air, trying to clear her mind as she emptied her lungs.

The cabin's sense of security enveloped her. She padded as softly as possible down the short corridor to the kitchen and great room. Nash had to be sleeping; he'd looked exhausted before she'd gone in for her shower. She stopped in the kitchen, pushed the heat button on the thermostat and set a pot of coffee to brew.

The silhouette of Greta's great head drew her attention to the far wall, under the large picture window that had been part of the cabin's renovation three years ago. Greta faced the window as she monitored the porch and woods, but looked over her hulking shoulder to acknowledge Patience's arrival.

Patience offered the dog a grin before she put her finger to her lips. She looked up at the loft and saw Nash's form was stretched out along the leather sofa, a thin throw over his torso and thighs. He hadn't even unfolded the sleeper into a bed. She stifled a giggle at the length of his frame on the couch, and went back down the hall to the guest room, where she yanked the comforter off the double bed.

Her intention was to cover Nash with the much more substantial blanket, but she paused once she'd crept up the steps to the loft, loath to wake him. She stood in front of the sofa, the thick down throw in her arms.

He looked so peaceful in sleep. Definitely Nash, and unquestionably masculine, but serene. His face was smooth, with no indication of the lines that often stamped it during the day. There was no sign of the professional hard-ass she'd witnessed in action last night, or early this morning. Nash Maddox was 100 percent male. She let her gaze drift over him, his form only half-concealed by the afghan her sister had crocheted. She paused her observation where his T-shirt rode up, exposing rock-hard abs covered with dark hair. Her breath caught and she let the thrill of sexual awareness run through her. His stomach teased her, shooting a pang of longing through her as she fought to keep her fingers from reaching out and—

"Are you going to keep staring at me, or give me some warmth?"

Patience jumped in surprise with a squeal. He opened one eye, his mouth curving.

She dumped the blanket on him. "There you go." But instead of leaving him be, she sank down onto the floor. "You know, this is a sleeper sofa. You didn't have to be so uncomfortable all night. Why didn't you take the guest room?"

"I need to have an uninterrupted sight line to the front door."

"Oh." Of course. He took his job seriously, protecting her. She looked down from the loft and saw Greta had moved to lean up against the oak door, a definite hindrance to anyone trying to enter the cabin. "It looks like Greta knows her business."

He rubbed his eyes and sat up, dragging the blankets with him. "Greta, at ease." When Greta cocked her head, as if trying to figure out why he was releasing her from her post, he added, "You're a good dog. Jeez, it's freezing in here."

"I fixed that. I turned on the heater on my way up here." She was in long johns and a heavy bathrobe, but he'd slept in...his underwear from what she could see. She noticed his grin. "What's so funny?"

"You. In a good way. This is the most rustic setting for a cabin and yet you've managed to outfit it with the latest in technology and convenience."

"If you're expecting me to apologize for that, don't hold your breath." She leaned her back against the sofa. Greta stood up, stretched and slowly climbed up the loft stairs. The huge dog placed her head in Patience's lap, and she buried her fingers in the thick, dark fur. "She is the biggest snuggle bug, aren't you, Greta?"

"Did you get enough sleep?" Nash asked.

She turned to look at him and his eyes blazed across the short distance between them. She glanced away. It was too easy to think he was looking at her with more than professional interest. She peered into Greta's liquid black eyes instead.

"Yes, thank you. I don't know the last time I went that long without sleeping. Do you realize we'd been awake for the better part of twenty-four hours by the time we got here?"

He chuckled, the sound low and sexy. "I sure do. Man, am I glad that my aunt and uncle are with the kids. I love my brothers and sisters, but it's nice to have to only worry about work, too."

"That's fair." Besides the constant sexual tension, the silent topic of the baby hung between them and she wondered when he'd talk about it again. If he'd mention the baby on his own.

"Is there coffee?"

"Yes, I'm sorry—in the kitchen, on the counter. I made a whole pot, but if you don't like regular dark roast there's a single-cup maker there, too. Help yourself."

He stood and she did, too, ignoring the part of her that wished she'd woken him up with something other than coffee. As he meandered down to the kitchen with the blanket wrapped around him she followed, as did Greta. She didn't see any skin but his muscular calves. Was it the baby hormones that made her want to touch said calves and maybe get more of a peek of what was under his blanket?

They stopped in the kitchen and she was transfixed by how much he filled the space. His scent overrode the coffee aroma and she had to remind herself for the umpteenth time that her sexual journey with Nash had ended almost three months ago.

"Are you able to have full caffeine? I mean, is the baby? Patience?" Damn it, he'd caught her staring and was making fun of her.

"I'm not in some kind of daze, you know."

He shrugged and then dug in the cabinet for a mug. He chose a dark green ceramic one she'd received gratis from a veterinary drug company. The most masculine cup in her cabinet. Of course he did. She couldn't blame him for being such a guy, but then again, he was. So. Incredibly. Hot.

Frustrated, she left the kitchen and took a seat in the living room's easy chair, next to the sofa.

"Patience?"

She shook her head. "I'm still a little groggy, I suppose. I don't usually sleep for twelve hours."

"Is it grogginess, Patience?" He padded into the living room with his cup of black coffee and sat on the sofa. When he leaned forward, his knees were a scant inch from hers, and his scent again transported her back to their night together.

"Nash, I'm not looking for a relationship any more than you are. We'd agreed that our night, that one night, was a onetime deal. I don't expect anything more from you. Honest."

"What if I'm looking for more? What would you say then?"

"That you're only doing this because of the baby. And in case I didn't make it clear, I'm raising it on my own. I won't ever ask you for anything. I told you because it was the right thing to do." She prided herself on always keeping things aboveboard. It was how she'd kept her identity as a child in a family of billionaires and the accompanying lifestyle.

"If you think for one minute that I'm going to say

okay to the Patience Plan, you don't know me very well."

She knew him enough, though. "You're already raising four kids."

"I am. And the two oldest will be out the door to college within the next two years, one right after the other. The boys could benefit from having a baby brother or sister. Nothing better for teenage birth control than seeing the responsibilities that come with a child."

"We didn't set a very good example. I mean, with the birth control part."

"So the condom didn't work. They usually do. And to be honest, were we as careful as we could have been? I saw you down at least two champagne cocktails that evening, and I know I had a few beers. Not that drinking is an excuse."

"But it sure let our inhibitions down." As soon as she said it, she grimaced. "Sorry. I tend to forget my mental filter when I'm tired. To be truthful, I would have done it all stone-cold sober." And she would have. She wasn't under the influence of anything now but the nearness of Nash, and she wanted to jump his bones.

"You've said nothing but the truth." He leaned over and placed his cup on the coffee table. But instead of settling back onto the sofa, he got down on his knees and placed his hands on hers, their faces level.

Patience's breathing slowed as her heartbeat sped up. It was as if they were in their own sensual bubble whenever he was around, and certainly when he got this close to her. She knew she should at least grasp at a semblance of professionalism, show him that she wasn't the same woman he'd been with that night. But she was that woman, and more.

"Nash."

He raised his brows very slightly and inclined his head, making his intent clear. But he wouldn't follow through until she said yes.

Instead, she closed the distance between them and kissed him first. His lips were firm but so soft, and at the smallest flicker of her tongue he opened his mouth to her. Patience let the chaos of the last two days go as she gave in to her need.

Nash's arms came up and he cupped her head, more firmly sealing his mouth over hers. They parried for the lead, their tongues waging battle, and she remembered at once why they'd been so good together.

So good it had made a baby.

She pulled back.

"What?" His eyes were still closed and he landed a kiss on her jawline, her throat.

"Nash, we've already agreed that last time was—"

She groaned as he kissed his way back to her lips. *Just a little more*, she promised herself. When his tongue filled her mouth, she wasn't sure why she'd ever resisted him.

Nash didn't allow himself to think of anything but the taste of Patience's lips as they continued to kiss like sex-starved teenagers. He wasn't going to suggest they go to bed again since he didn't have any condoms with him. But there were other ways to please her. He paused, pulled back from the kiss reluctantly, looked into her very liquid brown eyes.

"I want to taste you again, Patience. All of you." She answered him by shimmying out of her pajama bottoms and long johns, throwing off her hoodie as if they were in a cabana on a tropical beach and not in a cabin in the mountains.

Her heavy-lidded eyes opened far enough for him to see her want, her need. "Nash." She breathed his name as if she'd come to the end of a long search.

He knew he had. The taste of her lips, her skin, made him need more. Her moans and sighs guided his tongue, told him what she liked best, what turned her on.

His erection strained against his boxer briefs, but this wasn't about his release—this was all for Patience. He kissed his way down over her rounded abdomen, where he dipped his tongue into the indentation of her belly button. She cried out in need and he chuckled. "Not so fast, babe. Enjoy each—" he licked her hip bone "—and every—" he sucked on the skin just above her bikini panties "—bit." He kissed her through the flimsy fabric, purposefully blowing his breath into her, the satisfaction of making her squirm in response filling him with something he couldn't name.

She helped him get her panties off, then lay on the sofa, her legs spread wide. Nash paused, stunned by her beauty.

"Don't make me beg, Nash."

He worked his way back up her legs to the insides of her thighs, taking his time, leaving wet kisses where he knew she liked them. He'd memorized her every response and preference that night they'd shared, and still there was so much more to learn about her. He wanted to know all of Patience.

Every last bit.

Patience delighted in the contrast of the cool sofa beneath her and the white-hot heat of Nash's mouth on the insides of her thighs. Her nipples tightened, as taut as the need she had for this man.

For Nash.

"Don't stop, Nash. Please."

"Babe." He placed his mouth over her sex and swirled his tongue over her most intimate parts, swollen for him. Because of him. Her entire body was inflamed, aware of only Nash's skillful lovemaking and her urgency for release. She tried to hang on, to make it last, but like the relationship building between them, and the unborn child that they'd made, her response kept growing.

The initial waves of her climax began, and when Nash slid one, then two fingers inside her, the internal counterpressure catapulted her into a strong, breath-stealing orgasm. Her cries echoed about the cabin and she gasped for breath. As soon as she came down from the climax, Nash surprised her. Instead of stopping, he kept going, kept stroking and licking until she came again. And again.

He didn't let up until she begged him to.

Nash looked at her, his eyes glazed with the same feelings she had—but how could this be? He hadn't enjoyed the release she had.

"Babe, I can do this all day."

"I could let you, but I want to please you, too. While I still have the strength." She laughed then, a long, low rumble that reflected the depth of her sexual satisfaction.

"This was for you, Patience." He sat up and gently covered her with the blanket. "You're going to get cold."

She sat up and sidled closer. "Never. Not next to you."

He shook with his need for her and fought his instinct to move over her, to take her fully and completely. He wanted her so badly. He'd savored every last lick, every last taste of her. And still he wanted more.

"We don't need to use a condom anymore. I'm already pregnant. As long as you're clean? You said you were that night."

"As did you. And yes, I'm clean. But, Patience, we don't have to do this. We moved so quickly last time."

"By agreement." She leaned over and kissed him. The kiss was sexy and full of both their scents, with her musk still on his lips. Her hands reached down and stroked him, and he stopped worrying about consequences. He needed Patience, had to be inside her.

He stood up and they both got him out of his T-shirt and briefs. Patience grasped his buttocks and without preamble took him in her mouth. Her tongue teased and flirted before her lips closed around him with the perfect amount of pressure.

"Babe." He stroked her lush, sexy hair, held her to him as long as he dared. Reluctantly, he gently pulled back.

She looked up at him, puzzlement in her eyes. "Tell me, Nash. What do you want?"

He eased her back and lowered himself over her. She opened her legs again, this time to receive him. "As much as I love your mouth on my cock, I need to be inside you."

"Then do it, Nash. Take me."

He prayed there'd be another time to take it slowly, to spend all day and night with her. But not now. He entered her in one swift stroke and groaned with the sheer ecstasy of her tight heat wrapped around him.

"I've missed this, Patience." He began to move, and her hips met his as she gasped in pleasure. He didn't know where or when, but they became one, seeking a common goal: totally unity.

His climax came at him like a Mack truck on an empty highway, with little warning before the huge spasm of total abandonment hit.

This…this was what had been missing from his life. Not the sex, not the release, but the completion with Patience.

They lay together, Nash atop her, for several minutes as they both caught their breaths. Came down to earth. Only when Patience's thoughts turned back to why they were here in the cabin together did she nudge Nash to sit. As soon as he left her she missed him, and he was only inches away. But the omnipresent fear of being killed chased away her afterglow.

She stood and ran her fingers through her hair. Hair that his fingers had turned into an unholy mess. She couldn't keep the grin from her face. It'd been worth it.

Except now they had to face reality again. Only after she'd increased the distance between them by several feet and two easy chairs did she stop and face him.

"Nash, we're playing with fire here. With our emotions. There's no future for us, and we'd both do best to stick to our original agreement." She watched him as he stood and wrapped the blanket around himself. A pity, as his naked body was heaven-sent.

"Plans change, Patience. We weren't planning on you getting pregnant. Yet you are." Nash's face revealed no frustration, no recrimination. Just openness, honesty.

"Of course, we didn't plan for the baby. But facts are facts." She didn't like it that they couldn't be friends with benefits, either. This time had been a mistake. But it didn't feel like a mistake to her body. In fact, she'd never felt so at ease with a man as she did with Nash.

That enough was reason to guard her heart.

Patience looked at him, her hair mussed from their lovemaking, and it was all he could do to not kiss her again, let the desire build until they were making love on every surface in the cabin.

He stood, naked under the blanket he'd wrapped around himself. "I need to shower. When I come back, we're going sit down and hash this out."

But when he came back into the kitchen, after a quick shower and putting his jeans and flannel shirt on, the time to talk had passed. Patience was engrossed in a phone conversation and pointed at the fresh coffeepot as she spared him a quick glance.

He helped himself to a large mugful and added in some of the milk she had in her fridge. It was almond milk, but it would do. Paige had taken to almond milk the last year and he had to admit it wasn't the worst thing on the planet. He looked out the kitchen window and saw two deer meandering through the trees out back. The kids would love this cabin.

Crap. When he was with Patience it was easy to lose track of time. He needed to check on them. He took Greta with him and let himself out the side door.

"Hey, Uncle Jim. How are you and Aunt Clara doing?"

"We're great, the kids are fine. Paige and Maeve helped us get the boys out the door on time. Those two will fiddle about all morning, won't they?"

Nash laughed. "Yes, they will, but don't take any guff from them."

"Oh, they're polite. They just like to sleep a lot. I remember feeling tired when I was their age, but sleeping in was never an option." Uncle Jim and Nash's mother had been raised on a cattle ranch and had been expected to perform their share of chores from a young age.

"They're not having the same upbringing as you and Mom did, that's for sure."

"That's okay. It's not a bad thing to be able to be a kid a little longer. How's your case going?"

"I don't know—I'm about to head back into town and check it out for myself. I'm going to be on this assignment until we catch the bad guy. He's threatened our K9 vet twice. Greta and I are keeping an eye on her."

"I didn't realize your duties included bodyguard."

"They don't, not normally. But since Patience Colton is the department's K9 veterinarian, I've stepped up. The RRPD takes care of its own."

"I hear you. Dr. Colton took care of Sleepy, you know." Uncle Jim referred to the cocker spaniel he and Aunt Clara had had for almost fifteen years. They'd never had kids of their own and the little dog had been like a child to them. They'd had to put her down last spring after a cancer diagnosis.

"I didn't realize Patience was the vet who'd cared for Sleepy." He remembered his aunt and uncle's ordeal over the dog when it took ill, and how they'd brought it into Red Ridge after hearing about the K9 clinic being open to civilian patients, but he hadn't connected the dots.

"Dr. Colton was, and is, excellent at her job. She was also single at the time and very attractive." Uncle Jim was as subtle as a landslide.

"She is still both, in fact." Nash wasn't going to pussyfoot around it.

"Does that have anything to do with why you've taken such an interest in her safety?" Uncle Jim's voice had the same positive inflection his mother's had had. A sharp pang of grief tugged deep in Nash's chest.

His first instinct was to blow Uncle Jim off and make light of his query. But the man who'd helped Nash piece his and the kids' lives back together deserved more. Besides, Uncle Jim knew him well and would know he was lying.

"Yeah, it does. But don't say anything to Aunt Clara for now. I don't know how it'll go and I don't want to get her hopes up." Aunt Clara had done everything but hold a rally in downtown Red Ridge and Sioux Falls to find a woman for Nash. She was certain that the right partner would make his time raising the kids go more quickly, and help Nash through his grief.

She hadn't been wrong; his night with Patience had underscored to him how lonely he'd been. And how downright horny he was. Except his sexual needs and fantasies were always centered around Patience, ever since he'd started working more closely with her at the K9 clinic. As if their attraction to one another had always been there and only waited for the perfect time— the night after their last K9 training workshop—to come to the surface.

And now they were going to have a baby together.

"You still there, Nash?"

"Yeah, just checking on Greta. We're out walking through the woods."

"I imagine it's beautiful up on that mountain."

"It is, but again, please don't mention it to anyone. I've got to keep her here safe and sound until we know it's clear for her to go back to her home in Red Ridge."

"No worries there. Don't you worry about the kids, Nash. They're older and understand your responsibility to the community. Just do your job and we'll all be waiting for you when it's done."

"Thanks so much, Uncle Jim."

He disconnected the call and looked around the cabin's

perimeter for any signs of a prowler who'd come while he and Patience had slept. And made love. As cunning as the murderer was, Nash had learned over the years that someone being where he or she shouldn't always left a trace. It was very difficult for a human being to leave zero evidence behind.

"Greta, work." He moved her through the task of sniffing around the cabin and surrounding woods, but she never alerted to anything unusual. He was confident that she'd tell him if she smelled anything from the boat the man had used to dump the body.

Nash heard the door open and watched as Patience came outside. Her eyes were bright and her cheeks had the color of ripe peaches. Her rest had done her good. He shouldn't feel the resulting swirl of satisfaction over something so simple. Sure, he was here to help keep her safe, but he'd not been the one to make her sleep. It was just the paternal connection; he was happy the mother of his future child was doing better.

It couldn't totally be due to how hard she'd come in his arms.

"I need to go to the clinic." Patience walked up to him. They watched Greta sniff through a pile of dried pine needles. Nash called her to his side, where she dutifully sat.

"We can leave now, if you'd like. I have to head in to the station, and you do, too—you need to give your description to the sketch artist."

"I want to bring my car back here, Nash. I can't be tied to you forever." And yet she was. She carried his child. When would this new reality stop taking his breath away?

"It's not safe for you to go back and forth on your own. Not yet. And the killer knows your vehicle and will follow you here in a heartbeat."

"If he's still around. Don't you think he may have taken off for now? He has to know the entire county, the state even, is looking for him."

"That may be true, but I'm not willing to take any chances, Patience."

Her chin rose in what he knew was her unconscious signal that she wasn't going to bend. "I have choices here, Nash. Being pregnant doesn't change that."

Their eyes met, and besides the instant zing to his crotch that always accompanied eye contact with her, he felt something different. Something that they were building together.

Trust.

He shook his head. "I'm sorry, Patience. You're as knowledgeable as I am about this case at this point. And it's totally your call as to whether we travel together or solo. But you can't blame me for having an added interest, can you? You're pregnant with my baby."

"A baby I told you I don't expect you to help me with." Her gaze softened a notch. "Although I guess I haven't been too understanding. You've had a lot to process these last hours, too."

"Let's get to the station while the sketch artist is still there." Keeping to the business at hand suited him best.

He'd thought he wanted to have a heart-to-heart with her about how they'd handle raising the baby together, but she was right. He needed some time to process.

# Chapter 8

Glad that Nash had to focus on the road back into town, Patience used the time for self-examination. Something about him made her words come out ahead of her thoughts. She wasn't used to curbing her usual forthright manner, or having to engage her mental filter so much.

In her family and at the clinic, she was pragmatic, and prided herself on speaking her mind. It made life easier for all. The emotional tug-of-war she felt whenever she was around Nash called for a different tactic, and worst of all, her namesake. She needed to be more patient with Nash. He'd only just found out he was going to be a father, and hadn't had time to come to terms with the ramifications. Instead of being free to be a bachelor in six years as he deserved, when his youngest brother came of age, he'd have to start the clock over the minute the baby was born.

Her baby. She couldn't think about it as theirs, or about his paternity, without her emotions taking her to dangerous places. To a life where she'd have a partner to share everything with, including the joy of raising a child together.

"You're awfully quiet." Nash was barreling down the mountain road, obviously as eager as she was to be back in civilization. Greta sat in the rear, her canine seat belt keeping her almost one hundred fifty pounds from flying into the front between their seats.

"I'm trying to remember the exact details of the murderer's face, so that I don't mess up with the artist."

"You can't mess up. Just tell her what you saw, and you'll know right away if her drawing matches."

"You're right." It was easier, safer to talk to Nash about work. "How long before we catch him, do you think?"

She watched his profile as he made the turn onto the highway that was a straight shot into Red Ridge. "No telling. He's a professional, that much is clear. And I'm not a detective, so I'm not privy to all the details on the case, not as they happen. Unless it pertains to your safety. You know as much as I do. We can ask for a recap when we get there."

"That would be good. That should take about an hour, right? I do have to go by the clinic at some point today, Nash."

"It's too risky."

"Hear me out. You can drive me there in a police

vehicle. I'll wear a ski cap and borrow your jacket. I only need a half hour or so. I want to check on my patients and make sure my staff doesn't feel like I abandoned them."

"I doubt they feel that way."

"You know what I mean. They need to know I'm still around and should be called with any concerns that come up." Although she had to admit the staff at the clinic were very good at their jobs. "And I want my car back. Or at least a vehicle of my own. I'll rent one for the time being."

His face stilled. "That's awfully expensive. I doubt it's in the RRPD budget."

"I'll pay for it myself."

"Of course you will."

"Wait a minute—why does that sound like an accusation?" She'd had her share of being judged because of the Colton fortune. Some people had a hard time believing a wealthy person had the same morals as the average citizen.

"You're used to being able to pay for whatever you want, I'd assume. It's a fair assessment, isn't it? Your father is Fenwick Colton. He practically owns all of South Dakota."

"Not true. He owns the most successful energy company in the state, yes." Colton Energy was having some financial issues, but Patience knew her dad would find a way to regroup. A way that hopefully didn't include Layla marrying as part of some deal. "And do I have a trust fund? Of course—but as I've already told you, I haven't touched it except to take loans out for college and vet school. And due to scholarships and the K9 research I did, I was able to pay back into said trust fund entirely. I paid for my schooling, my town house and the cabin all on my own." She felt a niggle of guilt and blurted out its cause. "Okay, I used a little bit of the funds to renovate the cabin. It was better than accepting the huge McMansion my father wanted to give me after I graduated." She and all her siblings had offered to turn their trust funds over to Fenwick to help out the business, but he'd said all of them combined would barely make a dent in the issues.

"If I were your father and could afford it, I'd give you the world after such a great accomplishment."

"You obviously love your siblings, and I've no doubt you'd do anything for them. What am I saying? You *are* doing everything for them. You've given up a single lifestyle for them. But my father isn't as altruistic. He never supported me going to vet school. He was beyond annoyed that I refused to major in finance or business at university, like Layla did. Layla's our daddy's favorite—because she works for Colton Energy."

"I know Layla."

He said it in a neutral manner, but Patience read past his ambiguous demeanor. Everyone in town knew Layla; she was an assertive, take-no-prisoners businesswoman at Colton Energy. And unknown to Nash, she was secretly engaged to that slimy jerk Hamlin. The thought of it made Patience's stomach more queasy than the baby did.

"Tell me, if you're not close to your father, why do you still call him Daddy?"

His question caught her up short. "Habit's the easiest answer. But I guess I've never stopped being the daughter who wants her father's approval. I don't need it, and don't care about it now, but it would have been nice if just once he'd acknowledged my work, you know?" She shrugged. "Maybe it's a way to keep him smaller in my mind, to not have him be that bigger-than-life person that his reputation promotes."

"It must be hard being a Colton."

"Are you being sarcastic?"

"No, I'm serious. Everyone knows your family name, and makes immediate judgments."

"Except you. You've never given me the impression you think less, or more, of me because I'm a Colton. Except for this recent slam."

"I'm sorry, Patience." Sincerity laced his tone.

She shrugged. "It's okay. Just don't do it again." She heard the edge to her words too late. "My turn to be sorry, Nash. Knowing the Lake Killer is looking for me is affecting my attitude."

"Completely normal." He stared through the windshield and she knew he, too, felt extra stress—the stress of protecting her.

The road stretched out in front of them for the last thirty minutes of the drive.

"This is going to get old, Nash. Driving back and forth to the cabin. You and Greta need to be closer to town, in case of an emergency, don't you?"

"Not happening, Patience. And stop trying to manipulate your way out of it."

Underneath her independence she had a moment of serenity—or was it relief?—that Nash was going to keep her safe from the Lake Killer.

Sometimes it didn't hurt to have a partner.

Nash pulled into the station lot, killed the engine and turned to Patience. "Take as long as you need in there. I'll work out finding you a plain car to use for now. You're right, you need to be able to come and go as needed. But I'm only going to agree to this if you don't fight me on staying overnight with you at the cabin. You'll need at least two weapons—a rifle and your RRPD-issued .45—with you at all times and in the cabin. And if I have to remain in town past usual hours you'll have to stay near me, too. I don't want you at the cabin alone for any stretch of time."

Her face was a study in conflict as she bit her lip, her eyes bright with anger. "I'm not one of your siblings, Nash. And don't you need to get back home to them? Your aunt and uncle can't stay forever, can they?"

"Actually, they can. They both work from home and run their own business on their laptops. And this won't take forever. We'll catch the man you saw on the lake, Patience."

"Let's go." She let herself out of the car and walked up to the station.

Nash stayed in his seat for a minute. "We've got to give her space, Greta. But we're not backing down on the baby business." He spoke to the dog as he watched Patience go into the building, then turned and looked at his K9 partner. "We're going to have another member of the family. Two, if she'll ever agree to raise the baby with me."

"Pale blue eyes with a vacant look to them." Patience gave the sketch artist every single detail she remembered. She'd seen that kind of expression only once before, when she'd had to testify in court against a hardened drug dealer who'd shot at one of the K9s. Patience had saved the dog's life, since local police officers had brought the injured Malinois to her within minutes, a tourniquet around its left hind leg.

"Are you sure you saw the color in the dark?" The sketch artist kept moving her hand as she questioned Patience.

"Like I said, the moon was full and I was using binoculars. I'd gone out to see if the great horned owls were in their usual perch and instead saw this man dumping a body."

"You said he had short hair?"

"Yes. That was harder to tell, as he was wearing a dark ski cap, but I noticed blond or gray hair coming out around it." Her hands started shaking and the artist noted the fact.

"Take a sip of water. We can break at any time."

"I'm okay. I know you'll get a better likeness the more I remember, and that memory fades quickly." She hadn't expected it to be so tough, but the Lake Killer wanted her dead. Of course, it would be scary going over his appearance again.

"We've got a lot already. How does this look?" The

artist turned her smart tablet around and revealed what she had so far.

Patience gasped. "I had no idea you'd make it so perfect. Your talent is amazing. It's like you took a photograph of him!"

The woman smiled. "It's my job. Lucky for us, your observational skills are top-notch. Sometimes I barely get more than the description of eyes and a nose out of a witness, trust me."

"So we're done?"

She nodded. "For now. I'll get this uploaded to our system."

Patience thanked the artist and went in search of Nash. He was in a meeting with the chief and other officers, but saw her as she passed by the conference area, and waved her over. He motioned for her to take the empty chair next to his.

"Any luck?" he whispered, leaning close to her ear. The intimate contact of his heated breath on her skin made her self-conscious, but not before her body reacted. The warmth only Nash lit fired in her belly and reached out to her most intimate parts. She looked around, but the other officers paid scant notice to her as they listened to Finn, who was outlining the details of the case so far.

"Yes," she whispered back, then saw the image of the criminal flash up on the RRPD smart board. "It's there!"

Nash turned to look and Finn nodded at Patience.

"Thank you, Dr. Colton." He used her formal title in front of the others. "You've provided a detailed description to our artist. This is the man we're looking for, everyone."

"Chief, is there any chance this is also the Groom Killer?" One of the officers spoke up and Patience stiffened. The Groom Killer was why so many in town, including Layla, had canceled long-planned weddings and postponed announcing their engagements.

"Doubtful. We've just got information that the victim was wrapped up in drug dealing. We'll know more as soon as the coroner releases his report, but I think we're looking at a different case. But we're not sure about anything until proven, right?"

"When are we going to sweep the lake again?" Nash asked, and the chief called up the officer in charge of the lake crime scene.

"I'll let Officer Billings fill you in."

Tom Billings nodded. "Good afternoon, everyone. As the chief said, we've done an initial sweep and found no further bodies, but we're going to need to dive to figure out what our equipment was catching on. It could be a sunken boat, but we're not sure. Nash, I'll need you and Greta in the morning at first light."

"You got it."

Patience leaned close to Nash. "I need to go to the clinic now, and then I'll come back with you in the morning."

She heard his sharp intake of breath, saw the pulse pounding on the side of his temple. He didn't want to leave her side and she didn't want to lose the sense of connection to him. But they were both professionals and had a job to do. Whatever it would take to catch both killers.

Patience, like Nash, prided herself on putting duty first. But her vocation didn't keep her from wishing things were different. That she and Nash could spend time together, at her cabin, for reasons other than security.

Nash drove Patience to the K9 facility. Leaving her there dismayed him, but it was still light out and she wouldn't be alone for long. He procured her a car from the station pool, an old beat-up sedan that looked nothing like the late-model SUV she normally drove. That vehicle would stay parked in the RRPD lot, so if the murderer knew it was her car, he wouldn't follow her to the cabin.

"Here are my keys." She opened a desk drawer in her office and handed him her key ring. "It's touchless."

"I think I can figure it out."

"I didn't mean to insinuate you couldn't."

They looked at one another for a heartbeat.

"Is it always going to be this prickly between us?" He knew she didn't feel her best, being newly pregnant, but thought maybe he'd done something to tick her off.

She exhaled forcefully and it made the wisps of hair around her face float. "I'm sorry, Nash. It's been a little intense, hasn't it? I mean, I know we're both in the business of adrenaline rushes, you more so than I. But I'm used to having downtime each day after surgery, and the other day was insane. We had an emergency gunshot wound and..."

"And?"

She let her shoulders fall and leaned against the wall behind her desk. "And nothing. It sounds so tame after witnessing a murderer dump a body into a lake."

"Don't forget being chased and then stalked by the killer." He knew she'd already compartmentalized what had happened. It was the only way she'd be able to walk in here again and not curl up into a protective ball on her worn office sofa.

"Yeah, well, there's that, too. But none of this is really out of the ordinary for you and Greta, is it? Not that you see murderers every day, but you're more used to the break-ins and chasing vandals. Am I right?"

"You are. But there's nothing like the stress of an op that turns personal. This case was personal for you the minute you identified the man dumping the body. Speaking of which, I have more news."

"Oh?"

"Turns out it was a young student from the community college in Rapid City. Her name was Dallas Remington, and she was nineteen and suspected of dealing heroin."

"If she was in school in Rapid City, what was she doing way up here?" Rapid City was almost two hours away in the southwest portion of the state, mirror opposite to Red Ridge's location.

"Probably picking up a drug delivery. We've had a lot of heroin activity recently and this ties in with it."

"What a shame." Patience studied him and Nash had to admit he didn't mind it when her attention was on him. "You must worry about your siblings. The opioid epidemic is alarming."

He nodded. "I sure as hell do. Being a police officer never protects a family from crime, even though I wish it did. But it's frustrating to know so much about what it can do to a kid and not be able to do anything but educate."

"And some hope and prayers, too, I imagine." She had a soft smile that he remembered from after they'd made love the first time in the middle of the night. "You can't do it all, Nash."

"No one's asking me to. I do the best I can." He needed to get back to the station. "Text me when you leave here, and when you're safe in the cabin. Take your weapon with you, and make sure it's loaded. And please, above all else, don't hesitate to use it if you need to."

"Do you really think I'd think twice if I see that monster again?"

She had him there.

# Chapter 9

The next morning, they rose before sunup, and Patience beat him to the kitchen. When he walked in from his shower, the coffee was hot and she was at the stove.

"Good morning. I'm making some eggs—want one?"

"Sure, I'll take three if you have them."

She laughed. "Scrambled okay?"

"Perfect." He watched her out of the corner of his eye as he poured himself coffee. "You don't seem to be having morning sickness."

"Oh, trust me, I do, but it hits me at the oddest times. And I woke up craving eggs, so I'm not going to argue. My guess is that I need the protein."

"My guess is that you're exhausted from all we've been through, plus making a baby while you're at it."

He wasn't sure what he felt, standing in Patience's

kitchen at five thirty in the morning, but it wasn't unpleasant. A warmth pervaded the atmosphere and even Greta was perkier than usual. He nodded at her as she sat near the counter stools. "She bother you?"

"Not at all. I took her out for a quick walk while you were in the shower."

"You didn't have to. She would have waited for me."

"I figured as much, but she knows me and I knew you'd trust me with her." And she was correct—he'd trust his life with Patience, and certainly his K9.

"You know all of the RRPD dogs better than anyone, except for their handlers."

"That's my job." She served the fluffy eggs up on an aqua plate. "Here you go. And don't get used to it. I'm usually a quick yogurt or smoothie girl in the mornings."

"This looks delicious." He sat at the high counter and dug in. Between bites, he tried not to stare at her. Patience Colton first thing in the morning was a beautiful sight. "Thank you."

"You're welcome. Was the sofa comfortable? I see you gave in and used the pullout."

"I did. Greta is settling in, keeping guard at the front door. I have to say I never heard anything strange or out of place. Besides, Greta would have alerted if anyone tried to snoop around."

"Not happening. We've taken good precautions with the cars, and trust me, I made sure this place was off the map enough when I bought it. I needed a respite."

"Normally I wouldn't agree with you. Someone who's determined enough will always find who they're looking for. But this is very remote, even though I noticed you didn't say 'off the grid.'" He couldn't keep the grin off his face. Patience liked her creature comforts and Wi-Fi was included.

"No, I'm definitely not a doomsdayer! And as you noticed yesterday, I am a bit of a technophile."

"What's attractive about you, Patience, is that you don't have to have all the best, all the time. You'd never have taken the K9 position, or even be a vet, if you weren't able to put the needs of others above yours." The K9 clinic was practically brand-new and a sparkling facility, but it was still a vet's clinic. Her office sofa had already become worn in a short time from all the dogs she allowed on it.

"Thank you. No one's ever said that to me before." She sat next to him with her own plate of eggs. "I'm used to folks just assuming I'm a spoiled Colton. At least when I was younger. Now they take me for who I am, more or less."

Nash wanted to take her in every way imaginable. But that was a conversation he suspected wouldn't go over too well. Patience had made it clear that there was no hope for a relationship, or at least a repeat or two of their spectacular night together. Yesterday had been an anomaly.

He had no choice but to respect her wishes on that, but he wasn't going to give up on being a full parent for the baby. The question was how could he get past Patience's strength and independence to show her it was okay to lean on him for the baby's sake?

* * *

By the time Nash and Greta were at the dive scene, the lake was spotted with local fishing vessels, but not nearly as many as during the warmer seasons. Fall was wrapping up in Red Ridge and the morning chill proved it. In his dive suit and scuba gear, Nash wasn't looking forward to the water temperature.

"Greta, stay." Nash and Greta were on a police patrol boat with four other officers, anchored over the sight where the victim had been found. The RRPD and a local coast guard unit had guarded the area since the night of the murder. A basic drag of the lake hadn't revealed any more bodies, but a couple sonar hits in this area had alerted the RRPD that there might be something still hiding in the lake.

Greta let out two sharp barks, her signal that something was going on below the water. RRPD Officer Cathy Schwab was working the bottom of the lake, and Nash was up next.

"Has Cathy found anything yet?" Nash spoke to Tom Billings, the officer in charge.

"Yes, but I couldn't make out what. She's coming up now." Tom looked overboard to where the diver's figure was visible as she rose from the lake's bottom. He held his headset tight to his ear.

"It could be why Greta is alerting, but we'll be on the lookout for anything off." Nash spoke to the team as much as to himself. He trusted Greta's instincts and didn't believe she'd alert over Cathy's movements.

"Nash, you ready?" Tom spoke as he checked Nash's oxygen tanks while they waited for her to surface.

Within seconds she was alongside the boat and the two other officers hauled her back on board.

Officer Schwab stripped off her hood and mask as the dive team worked to untether her safety line and attach it to Nash's harness. "There's definitely something there, and it looked like a fluorescent orange flag marks the spot. But I had to surface—I was out of air and feeling hypothermic. I felt cold almost right away, Nash. Don't expect to stay down for too long."

"We need heated wet suits." Nash knew he'd stay as long as he could in the icy water, but the department rule was safety first.

"Funding is everything. Why don't you ask Dr. Colton while you're hanging with her? She can get her father to throw us some support." Tom referred to the fact that Fenwick Colton had almost single-handedly donated the funds to pay for the new upgrades at the K9 training center, making the decades-old building practically brand-new, with a full extension and indoor training pool. It was where the team practiced this kind of dive.

"I'll get right on that." Nash's reply made the entire team laugh. "I'm going in. What do I have, ten minutes?" He looked at Cathy.

She nodded. "It's the most you can hope for in these temperatures."

Nash put on his mask, made sure the underwater breathing apparatus was working and gave Tom a thumbs-up.

He plunged into the water. As much as he'd braced for the shock of the cold, nothing ever prepared him for it. Grateful for his wet suit, he got to work. The lamp on his headgear lit up the surrounding area, clearer than usual. The cold temperature affected the sediment and dirt twenty feet below the surface, too. Still, he waited for a light cloud of dirt and sand to settle. Once it did, he focused on the area Cathy had directed him to, and within seconds saw the flag she'd been talking about.

"Eyes on flag. Going there now." He had to modulate his breathing in order to talk. He kept communication to a minimum when he dived.

Nash swam to the flag, a triangular orange cloth attached to a long white flexible pole. He found two sealed containers at the base of it, nestled against a large boulder, and reached down to see if he could lift them. They were light enough, and upon further inspection, he saw they were waterproof ones used by divers and fishermen.

"Nash, abort mission and surface now. Repeat, abort mission." Tom's voice sounded in his earpiece.

He felt a sharp tug on his safety line, another emergency signal that demanded he surface immediately.

"Why, Tom?" he asked over the comm unit. He had seven minutes left on his watch. But there was no reply from Tom, not even a rush of static. As dive master, Tom's orders were sacrosanct. Nash grabbed one of the boxes and prepared to surface.

Before he could, the large form of Greta appeared, swimming straight for him. Why had Tom deployed Greta while ordering Nash to surface? He signaled for her to surface, too.

Greta either didn't see his hand signals or ignored

him, completely unlike her. As she swam not to him, but past him, Nash turned. Adrenaline surged when he saw her target—another diver, male, who was not RRPD. The man held a knife in his hand and Nash realized that must have been the tug he'd felt—his line had been cut. That same knife meant trouble for Greta.

Greta had the other diver's arm in her teeth and was making for the surface with him when he saw the man strike her head with his free hand. Nash feared she'd been stabbed and knew Greta needed air, so he signaled her to surface while he went after the assailant.

The thug knocked the container from Nash's grip and grabbed the second one, wielding his knife in a clear message: he'd kill Nash for the boxes. Nash didn't have body armor on, and even if he had, it wasn't bladeproof. He was a strong swimmer and diver, even with the weight vest. But he found himself struggling to breathe, and at the same time, his tank issued a loud warning alarm. The thug had cut his air off, too. He had no choice but to surface. And pray that Greta was okay.

Patience stood on the edge of the lake, watching as the RRPD launch approached the small dock. It was all she could do not to jump into the water to reach Nash sooner, to hell with the cold. If not for their unborn child, she would. When she'd heard the alert over the clinic's sound system she'd had to fight off the urge to throw up. Greta was injured, and that meant Nash had been in harm's way.

As the boat cut across the usually placid lake, sadness hit her that what had been her secret serenity spot had turned deadly overnight. Literally.

Greta wagged her tail as the boat neared, even though her head was held by Nash, keeping her still. Thank God, Nash appeared none the worse for wear.

Patience ignored the other dive team members, focused solely on him. She made eye contact with Nash as the boat came alongside the concrete pier. It wasn't necessary for her to jump into the vessel, but she wanted to. Best to keep it professional, though, since Greta didn't appear seriously injured.

"You okay?" She wanted him to know she cared. He was still in a wet suit, but it was unzipped, his RRPD jacket and ski cap providing warmth.

"I'm good. Greta got stabbed." He held the dog's head in his lap, pressing a gauze bandage to it. The red stain that spread on the white fabric told her he was keeping it under control, but she suspected Greta was going to need stitches at the very least.

Greta looked up at her with soulful eyes and Patience smiled. "You're going to be just fine, girl." She returned her attention to Nash and the dive team. "Did anyone see what happened to her?"

"I did." Nash stood and helped Greta get off the boat. Patience pointed for her to lie down on the lowered stretcher, which Greta did with her bulky frame as gracefully as any sugarplum fairy in *The Nutcracker*. Patience buckled the dog onto the cot before she stood and pressed the button to raise the stretcher to working height. Nash went to push Greta but Patience put her hand on his arm. "They've got her."

Two vet techs expertly moved Greta up the pier and onto the ramp at the back of the clinic.

"I think she's fine. It looks like she just got a cut on her scruff. An unknown diver attacked me and her. They made off with containers we discovered. A patrol was dispatched to intercept the diver but they've found nothing." Nash issued the report with professional expertise, but she saw his pallor, the pulse at his temple throbbing under his skin. He'd obviously been through an event, and with the cold conditions could go into shock. He needed to warm up.

"I've got her, Nash. Go get a hot shower and find us when you're dressed."

She didn't wait for him to respond, but instead ran to Greta's side. All the K9s were vital to the RRPD's work and she treated them all as if they were her own. But now Greta had achieved a new status with her— she was her baby daddy's K9. Patience knew the pain it caused Nash to have his partner hurting in any way.

She walked behind Greta's gurney to the clinic. She couldn't pinpoint when or where it had happened, but Nash's well-being was inexplicably important to her. It wasn't just because of the baby, though that was the easiest explanation for the fear that had rocked her when she'd heard the alarm call for Nash and Greta.

She quickly glanced around the clinic and to its farthest visible bounds, quelling her anxiety over the Lake Killer. He was nowhere in sight. For now.

Patience quickly ascertained that Greta's cut was superficial. As she cleaned the small wound, she wondered how Nash had checked out with the EMTs the RRPD called in. If he had to go to the ER, she'd be the one to get him to the cabin tonight.

She and Greta walked to her office, where Greta settled down and Patience checked her emails.

"Nice headgear, Greta." Nash's voice made her stomach flip as he walked into her office and spoke to his K9, who'd taken up her favorite spot on the largest of three dog beds. Often Patience would have one of the dogs stay with her after it had been through either a daily drill with its partner or the monthly group training session. Patience knew the K9s needed to accept her as worthy of trust, so that they'd allow her to treat them in a worst-case scenario. Which, unfortunately, she'd done on several occasions.

"Greta's doing fine." She pushed back from the side of her desk, where she'd been working on the computer. "You were right. It was a very minor cut. And while I know the knife wound scared you, it was a clean cut and I didn't even have to stitch it."

"You were able to glue it?"

She nodded. "She's absolutely fine. But no diving until it's healed, of course. I'd give it a week, at least. We don't want to risk infection. Because it's on the top of her scruff she can't get to it, so I'll send her home without a cone. How does she usually do when she's hurt?"

"She only needed a cone after she was spayed." Nash was on his haunches next to his dog. "You did a good job today, Greta."

Greta's huge tail thumped against the floor and they both laughed.

"She's a special dog. What happened out there, Nash?" Patience was worried there might be more victims. She was haunted by it since the other night.

"No more bodies, if that's what you're asking." Nash's direct answer was predictable, but she still felt as though he could read her mind. And if that in turn meant he was able to read her heart, it spelled trouble. As she watched him love on Greta, she felt a tug under her rib cage, suspiciously near her heart. Baby daddy or not, Nash was a man she could fall for. If she'd lost him today...

"How did she get cut, Nash?" Staying in the present always proved handy for keeping the what-ifs at bay.

He stood up and walked closer to her. "There was another diver there, an unknown. Good chance it was the same guy who tried to come after you both times, but no way of telling with all the dive equipment on both of us. I couldn't see the color of his eyes. He cut my lifeline and messed up my tanks. I couldn't go after him, but between the other dive officer and me, the dive team was able to verify that it was a spot used to exchange drugs or money. Or both. I saw him swim off with two plastic containers before I had to surface."

His frustration was palpable in the small space between them. The clinic beyond her office was bustling as routine appointments were handled and techs walked dogs to and from the back fenced area and training yard.

"You're lucky you're still here, Nash." She didn't have to tell him it'd been a close call. And she didn't want to tell him how much it had shaken her. He'd been her rock over the past two days.

"If I'd seen him first, we'd have the contraband, if that's what it is. And he'd be in cuffs." His gaze never faltered. "If something had happened to me, what would you have done? I mean, about the baby?"

She saw the question in his eyes, deeper than the one he verbalized. He wondered if she had been worried about him.

"I'm glad you're okay, if that's what you're asking. If the worst happened—and it didn't—nothing would be different. I would raise the baby like I'm going to. On my own." She took a step back, but her calves hit her chair and she wobbled. When he grasped her upper arms and steadied her she felt the connection to her very center. A whoosh of air left her lungs and the tension left her body. Nash was okay. He'd survived.

"Are you sure about that, Patience? Why are you still so bent on your independence?" His hazel eyes glittered. It reminded her of the night they'd spent together, of how intensely intimate it had been.

"Of—of course I'm sure. You say 'independence' like it's a bad thing." She couldn't help licking her lips as he stared at her. He looked hungry. Starving. Her body leaned closer, any resistance to her attraction to Nash futile.

"I think you're might be overlooking the obvious."

He closed the gap and his lips came down on hers with the most delicious amount of purpose. She wrapped her arms around his neck and gave the kiss, the embrace, Nash her all. It was too hard not to.

Nash loved the feel of Patience in his arms, and liked the taste of her lips even more. He nudged her lips apart with his tongue and hers was there, waiting for him. The friction of their tongues after a life-threatening scenario proved as intimate as making love, and he pulled her against him, not satisfied with just mouth contact.

Patience groaned and the sheer need in her voice mirrored what he felt, as his desire for her went from a spark to combustion in two seconds flat. He wanted— no, he *needed*—her to feel what he'd experienced in the lake, under the water, too far from her. The pure terror that he might never see her again, never hold her like this. That he might never meet his unborn son or daughter.

Patience pulled back and removed her hands from around his neck, but at least she let them rest on his chest as she stared at him. A small comfort. Did she have any idea how desirable she was? Her eyes were big and dark, shining from the ardor of their embrace, and her lips were swollen. He was proud of that, that his kiss did this to her.

"What?" He bent to nuzzle behind her ear, inhaling her scent.

"Nash." Her hands were firmer this time as she pushed on his chest, just a little. "We're at work."

"So?" He watched her eyes reflect arousal, amusement, frustration. He took a step back and shook his head. Had he suffered from more oxygen deprivation than he'd initially thought? "Heck, Patience, I'm sorry. You're right. I think the dive, and how messed up it got, has me leaving my manners at the door."

"It's not your manners, Nash." She looked at her door before running her hand down his arm in a conciliatory gesture. "It's the fact that we could be seen at any point. It'd be one thing if we were, you know. A couple. I don't want anyone to get the wrong idea."

A chill ran down his back, quickly followed by a rush of heat. "Whatever."

She shook her head. "I don't mean it like that, Nash."

"Like what? Like you have absolutely no interest in getting to know me past the sex we've shared? Like you're embarrassed to be caught with me, a regular kind of guy without a trust fund?"

She blinked and swayed as if his words were physical. Remorse flooded him, but he held his ground. Patience needed to get used to him being around, because she was going to have his child and he was going to be a participatory father.

"You know I don't care how much is in your, or anyone else's, bank account." She looked away, as if it were her fault he'd snapped.

"I know you don't. I'm sorry. It's been a long day. It wasn't fun, this dive."

She nodded. "Are you okay to drive?"

"Yes. If I had any doubt, I wouldn't."

"Okay, then, I'll see you back at the cabin. Do you mind if Greta stays with me? I'd like to keep an eye on her for the rest of the day, just in case she shows any other effects of the dive."

"That's fine." He had so much to catch up on at the station, and he wanted to be home when the kids got off school. His aunt and uncle were doing a great job, no doubt, but he didn't want any of his siblings to think that he'd abandoned them. "I've got to stop in and see the kids."

"Of course you do. Normally I would insist you go back home, but I have to admit I'm worried, Nash. I keep thinking the Lake Killer is behind the next corner. Since I can't go to your place, as the kids' safety comes first, you need to do so. And take whatever time you need to."

"I didn't peg you as the maternal type." Of course, he'd only ever interacted with her in the clinic during training and Greta's exams, before their physical relationship began.

"You don't seem like the fatherly type, either, but you're doing it." She tilted her head. "We don't know one another very well at all, do we?"

"Oh, I'd say we know one another *very* well." He winked at her and enjoyed watching the blush color her cheeks. Patience Colton was worldly and sophisticated, yet still humble and very flirt-worthy. "Seriously, I do feel like I've known you longer than I have." Yet she spoke the truth: they needed to know one another better.

"We've worked together a long while—what, at least the past three years, since I got out of vet school, right?"

"Something like that." He remembered hearing that she'd been a prodigy of sorts and completed college and vet school earlier than most. But there wasn't time to talk about it now. They both had work to do.

"I'll see you later." He knelt and scratched Greta under her chin, to avoid disturbing her cut. "You be good for Patience."

"See you back h—at the cabin." Patience almost said *home*. She watched him, something alight in her eyes that he didn't want to explore.

He left her office and told himself the pang deep in his chest had to be from Greta getting hurt this morning. It wasn't as if he couldn't live without Patience Colton.

# *Chapter 10*

Patience sat in the booth at the front window of the restaurant. As she watched her older sister walk into their favorite Red Ridge café she couldn't keep the smile from her face. Nash would be angry if he knew she'd sneaked out of the clinic to meet Layla for a late lunch, but Patience had taken precautions by wearing a bulky hooded jacket and driving an RRPD civilian vehicle. She hadn't noticed anyone following her, and felt reasonably safe in the local restaurant.

She waved Layla over from the hostess's desk.

Patience's only full sibling, Bea, was as eager as their father for the Groom Killer to be caught, as it was eating into her bridal business, too. But Bea, compassionate and kind, was nothing like Fenwick. Patience spent time with Bea as she was able, but Bea had never been the sister she'd bonded the most closely with. Layla had. She saw Blake often enough, as Juliette was an RRPD K9 officer, and their youngest sister, Gemma, came around to the clinic every now and then as she spent her time fund-raising for animal causes. But neither Bea nor Gemma knew her like Layla did.

Patience thought she and Layla had bonded because they'd both inherited the Colton drive. Layla, as VP of Colton Energy, directed her strengths to the family business, while Patience threw herself into the K9 clinic. Patience had never had an interest in business at all but from a career standpoint understood Layla's need to succeed.

They were so different people often forgot they were sisters, even with the same last name. Layla was polished from head to toe. Her blond bob was sleek as ever today and contrasted sharply with her ice-blue power suit that matched her eyes. She had never given a nod to living in a more rural area by adopting comfortable shoes or cowboy boots, and was wearing her classic black designer stilettos. Sometimes Patience wondered if Layla hid her sweet nature behind her corporate look. Layla was determined to keep the family business going no matter what.

"Hey, sis." Layla kissed Patience on the cheek before she eased into the booth after grabbing a napkin and wiping the seat off. She grinned at Patience. "It's wonderful to see you. How are you doing?"

Patience froze. *The baby.* Would Layla see it? Notice her big belly?

"I'm great. I missed you."

"I've missed you, too. Let's order so that we can talk." Layla opened her menu, but then craned her head toward the large blackboard behind the coffee bar. "What are today's specials?"

"Pan-fried trout, an endive-and-citrus salad and their carrot cake."

Layla turned to face her. "Split a slice with me?"

"You know it."

The waitress delivered ice water and asked for their orders. Patience wasn't sure about fish with the baby, so she stuck to a plain grilled cheese, while Layla went for the endive salad.

"We're going to split a piece of the carrot cake later." Layla handed her menu to the waitress, as did Patience.

Once the server was out of earshot, Patience spoke. "It's okay to wait to order dessert. Are you afraid it'll disappear before we get to eat it?" She couldn't help poking at Layla. It was what they did—criticizing one another so that no one else could surprise them with their slams. It was an old habit from when they were kids and bullied for being so wealthy. They'd never told their father or mothers about it because they'd begged to go to the public school and had all their friends there. But they also had a few enemies.

"You know my sweet tooth. And why aren't you drinking your usual diet soda?"

Darn Layla and her sharp power of observation.

"I thought I'd try to be healthier. Besides, the caffeine's been bothering my sleep."

"Really?" Layla's perfectly made-up face was breathtaking in its beauty and Patience wondered for the millionth time why her sister would agree to marry Hamlin Harrington just to save Colton Energy. How could she sign away her own happiness that way?

"Hmm." She was not going there with Layla. Not today.

"You look like you're disappointed in me again, Patience. Please tell me we're not going to rehash the Hamlin issue."

"I have no intention of that. Not at all. But really, Layla, you just called your own fiancé an 'issue.' You can't tell me you're in love with the man."

"Some things are more important than personal happiness. Like family and legacy." Layla's resignation saddened Patience.

"Layla, please know I only want what's best for you. You deserve to be happy. When it's the right person, it's not a sacrifice."

Layla flashed her a surprised glance. Shoot. She'd meant what she'd said, more proof that she was getting in deep with Nash. Too deep.

"Wait, what? You're dating someone, aren't you?" Layla leaned over the table, her pearls glistening as the midday sun shone through the café's front window.

Patience held her eye contact without flinching. "No. Absolutely not."

"Come on, Patience. Spill it."

"There's nothing to spill. I'm single, unattached." Liar. At least where the baby was concerned.

Layla kept giving her the look that only a sister can. The "I'm going to sit here and wait until you dish" look.

Patience groaned. "You have to promise not to tell

Daddy." No matter how angry she or Layla got at their often absent father, they still referred to him with their childhood label.

"Cross my heart. As long as you stop harassing me over Hamlin."

"Deal. But you can't tell Bea, Blake or Gemma, either. I mean it." Patience took a sip of water. It was the most fortifying beverage of choice, since caffeine and alcohol were off-limits. "I'm pregnant."

Layla's expression didn't change. She blinked once, twice. "Shut. The. Front. Door."

Patience nodded, and before she knew they were threatening, tears spilled down her cheeks. "I wasn't planning it, of course. In fact, we used precautions."

Layla squealed with delight and got up to come around the table and give Patience a warm hug. "Congratulations! This is very exciting." She sat back down and took a drink of water.

"I'm glad you're happy about it."

"Cut to the chase. Who's your baby daddy?" Layla at least had the sense to keep her voice low and limited to their booth. Patience looked around the full café. Most of the customers were strangers or distant acquaintances. No threat of anyone they knew overhearing, anyway.

"I don't want to reveal that yet."

"Is he going to step up to the plate and help you with the baby?"

"Why do you assume I want or need help raising a child?"

"It's me, Patience. Your loving sister. We're Coltons.

We like to have children. It's the raising them right that we struggle with. All I'm saying is that it might not be a bad idea for you to have the other parent there alongside you to balance your quirks."

Patience laughed. "That's not an understatement." Fenwick had always meant well, but he'd been an absent father at best, always putting work first. "Daddy's still a business-first guy, but he has seemed happier lately, when we're all together."

"What, at Christmas after a few single-malt scotches?" Layla shrugged. "We're a modern family. It's a miracle we all get under one roof together to celebrate anything these days."

The waitress brought their food and they paused until she walked away.

"Have you heard anything on the Groom Killer?" Layla spoke as she smoothed three paper napkins over her lap and suit front.

Patience laughed. "I'm amused at how you treat that suit. And admit it—you're excited about being an auntie." She didn't want to talk about any killer during her time with Layla.

"Yes, once the shock wears off, I will pester you for a list of what you'd like for the baby. So, no news on the case?"

"No, nothing new, but you should know I'm going to be living at my cabin for the foreseeable future." She explained what had happened. Layla's eyes widened when Patience said "Lake Killer" and she put down her fork.

"You could have been killed, Patience! You have to come stay with me." Layla shuddered. "It can't be fun having a stranger, even a cop, stay with you day in and day out."

"Are you kidding? Did you hear what I said? I can't stay at Nash Maddox's because he's got four young siblings at home. We can't risk the killer following me there. No way do I want you in danger, either." She personally felt Layla had enough on her hands with her slimy fiancé, but kept the thought to herself. "Besides, it's part of my job description, even if it's unusual. I know the RRPD K9s and their handlers as well as I know my family. We're a team and we help each other."

Layla sighed. "I wish I had that. The work-is-a-family thing. You know I love my job and the challenges it brings, but I can't say there's a lot of camaraderie at Colton Energy."

"It's all about pleasing one man, that's why. Fenwick Colton. And you and he are working together all the time, with just your staff to support you. I work for the community when it comes down to it. The RRPD and the K9 teams all serve the public. We have to work together, no matter the personalities."

"Are you going to be able to work there after the baby comes?"

"Of course. I'll need to find childcare, of course, but nothing more than any other working woman faces. And I make a good living." She thought about her vet techs and some of the RRPD support staff. They often struggled to make ends meet, and affordable day care was often an issue.

"You don't have to work, Patience. You could take a leave of absence. In fact, maybe you should do it now.

You can disappear for a while, go abroad until they catch the man you saw on the lake. Did you tell Daddy about all of this?"

"No, not yet. I don't want him, or you, thinking that the clinic is more of a liability than an asset."

Layla stared at her. "Even I know it's not a business asset. Red Ridge needs your clinic, and I'll do my best to keep the funding on track. It's not about that, anyhow. It's your mother's legacy to the community."

"You won't be able to do anything if Daddy says to shut it down."

"There are other sources of funding if he does, but he won't. He has his hands full right now."

"Like trying to make sure he keeps Hamlin on his side and supporting Colton Energy?"

Layla's gaze sharpened. "We are going to have to agree to disagree on my choice of future husband. Hamlin can save Colton Energy."

"I'm sure Daddy can find another way, Layla. You can't tell me there's a lot of chemistry between you two!"

"Sex isn't everything."

Patience tried not to frown. She loved Layla and wanted her to be happy, not chained to a false sense of duty.

A movement outside caught her eye and she noted a tall woman walking two dogs. Two very familiar dogs. Her pulse quickened. She would know the adult Belgian Malinois, Nico, anywhere. She'd helped when his mother had whelped him and his littermates, and done a lot of the initial training, which was continued by Danica Gage, one of the Red Ridge K9 center's dog trainers. Patience was certain the slightly smaller dog next to him was definitely the Malinois pup that had been stolen along with Nico, back in May. The puppy would be that exact size by now.

"I'm sorry, but I've got to go, Layla." She stood up, ready to break for the door.

"I do, too. Wait—are you okay, Patience?"

"Yes. I'll call you later, promise. Pay the check, will you? Next time's on me!" She ran from the café, ignoring the cold wind that whipped down Main Street.

Lucky for her, the dogs weren't with the dangerous Larson brothers, who Patience and Danica believed had been behind the theft. And the dog walker had been stupid enough to leave the dogs tied outside the café. The woman was nowhere to be seen, but Patience wasn't waiting for her to return. She approached Nico with confidence, but carefully, just in case he didn't remember her.

"Nico."

The dog cocked his head, his intelligent expression the same as she remembered. After a few moments she held out her hand for him to sniff, which he did, then immediately licked, adding a happy yip to the affectionate gesture. He remembered her!

"Good boy."

The younger dog followed suit, doing whatever Nico did.

"Come on, boys, I'm springing you two loose." She unwrapped their leashes and hurriedly led them to her loaner car from the RRPD. There were no safety buckles for them like she kept in her vehicle but she'd take her chances. Her hand shook as she put the key in the ignition. She couldn't risk getting caught by the woman the Larson brothers had hired to walk the dogs. Anyone associated with the criminal twins couldn't be trusted. Patience was likely to be shot if they caught her. They'd long been on the RRPD's radar, but were great at covering their tracks. One day, one or both of the twins would slip up.

Once she was driving away, she let out a huge sigh, followed by a whoop. She'd gotten Nico and the puppy back for the K9 training center!

Frustration ran its familiar hand down her spine when she remembered she didn't have a hands-free phone in this car. She'd have to wait until she got back to the clinic to call the police department.

With a jolt she realized that when she thought about letting the team know she'd gotten the dogs back, she wasn't picturing Finn or any other officer, or one of her veterinary staff. The only person in her mind was Nash. To be fair, as frightened as she was of the Lake Killer, Nash occupied the bulk of her waking thoughts.

"Where's Dr. Colton now?" Nash stood in front of the receptionist, his heart pounding. He'd driven back to the clinic within twenty minutes of arriving at his desk. When Finn walked in and told him that Patience had "found" Nico and the puppy, now five months old, he'd been elated.

It was about time the Larson twins saw their own machinations used against them. But then the chief had gone on to explain how Patience had acquired the dogs, and Nash thought his head might explode like a cartoon character's.

"She's back in the kennels, checking on her patients." The receptionist gave him an easy smile. "Did you hear she found Nico and the pup?"

The woman's exuberance tamped down some of his ire, but not enough to keep him from making a beeline for the area.

He found Patience kneeling at the lowest row of kennels, placing the Belgian Malinois puppy in its new enclosure. The dog looked like it had as a pup, but was so much larger.

Patience must have heard Nash enter because she looked up, her hand still rubbing the pup's chest. The triumph in her eyes threw ice water on his fury.

"Hey, Nash. So you heard?" She smiled and all—well, almost all—the words of anger he'd been ready to spew, accusing her of putting herself and the baby at huge risk, dissolved on his tongue.

"Son of a—" He stopped himself and knelt next to her. Peering into the crate, he saw the pup that Danica Gage had just started to work with before he was stolen. "He's so much bigger. They both check out okay?"

Patience nodded. "Yes."

"Where's Nico?" He was relieved the adult Malinois was back in the RRPD K9 family, but not that it put Patience in more danger than she already was. Noel and Evan Larson were despicable, cruel men.

"Out in the back field. Danica couldn't wait to put him through some training exercises, to reacquaint them both."

"She must be over the moon."

"Yes, for sure." Patience closed the kennel door. "Have a good nap, buddy."

"Do you think he'll settle back in here that easily?"

"We just wore him out on the agility course. He's not had any formal training since he was stolen, from what we could tell. But he's eager to learn, trusts us and will pretty much do whatever Nico does. In fact, it's fair to say that Nico saved both of their lives. He didn't fight the Larsons, but followed the training we'd already given him, which protected the pup."

"He have a name?"

"Not yet. We'll go through our usual process to name him." The RRPD's policy to name K9s involved the community. The dog's photo would be put on social media and Red Ridge citizens were asked to offer suggestions. The elementary schools were all involved, with each classroom coming up with one name to put forward. The chamber of commerce voted on the final choice.

"The Larson twins are going to have a fit when they see that." Nash stood and helped her up. "Speaking of which, the real reason I came back today wasn't to see the dogs, Patience."

"I thought maybe you were still worried about Greta."

"I was worried about *you*. You know who the Larsons are, what they're capable of. If one of them had seen you take their dog, I could have lost you both."

"Us…both?" She stared at him for what felt like forever. "I wasn't thinking about anything but getting the dogs back to where they belong. God knows what they went through with those men."

"I don't care about that. I care about you. And the baby." His insides felt as soft and warm as her eyes appeared. What was it about Patience Colton that made him forget his reason for coming here? That made him think he could willingly fall into a serious relationship with her, something more than co-parenting?

"Okay. I hear you. You're not the only one getting used to the baby, you know. I only knew about him, or her, a few hours before you did."

"I know you said you thought you missed your two periods due to stress, but you should know your cycles better. You know about period apps, right?"

Her eyes widened and her mouth lifted on one side. "Look at you, all knowledgeable about the menstrual cycle."

He refused to be embarrassed for his lack of ignorance. "I've been raising teenage girls for the last five years. They each started their cycles under my watch. Of course, I know just about everything a man can regarding periods."

Patience's smile softened and she placed her hand on his cheek. "I've underestimated you. I'm sorry."

A loud *bam* cracked through the air as the swinging door from the reception area hit the side of the kennel wall. Patience jumped and her heart froze when she identified who'd slammed it open.

Noel and Evan Larson entered the room and walked toward them with menace stamped on their faces. "I want my dogs back. Now." Noel, known to be the ring-leader, spoke as Evan glowered.

"Hold on a minute. Who let you in here?" Patience said. Nash placed his hand on his holstered weapon, letting his body language speak to the twins.

"They cleared us at reception. Don't worry, I gave them my gun for safekeeping." Noel's sarcastic smile angered Nash. The Larsons had a bad reputation and were suspected of drug dealing in Red Ridge, and had been connected to murders, including the Groom Killer's. But their alibis were solid on the murders and there wasn't enough evidence to nail them for the drug crimes—yet. But wherever trouble was, there were the Larsons.

And they'd taken two of the K9 training center's dogs. That was fact.

The Malinois puppy growled from his kennel.

"They were never your dogs, Noel. They belong to the county and to the RRPD." Patience spoke as if she dealt with hardened criminals every day.

Noel pointed an accusing finger at her. Nash wanted to snap that finger in half, but stood his ground and let Patience do the same. He completely trusted her instinct and abilities, even with a big bad bully like Noel Larson.

"You stole them from in front of the café. My dog walker saw you! They have microchips proving my ownership."

"Calm down, Noel. You're right. That's the best way to prove canine identity and ownership. Nash, will you escort Noel and Evan to Exam Room One? I'll bring the dogs."

Nash's gut tightened. He knew the Larsons weren't

that ignorant—they would have had the dogs micro-chipped by another veterinarian as soon as they'd captured the puppies. But there was no doubt that these were the two that the Larsons had stolen. How would he keep them from the thieves, from danger? And how could he stop Patience from placing herself between the dogs and a dangerous man?

# *Chapter 11*

Patience was quaking inside, but damned if she'd let the Larson brothers see it. The jerks had kidnapped these precious dogs and tried to pass them off as their own. Worse, they'd paraded them around town as if there were no repercussions for stealing dogs. When, in fact, they'd stolen police property.

She was beyond grateful that Nash let her take the lead and didn't challenge the Larsons or kick them out of the clinic. It would have totally been within his purview to do so, since they were acting in a threatening manner, and doing so on county government property. And with the suspected illicit drug connection between the victim she'd seen dumped into the lake and the Larsons, Nash must want to see Noel and Evan behind bars. But to his credit, he stayed cool, while shooting her reassuring glances.

He believed in her.

As if she were a foot taller and a hundred pounds heavier, she entered the exam room with Nico and the younger dog on leashes. Nash stood near the door, while Noel Larson's hulking frame was braced in the center of the room, next to the exam table. Evan leaned against the wall.

"This won't take long." She took the scanning gun from a counter drawer and turned it on. "We agree that whatever this reveals, we're all good with it, right?"

Noel met her gaze and she saw fury, indignation and the promise of revenge in his eyes. He really thought he was going to walk out of here with the dogs he'd stolen, after having one of their best K9 handlers knocked out? The memory of Danica's pain and suffering made Patience see red.

"Right, Noel? Evan?" She used all her willpower to keep from snarling at them.

"Right," Noel grunted. Evan refused to speak. Their reluctance would have been laughable if they weren't such vile men.

"Nico." She gave the hand signal for him to stand in front of her, and when he complied, she waved the wand over the space between his shoulder blades. A digital readout reflected a unique ID. She held the display up for the Larsons to see.

"This is a code assigned only to our K9 clinic."

"That's impossible! I had microchips put in those dogs the minute I got them!"

*Yes*, Patience thought. *Right after you stole them from*

*us*. As Noel complained, Evan pushed back from the wall and stood alongside his brother.

She sensed more than saw Nash close the short distance and step between her and the men.

"Tamp it down, Larson." Nash's deep baritone was smooth and professional, but to Patience, it was the definition of pure security. Nash had her back, and she and the dogs were safe.

Noel took a half step back, clearly struggling with his temper. "Wave that wand of yours over his entire body. You'll find my microchip."

"I'm happy to do that, but it doesn't matter if another microchip shows up or not. K9 property takes priority unless there's a legal contract giving ownership to a civilian. You're a civilian and there is most definitely no contract between the RRPD, the RRPD K9 training center or Red Ridge County and you. These are not your dogs, Noel." She stared at him, refusing to budge.

Noel Larson wasn't the first person she'd had to take dogs from, but in past cases it'd been because the owners had neglected or abused their animals. Noel had taken care of these dogs well enough—they'd been fed—but he'd held stolen the canines. They weren't his.

He glared at her. "I get what's mine, Doc. Don't forget it." He turned to Nash. "And you—you have nothing on me or my brother. Screw you." With that, he and Evan left the exam room.

She turned to Nash. "There's so much I wanted to say to him, but didn't. I deactivated their microchips from the Larsons, by the way, when I put in ours. I called the manufacturer and reported the Larsons' identification as illegal. It's official—they are RRPD K9 property again. As they always were."

Nash gently turned her around.

"Thank God you thought so quickly. Let me do this for you." His warm hands settled on her shoulders, massaging her tension away.

"Why are there such awful people in the world?"

"Who knows? What matters is that you handled them perfectly. Trust me, given enough time and more evidence, those two are going to end up in jail, if I or my fellow cops have anything to do with it."

"I know." She did know, and more, she trusted Nash. She turned around and gave him a quick kiss on the lips. "And I know I'm contradicting my edict to be professional, but you know what? I don't care. Noel scared the crap out of me."

"You were incredible with him." Nash's eyes shone with intensity. "You know your stuff, Dr. Colton."

She laughed. "When it comes to the animals and especially K9s? I hope I do. It's my job!"

"I'm going to make sure he's off the property. Promise me won't put yourself on the line again today? I'd like to meet you safe and sound at the cabin."

"I'll be there when you get there."

He gave her a firm kiss goodbye. Patience wished it could last longer. The only time she didn't think about the Lake Killer was when she was in Nash's arms.

Nash didn't get to see the kids until much later. He was relieved that he'd been at the clinic when the Larson twins had shown up. If his hackles weren't already up from the Lake Killer case, the Larsons would do it. The twins were bad guys and at heart, bullies. He made a mental note to ask Patience if there was any way they might know about her cabin.

He'd taken a circuitous route home, practicing evading techniques he'd learned at the police academy. He couldn't risk the Lake Killer showing up and following him. Threatening the kids. He'd missed them, for sure, but to his surprise he'd been so completely absorbed with the case he hadn't spent a lot of time thinking about them. Knowing his aunt and uncle had them helped.

*You don't think about anything but Patience when you're with her.*

He took a minute as he got out of his car in the driveway. Sure, he thought about Patience a lot, but wasn't that normal? She was carrying his baby!

"Nash!" Troy jogged down the driveway toward him, all limbs and squeaky voice at twelve years old. "I didn't know you were coming home." He stood awkwardly in front of Nash at an age where he wasn't sure how to show affection.

Nash immediately enveloped him in a bear hug, kissing the top of his head. "Hey, bud! I had some time and wanted to make sure you hadn't tied up Uncle Jim and Aunt Clara. You behaving?"

"Yeah." Troy shrugged out of the hug, but his grin split his face. "Paige and Maeve are keeping things going, but Maeve thinks she knows it all."

Nash laughed. His younger half sister had recently scored perfectly on the PSATs and was obsessed with the naval academy and all things military. She also had a very strong maternal instinct, which she practiced on the boys.

"What about Paige?"

"She's always at swim practice or studying." Paige, a senior, had two athletic scholarships and was hoping for more by spring semester. Nash was proud of his sister and overjoyed that something was going so right for them. Losing their parents in such a tragic manner five years ago had cast a long sad shadow over their teen years. But they'd pulled out of it, thank God.

"How's school going for you?" Nash was careful to not specifically ask about the bullies Troy had been plagued with. While he was at the top of his class academically, his brother had yet to find his place in any sport, music group or other extracurricular activity. But he was clear about wanting to go to college, at least. He'd shown an interest in marching band, and Nash planned to support him in joining it when he was eligible at the end of eighth grade. But as a seventh grader, Troy was in the thick of middle school growing pains.

"It's fine. We got to use the Bunsen burners in science lab today."

"That's fun." Nash put his arm around his brother as they walked into the house.

Maeve was predictably at the family calendar, adding the *washi* tape she was fond of to the next week.

"Hey, Maeve."

"Hi, Nash!" She gave him a quick hug before turning back to the monthly schedule. "I just filled in the activities for next week for Aunt Clara and Uncle Jim. I thought you'd still be gone."

"I probably will be. I'm working a tough case and I can't take time away until we solve it."

Maeve's eyes lit up. "Is it about the Lake Dumper?"

"The what?"

"Hashtag Lake Dumper. It's all over social media. It was in the digital paper yesterday. It says he's tied to a major drug ring, that he disappears into thin air and that he is also a serial killer."

Nash shook his head. He hadn't had time to even think about the press, much less scroll through community posts about the case. "You know you can't believe everything on there, right?"

Maeve looked at him as if *he* was the teenager. "No, but where there's a hashtag, there's a story." Maeve wasn't yet sure what she wanted to do if she went into the navy, but he'd place his wager on Intelligence or JAG Corps. She was as stellar a writer as a negotiator.

"Keep it under your hat that I'm on it, okay?"

"Of course."

Aunt Clara walked into the room. "There's the puppy snatcher."

"Aunt Clara, thank you so much for helping me out here. I really appreciate it." He hugged and kissed her. "What the heck are you talking about, 'puppy snatcher'?"

"Noel Larson's mother was down at the café, spouting off about how her son's dogs were stolen. She doesn't know me from Adam, or rather Eve, but I paid attention in case it's something you could use. I know those Larson boys are up to no good. They've never had a good reputation. Neither did their grandfather."

"I appreciate you trying to help, but like I just told Maeve, you can't believe everything you hear." One thing about a small town was that word traveled fast, but it could often be misleading. "Where's Uncle Jim?"

"He went to check on our house and get us some more clothes. The nights have been cold and I wanted my flannel pj's."

"Is the woodstove working okay?" He walked over to the stove in the middle of the large living room.

"It's fine, but you know we don't like to leave it burning overnight. We've gotten used to our gas heat, let me tell you."

Gas heat was something Nash wanted to add to the house, but until the girls got situated with college and he knew how much it would be out-of-pocket for him, he was holding off. If Maeve's appointment to the Academy came through, he'd have more than enough for both boys' educations and to upgrade the house.

"There are down blankets in each of the bedroom closets." The last thing he wanted was for his relatives to be the least bit uncomfortable. They were sacrificing so much to help him out and always had. "I don't know what I'd do without you and Uncle Jim to help me. I wouldn't be able to keep my position as a K9 officer without you."

"We're family. It's what we do. Speaking of K9, where's Greta? You didn't leave her in the car, did you?"

"No, she's back at the clinic. Dr. Colton is keeping an eye on her. She got a minor injury this morning and needs a little TLC."

"Greta's okay, right?" Jon walked into the room,

grabbed an apple off the counter and bit into it, all while quizzing Nash. "I miss her the most. Not that we don't miss you."

"Gee, thanks, bud. Come over here and let me wrestle you."

Jon, thirteen, had started to eat like a horse and had grown four inches this past summer. He got close enough to Nash to lean in for a brief hug. Something in Nash's heart twinged with regret. As tough as the last five years had been, they had also passed in the blink of an eye. The kids were getting older and didn't need his constant care. Sure, the teenage years meant he had to stay present and vigilant, but it was nothing compared to the first crazy years of meal after meal, helping with homework, the chauffeuring. Paige had picked up a lot of the slack with the driving lately, and soon Maeve would be able to, too.

"I miss you guys."

"Miss you, too."

"But?"

"We love having Aunt Clara and Uncle Jim here. She made us cookies last night."

"That's what they really like about me." Aunt Clara laughed from the kitchen, where she was making herself a cup of tea. "Can I get you a coffee?"

"No, I have to get back."

"Are you staying at the station overnight?" Jon lifted the lid on the cookie jar and grabbed a handful of the cookies Aunt Clara had baked.

"Whoa on all those sweets—how about leaving some

for your brother and sisters? And no, I'm not staying at the station. I'm staying with Dr. Colton, actually."

"Patience?" Maeve's eyebrow rose in query.

"Yes." He waited for the firing squad.

"She's a fox!" Trey exclaimed, his face reddening.

"She's so nice. She let me help train the dogs the last family day." Maeve's thoughtful expression warmed his heart.

"Way to go, Nash." Jon held up his hand, waiting for his to fist-bump.

"Hold it right there. I'm staying with her as part of my job. There's a big case going on with the clinic, and besides adding some extra protection, I'm gathering evidence." A twist of the truth, but he had to keep his siblings off the trail they always focused on: finding him a girlfriend. Or, worse, a wife. He chalked it up to wanting a more permanent mother figure in their lives, but as Paige and Maeve matured, they seemed genuinely interested in his well-being. Sweet, but unwarranted. He was a bachelor.

After enjoying an early dinner with them and having a few words with Paige when she came home from swim practice, Nash headed out. He still had one more stop before the cabin.

# *Chapter 12*

After a long day that included Nash's dive, Greta's injury and the Larson twins, Patience enjoyed the peaceful respite of the cabin. She'd paid heed to Nash's insistence that she take every precaution to make sure she wasn't followed. She hated the constant feeling of being watched that had plagued her since the night of the crime.

As she walked Greta around the clearing, she remained alert to every sound coming from the forest. The familiar birdsong as the sun began to set, the dropping leaves and pine needles, the chatter of squirrels that were still out and about, busily harvesting cones and acorns until the temperatures dropped low enough to signal winter's arrival. The thrum of an engine made

Greta alert, her posture frozen as she faced the source of the sound.

It had to be Nash. He'd texted he was on his way, but Patience's spine tingled and she struggled to draw a deep breath into her lungs. The tension of the last few days was getting to her.

When the familiar shape of his Jeep turned into the clearing, she let her shoulders relax. Greta's happy bark confirmed that her handler, Nash, was driving.

"Come on, girl. Let's go greet him."

Nash got out of the Jeep and Patience let herself enjoy the warmth that rolled over her, as easy as his long strides as he walked to her.

"Hey, Greta." He bent over and greeted his partner with unabashed affection. "How you feeling, girl?"

Greta wagged her tail, making her entire body wiggle.

"She's doing great. I think we'll get away without the cone of shame around her head. She hasn't made any attempt to paw at her wound."

"You're a smart girl, aren't you?" He straightened up and the light in his eyes had nothing to do with Greta's cut or how it was healing. The thrill that thrummed through Patience was undeniable. Nash was feeling the same attraction as she.

"I can't thank you enough for taking care of Greta today."

"I'm just glad you're both okay. That was a very scary situation you were in."

He nodded. "Yeah, it was. If the jerk had been any closer or stabbed Greta an inch or two deeper, it would have been a different outcome."

"That's not what I meant, Nash. You could have been killed."

"As you could have been, Patience, if I hadn't been there when the Larson twins stormed into the kennel, I'm not certain Noel wouldn't have assaulted you to take those dogs."

"Unlikely. I had the staff around, and he was on my turf."

"It's not about what either of us thinks, is it?" Nash stepped up next to her. "It's what we're feeling, why we're both worried about each other so much."

Was the great bachelor Nash Maddox going to admit he had feelings for her?

"It's only natural, I suppose." She didn't want to share her feelings, not completely, not yet. It was still early and hard to know if she was experiencing baby hormones, lust or early signs of something deeper and more lasting.

He smiled. "A baby changes everything, doesn't it? It's clear to me we're both worried whether or not the other is okay because we're so focused on the child's safety."

Tears sprang into Patience's eyes at the sting of his pronouncement. He'd been thinking about the pregnancy, and the baby's safety, which meant her safety, too. Not about her as an individual or possible partner. Before he could see the tears pooling she stepped away and headed back for the house.

"Patience, wait." He caught up to her on the porch. "What did I say?"

"Nothing, Nash. You said nothing. It's not important."

* * *

Nash couldn't ignore the tangle of emotions roiling in his gut. But even more, he couldn't brush off the obvious hurt and pain he saw his words had somehow caused Patience. He thought she wanted him to respect her need to be a single mom, and he'd just done that, hadn't he? Her eyes moved away, to his Jeep, and he followed her gaze.

"What's in the back of your car?"

"A few things I thought we'd need before long." Pride warred with trepidation as he tried to decipher her. "I'll bring them in later. We need to eat, and I'd like to make you one of my specialties."

"Oh?" Her eyes didn't look like she was about to break into sobs any longer, so that was a start.

"Pasta carbonara. The kids love it and it's quick. Plus it's really good with a bottle of cabernet. I know you can't have alcohol now, so I brought some sparkling grape juice."

"That's thoughtful of you."

"I've also got a few things to unload. Give me a bit of time and I'll get dinner going."

She didn't say anything, but retreated into the cabin and, he suspected, to her laptop, where he knew she spent dedicated time each evening entering her notes on patients and general clinic work. He hurried to the car and started to unload.

When he entered the cabin with the first of his goods, Patience was nowhere to be seen. Just as well, since he wanted to surprise her with everything. As he brought in the last of his purchases, she wandered back into the great room, her phone at her ear.

Her eyes widened at the pile of gifts he'd come bearing.

"I have to go, Layla. I'll call you back." She disconnected from her sister and turned her stunned eyes to him.

"What the hell is this supposed to be, Nash?"

Patience stared at the Christmas-size pile of baby products in front of the cabin's fireplace. She couldn't help herself from going to it, passing close enough to Nash to feel his body heat, but ignoring her instant physical reaction.

"You bought all of this on your own?"

"Yes."

Nash was raising his siblings, but they'd all been beyond baby and toddler stages when their parents had died. A high chair, baby swing, car seat. Diapers, baby wipes and a baby wipe warmer. A huge box with *Baby Spa* printed on it depicted a fancy tub complete with a shower faucet and jets. And there were other items she couldn't see, on the far side of the pile. She looked at him.

Nash stood behind the sofa, framed by the fading daylight that streamed in through the picture window. His face was partially in shadow, so it was hard to tell what he thought, or to see any hint of his motive for buying out the single Red Ridge baby supply store.

"Why, Nash? You know, the baby's not bigger than a peach right now."

He stepped into the light, his hazel eyes bright with intent, but she still wasn't sure. Why had Nash gone to this trouble?

"I'm a planner, Patience. It's part of why I like working with the K9 unit so much. It's about more than me or my skills. I have to train Greta every day and do the monthly training to keep us both at top form. I've kept my household running for the past five years, with all four siblings' schedules and my workload. The only way I've done it is by having a plan for everything. A baby is no different. It needs routine. The other thing I've learned is that the right tool for the job is essential." He paused to shake his head and chuckle. "When I was living on my own, before my parents' accident, I had a few plates, one pot, and I was the master of microwave cooking. But kids need three solid meals a day and frozen meals weren't going to cut it. I moved back into my parents' house and found that the kitchen was like driving a Cadillac after using a bicycle."

"But you don't have to do this. I already told you, I'm prepared to raise the baby myself."

"You haven't heard me, Patience. I get it—there's been a lot going on since the Lake Killer. We haven't had time to be together and talk about our circumstance."

"You're calling my pregnancy a *circumstance*?"

"No, I'm referring to how we're going to handle the baby. You know this. What are you afraid of?"

His words lanced her resistance to him. When he closed the distance between them, she willingly went into his arms. Tears pricked at her lids for the second time since he'd come home, and she let herself lean against him and he held her tight. "I'm all over the place. It's the baby hormones, it's knowing a killer wants me dead, it's being confronted by Noel Larson. It's seeing that poor woman dropped into the freezing lake. And yet the most important thing that's happened is that I'm going to have a baby."

"It scared the heck out of me when you were in the clinic and they were coming after you," Nash murmured in response. "And when Noel Larson tried to bully you, it was all I could do to keep my cool."

His palms moved in circles between her shoulder blades and she yielded to his touch, wrapping her arms around his waist and pressing her cheek against his chest. He was a full head taller than her and they fitted together perfectly. His breathing and heartbeat were steady, another reassurance.

"I never felt more frightened than when it came over the emergency response system that you'd suffered a diving casualty. If anything had happened to you, the baby would never know its father, Nash."

She lifted her head to look at him at the same time he moved his hand to cup her jaw. The comforting vibe between them turned to sizzling heat in the blink of her tear-filled eyes, and a zing of awareness hit deep in her belly, pooling between her legs.

Nash must have seen the want in her eyes as he lightly kissed her lips. "Are we giving this a go, Patience?" His deep baritone stoked her need to a white-hot flash point.

"Oh, yes." When his mouth covered hers she stopped

thinking, stopped worrying about how they'd take care of the baby. Stopped revisiting the sheer terror that gripped her at the thought of anything happening to Nash. She embraced the moment, the very sexy, delectable moment.

His tongue was hot and insistent as he probed the depths of her open, willing mouth. His hands, so very talented, stroked her from her shoulders to her ass, and when he moved one hand to cup her breast, she groaned. She let go of his shoulders and lifted her top over her head. Nash unhooked her bra and his hot mouth seared a path from her throat to her nipple, his tongue stroking it from hard to throbbing. She ground her hips against his erection and he pressed back, his need as demanding as hers.

"My bedroom, Nash. Please."

Nash had never felt the need to please a woman the way he did Patience. Their first time together had lasted all night and he'd made sure she'd been satisfied, as he always did with his partners. The best lovemaking was two-way pleasure. Their lovemaking in the cabin the other day had been a release they'd both needed, and reassurance that their one-night stand hadn't been a passionate fluke.

This was different, on a whole other plane. As if Patience's physical response to him meant more than the fact they shared a smoking-hot chemistry.

Her room was pure Patience—feminine pale yellow walls, contemporary clean lines, the aroma of fresh flowers present but not overpowering. He shrugged out of his shirt as he stood facing her at the foot of the bed and unbuckled his belt. Patience grinned.

"Let me help you with that." She slipped his belt out of its loops and unzipped his pants. As he shoved them down, she shimmied out of her scrubs, revealing a grape-colored thong with a lacy front panel that revealed dark curls with the same hint of red as the hair that framed her face. He got rid of his boxers, freeing his erection.

Her hands wrapped around him and he closed his eyes, tilted his head back. "Patience." At this rate he was going to come before he had a chance to join with her, and that would be a pity. He needed to be one with her again.

Her hands shifted to his chest and he moaned in disappointment, until her hot mouth took him. She made him want to do everything he could possibly imagine with her, for her, to her. After he cried out a second time, she stood and gently pushed him onto the bed.

He moved backward on his elbows until he was at the headboard, watching her the entire time. Her breasts, full and luscious, swung in rhythm to her steps as her long, lean legs covered the distance to her end table in only a few strides.

She climbed onto the bed and lay next to him. He ran his hands through her hair, kissed her deeply. Her taste and scent were heady, clearing his mind of anything but his unending need for her. He pressed her back into the mattress, covering her with his body.

"Nash." She tried to grasp his length, but he brushed

her off, working his mouth and tongue on her skin, from her lips, her throat, lingering at her breasts.

"Not yet, babe." He suckled at her nipples, smiling against her smooth skin each time she groaned or cried out in clear delight. Tortuous pleasure; he knew it well with Patience. She always made him need her so much it hurt in its intensity.

"Nash, I need you inside me."

"Patience, Patience."

He licked the valley around her navel, marveling at the soft curves where her belly had been washboard flat the first time they'd made love. It had been a detractor to him when women he dated, never seriously, alluded to having a family. He'd had no desire to be anything but a bachelor, and was holding out for all his siblings to be raised. Yet the physical evidence of Patience's pregnancy, with a baby they'd made together, took his desire for her to a level he'd never experience before. It was a hunger, this need for the beautiful woman in his arms.

He took in the very essence of her, and when he placed his mouth over her she writhed and gently moved her hips as he tasted her.

He'd never satisfy his hunger for Patience.

Patience thought that Nash's mouth on her nipples had been the single most sensual thing she'd ever known. Until he moved to the pulsing spot between her legs and devoured her with his hot, wet, eager mouth. There was no room for thoughts of anything but Nash, her need and the hope for mind-blowing fulfillment.

The orgasm came fast and hard as he licked her,

and she screamed her release even as she reached for him, wanting more. Nash didn't fight her this time but knelt between her legs, his arousal insistent against her quaking center.

"Nash, please." She arched her hips, unwilling to wait a second more.

"Babe." He thrust into her, stretching her wide and filling her depths with heat that reached to her soul. They moved in perfect unison, their bodies resuming the pace that was uniquely theirs.

Nash's skin became slick with sweat and she loved that she made him want to work so hard for her, loved that he fought to please her each and every time. With him she was able to let go of any inhibitions she'd ever had and just be herself, let her body do what it needed to do for completion.

Her release started in a low, forceful wave that rose to an untenable pitch until she shattered, shouting in pleasure with a breathless effort. Nash kept moving for a few more seconds, until he cried out, her name echoing about her room.

"We make a good team." Nash stroked her throat, ran his hand down her rib cage, over her hip as they lay face-to-face, coming down from their most recent sexcapade. He knew it was more, that this wasn't anything like the one-nighters he'd pulled with different women over the last five years.

His "sexual maintenance" dating had ended with that night with Patience. And now this.

She smiled in the dim light, two flickering battery candles making the room the perfect backdrop for such a sexy woman. "We are at that. When we're working together."

He shoved himself up into a seated position, his back against the headboard. Patience followed suit. "About that. I'm not asking you to commit to me, or anything like that. But I'm going to be an active father for the baby. It's not in my being to ignore a child I've fathered."

She looked at him, stroked his cheek. He needed to shave, but had loved rubbing his five o'clock shadow against the insides of her dewy thighs. "This is what's so attractive about you, Nash. You always want to do the right thing."

"But? I hear the 'but.'"

"But you need to be practical. You're a hard-core bachelor. You said so yourself the night we got together. In five, six years you'll be free of raising your siblings."

"A lot has changed since we met. Since that night."

"Well, yeah. I'm pregnant."

He shook his head. "It's more than that. You and I— we've gotten closer. Don't you feel it?"

She wouldn't meet his eyes and he held his breath. He'd pushed too far. And while it should concern him that he was actually trying to prove to Patience that he wanted anything but freedom from being a father, it didn't. It felt right.

"I don't know, Nash. What you said—about a lot having changed since we met. It's true. And I so appreciate that you're already preparing for the baby's arrival. But it's at least six months off, and then there'll be so much round-the-clock care that it's a tough time to try to figure out what either of us is going to do. I don't know how I'll be as a mother, but I do know I'm going to give it my best shot."

"That's all I'm asking you for, you know. I need you to give me and the idea of us co-parenting a decent shot."

She met his gaze and beyond her trepidation he saw a glimmer of hope. Maybe the seed of trust. "I'll try."

"That's all we can ever do."

A low growl sounded in the front of the cabin and they both sat up.

"Does she normally growl at deer or wildlife?" Patience's hopeful question was laced with trepidation.

"No." Nash's inner alarm screeched. Greta's abilities rarely failed him. There was an intruder on the property.

# Chapter 13

Greta's sharp bark cracked through the air and Nash was up and dressed with his weapon in hand in under fifteen seconds. Patience's eyes widened, but she didn't show any signs of panic. She rolled toward the nightstand, where she'd put a gun safe, and punched in four numbers, unlocking it. When he saw the .45 in her hand, he motioned toward her clothes, strewed on the floor.

"Put those on and only come out after I tell you it's clear."

Greta's barks grew more insistent and he shoved his feet into his shoes, then put on his body armor. There was no telling who or what was on the other side of the cabin door.

"I'm going with you. Greta can guard the house. She can't go back out on patrol with her cut."

"You are not going anywhere. Do you have any body armor with you?"

She shook her head. "This weapon and the gun safe are all I took from my office."

"Then you do not leave this room. No matter what, Patience." He couldn't argue with her. There was an intruder and he had to take care of it.

Patience waited until she heard Nash shout and the front door open and close. Then she carefully crept into the short hallway and headed for the main room, her weapon in front of her as she cleared every nook and cranny in the cabin on her way forward. Just like her veterinary trauma training, the police training enabled her to perform as though she did this all the time.

Greta mostly maintained her alert stance at the front door, but once or twice paced to the picture window, which looked out onto total darkness.

Patience heard voices and Greta barked, two sharp, deliberate sounds. She jerked, unable to control her reaction. In the confines of the cabin, the big dog's vocalization sounded like a thunderclap.

She heard more voices as she waited, her weapon pointed at the door. With slow, deliberate steps she approached the kitchen sink and island counter and sank to her knees, using the granite surface for support. Anyone who walked into the cabin would have to get past her gunfire.

Three loud bangs sounded on the front door. Patience steadied her aim.

"Patience, it's Nash. I'm coming in."

Okay, so why didn't he just do so? She wouldn't shoot him.

The front door opened as Greta watched, and the dog didn't bark or whine. But Nash was behind a man Patience knew too well. She stood and lowered her pistol.

"Daddy."

Fenwick Colton's face was partially obscured by the custom cowboy hat he wore, always a part of his wardrobe no matter if he was in sweatpants or a tuxedo. Tonight he was in his usual business suit with a lariat. The sterling silver hawk bolo tie at the base of his collar was his signature symbol. The raptor suited him, as she'd never known her daddy to be anything but focused and predatory.

"Hey, short stuff. Since when do you have your own personal guard?" He shoved a thumb over his shoulder, indicating Nash.

"What are you doing here, Daddy? You could have been killed by either one of us." Typical of Fenwick, he hadn't called first. If he wanted to see her, he just showed up on his own timetable. Although he usually asked her to come to the office or stop by his estate. And almost always passed the message through Layla.

Concern ratcheted Patience's tension tenfold. "Oh, no, is it Layla? Is she okay?"

"What? Of course she's okay. At least she was when I left the office almost an hour ago. Right before I came here. I forgot how crazy the turns are. Next time I'll drive my four-wheel drive."

"How did you know I was here?" Layla must have told him, but Patience wanted to hear it from him.

Fenwick loved nothing more than playing "I've got a secret," being a disciple of the "knowledge is power" school since forever. If he'd found out she or her siblings were in trouble, or more likely planned to get themselves in trouble, when they were teens, he'd lord the information over them for the remainder of the time they lived at home.

"Layla mentioned it. She said you needed some space, so I didn't expect this young man to be here. You okay, fella?" Fenwick looked at Nash with genuine concern.

Nash remained silent, but Patience was pretty certain she sensed the heat of his frustration and anger, for his eyes sparked and his mouth was pressed in a frown.

"You should have called first, Daddy. We've been over this." And they had. She'd told him not to visit her at her small townhome unless he called and they had standing plans. Same for the cabin. Fenwick thought the world revolved around him and paid little heed to his children's, or their guests', concerns. Not that she'd had a lover over lately, but Patience valued her personal space.

"Do you have any bourbon?" Her father walked into the cabin. "And why the heck are you flashing a gun at me, Patience?"

She sighed and put the weapon on the counter. She opened the cabinet over the refrigerator. "I think I still have the bottle you brought with you the last time you were here." And the only time. Fenwick had checked out the cabin when she'd built it, but that was it. She found the bottle of his favorite drink and poured him two fingers.

"Here you go, Daddy." She placed it on the island and saw that Nash had quietly come in and closed the door. Greta lay against it, back to her preferred location.

"Aren't you going to join me?" Fenwick looked at her, and she saw how little he'd aged over the years since she'd left home. No wonder he never had a problem finding a date or his next wife.

"No, but I'll have a ginger ale." She caught Nash's glance and saw the surprise. Had he thought she'd told her family? Only Layla knew about the baby.

"How about you—what did you say your name was?"

"Nash. Nash Maddox. And I'm afraid I have to pass, too, as I'm on an active case. I'm with the RRPD."

"Haven't we met? I have a few relatives on the force." Fenwick's attention went to Greta. "She's beautiful."

"And a K9, too." Nash looked like he'd rather converse with a billy goat.

"Thank you for the work you do. Red Ridge is lucky to have such a fine police department, and we have the best K9 facility in South Dakota." Fenwick's skinny chest puffed at his boast. He'd funded most of the recent upgrades at the training center and clinic. And now Colton Energy faced bankruptcy.

"The training center is vital to the county's security, Daddy." Patience couldn't help the verbal prod. He threatened to cut off funding whenever Colton Energy hit a rough patch, which she found stressful and unnecessary.

"Of course it is, but you know that if I don't keep my

company going, I won't have anything to give. No worries, though. Your sister Layla is a true Colton." He held up his drink to Patience, then nodded to Nash. "Cheers."

"Cheers." She and Nash toasted with their sodas, but all she wanted to do was throw her drink in her father's face. It wasn't like she wasn't used to his self-centered ways, but his high-handed manner was over-the-top, even for him. For him to throw Layla's willingness to marry the creepy Hamlin around like a badge of honor made Patience sick.

After he took a healthy swallow, Fenwick looked around the kitchen and living room. "I forgot how excellent a job you did on the renovation. This is a very nice getaway for you."

"Why are you really here, Daddy?" She knew how to pin him down after years of practice. Fenwick didn't even bother to feign ignorance, or pretend he'd come on a friendly visit.

"You know about your cousin Demi, right? The trouble she's in?"

"Of course I do. But which part are you talking about?" Demi Colton had been branded by the town as the most likely candidate to be the Groom Killer. The first victim, Bo Gage, had been her fiancé until he'd left her for Hayley Patton. The breakup gave Demi motive, along with some circumstantial evidence. Her name had been written in the first victim's blood by his body, and a piece of her jewelry had been found near the crime scene. Plus, more than one witness put her at a few of the murder sites. But Patience liked Demi, and if her gut was correct, Demi was innocent. A couple months before she'd fled, Demi had brought in an injured animal for Patience to care for, and her demeanor bespoke her compassion and integrity. Not the characteristics of a serial killer.

"You know very well I'm talking about the Groom Killer herself. Demi Colton." Fenwick took another hefty swig before pointing his finger and glass at Nash. "Your colleagues need to get their crap together and arrest her. What the hell is taking you all so long? Now we have a second murderer on our hands."

Before Nash could respond, Fenwick turned back to Patience. "Finn filled me in." No apology, no expression of concern for her well-being. *Typical Daddy.*

She saw Nash's spine stiffen and for a second Patience thought he might answer Fenwick with some hard words of his own.

"You're right, Mr. Colton. It's a team effort, and the RRPD is working around the clock on this case. We'll catch the murderer, sooner than later."

"'Sooner' is not soon enough. How many more innocent victims will it take? Demi's clearly the one you want. What's keeping you from bringing her in for questioning? She's been spotted enough in town that no matter where she's hiding out, it can't be too far away. Do I have to remind you that you're speaking to the mayor of Red Ridge?"

"No, sir. But obviously you need reminding that as mayor, you need to discuss this with the chief of police." A muscle strained in Nash's jaw. Her father needed to leave.

"Daddy, did you come all this way because you knew

Nash was here with me? This is a crappy way to throw your weight around." Nash might not want to dress her father down, but nothing kept her from doing it.

She was glad she'd kept Demi's K9 clinic visit to herself. It wasn't relevant to the case in any way except to challenge the stance that Demi was a rough-around-the-edges hothead. Demi's brothers on the RRPD were in her corner, at least.

Patience only hoped Demi and her baby were okay—she'd been pregnant when she'd fled town and had had the baby on the run. That couldn't have been easy. Just last month Demi had been spotted in town, in disguise, with her baby in a carrier. Patience hoped the real killer would be caught soon so that Demi and her infant could come out of the shadows.

"I heard you were living up here for the time being, yes." He glared at Nash. "And I was told she had the finest K9 team with her. Now I'm not so sure."

Nash didn't reply with words. His own glare said it all. Patience almost laughed at how her father actually balked. Fenwick Colton wasn't used to being shut down by someone he considered a subordinate. Even though no RRPD officer worked directly for him, he acted as if they did and didn't have a problem putting pressure on Finn to keep or fire officers on a whim. As mayor, it was in Fenwick's purview to do so. Fortunately, Finn was a man of integrity and usually able to keep Fenwick mollified, while not letting the mayor's opinions negatively affect the RRPD.

"Daddy, it's going to take you the better part of an hour to get home. I know you've had a long day. Why don't you have a bite to eat, then head out?" Fenwick was an early bird and she hoped he'd take the hint. She didn't want him driving right after downing the scotch, though, so she brought out some cheese and crackers.

"I wanted to know you were safe, daughter. Don't believe me, but it's true. At least you're in a secure location, save for the woods. Though a man would have to be crazy to try to scale the mountain to get here on foot." He munched on the snack.

"You know I've got cameras all over the place." She mentally kicked herself for not checking the security system's monitor before Nash ran out to find her father. They wouldn't have been so worked up and would have seen it was him.

"The murderer you saw on the lake followed you to your town house, I heard. So you two decided to hole up here?" Daddy was a dog with a bone. He thrived on details.

"Not exactly." As she replied, Fenwick got up from the island stool and walked around, looking at the place. He wasn't one to sit still for long.

Still energetic and wire thin, he never had a short-age of women who wanted to be with him. She and Layla had compared notes and agreed their father wasn't going to have a fourth wife. He saw potential mates as future divorce adversaries—money grabbers. And Patience would like to think he was afraid of another broken heart, though he never displayed anything that indicated it.

"Nice touch with the gas insert." Fenwick stalled, and for the first time Patience wondered if he wasn't a little lonely. Unless he had a date on his arm, he went home alone to the expansive mansion she'd grown up in.

He stood in front of the fireplace, then turned to look out the picture window, where the porch lights illuminated the Appalachian chairs and rocker. "And the porch looks like a nice place to start the day."

"It is..." She almost choked on her words as she saw the huge pile of baby supplies beneath the window. She'd forgotten about Nash's shopping spree.

Her father's hawkish gaze missed nothing. When he turned to face her, he assessed her, pausing when he got to her belly. Incredulity and comprehension played across his features.

"What's with the kid stuff, Patience?"

Patience swallowed as she faced down the first adversary she'd ever known.

# Chapter 14

Nash wished Fenwick Colton would magically disappear. Why couldn't the man see his daughter as the beautiful woman she was? Instead, he treated her like she was his possession. *Enough.*

"I brought the supplies here. They're mine." Nash spoke up, seeing the consternation on Patience's face. Her cheeks were flushed and she bit her lower lip so deeply he expected to see blood. The least he could do was buy her time. If she didn't want to tell her powerful father that she was pregnant, he'd lie.

"Can I ask why?" Fenwick looked from Patience to Nash, then back to his daughter. She waited for Nash to meet her gaze, and when he did she nodded. She raised her chin and squarely faced her father.

"Daddy, you're going to be a grandfather."

Silence fell in tense shards, and Nash fought to think of something he could say or do to ease the stress he knew this caused Patience. She'd turned to him that first night they were together because she'd had a blowup with Fenwick and Layla. Something to do with Fenwick's business floundering and Layla agreeing to marry Hamlin Harrington, two things Patience believed were related. She blamed her father for pushing her sister to marry the much older businessman. Nash didn't want to get in the middle of family stuff; he had enough of his own. But the baby in Patience's belly was his.

Fenwick Colton and he were family by default. Holy hell, he'd never taken the time to think about that. His thoughts, his heart hadn't gone past Patience. And the baby.

"Well, I'll be damned. Congratulations!" Fenwick rounded the breakfast bar and took his daughter in what Nash thought was a genuine hug. Patience looked a little stiff, but she did hug him back. It was a start. When Fenwick released her, he looked at Nash. "I take it you're responsible?"

"We're both responsible for the baby, Daddy. I don't have to tell you how it works." Patience blushed and Nash bit back a laugh.

"No. No, you don't." Fenwick eyed Nash. "What are you going to do about it? As far as raising the child? My grandchild." Of course, Fenwick immediately claimed the unborn babe, another possession.

"Patience and I are working out the details." He walked over to her so that they'd face Fenwick together.

But her dad wasn't accusatory. He seemed bemused.

"Is that why you're here together? Besides keeping safe from the Lake Killer. You're figuring things out?"

"We're assigned to the same case, Daddy. I work with the RRPD on any K9 operation, technically, but this one is requiring extra time."

Fenwick gave his daughter a look that Nash knew probably melted his opponents in the boardroom. Patience stood her ground, and Fenwick turned to Nash.

"You're responsible for her now."

Nash saw red. Patience wasn't a commodity to be traded for a dowry. He refused to raise the tension in the room, though. And truth be told, he did feel responsible for Patience and the baby's safety.

"I'm responsible for me, Daddy." Patience certainly had the dog-with-a-bone DNA in her, too.

Fenwick waved his hand at both of them. "I would have preferred you did this the old-fashioned way, getting married first. But I also wanted you to join the family business instead of going to vet school." In what Nash suspected was a rare admission, the elder Colton's face fell as he contemplated his daughter. "And look at me. Two divorces, the awful, tragic loss of your mother, five kids, and I've not done well by you or your brothers and sisters. Who am I to say what's best?"

"Daddy, you did the best you knew how to do at the time. And we've all turned out okay, haven't we?"

Fenwick nodded. "That you have. Congratulations, my dear." He kissed Patience on the forehead, and Nash saw that she seemed reserved after such an emotional display by her father. This wasn't a family used to outward expressions of affection.

"Nash." Fenwick stretched his hand out and Nash shook it. "All I ask is that you do right by my daughter and grandchild."

"Yes, sir."

"Keep yourselves safe from the Lake Killer. And I mean business about the Groom Killer, Nash. The RRPD needs to get Demi behind bars. Red Ridge needs its sense of security back. We need people to feel safe to get married again."

"Is your father always such a prick?" Nash sat on the sofa next to her. Patience had distracted herself from her father's surprise visit by opening the pile of baby supplies after he departed.

"This is like Christmas, Nash. How did you know which swing to buy? I was at a friend's baby shower a while ago and she received four different swings, each supposedly the best." Patience hadn't paid attention to the discussion of timers and wireless controls. She'd dismissed it as useless information. "You know you've purchased the top-of-the-line swing, right? This has not only a timer but also a Wi-Fi speaker so that you can customize the baby's music. And it says here that the speakers will not exceed safe decibel levels." She pored over the service manual.

Nash's strong hands covered the text. "Answer my question, Patience. Do you think how your father behaved was appropriate?"

"Which part? How he arrogantly assumed we'd both do his bidding and work to get Demi arrested? Or how he threw his usual barb at me for being a 'mere' veterinarian and not working for the high-and-mighty Colton legacy?"

Nash looked at her with compassion sprinkled with a little bit of surprise.

"You're an amazing woman, you know that? I don't mean to put down your family, but it's fair to say that your father is a known entity in Red Ridge. You don't fit in his world, Patience. Money isn't your be-all and end-all. I get it. I have degrees in finance and computer science. I could have used my siblings as an excuse to follow through with my postcollege plans and gone to San Francisco or Chicago to get a moneymaking job. Bring in the bucks for my siblings, focus on their financial future. My aunt and uncle would have taken them in."

"So why didn't you?"

"Because I'm made of the same stuff you are. I knew the kids needed their closest family member, their half brother, more than they needed trust funds and college accounts."

"What made you pick law enforcement?"

"I was interested in white-collar crime and was beefing up my résumé with security jobs for high-end corporations. But it was too sterile for me. I wanted, needed, to work with real people every day. And I've always loved dogs, so K9 was a natural fit. I had just graduated the police academy when my folks were killed."

"Talk about divine timing."

"Yeah, it was, in an awful way. I had a regular paycheck from the get-go. And in total disclosure, the kids aren't without college funds. There was a life insurance policy that provided enough for each of them to attend a state school. Paige and Maeve are on the scholarship track, though, so the sky's the limit for where the boys will go to university."

His pride in his siblings touched her. "You're a wonderful father, Nash."

"Big brother, you mean. Yeah, I'm their parent, four times over. But I've had help. Besides my aunt and uncle, there are so many other family members and friends of my parents who've stepped up. My folks each had two siblings—that's a lot of babysitting power right there." He grinned, making what he did seem easy.

"I don't know how you've done it. Watch hours, duty assignments... They aren't all family-friendly."

"I haven't done anything anyone else wouldn't have." Nash's modesty made him all the more attractive.

"Give me a break. You've gone above and beyond and you know it."

"Which begs the question, Patience. Are you going to let me participate fully as the baby's father?" His question jarred her out of the bubble she wanted to stay in. Where she didn't have to make a big decision, where her heart wasn't at stake. Where a mad killer hadn't drawn a bright bloodred target on her back.

"Is this really the time to talk about it? There's a serial killer out there, another killer after me and the Larson twins after both of us. Why don't we get through the next few weeks and to the point where, hopefully, the Groom Killer is stopped and whoever I saw on the lake is apprehended? The Larson twins aren't stupid enough to come after us directly, but they might send their own thugs. To figure out how we'll manage the parenting—it's just a lot to take in."

"Come here." Nash opened his arms and Patience sidled up to him on the sofa, loving the unwavering strength he so freely gave her. Once her head was nestled on his shoulder, he spoke as he stroked her hair.

"Neither of us planned this, Patience. After these last days together, I'd say we have an attraction that doesn't come along every day. You don't want to settle down—I understand completely understand that, neither of us wanted to. It's okay to enjoy one another, draw fortitude from our bond, though, isn't it? And the baby will do better if his or her parents get along."

"I can't argue with that, but it's not that simple, Nash." She ignored the disappointment when he admitted he didn't want to settle down, either. And she wasn't ready to correct his assumption that she hadn't changed her mind about it, either. All she could think of was the fight she had in front of her to balance her career and impending mommydom. She'd fought long and hard to achieve independence from her father and the darker side of the Colton legacy, only to find out the K9 clinic in her mother's name was under threat of closure. "We have to catch the Lake Killer and the Groom Killer." As she said the words, she still couldn't get her head wrapped around the fact that two murderers were on the loose in Red Ridge.

"Speaking of that, I have some updates from Finn. I didn't want to say anything in front of your father. We believe the Lake Killer is an operative for a North American heroin and fentanyl distribution ring. He's an expert at disguises and disappearing as needed. We're getting closer to him, Patience."

She shivered. "I hate being so close to such evil, Nash."

"I know. Let me do the heavy lifting, worrywise, for you. The only thing you have to concern yourself with is staying safe and healthy. Trust me as your friend to take care of the rest for you."

"You can't charm your way out of this one, Officer Maddox." She playfully punched his jaw. His stubbled, sexy jaw.

He caught her fingers in his teeth and his tongue circled the tips, shooting mind-numbing awareness to the spot between her legs.

"Who said anything about charm?" He tugged on the tendril of hair he'd been playing with until their lips met. Patience had no argument. The next days and weeks would be scary until they caught both killers. She'd take comfort in the security of Nash's arms while she could.

The next week Patience drove to her prenatal checkup with a combination of nervousness and hope in her belly. She laughed as she realized something else existed inside her—the baby. Was it a boy or girl? She and Nash were minutes from finding out.

As much as she tried to convince herself she could do all of this on her own, she was excited to know Nash would be here, would see the baby for the first time with her.

It was hard to imagine life before, without Nash, and

now it was impossible to conceive that he wouldn't always be at her side, as their child was born and then grew over the years.

Her heartbeat sped up and it wasn't from distress. Maybe it would have a year, six months ago. Before she'd been with Nash. She was a different woman, with a fresh perspective on life and the importance of appreciating those who meant the most.

Nash was definitely in that category.

She spotted Nash's car in the ob-gyn's parking lot and pulled up next to it. Nash rose to his feet when she entered the reception area, a copy of *Your Baby* in his hands. The sight of such a big strong man holding a magazine about babies made her smile. And then tears formed in her eyes.

"Patience. What?" Nash stood in front of her, clutching the periodical.

She shook her head, wiped her eyes. "Nothing. Hormones. I'll get checked in—give me a minute."

As soon as she'd given her insurance information she sat beside Nash, clipboard in hand.

"You have to fill that whole page out?" Nash eyed the questionnaire.

She fanned the multipage document. "More like three pages. The doctor needs to know my entire history, plus how I'm feeling."

"And how are you feeling?" His concern touched her and she fought tears again.

"I'm good." Grateful. Hopeful. But hopeful for what? That the baby enjoyed perfect health? Or that

Nash might actually be a permanent part of her, and the baby's, life?

"Patience?" He refused to allow her off the hook that easily.

"It's just the hormones. And let's face it, we've had a lot going on." She looked around the room at the other waiting mothers, in various stages of pregnancy. She kept thinking she looked the same as usual, but in fact, anyone could see she was pregnant. Her belly was fuller and starting to protrude like a basketball.

"We have." His tone matched hers—low and measured. But still, there were plenty of ears to catch their conversation and this wasn't the place for police talk.

Her hand paused over the question about family history. "Nash, do you know if anyone in your family had any birth defects, or congenital disease?"

His brow furrowed. "Not that I know of. All of my half siblings are healthy as horses, as you've seen. Since I don't have a biological full sibling, I don't know about anyone but me, and from what my dad told me, my mother had no problems with my birth. She died when I was a teen, long after their divorce. I'd lived with both of them on an alternating schedule up until her death. My dad remarried a year later, and he and my stepmom had all four kids pretty quickly."

"I'm sorry, Nash." Patience had never thought to ask him about his parents and why his dad had remarried. And now all three parental figures in his life had passed. "The baby must mean that much more to you."

"You understand that better than me." His gaze left

hers and he looked around the waiting room. "We'll talk about it later."

"Yes." She finished filling out the form and realized she'd underestimated how much could go wrong with a pregnancy. As a medical professional herself, working with animals, she understood the basics. But she hadn't taken the time to apply it to her situation, to her baby.

"Ms. Colton?"

"That's Dr. Colton." Nash spoke up and Patience blushed. The nurse looked at her file.

"I'm sorry, Dr. Colton. Follow me."

Patience stood, and with Nash at her side walked into the examination room, where they'd find out how their baby fared.

Nash hoped like heck that Patience didn't see how freaking nervous he felt. Thankfully, she couldn't see his sweating palms, or feel how tight the muscles in his chest clamped down on his rib cage. He'd watched countless canines whelp pups, and he dealt with kids on a daily basis. But his siblings weren't babies and puppies were…pups. Not a human baby with an entire life in front of it. His father and stepmother had made it look so easy when the kids were young, when the house was a complete cacophony of toddlers and babies. He'd come in later, when they were old enough to dress themselves and eat from a plate.

"Do I need to put on a robe?" Patience appeared fine, her usual confident self, except for the way she kept biting her lower lip. At this rate she'd gnaw it off before they got to the ultrasound part.

"No, that isn't necessary. You'll pull your waistband down so that the doctor can measure you, and then he'll put some gel on it for the ultrasound. That's it. Are you interested in knowing the sex of the baby?"

Patience's gaze flew to Nash's. "What do you think?"

He gulped. "I don't know. I guess it's a good idea, to be prepared."

"But the surprise of finding out at birth might make it more fun, more to look forward to."

The nurse cleared her throat. "I'll let you two talk about it while you're waiting for the doctor. He had a late delivery last night—early this morning, actually— so we're running about fifteen minutes behind. We'll be back shortly." She left the room.

After Patience scooted up onto the exam table, Nash sank into the chair. His knees never wobbled, never behaved like jelly. Did all new fathers-to-be go through this?

"Nash, are you okay?" Patience's concern pierced his nerves.

"Yeah, I'm good. I'm not the one carrying our kid in my belly. You're the one we need to focus on."

"It's not just about me, Nash. Yes, the baby and I are in this together. But you're the dad. It's okay if you're feeling shaky about it."

"It's not because I already am raising four kids, Patience. I'm not disappearing on you. I'm in this for the long haul." Annoyance made his temples pound. He hated it when she fell back upon her belief that he wanted nothing to do with more kids after he finished raising his siblings. Sure, he hadn't planned the pregnancy any more than she had, but it was what it was.

"I know you are. It's not a part-time dad who does all the research you've been doing, or who is so determined to equip the baby with the supplies you've purchased." She smiled from the exam table, her hand on her belly in a classically maternal pose. Her beauty made his heart hurt.

"The baby is going to be beautiful, Patience. Like you."

"Healthy is all that matters. And yes, the baby is already beautiful. We're going to see it today."

"I read that the first appointment is usually just a fetal heartbeat check—it can be too early to see a whole lot."

"Yes, if we'd planned this and were here for the first time when I'd just missed my period. But this is two missed periods out, so I'm at least fourteen weeks along, maybe even sixteen. My periods have never been regular, so we'll have to see what the doc says."

"Do you want to know the sex, Patience?" It was her decision. Nash would love to know, but he wasn't the one who had labor and delivery to get through. Maybe she needed the surprise to wait.

She worried her lower lip again. "My instinct is yes, of course. I'm a K9 vet and it's my job to know what our bitches are having, their health, all we can find out before the pups are born. The baby isn't a puppy, though, is it?" She looked at him and he got up and went to her.

"Come here." He wrapped his arms around her and she leaned into him, her head on his chest.

"Thank you for coming today, Nash. It's so much to…"

"To absorb." He rubbed his lips on her hair, breathed in her ginger-spice scent.

"Yes. I keep telling myself I'm a professional and this is nothing unknown to me, except for the fact that I'm having the baby. But it's all uncharted territory. All those books with the pictures of the pregnant woman sitting in deep contemplation of her baby, they're stressing me out. I haven't had time to do anything but survive these last weeks."

"We're working on it, babe." He resolved to put the Groom Killer and Lake Killer in their rearview mirrors as soon as he humanly could. His work colleague, the mother of his child, deserved at least that much.

Wait—was Patience his partner only in work and making the baby, or more?

He shoved the questions down. Today was about their baby and figuring out what they needed to do next.

Three quick raps sounded before the door opened and Dr. Girard entered. "Dr. Colton and…"

"Nash. Nash Maddox." He shook the doctor's hand, and then Patience did.

"Dr. Girard."

"Well, congratulations to you both. Your urine test was positive, but you already knew that, I assume. I see you've missed two periods."

"Yes. There wasn't an open appointment before today, and the receptionist told me I could do a same-day walk-in sooner, but I've been involved in a case at work."

"You're the vet at the RRPD K9 facility, right?" He reached for his stethoscope. "There's been a lot of excitement in Red Ridge lately, according to the news. Breathe in." He continued the exam as he peppered her with questions. Nash's impatience grew, but then he figured out that the doctor was developing a rapport with Patience. He recognized it because it's what he did with citizens during his police work. Put them at ease, let them know they could trust you.

"That's me. And yes, we've been busy." Patience lay flat at the doctor's invitation and pushed her waistband down low. Dr. Girard pulled out a tape measure and ran it from her pubic bone to the top of the baby bump. "What am I measuring?" she asked.

The doctor smiled. "You're more than four months, from this, but let's see what the ultrasound says. This will be cold." Without further comment, he squirted clear gel onto her belly and fired up the ultrasound machine.

"Have you two decided if you want to know the sex?" He moved the paddle up and down Patience's belly, and Nash was torn between watching her expression and the image that began to take shape on the screen.

"Yes. Yes, we do," Patience answered, and Nash's stomach flipped. It was the same kind of anticipation he had while watching one of the kids participate in an athletic or academic event. Excitement for how it could turn out, joy at watching their achievement.

"Well, folks, here's the deal. You're measuring larger than a typical four-month fetus."

"It's not older than that—before this baby was conceived I hadn't had sex in at least a year." Patience's declaration brooked no reaction from the doctor, but Nash's insides tightened, then erupted in what he could only describe as a glow. She'd picked him to ease her loneliness with, as he had picked her.

"It's clear to me that you conceived when you think you did. The fact is, there's more than one baby here."

Patience almost sat up and grabbed the paddle from Dr. Girard.

"What? How many?"

"Two. You're having twins. And you're ready for the sex?" He narrowed in on one baby, and she stared at the screen. "Here's a boy."

Tears slid past her lids, and she blinked so that she wouldn't miss one bit of seeing her babies. *Her babies.* Nash's babies. She looked at him. His gaze was transfixed on the screen, and in the dim light she couldn't tell if he was especially pale or just reflecting the monitor.

"And here's a girl. So, fraternal twins, a boy and a girl. Both are measuring right where we want them to be."

"How have I been pregnant with twins and not realized it sooner?" She blurted out her thoughts before she had a chance to process.

"Good genes is my bet. And you're very healthy, active. It's easy to mistake a pregnancy for stomach upset, the flu or none of the above. The bottom line is that you're doing great and so are your babies." He wiped the gel from her belly and helped her to sit up.

"Will I be able to work until term?"

"We'll take it a week at a time, but my guess is no. With twins it can get tricky toward the last trimester, if not sooner. We want to keep your babies inside until we know their lungs are fully developed. Patience, you're doing great. Hopefully you'll be the mother who goes full-term without a hitch, besides getting uncomfortable the last few weeks. But we have to monitor you, the babies. If anything comes up that necessitates bed rest, then that's what we'll do. For now, enjoy it and be glad you're out of the woods for morning sickness. These next several weeks can be very exciting and a great time to get ready for the babies."

Patience listened with half a mind as the doctor reassured her. She couldn't stop looking at Nash, seeking the warmth of reassurance in his glance. But her search was in vain. He looked like a man with shell shock. More like twin shock.

Adding one child to the four he was raising was a tall order. Might twins be too much for even Nash's indomitable strength?

They walked out of the ob-gyn clinic together and Nash stood with her near the beat-up sedan. "We'll get through this, Patience." Sure, he was thrown off balance. Twins. Yet nothing, not one thing, was more important to him than her well-being. He had to make her see she wasn't alone in this.

Her teary eyes made his heart hurt. "Twins, Nash.

Two babies. There's no way you're going to be able to handle two in addition to your four siblings."

"Hey." He cupped her face. "That's my decision, not yours. All that matters is that you're healthy, the babies are healthy. That's it. We'll get the killers in no time, trust me. These past weeks will seem a blur, but they'll be over. And then we can live life the way we want to." He kissed her gently, not caring who saw.

As he drove away, he wondered if they'd agree to what kind of life they wanted for the babies. First, Red Ridge had to be safe from two murderers.

# Chapter 15

Patience was used to coming in on weekends, as she did most days all year round since she'd started working at the clinic. But she had to admit that she'd gotten used to the life she and Nash had carved out in the cabin over the past weeks. Leaving the warmth of Nash's arms this morning had been difficult. He'd let her go alone because she was heading straight to the clinic, to a safe place. Fortifications around the fences and gates, as well as the entranceways, made it much more difficult for the Lake Killer, or any intruder, to get past.

She and Nash had fallen into a comfortable routine over the last few weeks since the ob-gyn appointment, with no further threats from the Lake Killer or the Larson twins. The ongoing threat never left her awareness, though.

As much as being with Nash each day and each sexy night made her want to believe it'd always be like this, Patience couldn't allow herself to grow complacent. She did let herself enjoy her work, though. Wearing extra roomy scrubs she'd purchased meant that, so far at least, no one had asked her if she was pregnant. If they did, would she tell them there were two? How could she not?

She'd had to move the monthly community-wide K9 training day to a Saturday. Red Ridge citizens signed up months in advance to learn from the K9 experts. But since Patience had spotted the Lake Killer, the workload and security requirements made training with civilians during the week nearly impossible. The RRPD was stretched thinner than ever.

She made the drive from the cabin in just under fifty minutes, thanks to the clear roads and lack of precipitation. She headed for the postoperative board to see which patients were still in-house, and then over to the kennels.

"*Good* morning!" Gabby, the parrot, stretched her red wings for Patience, begging for an affectionate beak rub from her. Patience complied, stroking the smooth surface, careful to keep her fingers clear of the edges of Gabby's marbled gray-and-white beak.

"Morning, Gabby. I've missed you, too."

The macaw made kissing noises, like two lips smacking together, and Patience laughed. "I'm not that stupid. You nicked me the last time you asked for a kiss, remember?"

"Hey, sister." Blake, her younger brother by two years, stood in the entrance.

"Hi, Blake. How are you doing? And where's Juliette?" Juliette's K9 partner, Sasha, had recently injured her paw, so the beagle was doing some light training with Patience before being cleared for regular sessions at the training center.

"They stopped just outside to say hi to someone, so I thought I'd come see you privately for a minute. Because the real question is, how are *you* doing?"

Patience straightened. Her brother's eyes and fair coloring matched their father's. He resembled Fenwick more than she did, but despite being wealthy in his own right, Blake couldn't be less like the selfish, money-seeking businessman.

"I'm fine. Let me guess. Dad's been bugging you?"

"No, but he did call me." She watched her brother's gaze fall to her belly. Her much-extended belly. She realized her baggy scrubs weren't cutting it. By her count she was almost eighteen weeks pregnant, and none of her jeans or fitted pants were able to be zipped up any longer. She'd have to make a general announcement soon.

"Yes, I'm pregnant. It's true. But what Daddy doesn't know yet, what I didn't know when I saw him, is that I'm having twins. What else did he tell you?"

Blake shook his head, a wide grin splitting his face. He enveloped her in a big bear hug. "Twins? That's great, Patience. Congratulations." When he let her go, he looked at her and she saw that he was sincere. No judgment or recrimination. Just joy.

"Thanks. I have to admit it's come as a surprise, but I'm getting more excited about it." She braved putting a palm on her belly. "And I guess I can't really hide it too much longer."

"No need to hide it. It's your life." Blake paused, his own hand on the door of an empty kennel. "It's none of my business, sis, but are you and the father, uh, an item?"

"Daddy didn't tell you who the father is?"

"He may have mentioned a certain K9 officer's name in between a string of cursing, yes."

They both laughed. Patience nodded. "Yes, Nash is my baby daddy. *Babies'* daddy. It's a boy and a girl. But don't get the wrong idea about Nash and me. He's insisting on being involved with the babies, but he's got four kids of his own to raise."

"I don't know Nash Maddox well, but I've met him a few times and he doesn't strike me as the type to blow smoke, Patience. He'll be there for you. Why wouldn't he?"

Because she wouldn't let him. Because she wanted to keep her independence. Because she needed her autonomy in all areas of her life. "You know I have a tough time with men, Blake."

"Aw, sis. Nash isn't our daddy. It's hard for us to see that there are men who really give a fig about their kids and are devoted to their wives. We didn't have that example. But there are good guys. Nash is one of them."

"How about you, Blake?"

His glance slid away. "I'm doing my best to be a good partner and father. Finally." He'd recently fallen for K9 officer Juliette Walsh, who'd had his child three years earlier. But Blake hadn't known about his kid until he and Juliette connected again. Patience knew it had been hard on all involved.

"You got your happy ending, Blake. I'm happy for you."

He nodded. "And you can have yours, too, sis."

Nash let the boys out of the Jeep and looked around the clinic's training yard. Patience stood with two other trainers, their attention on a pair of young pups that were joining the RRPD K9 team.

"Can Greta run with us?" Troy looked at Nash.

"No, but you can walk her over there on her leash." He let Greta out of the back and handed the lead to Troy. "Remember, she's your responsibility until you get her to Dr. Colton."

"Doc Patience lets us play with all the dogs."

"That's when you're here for a family day, or to help with the other clinic patients. This is an official K9 training session for dogs who've been under veterinary care. It's a privilege to be here."

"We heard you before." Jon was being a snarky teenager, which Nash could usually brush off. But today it annoyed him.

"Watch your tone, Jon."

"Sorry." The teen's mumble felt like a victory. Nash had been through such emotional upheaval with Paige and Maeve when they were that age. So far the boys seemed so much easier to handle. but he knew that one wrong, impulsive decision on their part could change the whole trajectory of their adolescence.

As they approached Patience, she turned, and he saw

her profile in the full sunlight. She wore scrubs with a hoodie that had the K9 clinic logo emblazoned on the front. To the casual eye, or someone who didn't know her well, she might appear to have grown thicker around her middle. Not unheard-of as people hit thirty years old; Nash heard so many of the officers at the RRPD complain about having to cut back calories and increase their workouts to maintain professional standards in uniform. But Patience's belly was more pronounced today, and he couldn't keep the grin off his face. That was their babies growing inside her.

His breath whooshed out of his lungs as he saw how her eyes lit up when she recognized the boys, and then him. Knowing the swell of her belly was from their lovemaking added oxygen to the ferocious protective flames he'd felt since finding out she was pregnant.

"Nash, are you and Greta going to do agility or signals first?" Officer Juliette Walsh, who was dating Patience's brother, walked up and stood next to him, watching the scene unfold.

"I haven't decided. How about you?"

Juliette nodded at the beagle on her heels. "Sasha and I are going to work on signals today, aren't we, girl?" Sasha was a narcotics dog and her expert sniffer had kept a lot of illegal substances out of the hands of Red Ridge teens.

"Life will be better for all of us once we shut down the drug ring," Nash stated. Juliette knew as much as he did, and probably assumed the Larsons were responsible, but it wasn't their place to indict without evidence and a solid case. Most of that was left up to the RRPD detectives. K9 did the heavy lifting as far as drug detection and interdiction, as well as search and rescue to include diving.

"It sure will be. I'm sick of anyone around here thinking they can take advantage of the good people of this town." Juliette looked over at Patience, then back to him. "I hear you've been spending time with Blake's sister, Nash," she added with a smile.

"Greta and I were first on scene when she witnessed the Lake Killer dumping the victim, yes." He suspected Juliette wasn't referring to the Lake Killer case, though.

His colleague grinned. "I'm just busting on you. Blake's father couldn't wait to tell us he'd been to Patience's cabin, and that he'd run into you there."

Nash froze. Had Fenwick blabbed about the baby before he and Patience had had a chance to tell their relatives themselves?

"Before you get all upset, Patience let Blake know about my future niece and nephew—when Blake and I can finally marry, that is. He couldn't keep it to himself. I'm so excited for you both."

Nash smiled. "And count on me doing everything in my power to keep Patience and the babies safe through this case and beyond."

"I've got your back if you ever need it," Juliette said. "See you on the field. Come on, Sasha." They walked away and Nash took a few moments to calm down.

Patience needed him to be the calm and cool one, not a hothead. He saw the boys talking to her as they stood with Greta, Juliette and Sasha, and immediately relaxed. They were all family now, no matter what happened between him and Patience.

\* \* \*

For the next few hours Patience helped out at the K9 training center, working with the handlers and trainers to put the dogs into every conceivable situation they'd face on the street. Drug and bomb detection, search and rescue, guarding. She got a kick out of watching Jon's and Troy's expressions when the usually laid-back Greta turned into a focused, take-no-prisoners attack dog and grabbed the heavily padded arm of one of the trainers.

"Are we going to do any water training today, Dr. Colton?" Jon Maddox's face resembled Nash's so much she wondered if either of the twins would look the same.

"No, Greta's had enough real time in the lake lately." With a chill that had nothing to do with the crisp autumn day, she realized Greta might have more diving to do if the Lake Killer came back. Looking past the fences, she wondered if the thug was out there, watching from a hidden location.

"Hey, what are you thinking?" Nash was next to her, close enough to touch her, but not doing so. He was professional if nothing else. But with the thought of such a bad guy being out there, she wanted to lean against Nash, let him take care of protecting her and the twins.

Where on earth had that come from? The baby hormones were making a mess of her self-reliance pact with herself.

"I'm thinking it's time to bring everyone in for the potluck lunch. Are your sisters coming to join us?"

"Not today. Paige has senior class activities and Maeve is with a study group. Which reminds me—I'm signed up to chaperone the senior Fall Fest dance. I was hoping you'd join me."

"Are you asking me out on a date?"

"I'd never do such a cheap date, if it was a date. This is a way to be able to keep an eye on you and also let you get to know my siblings. Meet them on their turf, so to speak."

"How are you going to explain my baby bump to the other PTA members?"

"Do you care?" His eyes blazed with molten heat and her body's immediate response made her sit down on a nearby bench. "Are you okay?" His lust turned to concern so quickly that Patience had to laugh.

"I'm good. Just adjusting to all the changes." She rubbed the tops of her thighs before pressing her hands into her lower back as she stretched her legs out in front. "I needed to get off my feet for a bit, that's all."

"I'm going to be by your side through all of this, babe."

"We'll talk about it later, Nash."

He said nothing. Patience would figure out he wasn't going anywhere. Nash just had to keep showing up.

# *Chapter 16*

After the training center potluck, Nash left Greta with Patience for protection and took the boys home. He'd tried to convince himself that it'd be okay to bring Patience back to the house for dinner, but it would be a stupid move with the Lake Killer still at large. And now he had the Larsons' dog walker to worry about.

It was past dark when he drove up the mountain to the cabin. The only way to see was with the Jeep's brights on, given the tree branches reaching out from both sides of the asphalt. As he approached the turnoff to the graveled road that led to Patience's front gate, he was startled by a huge lumbering figure that came out to block the road.

Acting on pure instinct, he hit the brakes and the horn, staying focused on the figure as his vehicle came to a rough halt. It wasn't the Lake Killer or a Larson twin, though. A huge black bear stared him down from its stance in the center of his path, and he had the distinct impression it was sizing him up. It lifted its snout in the air as if it could tell who he was by his scent. Only then did Nash notice a smaller bear, about the size of Greta, meandering through the headlight beams. A mama bear with her cub, out for the last of the autumn feeding before they had to go into hibernation.

Nash took his hand from the wheel, no longer interested in honking. As he watched the scene play out, an unexpected rush of compassion rolled through him.

He loved his siblings and had accepted long ago that it was his role to help raise them. And he'd planned on years of bachelorhood, once the kids left for college and whatever their lives might bring. All this he expected and looked forward to. Discovering that he and Patience had created a baby had been a huge surprise, but to his shock, it wasn't a bad thing.

The mother bear and cub moved in unison, working their way across the road and back into the dark woods, as if he didn't exist. The natural beauty of it moved him.

As much as he had a family, raising his siblings, Nash wanted more. He wanted to feel so in tune with another that she'd know he'd always be there for her. And he loved the idea of waking up to a sensuous woman like Patience Colton every morning. And going to bed with her every night.

Nash wanted more than he'd ever thought he would.

As he put the car back in Drive, he realized that it wasn't what he wanted that mattered. This inexplicable emotion he had for Patience and their unborn children was his problem. His job was to be whatever Patience needed him to be. She'd made it clear that she valued her independence above all.

Patience wasn't much of a cook except when she came to the cabin, the one place she ever felt she truly had the time and space to prepare a proper meal. She took in the huge bowl of pasta carbonara she'd prepared, and while a nice glass of red wine would have been nice, it was easy to forgo for the health of the babies. Her stomach growled and she dug in.

As she twisted a second forkful of pasta, dripping with melted Parmesan, on her plate, Greta let out her warning barks. Patience paused midbite and looked at the monitor atop the island counter. Expecting to see Nash's Jeep, she felt her heart slam into overdrive when she saw an unfamiliar red pickup creep up the drive.

She dropped the fork and ran to the bedroom, where she retrieved her weapon from the safe. After making sure it was locked and loaded, she made her way back to the kitchen and turned out the lights. How had she gone from routine K9 surgeries to needing to draw her weapon multiple times in a few short weeks?

"Greta, here." She pointed to the floor behind the kitchen island to offer the dog the most protection. "Quiet."

Greta sat but remained alert, and Patience wished she could read her mind. Wished the dog could tell her what she smelled and what she heard.

The computer display lit up as the motion detector

light turned on, and she grabbed the monitor and put it on the floor next to her so that it wouldn't give the intruder a clue as to where she was, or if she was in the cabin. Her car was parked around back, so it wouldn't be obvious to anyone that she was home.

Unless this was Nash and he'd taken one of the RRPD pool vehicles. In which case she was going to berate him. Patience glued her gaze to the screen, and felt her stomach sink when she didn't recognize the person who got out of the vehicle. It was a male, over six feet tall, and he held a gun in his right hand. But it wasn't Nash. Patience immediately called 9-1-1.

"Nine-one-one. What's your emergency?" Frank's voice, sure and calm.

"Frank, it's Patience Colton. I'm in my cabin in the mountains and there is an intruder with a weapon, looks like a Colt .45, approaching my front door."

As she relayed the information, a gunshot cracked through the air, followed by loud pounding.

"He's breaking into my house!"

"Are you armed, Patience?"

"Yes." She braced her elbows on the island and aimed at the front door. The wood splintered and shuddered as it resisted the thug's attack, but within seconds the door burst open. The porch motion light backlit the man, and Patience thought she recognized his profile as that of the same suspect who'd been caught on security cameras at the clinic, running Nico and the puppy to a getaway car. One of the Larsons' henchmen. She watched him break into her home with a surreal detachment.

"Stop! I have a weapon."

Greta whimpered next to her, clearly wanting to break her silence and lunge for the intruder.

"You don't steal someone else's property and think you'll get away with it." Another gunshot rang out and granite exploded no more than a foot from her.

Patience was done with talking. She fired at the figure, aiming as she'd practiced countless times on the RRPD range and during the K9 exercises. It wasn't expected that as a veterinarian she'd ever have to fire a weapon, and it wasn't something she'd ever wanted to do until now.

The man jerked, and she wasn't sure if she'd hit his shoulder or his leg, but she saw his arms drop as he fell backward onto the porch. She took her flashlight and shone it at him. His weapon was a foot away, out of his hand. Patience couldn't send Greta to investigate, not yet, not while he could still be conscious and reach for that gun.

"What's going on, Patience?" Frank asked over the phone.

"I've shot the intruder. He's down, half in and half out of my cabin. I believe he's one of the Larsons' henchmen. We'll need an ambulance along with the RRPD."

"Both already on their way. Nash is almost there."

Nash had heard the call on his police radio, she was certain. He'd probably missed the shooter by minutes.

Dispatch must have heard the shots over the phone and sent the ambulance, per standard operating procedure.

Patience carefully crawled around the island and to the sofa on her belly. The bulge that felt like an eggplant was undeniable. The babies. She could not—would not—risk her children. She had to make sure this person was disarmed.

He groaned, his eyes closed. The gun was inches from his outstretched hand, near the back corner of the sofa, on the hardwood floor. She'd hurt him, but how badly was impossible to tell.

Two more feet and she'd be able to grab his weapon, then have Greta guard him until the EMTs and the RRPD arrived. She timed her movements with his groans, hoping to hide the sound of her crawling. Peering from behind the sofa, she ascertained that he had no other visible weapons. His left shoulder was soaked with blood, where she'd hit him.

Finally, she was only a few inches away, stretched out on her side with her gun ready to fire again. Her fingers stretched for his weapon—and his arm swung to hit hers.

"Greta!" Patience swiped his gun and sent it skittering across the hardwood as Greta bounded from the kitchen area, leaped over Patience and landed on the assailant's chest. The man cried out in pain and surprise. Greta stood her ground as trained, and Patience let out a quick sigh of relief. He wasn't going anywhere as long as Greta was on him.

She moved back to the kitchen and turned on the lights, just as a pair of headlights swept up to the porch. A door slammed and Greta let out her signature bark that was only for Nash. She'd done her job.

Nash's heart had been in his throat the entire time he'd raced up the mountain, fighting to get there before the Larsons' thug hurt Patience, all thoughts of the bears behind him. He'd known fear for his siblings when they'd initially struggled to regroup after their parents had been killed. The occasional case or law enforcement situation shook him up. But nothing came close to the abject terror that had clutched him the moment he'd heard the dispatch call in response to Patience's distress over the radio.

He'd also heard that she'd neutralized the killer, with some help from Greta. Thank God.

As he pulled up in the clearing, his terror returned in an icy wave at the sight of the downed criminal, Greta with two paws on the man's chest.

Nash got out of his Jeep and ran up to the porch.

"Good girl, Greta."

She didn't acknowledge him; she was in work mode and her job was to keep this loser pinned down. Nash recognized the man as a thug paid by the Larsons, but had to know Patience was okay. He searched the immediate vicinity for her and it was a full second before he met her gaze across the room. She stood in the kitchen, her hair in a disheveled ponytail, stomach bulging under her tight white T-shirt. The babies. She and the twins were okay. It was all that mattered.

"You all right?"

Patience nodded, and offered him a shaky smile. "We're good. Just keep him away from me, okay?"

His pleasure.

"What the hell did you think you were doing?"

This particular henchman had done the Larsons' dirty work for a long time. He had a rap sheet a mile long. Problem was he was sneaky and wily, and for years had eluded conviction for the many felonies he was suspected of committing. Not any longer.

"Screw you." Even in his pain and with a pretty nasty gunshot wound, the criminal was still a jerk. A jerk who could have killed Patience and the babies. Pure unadulterated rage hit Nash sideways. It was primal.

"Nash." Patience's voice reached him and he forced the emotions into the compartmentalized box they had to go in, until he could examine them later. Right now he had to focus on getting the intruder the medical care he obviously needed and arresting him.

Sirens pierced the stillness of the mountain forest and an RRPD unit, followed by one of the Red Ridge hospital ambulances, pulled up next to his Jeep.

Juliette Walsh and her K9 partner, Sasha, ran up to the porch and nodded at Nash. "Patience okay?"

"She's fine—see for yourself."

"I'll take your word for it." Juliette took over the scene, directing the EMTs and two other RRPD officers she'd brought with her. Within twenty minutes the thug was on a stretcher and en route to Red Ridge Hospital. Under RRPD escort, of course.

Patience had never seen this side of Nash before. Outwardly, he appeared himself, an even more content version of the Nash who routinely juggled four kids, a law enforcement career and K9 handling protocol. It was the tightness in his throat muscles and the way he kept clenching and unclenching his fists that clued her in.

As soon as all the first responders had left, Patience pulled out duct tape and large plastic leaf bags. "Here, help me patch up the doorway. We're going to have to make do with it tonight. I'll call in a repair on it tomorrow."

"I'll make the repair tomorrow. We don't want any strangers here."

"Larson already found me." She paused and looked at Nash. "And I heard that there have been sightings of the Lake Killer in the eastern part of the state. It doesn't sound like he's looking for me anymore."

"We thought we'd taken care of the Larson twins and the dogs when we sent them running from the clinic. That didn't work out so well." Nash peeled out a length of tape and ripped it with his teeth.

"Here." She handed him a box cutter. "It's easier on your teeth."

He grimaced.

"Wait, Nash—stop." She placed her hand on his arm. "What's going on with you?"

For a moment she thought he was going to just ignore her, keep adding tape to the tarp-like contraption the front door was becoming. Finally, he lowered his arms and looked at her.

"I wasn't here for you. Before you tell me that it's okay, don't. I know it's impossible for me to be everywhere, and you and our children are going to face dangerous situations that neither of us see coming. Not so insane as this—" he waved at the door "—but life isn't safe, not all the time. I'm a cop. I know this."

"If you're not beating yourself up about not getting here before I had to shoot him, what is it, then?"

"It hadn't hit me yet just how much responsibility a family is. That sounds stupid coming from me, right? I worry about my siblings all the time. Are they getting enough affection? Am I listening to them? Do they feel they can come to me about anything from drugs to sex? Have I handled the girls okay? You know, the female necessities—periods, gynecological health, how to handle boys who are rude to them. Will I be able to be enough of a father figure for the boys?" He paused, his hands on his hips, his face down. When he looked up at her again his eyes glittered with angst. "No matter what, I know that whatever I can do for the kids is good—it's better than what they'd have without me. These babies, our children, it's different. It is totally my responsibility how they turn out."

"Hey, come here." She tugged his arm until he shifted, and she led him to the sofa.

"I don't want to sit down, Patience. I need to move."

"You can move all you want in a minute. Let me have my say."

He complied, but his face was screwed up in an expression of pain that told her she had only a few minutes to talk to him.

"First, you don't have to worry about the babies if you don't want to. I've already told you that I don't expect anything from you. Not in a hard or mean way, but in a real, I-can-handle-this-myself way." She ignored the tug at her conscience. Yes, she'd appreciated him being near and protecting her. More than she'd ever imagined. But she didn't need him to keep her safe. Hadn't she just proved that?

"Second, you're doing a great job with your siblings, by all accounts. Word gets around the RRPD and I've never heard anyone say anything other than very complimentary words about how your siblings behave. You're raising fine kids, Nash. Which brings me to three."

He grunted and she couldn't help but laugh.

"You're going to be a wonderful father. I get that you are the forever bachelor, and trust me, I'm not looking for anything permanent with a man." *Liar.* She hadn't been, but being with Nash all these hours and days had added up. Her heart was getting too used to him. "But we've created these babies together, and I think between the two of us we'll work it out. Lots of people co-parent."

"Are you done?"

She let out a sigh. "Yes."

He got on his knees in front of her and cupped her face with his hands. "I never want to feel the terror I did driving up this mountain again. Ever. I thought... I thought I'd lost you, Patience." Nash didn't finesse his move; he crushed his mouth to hers.

Patience kissed him back, hoping her lips conveyed her belief in him.

But it wasn't Nash she was worried about. Tonight's intruder was tame compared to what still lurked out there. The Lake Killer. She knew he'd never give up until she was dead.

# Chapter 17

Nash mentally fought against leaving Patience the next day. His only conciliation was that they'd made love until midnight, after which he'd been able to hold her through the predawn hours.

He leaned back in his desk chair at work and appreciated the creaking that usually annoyed him. It grounded his spirit, reminded him that nothing had hurt Patience or the babies last night.

They'd agreed to table the discussion on what they were going to do about their relationship, at least until the Lake Killer was captured. As single parents, working as a parenting team, or as more. The "more" part had him stymied.

He was afraid to approach Patience with what he wanted, what he thought might be best. She should move in with him and the kids. It made the most sense. His house was equipped for a family, and would easily incorporate the twins.

"Maddox, I need to you go over to Hamlin Harrington's house with Officer Walsh." Chief Finn Colton stood over him. Jeez, he hadn't even heard his boss approach. Nash stood.

"Yes, sir."

"Hamlin says he caught Demi Colton red-handed after she broke into his house. She took off before he could catch her."

"'Catch her'?"

"Yeah, I feel the same as you. It's a good thing that woman can run. If she was indeed the person who was there. He's positive she'll show up on his security camera's footage, so head on out there and find out what you can."

"Sir, I understand that catching the Groom Killer is our top priority, but I'm working the Lake Killer case at the moment." He never questioned an order, but there was no way he'd take his focus off the Lake Killer case unless absolutely necessary. Although he couldn't defend his motives fully, not until Finn knew that Patience carried Nash's kids.

"I know you're providing protection for Patience, and that's a standing requirement of the Lake Killer case. But our good K9 vet is safe at the clinic and I'm shorthanded. I need to you to interview Hamlin, and then corroborate it with a statement from his son, Devlin."

Finn must have seen the stress on his face and interpreted it as friendly concern for Patience. Not too long ago Nash would have had no problem convincing himself the same. But after making love to her with such frequency and need over the past weeks, seeing those two babies on the ultrasound screen, hearing their heartbeats, Nash knew he couldn't dismiss his bond with Patience as merely friendly.

But what was it?

"Devlin's easy enough to pin down," Nash said. Harrington's billionaire status meant all of Red Ridge knew his family, too. His son, Devlin, ran his portion of the business in town. "I can catch up with him in his office."

"I knew I could count on you, Nash. If you need to break away to help Patience or the other case, do so."

"I'm on it, Chief."

"You and Juliette be careful out there, Nash. There's no telling what that man is thinking half the time. And we need to find out what Demi's looking for. Why would she risk her life to break into Harrington's mansion? It's practically a fortress." The chief shook his head. "He's convinced she was trying to kill him."

Nash knew this couldn't be easy on the chief; Demi was his cousin. But Finn Colton was always professional.

"Hamlin Harrington's always been a little off-kilter." He didn't want to come right out and say he thought the dude lived in a bubble that a lot of money bought.

"That's not our job, Nash." The chief didn't argue with his assessment of the senior Harrington, though. The RRPD received its share of house calls out to his home. Harrington seemed haunted by the possibility of being kidnapped or killed for his fortune.

"Got it, Chief." When his boss left, Nash signaled to Greta. She stood up from her resting spot and came to his side.

"You're ready to work again, aren't you, partner?"

Her large Newfie tail thumped in agreement.

Patience pulled into the K9 clinic parking lot and saw no handlers or dogs in the training center's large fenced area. There hadn't been more training scheduled for her since Saturday, a good thing, meaning all injured K9s were back on duty.

She grabbed the caramel decaf latte she'd bought for herself and the dozen doughnuts for the training center and clinic staff. After the shock of the attempted break-in, plus absorbing the fact she was having not one but two babies, she'd needed something fun to distract herself. Treating the employees to a sweet seemed to be the perfect choice.

Balancing her bag, coffee and doughnuts, she closed the car door with her hip.

"Patience."

The female voice came out of nowhere and startled her. She turned on her heel to face a woman dressed entirely in black, with a hooded jacket. Only after she pushed back her hood did Patience identify her.

"Demi!" Her cousin, wanted for questioning in relation to the murders of several would-have-been grooms in the Red Ridge area, stood in front of her.

Demi didn't look like a killer. Her pallor and shadowed

eyes reflected the burden of accusation without evidence, the constant stress of life on the run.

"Patience. I'm sorry, I didn't mean to frighten you. It seems I have this effect on people lately."

Patience put the box, purse and coffee on the hood of her car. "I'm not afraid of you, Demi. I know you better than most, and I've never thought of you as anything but a sweet person." They hadn't grown up together, since they came from opposite ends of town and the Colton family tree. But she would never forget how Demi had brought in that injured stray dog right before she'd fled. In Patience's mind, a woman capable of cold-blooded murder wouldn't be so concerned about a poor animal.

A ghost of a smile crossed Demi's pretty features. "The rest of Red Ridge doesn't agree with you."

"Who cares?" As Patience spoke, her gaze caught on Demi's black sweatshirt. A bounty hunter, Demi never appeared anything less than fully capable of the athletic feats her work often required of her. Fugitives weren't always the acquiescent type. Demi's stomach protruded under her zippered hoodie as if she'd been indulging in the doughnuts on the car hood. But her bump moved.

"Before you ask, yes, this is my baby." Demi hadn't missed Patience's observation. She turned and unzipped her jacket far enough that Patience could see the tiny face. The baby was cocooned in a sling up against her mom, covered by the jacket.

"How old?"

Demi stood up straight. "Four months. Don't ask me more—I'm not going to tell you."

Patience studied the baby. Demi had been jilted by

Bo Gage right after they'd gotten engaged. He'd dumped her for Hayley Patton, a not-so-nice local girl. It must have been humiliating for Demi. But no way had she killed Bo or the other victims, as many accused her of doing. "You know I don't think you're the Groom Killer, Demi."

"Yet you don't know, do you? I certainly have motive. First, I'm left practically at the altar, then my ex-fiancé shows up dead. What I want to know is why no one's looking at other potential suspects."

"I'm sure the RRPD is looking at a lot of people. But it's not that simple. You've heard about the murder here—" she motioned toward the lake "—about a month ago?"

Demi nodded. "Yes. I heard that you're the only witness."

"Word sure gets around in Red Ridge." She didn't confirm or deny Demi's comment. "You know you're wanted for questioning, right?" Patience didn't have authority to arrest or even compel Demi to report to the police. But she hated seeing her cousin, a new mother, so torn up, obviously being accused of something she hadn't done.

Demi nodded. "I know. If you need to call the police on me, go ahead. To be honest, the running gets old. But I have to gather information no one else is willing to."

"What do you mean?"

She held up her hand. "Sorry. I'm thinking out loud. I came by for two reasons. First, to see how the dog that I brought by is."

"He's fine. He made it and was placed with a family

soon after you dropped him off. That was a kind thing you did, Demi."

"My other motive for seeking you out is that I need you to tell your father to back off. I'm not the Groom Killer, and by funneling everyone's attention on me he's keeping us all from finding the real murderer. That's why I'm so reluctant to walk into the RRPD on my own. Chances of me being held are high, with the town gossip stirred up and your father's pull. I don't want to be apart from my baby."

Patience couldn't argue with her, on any of it. Fenwick used his weight as mayor to influence everything from the usual local politics to business deals. He saw no shame in playing judge and jury when the town was in such an uproar. There'd been no official weddings in Red Ridge since the Groom Killer struck. It was bad for local business, especially the bakery, florists and dress designers. But more, it damaged morale. Fenwick Colton counted on a happy town to be reelected.

"My daddy might only have his mayor position when it all is said and done. His energy business is floundering."

"Yeah, that's been going on for a good while now. Hamlin Harrington hasn't helped—he's done everything to undermine your father's corporation."

"Why do you say that?"

"Doesn't Layla fill you in? Colton Energy has been bleeding funds for over two years. Harrington was helping that, in the hopes he'd be able to buy the entire company out. Looks like it's going to happen, from what I read on the stock pages. My research into trying to clear my name has brought me down some interesting roads."

An icy chill ran across Patience's skin. She'd been overwhelmed by her own pregnancy and so busy since the Lake Killer that she'd not seen the writing on the ledger books. Her sister was planning to marry a very bad man.

"Thanks for sharing that with me, Demi. I don't suppose you want to come inside, get warm, have a cup of coffee?"

Demi shook her head decisively. "No, not possible, I'm afraid. I'll take a rain check, though. For sooner than later, if the RRPD figures out who the real killer is."

"I have faith that they will."

"I hope you're right." She turned to leave, then paused. "I'm okay, Patience. I have a solid place to live, and I'm keeping myself and my baby safe. It's what matters right now. Being a mother has taught me to value the most basic necessities."

"I understand." And she did, much more than Demi realized.

Her cousin's assessment of her form was quick, exacting. "I see that you do. How far along are you?"

Her hand instinctively went to her midsection. "Four months."

"You're slimmer than me, usually. Are you sure you're only four months along?"

Patience nodded. She didn't want to tell Demi it was twins.

"Well, congrats to you, too."

"If you need anything, Demi—"

"I know I can contact you, thanks. That's what I'm doing now. Please talk to your father for me. The resolution of the Groom Killer case depends upon it."

"I will."

Demi put her hood back on, ducked her head and hurried to a nondescript dark, beat-up truck. Patience was torn—she worked for the county and her clinic served the RRPD. No doubt many would say she should immediately call in Demi's location. But she trusted her gut, which told her her cousin wasn't the Groom Killer. But with all the evidence pointing that way, if Demi was innocent, then who was the Groom Killer?

Just as she'd witnessed the Lake Killer dumping a body, certainly someone in all of Red Ridge must have witnessed the Groom Killer in one capacity or another. The murders hadn't happened in a vacuum.

She looked at her latte, now cold, and the box of doughnuts on the hood of her car. It wouldn't make a difference if she delayed going into the clinic long enough to make a phone call. She pulled out her cell and hit the speed dial for Nash. He'd know what to do.

And she trusted him implicitly.

# *Chapter 18*

"**I**'m telling you both, Demi Colton stood right where you two are with a gun in her hand, ready to kill me." Hamlin Harrington spoke to Nash and Juliette, the massive river-stone fireplace in his great room a backdrop to his dramatic retelling of Demi's break-in.

"We aren't doubting how you felt, Mr. Harrington." Juliette spoke up as Nash took Greta around the room, sniffing for anything unusual. The security camera revealed that Demi had indeed entered the mansion via a back sliding door. But unlike how Harrington described it, she hadn't broken any glass or picked a lock—she'd opened an unlocked door.

"Then why do I get the impression that none of you at the Red Ridge Police Department are taking me seriously?" Harrington's face reddened, which Nash would have thought impossible on his perpetually ruddy skin.

"Of course, we're taking you seriously, Mr. Harrington. It's why Officer Walsh and I came out as soon as we could, and why Sasha and Greta are with us. We aren't going to miss a thing with their noses, trust me."

"What is she sniffing for, exactly?" Harrington wanted to channel his anger onto someone, and his annoyed expression focused on Greta.

Nash fought back a sarcastic response. Hamlin Harrington was a man of means who didn't take "no" for an answer, but Nash would be damned if he'd let the man take aim at his K9. At the end of the day, Harrington was a civilian and had no jurisdiction over the RRPD or its K9 officers.

"Come, Greta."

The dog trotted to his side and sat.

"Greta's been looking for any signs of drugs or other illegal substances that the intruder may have left behind."

"You mean like explosives?"

"Among many other things."

"It wouldn't surprise me that a woman like that brought in a lot of illegal substances with her."

"Well, our K9 doesn't agree with you. There's no sign of anything other than what you've shared and what your security footage reveals. Demi Colton was here, but she left without harming you or apparently taking anything. You're certain nothing is missing?"

"No, I'm not certain. Have a look at this place, will you? It'll take me a few days to figure out what she took." Harrington waved his arms at the heavily dec-orated interior, chock-full of what were probably ex-pensive paintings and sculptures. Nash wasn't into art, and had no idea what the various pieces were worth. He looked at Juliette, in an easy stance by Harrington's massive carved desk. The piece of furniture clearly came from another century, but the state-of-the-art computer and monitor atop it showed it had plenty of twenty-first-century use. Whatever Demi had come in here for, she'd either gotten it before Harrington inter-cepted her or she'd given up before she bolted. Nash doubted she had tried to harm Harrington. So far, every time the woman showed up anywhere she hadn't hurt anyone. The town chatter pointed toward her as the Groom Killer, but absolutely no evidence did.

And there was Patience's opinion to consider. Demi was her cousin, and while the two weren't close, it was clear that Patience trusted her. Patience made it clear that she thought Demi an innocent victim of town gos-sip.

"We'll take a few last photographs before we leave, if that's okay with you, sir." Juliette played the good cop very well, and Nash swallowed a snicker. He and Ju-liette had plenty to discuss on the ride back into town.

"You don't think Demi's guilty, do you?" Juliette spoke from the passenger seat as Nash drove them back to the station. She had another case to work and Nash could handle Devlin Harrington on his own. Nash hated that he wasn't the one splitting off and heading to the K9 clinic. To Patience.

"Honestly, no, I don't. But I'm not a detective and we don't have all the facts yet. It would make things a lot less complicated if we were able to question her."

"We have to find her first."

Nash let out a long sigh. "Yeah, I know. And we will. She's right here in town." He frowned. "What's with Red Ridge lately? Everything is being turned upside down. Our quiet part of paradise is definitely on troubled waters."

"We've got two killers on the loose, maybe more if one or both of them are part of a larger crime ring. It's daunting." Juliette stared out the windshield and Nash thought she looked as frustrated as he felt.

"But not impossible to solve." Nash valued looking at the big picture, then narrowing down to specifics. "Let's pull ourselves up to an eagle-eye view. Hamlin Harrington is involved in what local business at the moment?"

"He wants to bail out Fenwick Colton. Harrington's a corporate shark. He smells the blood of failing industry, and to him, it's opportunity."

"Right. But why? What's in it for him?"

"Interest back on the money he lent."

"What else?" Nash knew there had to be more.

"Power, I'd imagine. Men like Harrington love holding the keys to the kingdom, so to speak. Nowadays, if you're in control of a population's energy source, that's the epitome of power, don't you think?"

"I suppose." Nash pulled into the RRPD's lot. "Here you go. Nice work this morning."

"We all work well together, that's certain." Juliette got out of the car and let her K9 out of the back.

As he watched the two of them walk into the station, Nash's phone rang. Patience. If he were a sentimental man he'd swear little cartoon hearts like the ones in the quirky cartoons the boys watched burst from the phone.

"Hey, babe."

"Nash, this isn't a personal call. I just spoke to Demi Colton."

Nash's stomach twisted, no matter his thoughts on Demi's innocence. The safety of Patience and the babies was everything to him. "Where? Are you okay?"

"Of course I'm fine. I had just pulled into the clinic and she walked up to my car. You know I trust her. She's my cousin, and besides, she's not the Groom Killer, Nash. No way do I believe it. No matter what my father and the rest of Red Ridge think."

"What did she want?"

"She wants me to tell my father to back off, for one."

"That's fair, if she isn't guilty."

"Then why do you sound so disappointed?" Patience knew him better than he knew himself. It should frighten him, the way their bond exponentially grew, but instead he liked the warmth it shot through his chest.

"Because she needs to come in for questioning. It'd be best if I could get a statement from her, once and for all. Is she still there? On clinic property?"

"No, she left after only a few minutes. To be honest, Nash, if I were her I'm not certain I'd trust the RRPD right now."

"Excuse me? You're as much a part of the police force as I am, Patience."

"Sure, but you're not understanding what I'm saying. If I were Demi and the entire town was convinced I'd killed someone, even though I'm innocent, I wouldn't risk being taken into custody. Especially because…"

"Because?"

"She had a baby with her, Nash."

He immediately recalled the security footage from Harrington's house. "Then why would she risk going to Harrington's?" It didn't make sense to him.

"She's trying to figure out who the Groom Killer is, too, Nash. Because it's not her."

"I want to agree with you, Patience, but I have to follow this through to the end. We need all the facts." He told her what he'd been assigned to do. "I'm on my way to interview Devlin Harrington now. Don't worry, I'll be back at the cabin with you tonight."

She laughed. "That's the least of my worries. I can't stay up all night like we've been doing—I'm useless at work this tired."

"There's a big difference between 'tired' and 're-laxed.'" His teasing drew another laugh from her and he enjoyed the ring of her giggles over the connection. A small moment in the midst of a large, grim case, but it made him smile, too. With a jolt he saw that this bond with Patience wasn't just about the huge aspect of becoming parents together, or the danger of facing the Lake Killer, but more. As in he'd never felt like this about another woman.

"Yes, well, you've got me feeling both today, Nash."

"I'll see you later, babe." He disconnected and allowed himself to daydream about Patience's eyes as he drove downtown.

"Be a good dog, Greta, and have a nap."

Harrington, Inc. occupied an old bank building on Main Street that had been refurbished into office spaces. Nash decided to leave Greta in the back of the SUV, not wanting to be turned away by anyone at the swanky business.

Devlin ran the IT branch of the company for his father, but from what Nash knew, the oily son of a billionaire pretty much did whatever the heck he wanted. Devlin had a reputation in town as too slick for his abilities, and Nash had come face-to-face with Devlin's smarmy side personally when they'd played in a town softball tournament to raise funds for the K9 clinic. Devlin didn't know a softball mitt from a gardener's glove, yet he'd paraded all over the diamond as if he played in the major leagues. Nash wasn't in the mood for more of the same this afternoon. Not with two killers loose in Red Ridge, one directly targeting the woman he—

No, he wasn't going there. The mother of his unborn children was at risk, and the Lake Killer case needed closure. This sidetrack to cover some of the investigative work for the Groom Killer case had to be done, and Nash had no problem doing it. As long as he held Patience in his arms tonight.

"Good afternoon, Patti." He flashed a wide smiled

at the receptionist, a high school classmate he'd run alongside on the cross-country team.

"Nash Maddox! I haven't seen you in a while. I'll bet you're busy with the Groom Killer case, aren't you?"

"We all are. How's your family?" He wasn't afraid to use their personal connection and some good old-fashioned manners to get what he wanted.

After they caught one another up on their lives, he leaned in for the kill. "I'm here to talk to Devlin. Is he in?"

"He sure is." Patti didn't pretend her boss wasn't available, to his relief. "Four doors down the hallway, on the right."

"Thanks a lot, Patti."

"Anytime."

Nash walked along the corridor and took in the cushy surroundings, the open office doors, their occupants appearing hard at work as they sat or stood at computer desks. It was eerily quiet with no piped-in music since the workers he saw wore earbuds or headphones. He supposed it made sense. Still, it was damned creepy to have so many people working in a set space with little or no ambient noise. *Snap out of it.*

No matter how much he clung to police procedure, though, nothing could shake the sense of urgency he had to get to the bottom of both the Groom and Lake murders. Since the Lake Killer case came home to roost in his personal world, he'd been unable to shake a sense of foreboding.

Devlin's nameplate was on the wall next to his open door, and he stood with his back to the entrance. Nash took advantage of the opportunity to observe. Devlin looked at one of several computer monitors on his L-shaped desk. An open laptop displayed a familiar face that took Nash a mere heartbeat to recognize. Hayley Patton—the woman the first victim of the Groom Killer, Bo Gage, had been engaged to after Bo had dumped Demi Colton. Even if he didn't know Hayley from her connection to the murder victim, Nash knew her well because she was an excellent K9 trainer and he frequently worked with her at the center. Why would Devlin have Hayley Patton's picture on his laptop? Was it his screen saver? And again, why?

Nash rapped his knuckles on the doorjamb. Devlin turned on a dime and visibly blanched when he recognized him.

"Nash. What brings you into Harrington, Inc.?" Typical Devlin, invoking his billionaire family name by way of introduction. Very unlike Devlin, however, was how he jerkily slapped his laptop shut, making Hayley Patton's face disappear.

"I have some questions I need to ask you." He stepped into the office and watched as Devlin smoothed his hand over his shaved head with shaking hands. Odd. Devlin usually was the epitome of polished, to the point of creepy and oily.

"Have a seat." Devlin sank into his chair before Nash sat down. He'd definitely spooked the man and it had something to do with Hayley Patton. He made a mental note to see if there was a connection between Devlin and Hayley in Bo Gage's murder file.

"Thanks. I won't take too much of your time, but as you probably know, your father had a break-in at his home. According to him, Demi Colton broke into the house and threatened to kill him." He deliberately left out the part about Demi sliding open an unlocked door.

"Yes, my father told me. Have you or any of your colleagues apprehended her yet?" Accusation blazed in Devlin's beady eyes. The man's recovery from being caught with the image of a murder victim's fiancée on his laptop stunned even Nash. He'd witnessed plenty of human behavior over the years. Just because Devlin annoyed the heck out of him and most of Red Ridge, it didn't mean the man was a criminal.

It didn't mean he wasn't, either.

"We're exploring every aspect of the case at hand. To the best of your knowledge, does your dad have anything of interest to Demi Colton?"

Devlin smirked with his signature lip curl. "What doesn't he have is more like it. That b—woman's from the other side of town. I don't have to tell you that. And the entire Colton family seems to be after my father to bail them out. Some do legally, like Fenwick Colton. Others, not so much. Demi wanted drug money, I'd guess. When she didn't find loose cash, she was going to steal a painting. My father has a lot of valuable artwork."

Nash stared at Devlin, hard. "What makes you think she was attempting to steal any of your father's art?" Hamlin had said nothing marginally close to this, and the security footage only showed Demi rifling through Hamlin's desk, his home office, attempting to get into his computer. She'd been looking for something, all right, but Nash's law enforcement instinct told him it was in-

formation. Not cash or artwork. Red Ridge was a large
enough town at thirty-five thousand, but not big enough
for a drug addict to hope to turn around a valuable for
cash quick enough to get a fix.

Besides, Demi Colton had no record or history of
drug use. And she had a baby to worry about. That
could be enough motive for the money part, to feed her
child. But why risk going to Harrington's?

"Please, Nash, spare me the interrogation technique. Demi Colton is at the very least a burglar, and
at most…" He theatrically trailed off and Nash bit back
his own snarl.

"At most?"

"Come on, Nash. I'm in IT and even I can see the
trail. All you have to do is read the *Red Ridge Reporter*
twice a week. Demi Colton is the one consistent thing,
the common denominator, in all the Groom Killer murders. And she was dumped by Bo Gage—isn't that motive enough?"

"How do you know Hayley Patton, Devlin?"

Devlin's eyes narrowed, a remarkable feat considering how beady they were. "The detective sees a photo
and thinks he's onto something."

"I'm not a detective, Devlin. Just a cop closing the
loop on an intruder report. Answer my question."

"Hayley and I went to school together. We were
classmates, I'm sure you know. Two classes behind
you. She sent me her photo to airbrush—she wanted
her professional head shot freshened up. She said she
was applying for a new job. We have a couple of experts in digital imaging and I'm going to have one of

them do it. I just haven't gotten around to it yet, which is why I have her photo downloaded on my laptop, as a constant reminder. I tend to get distracted with running our IT department."

*Nice catch, liar.* Devlin's statement needed to be corroborated with Hayley, and Nash hoped it was another officer who'd have the honor. He wanted to get back to Patience, ASAP.

Nash nodded. "Any other reason you can think of why Demi would break into your father's home?"

Devlin's chest flattened. He'd obviously expected Nash to continue on the Hayley questioning. Nash wondered if Finn had anyone keeping tabs on Devlin. He would after Nash told him what he'd witnessed.

"I told you what I think. She's a druggie looking for a fix. If my father hadn't caught her red-handed, she'd have searched the medicine cabinet for painkillers."

"You mean opioids?"

"Yes, whatever. Does it matter? You know something, Nash? I resent that my father is the victim of what could have escalated to a heinous crime, and yet you're sitting here all smug and official, giving *me* the third degree."

"I'm so sorry you feel like that, Devlin. This is a standard line of questioning used for similar situations. We're trying to figure out why Demi Colton broke into your father's home, as you said."

"'As I said'? She broke in—it's on the video!" Devlin's tanning-salon skin color took on a ruddy hue.

Nash stood. "Thanks for your time, Devlin. If you

think of anything else, give me a call." He placed his business card on the glass-topped desk.

Devlin remained in his seat. "What I need, what Red Ridge needs, is for the police to get to the bottom of all of this and put it to rest. The sooner Demi Colton's in custody, the sooner I know I'll sleep better."

Nash mentally counted to five; Devlin wasn't worth ten. He leaned over the desk, just far enough to make Devlin tip back in his chair.

"It seems to me that your specialty is being your daddy's lackey, and what did you say you do? IT. It's wise to not accuse anyone unless you have the full facts of the case to back up your claims. In fact, it's defamation of character."

Devlin snarled. "A loser like Demi Colton wouldn't know what that means, much less would she ever come after me or anyone else in town for it. But okay, I get it. You want to do your job, show that our tax dollars are being put to work, go ahead."

Nash straightened, never breaking eye contact. Devlin's gaze slid away, his faux in-control corporate mask back in place. But not before Nash saw the flash of naked terror in the man's eyes. Devlin Harrington hid something behind his snarky exterior, and Nash couldn't wait for the RRPD to figure out what it was.

"Thanks for your time." He left, feeling Devlin's eyes drilling into the back of his skull. As if he hated him.

Not something Nash would expect from just a slimy businessman.

# Chapter 19

Later that day, Patience had finished with her routine vet checks. All the patients were doing well. A text from Nash indicated he wouldn't be able to break away from the casework Finn had assigned him until well after dinner. He didn't want her driving back to the cabin alone and she didn't argue. They'd drive together when he got off work, and she'd stay at the clinic under extra security until then. Except she wanted to go out for dinner.

Her stomach grumbled at the same time she felt a definite flutter in her belly. Patience laughed, unable to keep the joy from infusing her entire being. She called Layla from her office and was relieved to hear she could meet her for dinner at their favorite restaurant downtown. A couple hours with her sister would cure what ailed her—mental exhaustion from the case.

"Downtown" for Red Ridge meant Main Street, where several eating establishments were clustered. She and Layla met at the Rodeo Table, where Tex-Mex and Southwestern cuisine dominated the menu.

They each ordered fajitas—Patience, shrimp, and Layla, chicken—along with a side of guacamole to share.

Once they had the restaurant's signature *pico de gallo* salsa in front of them, Patience's news burst out of her mouth.

"I'm having twins." She watched Layla's face as she broke the news, and to her delight, sheer joy sparkled in her sister's smile.

"Patience, I'm so happy for you!" Layla leaned over the table and hugged her tightly, her sincerity evident.

"Thanks."

"I'm so excited. Twins!" Layla sat back down in the booth. "Have you told Daddy yet?"

"He knows I'm pregnant—he saw the pile of baby stuff Nash brought to the cabin. He wasn't so thrilled, to be honest."

"Daddy's a man who only has so much to give. And he's got a lot on his mind lately."

"The business still in free fall?"

Layla nodded. "Yes. But it's okay." She squared her shoulders. "Hamlin's going to bail us out." She didn't seem as confident about her fiancé as she had weeks ago. Or when she and Patience had exchanged ugly words about her engagement. The day before the night Patience lost herself in Nash's arms for the first time. When the twins were conceived.

"Layla, I haven't brought it up again because we got so mad at one another the last time we talked about your engagement. But really, honey, Hamlin Harrington? You're young, beautiful and kind. He's none of the above."

"But he has the means to save Colton Energy, which means your K9 clinic and training center will keep operating."

"You don't have to remind me of that."

"You know there are plenty of other ways we can keep the center up and running. The RRPD already has three grants they've applied for, and a couple of other private donors."

"That defeats the original pledge Daddy made to the center, for your mother." Layla spoke with a shadow of her usual feisty spirit. Maybe she'd finally begun to see the light, and it wasn't Hamlin Harrington.

"The center is dedicated to my mother. That will never change." And if her mom was still alive and able to see how Fenwick operated these days, all about his business, to the exclusion of his family, Patience knew she'd not give a fig where the money came from, as long as the donor was legit.

Unlike Hamlin, who had his fingers in so many pots it was impossible to tell which of his business dealings were legit or not.

"Daddy wants to be the one to always fund the K9 center."

"That's a noble thought, but if the money's from Hamlin, it's not Daddy's, is it?"

Layla frowned. The expression crumpled her pretty

face and for the first time Patience noticed tiny lines on her sister's skin.

"You okay, Layla? All of the financial stress has to be getting to you."

She rubbed her temples, eyes closed. "I'm fine. And I'm not about to admit to you that marrying Hamlin wasn't my idea at all. I mean, in the long run, Daddy is looking out for all of us, right? And plenty of people get married for sheer convenience."

"Give me a break, Layla. Listen to yourself. You're selling yourself out, like a slave or a prostitute. Unless... did Hamlin agree to a platonic marriage?"

She shook her head. "No, he hasn't. We haven't... you know, done much, and I don't think there'd be a lot in that department after we're married. He's in his midseventies."

"Do I have to remind you of basic biology, dear sister? Or tell you about Viagra? If you don't want to have sex with Hamlin now, nothing will change after the vows. Stop letting Daddy use you like this!"

Layla's eyes filled with tears, but while Patience ached for her sister's struggle, she wasn't backing down.

"See this?" She grabbed a white napkin from the table and waved it like a banner. "It's my BS flag and I'm throwing it on your belief. Daddy isn't going to accept you or outwardly love you any more or less because you go along with one of his dirty financial schemes. He doesn't have it to give, Layla. You could sell your firstborn to appease him and he'd still be Daddy."

Layla sniffed, took a sip of her iced tea. "You're right. Of course. It's just that..."

"What is it, Layla? Underneath your need for Daddy's approval?"

Layla looked at her with huge eyes and Patience picked up on her half sister's sorrow. "What will happen to me if Daddy's business goes belly-up? I'm not like you, with a skill I can take anywhere. All I know how to do is follow Daddy around and clean up his financial messes."

"Are you kidding me? That's a huge gift. Not everyone can take the tangle he makes of things and unknot it, transforming it into something useful. You've single-handedly turned around dozens of his damaging business deals, and kept the loan sharks from eating away at his earnings."

"I haven't done a good enough job or Hamlin wouldn't be my future husband."

Finally, Layla admitted her motive for marrying Harrington: she blamed herself for the problems at Colton Energy. Patience had felt that, but for Layla to voice it was huge.

She reached across the table and grasped Layla's hand. "Honey, you're doing a wonderful job for Daddy. But you have to do it for yourself first. Trust me, I learned that the hard way when I went off to college."

"And vet school." Layla wiped her eyes and managed a laugh. "I thought Daddy's head was going to explode when you refused all that money he offered you, wanting you to stay in Red Ridge and work for him."

Patience smiled at the memory. "He's never understood me, has he? All I've ever wanted to do, I'm doing. Work with animals and serve the community. Win-win."

"Daddy's all about the power. Yet underneath it, I have to believe he has a heart or else he wouldn't have endowed the clinic in your mama's name."

"No, he wouldn't have. But he's run out of funds, from all accounts. Care to comment?" Patience didn't expect Layla to divulge corporate secrets, but Fenwick had named all his children as heirs to his fortune. Which at the moment was at risk.

"If you're asking about your inheritance, don't worry. He put a good chunk of his wealth away for safekeeping. As for Colton Energy, yeah, he's in a boatload of trouble. Hamlin's not his only lifeline, you know. He's calling in favors and IOUs left and right."

"But it's not enough?"

Layla took a bite of fajita and chewed, obviously stalling. "We'll see." She poked at her food with her fork. "What about you, Patience? I know you're happy about the babies, but something's bugging you."

"Since witnessing the murder at the lake, I've been jumpy. That's all."

"And they still haven't caught the creep?"

"No." She didn't want to tell Layla how much the Lake Killer had affected her. No need to burden her sister with her concerns.

"I worry about you. I'm glad Nash is taking care of you. I have to admit I was afraid you'd let your independent streak keep you from agreeing to police protection. Even though you're obviously involved with Nash, it's a good sign that you accepted his professional help."

"What do you mean, good sign?"

"Maybe you'll break down and let him be the father and partner he wants to be."

Patience stared at her sister. Not from annoyance or humor, but flat-out shock.

Because she didn't know for sure what Nash wanted, but hearing the words *father* and *partner* fall out of Layla's mouth made her see the truth.

She wanted all of Nash. Friend, lover, father to her twins. Their twins. And she wanted it to be a permanent arrangement.

Had she waited too long to realize it?

The sun began to set after she arrived back at the clinic, washing the sky a pale peach and rose.

"Come on, Ruby." Patience led the stunning Irish setter, who'd had dental work done earlier, to the fenced-in area outside the clinic. She'd finally gathered the courage to walk out here on her own, the first time by herself since she'd witnessed the Lake Killer. In spite of her feelings of being watched, she felt safe at the clinic. And it wasn't night yet, so that helped.

Ruby walked carefully around the grounds, but got down to business in short order. Patience stood near her, looking out at the mountains beyond the lake. The water was as still as a mirror, reflecting the sky and stratus clouds.

A movement at the corner of her vision caught her attention and she instinctively tensed. And then laughed when she saw a herd of eight deer. They leaped over the fields just outside the woods that bordered the far left side of the clinic property. Something had spooked them. Probably a fox or coyote.

She eyed the fence that surrounded her and Ruby. Its purpose wasn't just to allow the recuperating dogs, when not on leash, to roam about without wandering off, but to keep predators out.

The deer darted back into the forest and she marveled at their speed and agility. Then froze. A tall man stood at the far edge of the woods. A man with silver hair stared at her. Even without binoculars, she had no doubt who he was.

"Ruby, come here." She tugged on the leash and got herself and the dog back into the clinic, locking the door behind her. One of the night-duty vet techs was down the corridor and she shouted for him to call 9-1-1, then get out of there. The Lake Killer didn't want anyone but her.

Patience hit the emergency siren button, located in the hall outside the kennels, and issued the command to hide in place and take cover. Then she handed Ruby over to another vet tech, instructing her to run, too.

Finally, Patience ran back to her office and got her weapon out of the safe. No way was the Lake Killer hurting her or her babies.

Nash strode through the K9 clinic, Greta at his heels. He'd made it there in record time after the emergency call came in. After checking in with the officers on scene, he'd convinced Finn that he and Greta were the ones to bring Patience out of the clinic. All the other K9 training center staffers were accounted for. As the evacuated team looked on, he'd donned body armor and suited up Greta, too. He was armed to the hilt. Nash's place was next to Patience, protecting her.

As was Greta's. The dog's gait resembled an eager trot as they approached Patience's office. Nash shoved aside the myriad emotions battling for position in his heart. Saving Patience required nothing less.

He knocked on her locked door. "Patience, it's Nash." He counted to two, prepared to break the door down. But she opened it first, and her face broke into a warm smile, just for him. Heat unfurled at the center of his rib cage and lit up his entire body.

Patience was a part of him. And she was alive.

"Hey yourself." Pulling her into his arms was as natural as breathing.

They embraced briefly, then he let Greta get some Patience love. She held the huge black, furred head in her hands and spoke sweet words to the canine. Her fingers gently explored where the cut had healed in record time.

"I hate that you saw that bastard again and I wasn't here." Nash's heart thumped in heavy agreement. He knew that Patience could take very good care of herself, no question. And she'd done the right thing, calling the RRPD.

"You're the reason I kept my cool enough to call it in and immediately come and get my weapon. It sounds like he's either been scared off or is waiting to break back in."

"We're not hanging around to find out. Let's get you out of here." Nash tapped his comms unit and spoke to

Juliette, who waited outside the clinic with the other officers. "I have Dr. Colton with me. Leaving now."

"Not so fast, Nash. Sit tight. Give us another minute."

Frustration pierced Nash. He knew he had to trust Juliette, for Patience's safety.

"Looks like we're holding in place."

"They've got it, Nash." She leaned against him. "How did your time with the Harringtons go? Let me guess—Hamlin's an arrogant ass and Devlin acted like he knows it all?" She was so good at distracting him, calming him down.

He laughed. "Pretty much, yes." He caressed her cheek with his thumb. "You know that Demi was really there, on his property. Technically, she broke into his house."

"If she did, it was for good reason. Trust me, now that I'm this far along with the twins, I understand what she's feeling, at least as far as being pregnant goes. No way would she risk her life or her baby's unless compelled to do so."

"I'm not arguing with you. Just saying that we need her statement at the RRPD."

"She doesn't trust anyone right now, Nash. I get that. To be honest, besides my sister, you're the only one I can fully trust. It's a tough place to be."

"You trust me?" He tried to go along with her attempt at conversation, but the whole time his mind was waiting for the signal to get her out of here.

"Of course I do. What I don't trust, who I don't trust, is the man I saw dumping that poor woman in the lake. Who I feel the RRPD may be apprehending as we speak. And I don't trust Hamlin Harrington marrying my sister. What kind of a man allows a woman to be bartered for his financial support to her father? A dowry is an archaic concept."

"It may be, but your sister is a grown woman. She has her choices to make, too."

"That's just it—she won't do anything to hurt Daddy." Patience sighed. "My sister and I are products of an absentee father. He was often physically there, for meals and such, but emotionally, mentally? All Fenwick Colton thinks about is how to keep himself at the top of the heap. Financial, political, community-wise, whatever. He may have been a kinder person when he was younger, when my mother was still alive. Who knows?"

"You think he married women so that they'd have a baby for him?" He saw that their dialogue relaxed her, so he continued to go along with it. What the hell was the rest of the RRPD doing? Where was the signal from Juliette?

"No. I think they figured out he wasn't all he'd sold himself to be. When they realized they couldn't fix him, they left."

"Yet you're in touch with your half siblings." The Coltons had a reputation as a tight-knit family. He'd never known the drama behind the billionaire clan.

"Yes, we all share a common bond, in that we survived having Fenwick Colton as a father. You saw him at the cabin, Nash. He's so self-centered."

"He might change when he meets his grandkids." Nash nodded at her belly. "How are you doing today?"

A smile wider than the lake spread across her face. "Wonderful. I felt them kick earlier. Lots of little flutters. At first I thought it was from drinking ginger ale—you know, the bubbles. But it was more definite. As soon as it happens again and you're with me, you'll have to feel for yourself."

His hands tightened into hard balls. The thought of feeling his children in her tight belly filled him with a sense of completeness he'd never known.

An explosion pierced the stillness and they both jumped. Patience screamed, "Nash!"

"Get down!" He watched as she grabbed her weapon and got under her desk. Hated that she'd already been through this, and had to again.

"Nash, we need you and Greta to clear the back hallway." Chief Colton's command boomed over the audio system. "Leave Patience in her office."

Nash leaned across Greta and grasped Patience's face. He kissed her firmly, conveying his total confidence in her. "I won't be gone long—I won't even leave the clinic building. But I have to make sure no one out there needs help. I'll be on the line with dispatch."

"Okay." Their gazes held and the words that matched the emotions he'd been afraid to name were on the tip of his tongue. But not here, not in the midst of this kind of danger. He'd tell her he loved her on his terms, not some criminal's.

"Sit tight. I've got to take Greta, but we'll be right back."

"I know you will. And, Nash?"

"Yeah?"

"I—"

"Don't say it, Patience. Not yet." He stood up and left, before he couldn't.

"I'm approaching the back entrance." Nash spoke into his mic as he cleared the corridor, as ordered by the chief.

"Be careful, Nash. We still don't have him." Finn's voice sent fear rocketing through his system, but he relied on his training and years of experience to ignore it. Patience's and the babies' lives depended upon him.

"Copy." Greta stayed at his side, ready to attack as she kept stride with him.

They came up to the kennels.

"Clearing the kennels." He opened the door and motioned for Greta to go ahead of him, to use her nose to find any sign of the Lake Killer.

"Copy." Juliette's tense voice let Nash know they were still looking for the killer. They all were.

He moved to follow Greta into the kennel, but a blinding strike to his skull sent a shaft of pain through his body, just as he was pulled backward, the kennel door slamming shut with Greta inside.

*Patience!*

Before he had a chance to resist, darkness captured him.

Patience sat under the desk for what seemed like hours, but according to her watch was only eight minutes. She regretted not using the restroom before Nash left. The babies were continually pressing against her bladder and it'd been foolish to not empty it before going into full lockdown.

But the Lake Killer was out there. Staying safe took priority over bathroom needs.

There'd been no other sound from outside, nothing from dispatch over her phone or clinic intercom. She trusted Nash and the RRPD security patrol implicitly. But it didn't keep the cold snake of fear from coiling in her gut and making her want to scream. She gripped the weapon in her hand, missing Greta's protection.

The silence grew along with Patience's trepidation. No further explosions or gunshots sounded from outside. Even the patients in the kennel were ominously quiet. She tried to reassure herself that it was a good sign; if Gabby, the parrot, remained still and not a squawk left her formidable beak, then chances were no one was hiding there.

Patience forced herself to draw in deep breaths, hold the air and then release it forcefully in an effort to center herself. She couldn't ignore her bladder any longer. The bathroom was just off her office. She'd be in and out in a flash. Quickly and quietly she used the restroom, making it back into her office within two minutes. She huddled under her desk again, weapon ready.

Greta's sharp, protesting barks shattered the silence and sent chills of fear through her. The sound reverberated across the clinic as Patience held her weapon in front of her, ready to shoot.

Two gunshots in swift succession sounded a split second before glass rained down on her office's tile floor. She'd been here before, knew what it meant. The Lake Killer was back.

It was now or never. Patience eased from under the desk, keeping her body behind the furniture, but enabling a clear shot at the intruder.

She balanced her arms on the desktop and faced the man she prayed she'd never see again. Not free and threatening like this. She wanted him behind bars. Now she'd kill him before he hurt her or her babies.

The Lake Killer pushed her office door open and stepped inside, dragging a limp body behind him.

*Nash.* Her entire life, her future, her love. He'd killed Nash.

His cold killer eyes hadn't changed, except to have gained more evil in their depths. He held his pistol but, instead of pointing it at Patience, aimed it at Nash as he dumped him on the floor.

"Put down the gun or I'll kill both of you." His voice chilled her even more than his eyes.

Clarity kept her panic at bay. She had to keep the babies safe. "Drop *your* gun. You've already killed him." She gripped her pistol, waited for him to comply, while never expecting him to. She took aim.

"He's still alive." The killer kicked Nash, who let out a harsh grunt, even unconscious. "The dog's dead, along with all the animals in your kennel, unless you come out now."

Nash was alive! She didn't believe for one minute the killer wouldn't harm her, but she also knew Red Ridge police officers were just outside, and hearing everything over her phone. Somehow, they'd make it through this.

"Put your weapon down." She repeated her demand.

"We put them down together."

She'd never trust him. Where were Finn, Juliette, the rest of the RRPD? She didn't know how long she could keep the killer talking, or if she'd be able to distract him from what he want. Her. Dead.

Despair rose and she saw dark spots in front of her eyes. What was the point?

Nash groaned again, and the sound of his voice even in pain fortified Patience's resolve. There were two tiny beings inside her. She had to do whatever it took to save her babies. Which meant she had to save herself. If she shot the Lake Killer, he'd fire back. Even with a reflexive shot from him, chances were good she'd be hit, too.

"Now. Put your weapon down." She spoke slowly, constantly looking for a way to distract the killer.

"Drop yours or I'll crush his skull." The killer stepped on Nash's shoulder to prove his point, eliciting another long groan from him.

"Patience, you there?" Finn's voice came over the clinic intercom.

"I'm here. Suspect refuses to comply." The killer's eyes never left hers, and she sucked in a deep breath. She'd have to kill him. She briefly looked at her weapon, made certain her safety was off, but it was too much time. She looked back at the killer in time to see him lunge toward her with an object in his beefy hand. It wasn't a gun or a knife.

*A syringe.*

She screamed and aimed her weapon at him, but not before the sting of the needle pierced her neck. As her world spun and began to drift, she heard the Lake Killer's promise.

"I told you I'd be back for you, you bitch."

# *Chapter 20*

Nash came to on the floor of Patience's office, his head throbbing, Greta's barking annoying as hell. His first thought was to get up and run, but to where? He heard Greta's barks, urging him to rise.

When he sat up the room spun, and he had to wait for it to stop. The Lake Killer... He'd knocked him out. Patience was gone, and the sight of her overturned desk chair and spots of blood on the floor terrified him. It also gave him the courage he needed to fight through the pain. Patience. He had to get to Patience. The bastard had her.

He moved as quickly as he could, which was too slow, too awkward. Leaning against the corridor wall, he caught his breath and remembered his comms unit, which he pressed with a trembling hand.

"Nash?" Finn's voice, if his battered brain was correct.

"Yeah. Hit. On head."

"Nash, stay there. We have eyes on the killer and we're moving in. Repeat, stay there."

*Like hell.* He pushed the kennel door open and Greta bounded out, but not to see if he was okay. She raced down the hall and disappeared.

She'd run out the back door. He leaned on the windowsill and saw her huge figure streak across the training field and through the open gate to the pier.

The lake.

*Oh, God, no.*

His plea wasn't answered as he looked to the water and saw a small motorboat moving away from the pier, toward the center of the lake. Steered by a man with silver hair, with the unmistakable shape of a woman slumped next to him.

*Patience.*

Nash immediately half hobbled, half walked to the exit. He'd never get to her in time, but Greta would.

"Nash, you still with us?"

"Where. Are. You?" He gasped with each step, his head screaming in pain. When he got to the door he walked out onto the deck and hung on to the railing, fighting for air. Struggling to keep Patience in focus. She was so still. A strangled sob squeezed out of his throat.

"Nash, listen. Stay put. The killer booby-trapped the clinic so that we can't move forward, not until we've cleared the area of explosives. You'll trip a detonation wire if you try to leave."

"I'm already outside." He kept going toward the pier, his breath returning. "She's in the lake with him. Greta's there."

"Copy that."

He ignored Finn and kept going. Nash got to the pier in time to see an image no man ever wanted to. As he watched, the Lake Killer dumped Patience's unconscious form over the side of his motorboat. It wasn't more than two hundred yards from the shore. Nash pulled out his weapon and took aim. He'd kill the bastard now.

Except Greta was swimming across the lake, and he saw her disappear under the surface. Fortunately, the Lake Killer wasn't interested in harming the dog, but only in escape, as he aimed his boat at the far shore and revved the engine.

Nash dropped his arm, knowing he'd never get a decent shot off now. He got himself into one of the RRPD launches, and as he started the engine, two officers and two EMTs jumped in next to him. The small motorboat rocked with their arrival, making Nash's stomach heave.

"We've got it, buddy." Juliette took over steering, and Finn shoved Nash onto the small bench as they raced across the lake toward where Patience had been dropped.

"Greta's doing her job, Nash. We'll get Patience out." Finn's voice was full of hope.

Nash clung to it. He had to believe she was still alive, that Greta would bring her up before it was too late. It was the single thread that held his sanity together.

They reached the site where she'd slipped beneath

the water just as Patience appeared to float to the surface. But it was Greta, nudging her up.

"Good dog, Greta."

"We've got her!" Juliette yelled, as she and Finn worked to bring her limp body aboard.

Nash's hopes were crushed when he saw the blue tinge to Patience's skin. It was the first Lake Killer victim all over again.

"No!" He pushed past them all, grabbed at Patience. Finn and Juliette pulled him back, giving the EMTs room to do their job.

"It's okay, Nash. Let them work." Juliette spoke as Finn held Nash's arms. "She'll be okay."

"How can you say that?" His entire life had died in this lake today and—

A loud cough was followed by sputters as Patience's lungs rejected the water she'd inhaled. Nash was afraid to look, but as the EMTs continued to work on her he saw her skin pinking up and hope crept back into his heart. When Patience asked for him with a raspy voice, Nash let the tears of gratitude fall.

They'd saved her.

Bright hospital lights and the smell of antiseptic greeted Patience as she woke up the next morning after a long night's sleep. The events of yesterday returned, and all she cared about was that the twins were safe, healthy. They'd survived the knockout drug the Lake Killer had stuck her with. As had she. She turned to find Nash at her side, watching her.

"How long have you been here?"

He gave her a slow smile as he stood and stretched, then came over to the bed and kissed her. "Awhile."

"More like all night?"

"Hmm." He kissed her again and she wished they were back at the cabin, alone, with the whole day in front of them to do nothing more than make love. She reached up to run her fingers through his hair and found a large bandage.

"Nash? What's this?"

He turned around long enough to let her see the large patch over the back of his shaved scalp. "I got a few stitches is all."

"And a concussion." She'd heard the EMTs talking on the ambulance ride to the hospital. Nash had ridden with her, and they'd checked him out.

"Minor. The outer swelling saved me from the worst."

"You saved me." She watched him as she spoke.

His face contorted into a grimace. "I wasn't there for you, Patience. Greta saved you."

She looked around the room. "Where is Greta, by the way?"

"She's at home. The kids miss her and she needed a day off."

"She saved my life." Tears welled and Patience knew she'd never be able to repay the dog.

"She saved us both." He kissed her forehead. "I'm going to go get some real coffee for us—there's a café downstairs. How does a caramel latte sound?"

"Like heaven."

"Be right back."

She watched him as he left, allowed herself the sight of his sexy backside. And realized she'd forgotten to ask if they'd caught the Lake Killer yet.

As she went to the bathroom, brushed her teeth and tried to make herself presentable, all she thought about was how incredible it would be if they were finally free of both the Lake and Groom Killers. She and Nash and the babies might have a chance at a real life, without the constant stress of being under attack.

As Patience walked back to her bed she heard the door swing open, and turned to give Nash a big smile.

And looked into the cold eyes of the Lake Killer.

Nash used his back to open the hinged door of the hospital room, holding two lattes and a bag of dough-nuts. He froze when he saw the Lake Killer there, and Patience's wide eyes. To her credit, she didn't give away that she saw him enter.

"You'll never get away with this."

"I almost did yesterday, you bitch."

"There are more witnesses now, and you'll have to kill them all. It's not going to work."

"Watch me—ahhh!" Nash threw the treats to the ground as he jumped on the taller man's back and hauled him down. He vaguely heard Patience scream and call for help. The killer fought him, but Nash had the element of surprise and managed to subdue and hold him until security guards rushed into the room.

RRPD officers arrived ten minutes later and took the Lake Killer into custody. Finn was with them, and waited until the room cleared to speak to both Patience and Nash.

"You two have been through the wringer. I'm ordering you both to take a week off, no argument."

Nash shook his head, still a painful move. The adrenaline from capturing the Lake Killer must have dulled the pain temporarily. "I can't do that, Chief. The Groom Killer's still out there, and I've got my kids to take care of."

"It's paid leave, Nash. No arguments." Finn's eyes twinkled. "And I understand congratulations are in order."

Nash saw Patience smile, and more—he saw the relief in her features. The target on her back was gone, her stalker behind bars. "Thank you, Finn," she said warmly. "I agree with you—we need a break. But like Nash said, this probably isn't the time for it."

"No arguments from you, either, Dr. Colton." Finn nodded at them before he turned and left.

Nash looked at Patience, who sank onto the bed. "This has been too much for you."

She waved away his comment. "I'm good. You heard the doctors—the babies are, too. I can go home later today."

Nash knew this was the time to tell Patience where he wanted "home" to be. For both of them.

Patience saw the gleam in Nash's eyes after Finn left. It was the look he saved for her, the one that made her know he was thinking of nothing, no one else. Only her. Patting the space next to her on the hospital bed, she waited for him to sit, then took his hands in hers. His strong, sexy, dear hands.

"Nash, what I was trying to say before, in my office yesterday, is that I love you. And it's okay that you don't feel the same—this isn't my way of trying to get you to be more than you want to with the babies. But I had to tell you." A keen sense of happiness unfurled from her center, as if her heart was exploding in fireworks. It was absolutely the best thing she'd ever felt or done. She loved Nash.

He gave her his signature wide, sexy smile that made all they'd been through the past month melt away. "Babe, you're not getting off that easy."

"No?"

"I love you, too. And you're not going to raise these babies on your own."

Delight and pure love washed through her. "I'm not?"

"No. These babies will grow up with four older siblings, and with both of us." He touched her forehead with his. "Now's not the time, Patience, but when you're better, and my head's not so messed up, I'm going to ask you to marry me."

"You are?"

"Yes." He claimed her lips, this time in a promise to last the rest of their lives. "What do you think about that, Dr. Colton?"

"I think that when you do ask me, I'll say yes."

\* \* \* \* \*

# WYOMING
# COWBOY SNIPER

## NICOLE HELM

For opposites who attract.

## Prologue

Dylan Delaney considered the scene around him an atrocity: Carsons and Delaneys of Bent, Wyoming, not just mingling in the same yard but celebrating.

Celebrating the marriage of his sister—an upstanding, rule-following sheriff's deputy with too good of a heart—to a no-good, lying, cheating, *saloon-owning* Carson.

The fact his sister looked so happy as she danced with her newly pronounced husband was the only reason Dylan was keeping his mouth shut. That and a well-stocked makeshift bar in the Carson barn that had been transformed into a wedding venue for Laurel and Grady.

Dylan had been bred to hate Carsons and what they represented his whole life. Delaneys were better than thieving, low-class, lying Carsons—and had been since the town had been founded back in the eighteen hundreds.

Dylan's siblings had always been too soft. Though Jen had held strong with him, Cam and Laurel were growing even softer in adulthood as they mixed themselves up with Carsons.

*Romantically* of all things.

Dylan had prided himself on being hard. On being *better*. Half his siblings had been happy to ignore the calling of the Delaney name, but he'd used everything he had in him to live up to it.

If it felt hollow in the face of his sister happily marrying Grady Carson, he'd ignore it.

"Worried about your precious bloodline, Delaney?"

Dylan sneered. Normally, he wouldn't. Normally, he'd be cool, collected and cuttingly disdainful of Vanessa Carson even breathing the same air as him, let alone addressing him. But the liquor was smoothing out just enough of his senses for him to forget he never engaged with the Carson he hated the most.

"Aren't you worried about catching a little law and order? Ruining that bad-girl reputation of yours?" Dylan smiled, the way he would have smiled at a dirty child who'd just smeared mud over his freshly dry-cleaned suit.

She wore the same shade of black as his suit, but not in a sedate cocktail dress that might have befit a wedding. He'd have even given a pass to a funeralesque sundress, because it was a rather casual affair all in all, and it felt like a funeral on his end.

But no. Vanessa wore tight leather pants and some kind of contraption on top that flowed behind her like a cape down to her knees. It knotted in the front above her belly button. A little gold hoop dangled there, mocking him.

He was so attracted to her, it hurt. He hated himself for that purely animalistic reaction that he'd always, *always* refused to act on. He'd dealt with cosmic jokes his whole life. This was just another one to be put away and ignored. He was stronger than the cosmos. Had to be.

She flashed a grin meant to peel the skin off his face. "My bad-girl reputation is rock-hard solid, babe." She sauntered around Dylan and the makeshift bar, then started looking through the collection of bottles and cans.

The hired bartender blinked at her, clearly caught off guard and having no idea what to do despite making a living from serving drunk and rowdy wedding guests. "I can get you what you—"

"No worries." She nudged the bartender away and rummaged around, then poured herself an impressive and possibly lethal combination of alcohol. She lifted her cup in Dylan's direction, which was when he realized he'd been watching her. She drank deeply.

"If that was for my benefit, color me unimpressed," he muttered, looking away from that long slender neck and the way long wisps of midnight-black hair danced around her face.

"Baby, I wouldn't do anything for your benefit, even if you were on fire," Vanessa said, her voice a smooth purr.

He refused to let his body react. "Someone's going to be carrying you out of here if you drink all that."

She laughed, low and smoky. It slithered through him like—

Like nothing.

"I could shoot you under the table, sweetheart."

"Wanna bet?" he muttered, forcing himself to stare ahead even though he could feel her come to stand next to him.

She laughed again, the sound so arousing he wanted to bash his own head in.

"I know you didn't just say that to me, Delaney. You're not that stupid."

Which poked at all the reactions he kept locked far, far away. Apparently the rather potent drinks he'd been downing in swift succession were the key to unlocking them. "I'll repeat it, then. Want to bet?" He enunciated each word with exaggerated precision as he turned to look at her.

She smirked, somehow a few inches shorter than him even though she always seemed to take up so much space. "Oh, I'll take that bet. How much?"

He named a sum he knew she couldn't possibly afford.

She rolled her eyes and waved a dismissive hand that glinted silver and gold with an impressive array of rings, including more than one in the shape of a skull or dagger.

He despised her. Every inch of her. Which he drank in against his will.

"Delaneys love to flaunt their money."

He flashed a wolfish grin, enjoying far too much the way her eyes narrowed as if preparing to ward him off. *Good luck, little girl.* "Chicken?"

Some little voice in the back of his head reminded him of propriety. Reminded him of his place in Bent and the fact that getting in a drinking competition with Vanessa would only end in embarrassment and trouble. It went against everything he believed and stood for, and he should just walk away.

He stood where he was and ignored that voice.

When he woke up the next morning, definitely not in his own bed, ignoring that voice was the last thing he remembered.

VANESSA WAS DYING. From the inside out. So, so many bad decisions made last night. But it was her brother's fault for marrying a Delaney. That she was sure of.

She groaned, rolling over in bed as her stomach roiled in protest. She'd had her fair share of hangovers, but this one was truly something.

And now she was hallucinating.

Had to be. Because there was no way on God's green earth that Dylan Delaney was in her bed.

No *Delaney man* was *naked* in her bed, in the middle

of her apartment above her mechanic shop. She looked to the left. There was her little kitchen, the hall with the bathroom door. She looked to the right, at the door to the stairs down to the shop, and in that line of vision was clearly a man.

As she blinked at that shape of a man next to her, it was Dylan's dark eyes that widened and sharpened. It was every gorgeous plane of Dylan Delaney's face that went very, very hard.

Vanessa closed her eyes tight, counted to ten in a whisper. It had to be a dream. It had to be an alcohol-induced mirage. It had to be anything but the truth.

But when she was done counting, Dylan was still there.

"Apparently bad dreams do come true," Dylan said, his voice all delicious rough gravel.

*Get yourself together. Nothing about Dylan Delaney is delicious.*

She watched, horrified, really she was horrified and not intrigued at all, as he flung the covers—*her* covers—off of him and stood, clearly having no compunction about being *naked in her room*.

With jerky movements, he pulled on his pants from last night. Last night. She'd...

"You can't tell anyone." If she'd been feeling better she would have kept that inside. Ignored the panic and held on to the upper hand. But she was *dying*, and she'd apparently slept with Dylan Delaney.

She remembered nothing. Nothing about last night beyond the wedding ceremony where her rough-and-tumble brother had promised himself forever to goody-two-shoes Laurel Delaney. A *cop*.

Beyond that, everything got fuzzier and fuzzier until...

*Best kiss of your life.*

Ha! She'd been drunk. How would she have known?

Dylan gave her one smoldering look—enough her heart started pumping overtime and her whole body seemed to blaze with heat. She could almost, *almost* picture them together, feel his big rough hands on her—

But Dylan Delaney, a bank manager, did not have rough hands. She was hallucinating. And was that a *tattoo* on his chest that disappeared as he pulled his shirt on and began to button it?

"Who on *earth* do you think I'd tell about this horrifying lapse in judgment?" he said disgustedly.

It didn't sting, because she felt the same way. Except *lapse in judgment* was way too tame. *Catastrophe of epic proportions* was more appropriate.

A catastrophe she would also blame on Grady, because if he hadn't married a Delaney, she wouldn't have gotten drunk enough to *sleep* with one.

Dylan was now completely dressed, and she was still naked in her bed. *Naked.*

"We'll both forget this ever happened," Dylan said. No. He demanded it, like she was a peon to be ordered about. But even she couldn't work up contrariness at his tone when *this* had happened.

"I don't even know *what* happened. We didn't really..." But he'd been naked, and she was naked so...

"I don't remember either. So we'll just say we didn't."

"But—"

"We didn't," he said firmly, patting down his pockets. "I have my wallet. No keys."

"Surely neither of us were stupid enough to drive."

"Surely neither of us were stupid enough to have someone drive us *together* anywhere." He sighed, running an agitated hand through sleep-tousled hair. He did not look like his normal slick self. He was disheveled and...

Appealing.

No, not that.

"Hate sex is a thing," she blurted, feeling unaccountably out of control and nervous. Which did not make any sense, but she couldn't seem to straighten herself out. It had to be the hangover and all the booze still in her system.

He scowled, and Vanessa didn't understand why her eyes wanted to track the small lines around his mouth or note the way dark stubble dotted his chin where it had been smooth last night.

There was something compelling about him. She'd admit it now and regain some of her control. They were polar opposites, and sometimes when polar opposites got drunk enough, they ended up attracting.

She'd swear off alcohol for the rest of her life right here, right now.

"Hate sex is not a *thing*. Not for me it's not."

"Apparently for drunk you it was."

He pinched the bridge of his nose. "I'm leaving. We'll never speak of this again. And if anyone saw us…"

"We lie," Vanessa supplied for him.

He seemed startled by that word, but what else was there to do?

Eventually, he gave a sharp nod. "Through our teeth." He turned and strode out her apartment door.

Vanessa stared at the ceiling, hoping she never, ever remembered what had transpired and willing herself to forget about it for good.

# Chapter One

*Four months later*

Vanessa Carson was not a coward. In her entire life, she'd never backed down from an insult, a challenge or a fist. She'd faced all three of those things practically since she'd been born, and yet none of it held a candle to this moment.

She sat in the driver's seat of her ancient sedan in the back parking lot of Delaney Bank. She preferred her motorcycle but... Without thinking the movement through, she placed her hand over her stomach. It was starting to round, just a little bit. No one else would notice, but she could tell. It wouldn't be long before other people would be able to tell, as well.

The morning sickness had been hell, but it seemed to dissipate more every day. She'd taken to eating better, and she'd sworn off alcohol for different reasons ever since that night. Her doctor said she and baby were healthy as a horse.

Luckily, she was surrounded by clueless men for the most part, so no one in her life had any idea. She was convinced it was paranoia that on more than one occasion she'd caught her cousin-in-law or new sister-in-law staring at her with a considering gaze when she did something like eat a veggie plate or pass on another hit of caffeine.

Paranoia or not, she had to face the music before anyone actually put the puzzle together. Had to. Before the music told him itself.

*You are not a coward.*

She repeated those words with every step toward the bank. She had never once stepped foot in Delaney Bank, would have rather chewed her own arm off—or simply driven the twenty-plus minutes to Fremont whenever she needed a bank.

But this wasn't about asking for a loan or sullying the white halls of such an upstanding establishment run by the Delaneys. It was about the very unfortunate truth.

She was going to have Dylan Delaney's baby.

For a few weeks she'd considered running away. Disappearing. Grady would likely try to find her, with her cousins Noah and Ty not far behind him. But it would have been possible if she'd played her cards right. Eventually, they'd have given up on her. Maybe.

But Bent was her home. Her life. Her mechanic shop was everything she'd built her life on. She'd paid in blood, sweat and tears for it. She wasn't ever going to let a Delaney scare her into running away.

*Your baby is half Delaney.*

She paused at the corner of the bank building. Ruthlessly, she reminded herself Dylan wouldn't want anyone to know that any more than she did. He'd agree to her plan. He had to. He'd *never* risk his reputation just to be a part of his baby's life.

Which was why she had to tell him. He'd be spiteful if he found out some other way. She needed this to be quick, easy and painless. Which meant she couldn't just stand here.

She heard a noise from behind her and turned to see a back door opening. Dylan stepped out, looking perfectly dapper in a suit with a briefcase clutched in his hand. He slid sunglasses onto his face in defense of the setting sun, his dark looks tinged with gold in the fading light.

She'd never understood her reaction to him—a tug, a *want*. No matter how much she knew she did not want the uptight, soft banker boy, something deep inside of her begged to differ.

Luckily, she was a smart woman who knew when not to listen to stupid feelings. She just needed to explain to him how things were going to be, and be done with him for good.

"Dylan."

He startled, as if he recognized her voice instantly and how incongruous it was at his precious bank. He immediately scanned the lot before turning his gaze to her.

When he'd seen there was no one else around he took a few steps toward her, suspicious and uncomfortable, but not sneery. She would have preferred a little sneery to get her back up.

"Vanessa," he said, his voice cool and clipped, though not nasty.

"Dylan. We need to talk."

He raised an eyebrow. Such a disdainful look, and yet she didn't feel that same animosity from him she'd always had when they'd been growing up. They'd avoided each other even more carefully than usual since Laurel and Grady's wedding, which was hard to do in a small town when your siblings were married. But they'd done it.

Still, there'd been a cooling of antagonism on both their parts. Perhaps they now knew a little too well where unchecked dislike could lead. Being apathetic worked a heck of a lot better.

But she wished he'd be nasty, so she could be angry and defensive instead of so nervous she felt sick.

*This is better. You can be calm and collected and show him he's not the only one with some control.*

"We really need to talk," Vanessa repeated when he said nothing. "Privately."

Again he scanned the lot and seemed satisfied no one lurked in the dusky shadows. "Follow me."

He used a key card on a pad outside the door he'd come out of, then pulled it open and gestured her inside. She went, chin too high and sharp, shoulders back and braced for a fight.

But it wouldn't be a fight. It would be a quick, informative conversation, and then she'd walk right out of the bank with this awful weight off her shoulders. She wouldn't run her mouth. She'd just say it plain.

He stepped inside, the door closing behind him with a definitive slap. With a nod, he moved down the hallway, leading her to another door—this one glass. Inside was a fancy office. Evidently his, since his name was printed on the glass.

"You know, in my shop I don't have to put my own name on the door to my office."

"I'm guessing, in your shop, you're not entertaining wealthy clients in your office."

She flashed him a hard-edged grin. "You'd be surprised who likes me doing the oil change on their car."

His lips pressed together. She couldn't help but remember him not as the slick, suited businessman who stood before her but as the rumpled, slightly shaken man she'd woken up with that morning all those months ago.

He set his briefcase down and took a seat behind the big, gleaming desk, then ran a hand over the lapel of his suit jacket. He looked impossibly elegant. He wasn't like his siblings. They were the down-home noble type. Laurel the cop, Cam the former marine and Jen the shopkeeper.

Dylan had style—with an edge to it. She didn't know why he stayed in Bent when he was clearly meant to be somewhere a lot more posh than this nowhere Wyoming town.

She didn't know why she had this odd memory of his hands on her feeling *right*.

Just insanity and liquor, she supposed.

"What did you need to discuss?" he asked in the cool, detached voice he'd almost always used on her. Even when they'd been in the same class in first grade, he'd spoken like that to her at the age of seven. Like he was inherently better.

It should have put her back up, but all she could do was stare at him behind his big desk, looking imposing and important in this big, fancy bank office.

She swallowed as an unexpected emotion swamped her. Regret. It was a shame the way her baby had been conceived because this whole Delaney legacy belonged to him or her too.

Money. The kind of reputation people slaved a lifetime to never live up to. The baby wouldn't even have to deal with being the first commingling of Carson and Delaney. Laurel and Grady would always take whatever heat people blamed on a foolish curse, because they'd promised to love each other in front of God himself.

Not everyone in town took the feud between the Carson and Delaney families as seriously as she did, and not everyone in town believed the old tale that if a Carson and Delaney ever fell in love, the town itself would be cursed to destruction.

A story passed down from generation to generation

since the Carsons had accused Delaneys of stealing their land back in the eighteen hundreds.

Enough people believed it to make it a *thing*.

The fact Bent hadn't immediately crumbled or been struck by lightning didn't soothe the most superstitious. They were still waiting for it. As for Vanessa, she was more of a take-life-as-it-comes type of girl. She'd deal with a curse if there was one, and she wouldn't be surprised if life went on as it always had.

"I know you're not here for the view. Or a repeat performance," Dylan said, shocking her out of her reverie.

Repeat... She clamped her jaw shut so it wouldn't drop. No one ever turned her off-center like this.

It was the baby softening all her edges. Which was fine and dandy, once she'd done her business. She was determined to be a good mother—the kind hers had never been—where her kid came first and foremost. And not one man was going to ruin that for *her* kid. She'd soften every last edge, sand off her tattoos and cut out her own swearing, drinking, idiot tongue if it meant giving this baby the kind of idyllic childhood she'd never had.

Which meant no strife with the father of the baby, even if Vanessa didn't plan on him being involved.

The best way not to have any strife was to be quick and to the point. She took a deep breath in and let it out, forcing herself to meet Dylan's dark, imposing gaze.

"I'm pregnant."

THE WORDS LANDED like a blow, the kind that had your ears ringing and your eyes seeing stars. Even as Dylan's brain scrambled to make sense of those two simple words, he desperately held on to his composure.

In business, composure was everything.

This wasn't business.

*Pregnant. Baby.* She was telling him she was pregnant and that meant…

He opened his mouth to speak, though he wasn't sure what it was he meant to say. No words or sound came out, anyway.

"I'm not asking you for anything," she said clearly. Her gaze was calm, direct, but he saw the way she clutched her hands together in her lap. For a woman like Vanessa she might as well have been shaking in her boots. "I'd rather—"

"Yes, I can imagine all you'd rather," he muttered. He glanced at her stomach where her hands were clutched. There was no evidence a child grew there, but one did and it was his.

His.

His heart squeezed as if gripped by some iron outside force, a mix of panic and awe. Mostly panic, he assured himself.

"But if I didn't tell you, you'd figure it out and assume. So I'm telling you. You don't need to worry or do anything. I'll keep your part in this a secret and raise this baby myself." Her hands squeezed harder, and he couldn't seem to bring himself to lift his gaze from them to meet hers.

"Yourself," he repeated stupidly.

"Yes. I'm capable. Maybe I don't look like the most maternal—"

"I'm not challenging you, Vanessa," he snapped, looking away from her hands. Her eyes were storms of a million things. Things he didn't want to consider.

But she was pregnant with his child. *His* child.

Hell.

"Regardless," she said, sounding surprisingly prim. "I

wanted to be clear that I'll be taking care of everything. As long as you don't yap, we'll be fine."

"Fine," he echoed. Fine. This was not fine.

She began to stand.

"Where the hell do you think you're going?"

She raised her eyebrows. "Home. I told you what I had to say and—"

"And you think I'd just step back and ignore the fact I have a child? You honestly thought you'd make your little announcement and that would be it?"

Her eyes went cool, the nervousness in her clutched hands gone as they came to rest on the arms of the chair. "Obviously, I considered you'd be obnoxious, but I held out hope you'd understand that yes, that's it. Because it's a Carson child."

He stood, pressing his hands to the shiny surface of his desk in an effort to center himself and leash his anger. "Half Delaney."

She folded her arms across her chest and gave him one of those patented Vanessa Carson, *you-are-a-bug-to-be-scraped-off-my-boot* looks. "Are you suggesting we cut the baby in half?" she asked dryly.

"I'm not suggesting anything. You're not giving me time to suggest anything. You've dropped your bomb and now seem to think you're going to waltz out of here and leave me to deal with the fallout."

"I believe that's usually how bombs are dropped," she replied. She was back to herself. Sharp, dismissive and oh so sure she was better than him.

But she hadn't been for a few minutes, and she was carrying his baby. His child.

A living, breathing *human being*.

He sat back down. The weight of it floored him. "I

can't… How long? It'd be…" He did the math. "You've been sitting on this for a while."

She shrugged. She wore jeans and a long-sleeved T-shirt. Heavy black boots. Even with her tattoos covered, she looked like trouble. She always had. He didn't know why he'd think pregnancy would change it.

He focused on her. On the gleaming silver skull ring on her thumb. The way her hair seemed all that much blacker against the fair, freckled skin of her cheeks. Sharp edges with surprising hints of vulnerability.

And she was carrying his child.

She sighed heavily. "Look, I don't know what you think sitting there staring at me is going to accomplish, but this is how things are going to be. I have the kid, tell people the father's some random out-of-towner. I live my life and you live yours."

"Knowing your child is mine."

"Consider yourself a sperm donor."

"I will not," he said, managing to keep his voice as even as hers. It was a hard-won thing. "I don't know if you're trying to be difficult or if it just comes naturally, but this is not a *small* thing. It's a huge, bomb-sized thing."

"You seem pretty calm and collected to me," she muttered.

"Years of practice," he said through clenched teeth. The lies he'd told and the things he'd seen. Yes, he'd had *years* of practice in how to appear calm when he was anything but. In control of a world that would not bend to his will—here in Bent or out there where he'd lived his secret life.

Now this. He wanted to be angry, but every time it spurted up, this strange weight settled over him. *Calm* wasn't the right word for it. There was something like a flash of her, from that night. Something he should re-member and couldn't. A softness. A rightness.

He shook it away, but he couldn't shake away the re-alization he didn't have a choice here. She thought he could walk away, turn his back on his own child, and he wouldn't in a million years.

Which meant he had to find common ground with the one person in this whole town—and possibly world—he wasn't sure he could.

There had to be common ground here though, whether he liked it or not. They had to find a compromise.

Something had changed that night, and not just the life it had created. The animosity between him and Van-essa had dulled. Or maybe it was watching Laurel and Grady these past few months. No matter how much grief they got from the town or Dad, they laughed and smiled and…didn't care. Something had changed inside of them so they didn't care.

Dylan had made a child. It was time to not care. "Van-essa."

The distinct sound of a gun being fired jolted them both. It had come from the front. Dylan was on his feet in seconds.

"Stay here," he ordered.

"Stay *here*?" Vanessa repeated incredulously. "You can't… Was that a gun?"

But he was already striding out of his office. He made it not even halfway down the hall before he heard foot-steps behind him.

He whirled on Vanessa. "I told you—"

"Was that a gun? We should call someone! Why are you running toward it?"

He didn't have time to explain, but she could call. "Go back to my office, lock the door from the inside and dial

911. Tell them you heard two shots fired in the lobby. One employee inside, not sure about customers. Go."

He nudged her back toward the office.

"Aren't you coming with me?"

"I have to make sure Adele—"

Two masked men slammed through the door from the bank lobby. It was a robbery. Possibly the stupidest of all crimes in this day and age. Surely Adele had hit the alarm and these two men would be caught before they even tried to leave.

Dylan glanced down at the assault rifles they each carried. Unless they'd shot her first. He felt the horror move through him, but quickly pushed it aside. Compartmentalized and assessed the situation.

Two armed robbers in front of him. The Carson woman, pregnant with his baby, behind him.

And he'd thought it was going to be your average Monday.

## Chapter Two

Vanessa tried to think, but unfamiliar panic tickled the back of her throat. Masked men with guns. She'd faced a lot of bad crap in her life, but this was a first. Fear had turned her body to lead.

"Office," Dylan said under his breath. He didn't look back at her, just ordered her to move.

But she couldn't. She was rooted to the spot by a mind-numbing panic that barely allowed her to suck in a breath. The guns. She wasn't usually rendered useless by the sight of guns. She'd shot her fair share, sometimes even carried one, and had been in the presence of them her whole life.

But these were so big, and they looked more military than recreational. She was sure she and Dylan were dead where they stood, and all the fight she was so certain she had in spades deserted her.

"Who are you?" one of the men demanded, gesturing his gun toward her. "Supposed to be one," he muttered to the other man. "Boss promised us it'd be one."

"What have you done to Adele?" Dylan asked.

Dylan's calmness was downright creepy. He didn't shake or seem panicked. Vanessa managed to keep a decent mask of not freaking out on the outside, but Dylan didn't seem to be acting. Easily, he stepped toward the two men, even as they aimed their guns at him.

Vanessa tried to swallow down the labored breathing that threatened to make too much noise in the quiet hall. She tried to move, but her body was still lead weight.

"Put the guns down and we'll make sure this ends well for everyone," Dylan said, still moving toward them, even as their fingers curled around the triggers. "Now, what have you done with my employee?"

Vanessa couldn't catch a breath. She and Dylan were going to die here in this hallway. Not just them, but their baby too. Her balance swayed and she had to squeeze her eyes shut and lean against the wall to find it again.

"Take them both?" one man asked the other.

The other seemed to consider it. "Only set up for one."

"Tricky business. Shoot her?"

Some awful sound escaped her throat, and she couldn't open her eyes or breathe. She was going to die. Her baby was going to die. Dylan was going to die.

*Fight. You have to fight.*

"Boss's got space. Rather take them both than get any blood on our hands till we know we can get away with it."

"Wasn't supposed to be two here. Boss's fault if we have to kill her."

Vanessa opened her eyes. She was still unaccountably dizzy, but she had to fight. For her baby. For herself. *Dylan.* "Are you seriously discussing whether or not to kill someone in front of said someone? What kind of criminals are you?" Vanessa demanded.

"Yeah, we'll take her," the bigger one sneered.

"Over my dead body," Dylan seethed, moving forward.

"I can arrange that," the sneering man said, jabbing the barrel of his gun right into Dylan's chest.

Vanessa went cold all over, even as she couldn't work out why Dylan was trying to save *her*. Just the baby, she supposed. Her teeth were chattering now, and she berated herself for being such a coward, but that didn't help give her the strength to push off the wall. To do anything. She could only stand here, shaking, falling apart, wondering why everything was spinning around her.

Except Dylan's profile. Something clicked off in his expression. It wasn't fear that overtook him, even though this huge, monstrous weapon was pressed to his heart. It was…determination.

"You should leave her. She's pregnant. You don't want to mess with that. I'm the son of the bank president. Think of the ransom you could ask for. You don't need her, and you don't need to hurt her." Then Dylan did the damnedest thing. He smiled.

"Dylan," Vanessa managed. The hallway seemed to be getting dim, and she thought maybe she was going to throw up. She tried to say something, warn somebody that it wasn't going to be pretty. But the world was moving. The walls. The floor.

"Pregnant, eh?" One of the men eyed her and she had to close her eyes again. She had to think of the baby. If she could get her brain to stop being a jumbled mess, get the panic to stop freezing her, she could barricade herself in Dylan's office and call 911.

These men would be able to shoot through the glass door though. She'd left her cell phone in her car. Did Dylan have his on him? He seemed like the type who wouldn't be parted from it. She opened her eyes, trying to study his pants to see if there was the hint of a phone in his pocket.

"She's a liability," Dylan said, still so damn calm while she was shaking. Had the lights gone out? Everything seemed so dark. "Any harm you cause her would come back on you tenfold. It's one thing to kidnap and demand ransom, another to harm a woman and her unborn child."

"Only if we get caught," the other man said, his smile going so wide half his mouth was hidden behind his black face mask.

Vanessa thought she could all but read Dylan's thoughts from the simple murderous expression he gave the man: *oh, you'll be caught.*

She'd never given Dylan much credit for bravery or having a backbone, but watching him face down two goons with giant guns, she realized she had to reassess her opinion of him.

"We need to get going. We should have been gone ten minutes ago. Stick to the plan, or the boss—"

"Yeah, yeah, yeah." The man holding the gun to Dylan's chest pushed him with it. "You're coming with us." He gestured toward the back door Dylan had led her through not that long ago. Dylan started moving toward it, the gun now to his back.

He didn't even look at her as he passed.

"We can't leave her, pregnant or not. She's seen too much. We have to take her with us. Come on, little girl."

The man not pushing Dylan reached out for her, but she flinched away. She wanted to deck him, but she couldn't manage to move her arms. She couldn't *move*, period. Bile rose in her throat.

"I'm going to…" But the room was something like black, and she wasn't on her feet anymore. Then something crashed against her head and painful stars burst in her vision, but it wasn't light. She heard Dylan say her name, but she couldn't seem to do anything but stay still—and then float away.

DYLAN'S FACE THROBBED in time with his heavy beating heart. He should have been able to fight them off, but he'd been trying to get to Vanessa to make sure she was all right.

Now his hands were zip-tied behind his back, and he was pretty sure his shoulder was dislocated from trying to fight that off. It was possible his jaw was broken from the butt of the gun being smashed into his face, but since he could move it, he'd hope for just a severe bruise.

He'd never be able to break the bonds on his hands or feet, or even loosen them, but he kept feeling around the back of the van, trying to find something sharp.

Trying to keep his mind off the fact Vanessa was unconscious on the floor of the van and carrying his baby.

They'd been in the back of the vehicle for at least fifteen minutes by his count, and Vanessa was still out cold. She was so pale. So...vulnerable.

He'd save her. He had to. His skills at survival had dulled somewhat these past few years of playing dutiful banker and protégé to his father. But he'd remember them. He'd bring them all back, and he and Vanessa would escape this mess.

Poor Adele. He hoped she was all right. Surely she'd have hit the alarm, even if they'd hurt her. But the two morons who'd abducted them had certainly taken their time getting out of the bank, and no one had shown up.

Well, someone would notice him missing. A Carson would surely notice Vanessa missing. Someone would notice she didn't come home and that her shop wasn't open. They'd see her car in the bank lot and know something was very, very wrong.

If he assured himself of those facts, he could concentrate on how they were going to escape. Because they *were* going to escape.

A quiet, gasping sound came from Vanessa's direction. Dylan scooted toward her. He wished he could maneuver himself to grab her hand, feel her pulse, but there wasn't enough room on the floor of the van.

"Vanessa."

She groaned this time, moving her head and then groaning again.

"Vanessa. Come on, sweetheart. Wake up." He tried nudging her with his elbow, but he couldn't lean that way without falling at every bump.

"Wh-what…?" She jerked at her arms, her legs thrashing wildly.

"Calm down. It's okay. I'm here. It's okay."

She jerked her gaze to him, all vicious anger hiding a little flash of fear. "Why would *you* being here make anything okay, Delaney?" she demanded, her voice rough. She looked around wildly.

"Just try to breathe. You fainted. Take your time to wake up. Then I'll help you sit up as best I can."

She sucked in a breath then let it out, eyeing their surroundings. The back of the van was all metal, and though the windows were tinted completely black, enough light shone through that they could make each other out. She moved her gaze to him.

"Fainted?" She tugged at the bonds on her hands as she moved herself into a sitting position—without his help—with a wince. "I've never fainted in my life."

"First time for everything. I'd imagine it had to do with—"

"How the hell am I tied up with *you* of all people?" She looked around, her expression one of panic with a steely disgust instead of that ashen terror from before. It was some comfort. "Where *are* we?"

"They took us both as hostages."

"Who's 'they'?" She pulled at the ties on her wrist again, then winced. She squeezed her eyes shut. "How did I get here? I can't..."

"What do you mean, 'you can't'?" He recalled that sometimes people with head injuries didn't remember what had caused them. Added to that, she'd fainted and suffered a trauma. Maybe she didn't even remember coming to see him at the bank. "You don't remember?"

"Remember what?" she snapped.

"What's the last thing you remember?"

She flashed him an impatient look, then her eyebrows drew together. "Man, someone did a number on your face." She seemed to finally understand he was tied up too.

"Yeah, yeah. We can talk about that later. Vanessa, what's the last thing you remember?"

She blinked, frowned. "I don't. Things are fuzzy around the edges. Fuzzy everywhere. I went to the grocery store this morning. Yeah." She closed her eyes and swallowed. "I'm not going to be sick," she muttered to herself, as if saying it aloud would make it so.

"That'd be preferable."

She frowned at him, but the confusion dominated her expression. "You look different. Your face is different."

"Must be the impressive bruising."

"No. You have lines."

"Lines?"

"Around your eyes. Your mouth. And that's some suit. Are we in Bent?" She tried to peer out the window, but she was still sitting and it was too black to see out of.

"You're supposed to be in college, aren't you? Somewhere out east. Yeah, that's what I heard."

"College?" Panic threatened. *College.* She was just a little confused. By over a decade.

"A fancy one, right? I certainly remember your dad bragging all over himself about it when I went to the store this morning. Dylan this. Dylan that. For my benefit. As if *I'd* be impressed."

"Vanessa. God." It was as jarring of a blow as the butt of the gun to his face had been. "What year do you think it is?"

"What kind of question is that? It's…" Her brow furrowed again, and she shook her head. "It's… I'm sure it's…" She looked up at him helplessly. "What's wrong with me?"

"You fainted. And you hit your head. Things are jumbled, but they'll clear up." He said it far more confidently than he felt it. She'd lost over a decade. That little trickle of panic turned into a full-on frantic clawing, but he ruthlessly shoved it down.

She'd just woken up. She was disoriented. The past ten years would come back. Everything with the baby would be okay.

It had to be.

"Got a phone on you?" he asked, his last hope at getting a message to someone.

"Why would I have a phone on me?"

Dylan swallowed down the bubble of hysterical laughter that tried to escape. He wouldn't panic and he wouldn't be hysterical. She'd be fine. She'd have to be. Surely pregnant women fainted and were fine, even with a little memory loss. Women had survived life on the prairie and what-have-you and had had plenty of babies.

Everything was going to be fine if he kept his mind calm, his body ready.

He'd been a soldier once. He could be a soldier again.

"Okay, no phone. Anything sharp?"

"There should be a knife in my boot, but I can't get it with my hands behind my back like this. Who took us? Why are we both tied up? I don't—"

"One thing at a time. Let's get free and then I'll explain everything." Hopefully. Maybe she'd remember once she fully woke up. He had to hope there really was a knife in her boot, and she wasn't remembering a knife in her boot from thirteen years ago. "Put your legs out."

She did as he instructed, straightening her legs out in front of her.

"Which boot?"

"Right. There's a slot for it behind the outside of my ankle." Dylan scooted forward, maneuvering himself so the hands tied behind him were close to her ankle. He'd have to kind of lean over her legs and brush up against her to get his hands anywhere near her boot.

It was uncomfortable and awkward, but the most important thing was finding the knife, if in fact she had one down there in the here and now.

She fidgeted just as he finally got his fingertips down the side of her boot. "This is weird," she complained.

"No weirder than what you don't remember," he muttered, concentrating on leaning this way and that and ignoring the sharp pain in his ribs where one of the goons had kicked him, and the fact his head was all but in her lap.

It took a lot of time, a lot of contorting and a hell of a lot of pain every time the van went over a bump, but he managed to pull the knife out of her boot.

He was sweating by the time it clattered to the floor

of the van, but he didn't wait around to catch his breath. The sooner he got them out of their bonds, the better. He leaned back, managed to grasp the knife. In a few swift movements, he cut the zip tie off his wrists.

Sometimes military training did come in handy in the civilian world. He wouldn't have guessed.

He didn't take a second to enjoy the feeling of freedom, however. He shook off the plastic and immediately cut the one around his ankle, and then freed Vanessa.

"Well. You move…fast," she said, as if that surprised her. "You better not have gotten me roped into this, Delaney."

"Quite the opposite."

"Figures. Always blame a Carson." She rubbed at her wrists, then delicately touched her fingertips to the side of her temple. She winced. "Some blow to the head."

"You folded like a card table and hit the ground before anyone could do anything."

She scowled. "I find that story very hard to believe."

"Well, I didn't knock you around and then tie us both up. But someone with guns *did* tie us up, so we need to be quick about getting ourselves out of this mess." But before they could do what needed to be done, she needed to recall one very important thing.

"You don't remember why you came to see me?" he asked carefully.

"I'm assuming these goons had a gun to my head, because that's the only way I would ever voluntarily go to see you. Unless you were being tortured. And I was invited to watch."

"Nice." Dylan sighed. This was going to make everything so much more difficult, but he didn't have time to get his nose out of joint about it. "I need you to understand something, okay?" He took a deep breath. If she really didn't remember years' worth of stuff, he doubted she'd believe him. He doubted a lot of things, but he couldn't let her go running around thinking it was just her. "You're pregnant."

She barked out a laugh. "Uh-huh."

"I'm serious. That's why we're together. You came to tell me."

"And why would I tell you… Oh. No. No." She shook her head back and forth. "You really expect me to believe I slept with *you*?"

"We were very drunk."

She shook her head, eyes wide. "I don't believe it. There's not enough liquor in the world."

"Okay. Don't believe it. But I need you to understand you *are* pregnant, it's thirteen years later than you think it is and bank robbers have kidnapped us to get a ransom. But I'm going to get us out of this, and when we escape you have to do everything in your power to keep the baby growing inside of you safe."

She went pale at that, but they didn't have time to keep discussing. The van had been moving too long, too far, and they had to make a serious jump-and-run effort here. She had to believe it, even if she didn't want to.

"It can't *be*," she whispered, pressing her hand to her stomach.

"But it is."

*Chapter Three*

Vanessa didn't believe him. Maybe things were all wrong—from the lines on his face to the nausea in her gut to the van they were trapped in—but she would have never slept with Dylan Delaney, even with a blow to her head.

And *he* would have never slept with *her*.

Dylan was fiddling with the door, looking serious and in control. He'd been beaten up pretty badly, but he didn't seem to pay it any mind. He wore a suit—and even though it was dirty and rumpled, she could tell it was expensive.

Her eyes stung, and it took a few moments to realize she wanted to cry. Everything was wrong, like a bad dream where only half the things made sense, no matter how real it all felt.

But cry? Not her. Not in this lifetime. She blinked a few times, and focused on the here and now. Not anything Dylan was claiming, but the fact they were tied up in the back of a van, and now Dylan was using her knife and his bloody hands to mess with the door.

"Can I help?" she managed to ask once she could trust her voice.

"Just sit back."

She scowled. She wasn't a *sit-back* kind of girl, but

she wouldn't have pegged Dylan as a take-charge kind of guy. Sure, to order people around maybe, but not to try and bust them out of a moving van.

How could this all be happening? She was about to demand he explain this and tell her the truth instead of his nonsense dream—lies—about her being pregnant with *his* baby.

She pressed a hand to her stomach, acknowledging that she *might* feel really off. But couldn't that just be the head injury? Couldn't Dylan have *caused* the head injury? Sure, he was all beat up, and he'd been tied up too, but...

She tried to remember. Tried to order her thoughts and memories, but the very last thing she remembered was flipping off Dylan's dad as she left the Delaney General Store.

Not her finest moment, but...

But nothing. The old jerk deserved it. She opened her eyes to the young Delaney jerk in front of her, still trying to jimmy the back door open. He didn't look right. He looked older. Was she really missing such a big chunk of time?

She looked down at her hands. There were pink marks and scratches where the zip ties had dug into her skin around her wrists, but otherwise her hands looked the same. Same rings she always wore... Well, maybe not exactly. She fiddled with a dainty-looking gold one in the shape of a mountain. She didn't remember that one.

She had to find some kind of center—both a mental one and a physical one. This weakness in both wouldn't save her, and it wouldn't fill in whatever memory blanks she had.

But the van chose that moment to rumble to a stop, followed by the engine shutting off.

*Oh, God.*

Dylan swore, then sat down on the floor of the van right by the doors. "Stand behind me," he ordered, like he knew what he was doing, like he could get them out of whatever this was. "Be ready to jump. On my signal, run as fast as you can for whatever cover you can find."

"What about you?" Not that she *cared* about Dylan, but...

He flashed her a grin so incongruous with the Dylan Delaney she'd grown up alongside, she could only gape at him.

The door made a noise, like a lock being undone. "Be ready," Dylan murmured, leaning back on his palms as he watched the door.

"What are you—"

The door began to open, and on an exhale Dylan kicked his legs out as hard as he could against the doors. There were twin grunts of pain as the doors hit something, but Dylan didn't pause. He flung the doors back open and jumped out.

"Go!" he instructed.

Because she saw one man on the ground, struggling to get to his feet, with a *huge* gun next to him, she did as Dylan instructed. She jumped out of the van and immediately started to run.

"Opposite way!" Dylan yelled. She turned, ready to do whatever Dylan instructed if it'd get her out of here, and watched in the fading dusk as his yell ended on a grunt as one of the large men landed an elbow to his gut.

Dylan Delaney, a hoity-toity Delaney who was getting a fancy degree and likely hadn't done an ounce of manual labor in his entire life, took the blow like it barely glanced off him. Then he pivoted, swept a leg out and knocked one large man on his butt. Dylan reared back a fist and punched the other guy in the throat, then whirled as the fallen man got back to his feet.

Vanessa blinked.

"Go!" Dylan yelled at her, and it got through her absolute shock at seeing him fight like he knew what he was doing. No, not even like he knew what he was doing. Like he was *born* to do it.

But there were angry men and guns, so she ran the opposite way she'd been going, toward the front of the van. It acted as a buffer between her and the men and gave her the opportunity to get away without them seeing exactly where she was going.

Dylan knew what he was doing—between the instruction to run this way and fighting off two men. What the hell? She shook away her confusion and focused on running as hard as she could. Her stomach lurched and her head throbbed, but the guns brought it home that she was running for her life here.

*And your baby's life?*

She couldn't think about Dylan's nonsense right now. She just had to get away. She ran hard, but the farther she ran, the darker it got. She had to slow her pace so she didn't trip. So she didn't throw up.

With heaving breaths, she slowed to a stop and pressed her hand to her stomach. She had a cramp in her side that felt like a sharp icepick. When she stopped, she was nearly felled by a nasty wave of nausea. Her head downright ached, and the stinging behind her eyes was back.

But she was in danger, and a Carson knew how to get herself out of danger. She swallowed at the sickness threatening, focused on evening her breath, then studied her surroundings.

She had run for the trees—the best cover she could find—but they were spindly aspens, and it wasn't ideal to be hiding behind even a cluster of narrow trunks. The van must have driven them up in elevation, but where? It was completely dark now, and she couldn't get a sense of her bearings.

Panic joined the swirl of queasiness in her stomach. She breathed through both. She could survive a night in the wild. She didn't particularly *care* to, but she could survive. As long as Dylan had taken care of those two armed men, she was safe enough. Anyone could brave the elements for one night.

*And if Dylan didn't fight them off?*

It was hard to imagine it. He'd moved like a dancer. A really violent, potentially lethal dancer. Dylan Delaney. She would have labeled him the prissiest of the four Delaney kids. Even his younger sister Jen had more spitfire to her than Dylan.

But he was claiming they'd slept together, that he'd impregnated her somehow, and then she'd watched him fight like a dream.

Touching fingertips to the bump on her head, where everything throbbed and ached, Vanessa had to wonder if the blow had caused hallucinations.

Either way, she was alone in the dark in the middle of the Wyoming woods. She lowered herself to the ground, leaning her back against one of the rough trees. It was uncomfortable, and a chill was creeping into the air.

It would be fine. There wasn't snow on the ground, and the leaves still clung to the trees, though they'd gone gold in a nod to fall. But they hadn't completely fallen.

Luckily, she was too nauseous to be hungry, though she wouldn't mind a drink of water. But she'd live. She was alive, and she'd live.

"There you are."

She would have screamed if a hand hadn't clamped

over her mouth. She turned her head to find herself face-to-face with Dylan. It was too dark to make out the individual features of his face, and yet she knew it was him.

"Shh. Okay?"

She nodded and his hand fell off her mouth.

"What happened? How are you… How am I… What is going *on*?"

Breathing only a little heavily, he scanned the dark. "I managed to incapacitate one."

*"Incapaci-what?"*

"I didn't have time to incapacitate the other," he continued, clearly not worried about how odd his word choice was. "Figured I had a better chance to catch up with you so we're armed."

And he *had* caught up with her.

He'd fought off two armed men like he belonged in some sort of action spy movie, run fast enough to catch up with her and now, in his rumpled, torn suit, was holding a giant semiautomatic weapon as if he knew how to use it.

"Who *are* you?"

He flashed her that incongruous grin again, just barely visible in the night around them. "Well, clearly not who you think I am."

THEY WERE IN TROUBLE. Dylan would be less worried about being stuck he wasn't quite sure where in the dark if Vanessa wasn't pregnant and sporting a hell of a head injury. He couldn't let himself dwell on that too much. All he stood to lose.

No, a good soldier focused on the mission at hand, not the future.

He hadn't had a chance to put his real talents to use, he thought bitterly as he looked at the gun. Knocking out the first guy and getting his weapon had taken more time than Dylan cared to admit, and when the second guy had hopped into the van and tried to run him down, Dylan's best choice had been to run, not shoot like the sniper he'd been once upon a time.

"I need an explanation," Vanessa said, and he knew she wanted to sound strong and demanding, but he heard the tremor of fear in her voice.

How had this day gone so far to hell so fast?

"I don't really have one," he said softly. None of this made sense to him. A bank robbery was foolish, but they'd gotten away with it. Except they hadn't taken any money. They'd taken him and Vanessa.

"More of one than I do."

Dylan sighed. He couldn't see well in the dark, but he was fairly the certain the other man had lost him in the trees where his van couldn't follow and headlights couldn't penetrate deep enough.

Still, Dylan needed to be on alert until morning. Maybe with daylight he'd be able to figure out where they were and get them home.

Surely someone knew something was wrong at this point, with both him and Vanessa missing, Vanessa's car in the bank's parking lot. Adele was likely hurt—he had to accept that more-than-possibility, and she didn't have anyone waiting for her at home. But maybe she wasn't fatally hurt and—

"Dylan. Answers." Vanessa gritted her teeth, and he wondered if it was to keep them from chattering.

"Still no memory, then?"

She was silent for a few moments, except for the rustling of her fidgeting. "No. I... No. My last memory is that morning in the store with your dad, but if I try to come up with a year or how old I am, it all jumbles up.

Some things make sense and some don't." Her voice trembled at the end, and she didn't say more.

"You seem to be missing about a decade. More than, actually. I've been home from…college for ten years."

"Why'd you pause all weird before you said *college*?"

"I didn't," he replied, irritated that she'd picked up on that. "Now, can we focus on the here and now?"

"I have *amnesia* and lost ten years plus off my life and you—"

"Just fought off two armed men who wanted to kick us around and use us for ransom. In the best-case scenario. Now we're alone in the woods with no supplies or help. Do you have any idea where we are?"

"It's too dark. It's too…"

He wouldn't let her panic, so he spoke over her. "The way I figure it we drove south out of town, and kept on that way since the sun was setting into the window when we left. That puts us close to Carson territory. Maybe."

"Maybe. But none of this looks familiar to me."

"That's okay. We don't want to be moving around in the night anyway. In the morning we'll have a better idea." One way or another. "How are you feeling?"

"Am I really…?" She paused, then audibly swallowed.

"Pregnant? As far as I know. You came by the bank to tell me. That's when these men came in. I hope they didn't kill Adele." He muttered the last to himself. "I was too hard on her. Sharp mind, abrasive attitude, sure, but she was always a stellar employee. I should have…" Not the mission at hand though. He blew out a breath. "You need to rest. Tomorrow might be a bit of a rough day. We'll have a lot of walking to do."

He moved from a crouch to a seated position next to her. He positioned the gun so he was able to hold it and wrap his free arm around her shoulders.

She tensed and leaned away. "What are you doing?" she demanded.

"Being your makeshift pillow, sweetheart."

"You think I'm going to sleep on you?" She sounded so horrified it gave him some semblance of hope.

"You may not remember, but you've done a lot worse on me."

She recoiled, and he couldn't help but chuckle. "If it helps, on that front, I don't remember either. It is no exaggeration that the night we were together was the drunkest I've ever been. Somewhere during the reception my mind goes black." Maybe he had a few flashes here and there of soft sighs or the silk of her hair, but she didn't need to know that.

She didn't lean into him, but she'd stopped leaning away. "I…"

"It's going to be a chilly night. We'll keep each other warm. Hopefully, you catch a few hours sleep. We move at first light. No ulterior motives. Just common sense and getting through this…ordeal."

"Are they going to come after us?"

Dylan wanted to lie, to reassure her. It was strange to want to comfort Vanessa, but she wasn't herself. She was pregnant. With a bump on her head. And amnesia. She was a mess, and everything in him had softened completely at that.

Still, it was important she knew what they were up against. "I have no idea. Which is why you need to sleep, and I'll keep watch."

"Don't you need to sleep?"

"I'll be just fine."

She leaned into him, slowly, almost incrementally. Eventually, her head rested against his shoulder.

It felt oddly comforting.

"Where did you learn to fight?" she asked, her voice thick with exhaustion.

Briefly, he wondered if he should keep her awake because of concussion concerns, but she needed rest. She was *pregnant*. And they had no food or water. Surely rest was better, and it wasn't like they'd get much anyway.

He didn't answer her question, and when she didn't push, he figured she'd fallen asleep.

Funny, Vanessa was one of the few people who probably wouldn't be horrified by where he'd learned to fight, by all the lies he'd told. She'd love it.

She'd also tell his family with relish and glee, regardless of the accidental pregnancy.

Why that made him want to smile in the middle of this mess, he didn't have a clue.

# Chapter Four

## Back in Bent

Laurel Delaney parked her police cruiser in front of Delaney Bank and glanced at the man in the passenger seat.

Deputy Hart didn't know it yet, but she'd asked him to be her second on this call because soon enough she'd have to disclose her pregnancy to her superiors. They might let her continue to do some light detective work but not in the field. Desk duty. *Ugh.*

Regardless of how she felt at having to sit things out for *months*, Hart would be a good replacement for the duration of her desk duty and maternity leave. Yet that didn't make it easy to accept someone else taking the role she'd worked so hard for. Bent County only had one detective spot, and she loved it.

Sometimes you sacrificed what you loved for who you loved. She may have only just found out about this baby, but she already loved the child she and Grady had created with everything she was.

Which was why Hart would take the lead on this case. Probably best regardless of her physical condition, considering the man who'd called it in was her father.

Dad stood in front of the bank, looking grave and irritated. His patented look.

He didn't know about the pregnancy yet—no one but her and Grady did at this point. Dad wouldn't be happy. But then, nothing about his children's choices of significant others lately made him happy. Dylan and Jen were his only hopes. Laurel and Cam had been relegated to black sheep at best due to their choice to connect their lives with Carsons.

It hadn't been a choice, falling in love with Grady. Though she supposed they'd chosen to center their lives in that love.

Laurel sighed and gave Deputy Hart a thin smile. "I'd ask you to take the lead, but my dad is only going to want to deal with me."

Hart grinned. Laurel knew he cursed his baby face, but she thought it'd often work in his favor as a detective. People underestimated the sharp mind and conscientious attention to detail underneath. "I'm counting on it," he offered cheerfully.

Laurel rolled her eyes but got out of her car. Darkness had settled around the bank, but the lights were still on. She took a deep breath of fresh air and shored up her patience to deal with her father.

"Dad."

"Laurel." He didn't even give Hart a cursory look. "Took you long enough."

"You said it wasn't an emergency."

Dad merely shrugged. "Have you heard from Dylan?"

"No, but I wasn't expecting to. Why don't you tell me what you think happened?"

"I don't know what happened," Dad snapped. He smoothed out his features, clearly remembering that it wasn't just her in his audience. He had to play the role of upstanding Delaney for Deputy Hart. "I was driving home from the airport after my meeting in Denver. I passed the bank and saw the normal lights on instead of the security lights. So I pulled in, thinking someone had forgotten to switch over to closing lights, but the door was unlocked and no one was inside."

"And you suspect foul play?"

Dad pressed his lips together, a sure sign of irritation. "I don't know what to suspect. Neither your brother nor Adele will answer their phones. The safes are all closed and locked, and nothing appears out of place, but the evening paperwork wasn't done, so I can't be sure if every dollar is accounted for."

"So it was just Adele and Dylan working?" She nodded at Hart to start taking notes, pleased to see he already was. He was going to be a good replacement. Just hopefully not so good she couldn't get her detective spot back when she returned from maternity leave.

But that was so far away. She didn't need to think about it now.

"As far as I know. Adele was scheduled to close. Dylan wasn't scheduled, but it's not unheard of for him to be here until close. Still, we didn't have any meetings, and he tends to check in with the foreman at the ranch before the foreman's done at five."

"Why don't Hart and I take a look around? Have you been home to see if Dylan's there?"

"No, but I called George and he hadn't seen him."

Laurel felt the first little tickle of worry at the base of her spine. "Hart, I'll take the inside. You take the outside. Dad, do you have security tapes?"

He puffed out his chest. "Of course. I haven't had a chance to look at them. I called you once I realized my bank had been abandoned and unlocked for who knows how long."

"Pull up the footage," Laurel instructed, stepping inside. She began to look around the front counter. Though she'd never planned on following her father's footsteps at the bank, she'd spent some time working as a part-time teller when she'd been in the police academy, since Dad had refused to pay for that.

She knew her way around, and nothing appeared out of place. It didn't look like your typical burglary. Surely it had just been someone's mistake. She couldn't imagine her brother or Adele Oscar, one of Dad's higher-up employees, being that careless. But maybe if there'd been an emergency elsewhere?

Yet there was the gut feeling that had gotten her through her years as a deputy, and now as Bent County Sheriff's Department's detective, that told her something was off. That this was more than an oversight.

Hart appeared at the front doors. "There are two cars in the employee lot out back," he said. "You want to come see if you recognize them?"

Laurel nodded and motioned Hart to follow her through the back hall that would cut through the bank to the back lot. She passed Dad's office and stopped when she saw him scowling and punching at the computer keys.

He looked up and, though his face was scowling and angry, she saw the hint of worry in his gaze. "I'm not sure what happened, but there's no footage today. It appears the cameras were turned off last night."

"Purposeful?"

Dad shrugged. "I don't know. I suppose it could be an accident, but whoever did it had access."

"I'll need a list of anyone who has access and opportunity to turn on or off the cameras. Hart, sit down with him and write down everyone who had access. I'm going to check out the cars." She moved through the back hallway briskly, that gut feeling diving deeper.

She immediately recognized the first vehicle, her brother's sleek sports car. It was enough to make her feel uneasy. Why would Dylan have left his car behind? Still, she could have come up with a few reasons. But the second car, parked farther down, made her stomach flip over in absolute police-level concern.

What was Vanessa Carson's car doing in the Delaney Bank parking lot? That wasn't just abnormal—it was unheard of.

Laurel immediately pulled out her phone. When the rough voice answered, the noise of his saloon a steady hum behind him, she couldn't smile like she usually did. "Grady."

"What's up, princess?"

The nickname didn't bug her anymore, but this feeling did. "Have you seen Vanessa today?"

"Van? Hmm. Guess not, but I wasn't expecting to." There was a pause. "What is it?"

"I'm not sure. Can you send someone to see if she's at her shop and give me a call back?"

"Laurel, do I need to be worried?"

It was her turn to pause. "I'm not sure."

"But you are. Worried, that is."

"Call me back, okay? Love you."

"Laur—"

She couldn't sit on the phone and argue with her husband. She marched back inside to her father's office. "It's Dylan's car and Vanessa Carson's."

Hart's eyebrows rose and Dad's face turned a mottled red.

"Are you telling me—"

"I'm telling you those are the cars left in the lot, and both people are unaccounted for. We need to find Adele Oscar. If she was working, and her car's gone, we need her story. If she won't answer her phone, we'll have to go find her."

Hart nodded. Laurel looked at her father. "Lock up. Go home. I'll let you know when I've got more information."

"I demand—"

"Go home, Dad. Let us investigate." She pushed Hart toward the front doors and to the police car.

She had a bad feeling Adele Oscar had something to do with this weirdness. Now they just had to find her.

# *Chapter Five*

Vanessa awoke to a barrage of bad feelings. Pain, sharp and relentless, in her head and against her eyes. A roiling queasiness that seemed more familiar than not. Hunger. And a nasty crick in her neck.

She groaned in protest as her bed seemed to move out from under her. When she opened her eyes against the warm glow of sunrise, she realized she wasn't lying on a bed. She was on the cold, hard ground, curled around and tangled up in a very warm and comfortable Dylan Delaney.

He was staring at her, and she could only stare back, because if she moved she would throw up.

There was a prickle at the base of her spine, and a warm wave of…something low in her stomach.

His eyes were dark brown, closer to black. Had she ever noticed that before? He had the scrape of a five-o'clock shadow, which still didn't hide that sharp cut of his jaw. She had the insane urge to touch her fingers to his cheek to see if the bristle of whiskers would be as rough as it looked, if his cheekbones were really that sharp.

It was something elemental inside her, as if she simply belonged here and he belonged there. She should touch him because he was hers, looking dangerous almost. Like a pirate or an outlaw out of time. As if he'd whisk her away and she'd never fight back, because this was exactly—

Dylan Delaney? Dangerous? Her not fight back? What a laugh. She was clearly delirious.

"It's morning," she managed to say when he didn't move or say anything, just kept staring at her with dark eyes that seemed to go on forever, a century of secrets and longing.

Some bump on the head she had.

"That it is." Carefully, with a gentleness that touched her even though it shouldn't, he disentangled himself and got to his feet. Then he held out a hand and pulled her up.

She closed her eyes against the wave of nausea, tried to swallow against her cottony mouth.

"You don't look so good."

She wanted to be insulted, but she felt way worse than that.

"I want you to stay here," Dylan instructed.

Normally, instructions got her back up, especially delivered by a high-and-mighty Delaney, but there was something about his that made her feel safe.

"I'm going to find some water," he continued. "You stay put and look around and think about if anything looks familiar, okay? The gun is right there if you need it."

Again, some part of her brain insisted she argue with him, but it was buried deep underneath a fog of exhaustion. "Okay."

He nodded and headed off for the pines.

"Wait. How will you find your way back?"

His mouth curved, that ironic twist of humor she had yet to figure out. "I'll manage."

She wanted to believe he was stupid. That he'd get lost and she'd be left alone. That'd be preferable, wouldn't it? Fending for herself rather than teaming up with a Delaney.

But as he disappeared, panic bubbled in her chest. Just about any company was better than no company in this particular situation.

She tried to focus on the task he'd given her. Find something familiar. But the aspens and pines and rocks could be any in Bent County.

The sky was blue, the sun slowly warming up the air. Maybe they weren't even in Bent County. Maybe they weren't even in *Wyoming*.

She wrapped her arms around herself, trying to squeeze away the panic.

Would she know where she was if she wasn't missing chunks of time? She closed her eyes, trying to work through the years that were apparently missing.

But all she saw was Dylan's face. The dark whiskers, his dark eyes. Something lurking behind them that called to something inside of her. A certainty and a calmness that steadied her when she wanted to fall apart.

She didn't want him to find his way back, or so she told herself, but she knew he would. She was certain he'd return with water and that enviable certainty.

She was hungry and thirsty and *insane*. She opened her eyes, shook away Dylan's face and focused on survival.

He was going to find some water. Even if his crazy story about her being pregnant was true, she could survive a few days without food. But she needed water.

She sucked a breath in, then out, finding deep breaths helped the queasiness.

Pregnant. She placed a hand over her stomach, trying to divine if there was any truth to it. Sure, queasiness could be morning sickness, but couldn't it also be the aftereffects of the blow to the head? Couldn't that account for the exhaustion, as well?

Wouldn't she know on some deep maternal level if there was a human being growing inside her? She didn't know. She didn't feel certain either way.

But why would Dylan make up this ridiculous story about being the father of her supposed unborn baby? He wouldn't want that, even as a joke. Even if she was missing chunks of time, there was no way her feelings about Dylan, or his about her, had changed so drastically either of them would want to be parents together.

She gingerly touched a finger to the knot on her head, then winced at the pain from even the lightest touch.

Everything was so messed up, and instead of being her usual alert, tough, kick-butt self, she felt like a blob of uselessness.

She leaned against the tree, then went ahead and slid to the ground so she was sitting next to the gun Dylan had propped against it. What could she do but sit here and wait? Cry? She certainly wanted to, but she'd never let a Delaney see her cry if she could help it.

So she breathed. She kept looking around the small clearing trying to find something familiar, and she waited. She listened for footsteps and Dylan's return, but she heard nothing except wind and occasionally the faint sounds of scurrying.

Something puttered nearby. Wait. Was that a car? Definitely an engine. Slowly, Vanessa got to her feet. She began to follow the noise, leaving herself a trail to get back to the clearing, because she knew a thing or two about not getting lost in the woods or mountains.

It didn't take her long to get to what appeared to be a road. Dirty and bumpy. Clearly not used often, but similar to the one that ran up to the Carson cabin. Again, she looked around. She wasn't near her family's cabin, she didn't think, but they were definitely in the mountains. Isolated.

And then, almost as if she were walking through a dream, a car appeared. A sleek sedan, so out of place in the rough yet breathtaking Wyoming mountains. She *was* in Wyoming. Somewhere close to home. She had to believe that.

The sedan rolled to a stop, and the tinted driver's-side window slid down. The woman's face behind the steering wheel didn't look familiar. Vanessa squinted at her, searching for some kind of recognition.

"Hello there." The woman smiled, though it struck Vanessa as too sharp for friendliness.

"Hi."

"You seem..." The woman trailed off and looked around. "Lost. Alone."

"I'm not alone."

"Oh?"

Something about the way the woman jumped on that made Vanessa nervous, and really made her wish she'd thought to bring the gun. Silly. What could this woman do to her? She was help. Salvation maybe.

"We are lost though. Do you have a phone so I could call someone we know to come get us?" If she remembered anyone's number—the ranch. She knew the number to the ranch. Surely that hadn't changed, if it had really been years since she could remember. Noah or Ty would help her.

"I'm afraid it doesn't have any service up here." The woman's expression changed, but Vanessa couldn't read it. There was an element of sheepishness to the shrug, but it was too...pointed.

Vanessa took a step back from the car.

"I can give you a ride back to town," the woman offered. "If that's where you want to go. I was headed up to my cabin, but you look like you need some help."

Vanessa glanced back at the pines. She could take the offer, and then send someone back to get Dylan. Surely it'd be the smart, rational thing to do. Wasn't she positive Dylan could take care of himself?

"What town?"

The woman cocked her head. "Are you okay?"

"Could you wait?" she asked, wincing at her own idiocy. "I just need to get the man I'm stranded with."

The woman studied her. "You've got quite the bump on your face. You sure you want to get him, Vanessa?"

"He had nothing— You know me."

The woman's eyebrows drew together. "Of course I know you. I know we're not exactly *friends* or anything, but I've lived in Bent since I took a job at the bank."

Vanessa took another step back. Her instincts were all off, but this felt wrong. Of course Dylan Delaney felt right, which *had* to be wrong.

Nothing made sense. Nothing. The mention of the bank made her stomach clench—not in its normal disdainful way when faced with anything having to do with Delaneys either. Something closer to fear.

"You're hurt," the woman said, and though her voice itself was gentle, something in the tone was harsh, grating. "And scared. Let me take you into town. To Rightful Claim. Oh, wait, your brother doesn't live there anymore, does he?"

"I…" Grady. Grady didn't live above Rightful Claim anymore? The saloon he ran was his heart and soul. Where would he have gone? The Carson ranch, maybe. She opened her mouth to ask, but then decided better of it. She didn't know this woman, and no matter what she knew about Vanessa, she gave her an uncomfortable feeling. Vanessa had never been one for parading her weaknesses to strangers, and this weird memory loss was quite the weakness.

She might be all messed up in the head, but she'd always trusted her uncomfortable gut feelings before. Head injury or not, some form of amnesia or not, she had to trust her internal feelings of right and wrong.

"Vanessa!"

It was Dylan's voice. She wanted to run toward it, no matter how little sense that made. "Hold on," she mumbled to the woman. She walked back the way she'd come. "Dylan! I found a road."

It only took a few minutes before Dylan appeared, something like fury dug into the lines in his face. Until he saw the car. He rushed toward it.

"Adele."

That name rang some bell deep underneath the fog in Vanessa's brain, but the woman's face still didn't. But Dylan knew her. Maybe Vanessa should be relieved.

But all she could feel was regret he hadn't grabbed the gun she'd left behind.

"You're all right," Dylan said to the woman, coming to a stop just a few paces in front of the car. Surprise and then something like suspicion flashed over his face. He glanced at Vanessa, then back to the driver.

"We're just worried sick, Dylan," the woman said, suddenly sounding scared and just that. Worried sick. "What on earth happened?"

Vanessa frowned at the woman. She'd changed her tune now that Dylan was here. Put on this little panicked act. She hadn't been at all panicked or surprised before.

Vanessa didn't buy it for a second. "I—"

"You'll drive us back into town, then," Dylan said with

that commanding tone of voice that made Vanessa want to roll her eyes. *Men.* Delaney men at that.

But he hadn't grabbed the gun and this felt all wrong. He needed to know, to see something wasn't right. "Dylan—"

He was already opening the car door to the back seat. "Adele will drive us back to town." He took Vanessa's arm, pulling her to the car. "She works for me at the bank. She'll get us back."

"Dylan," Vanessa hissed as he pushed her gently into the back seat. "I don't think—"

He slid inside next to her. "To the hospital, Adele. Vanessa needs to be checked out."

"Of course."

Vanessa didn't trust the odd smile Adele flashed into the rearview mirror, but she kept her mouth shut.

DYLAN FIDGETED—SOMETHING he almost never did. But the fact Adele was safe and whole, and here, struck him as wrong. It had all his senses on high alert, waiting for trouble.

Beggars couldn't be choosers though, and Vanessa needed a hospital, enough so he didn't think it prudent to wait to go retrieve the gun he had left. Once he got Vanessa checked out, he'd be talking to Laurel about what had happened anyway.

Besides, what could one middle-aged woman do to the two of them? He didn't consider himself invincible or anything, but two-against-one odds were already in his favor. Add his military training and he was sure they were good, even if she had a weapon.

Weapon? Adele? This was ridiculous. What reason would Adele have to hurt them? She'd worked for Delaney Bank for over a decade and slowly worked her way up the ladder. She could be a little harsh and abrasive, but she did her work meticulously. She was devoted to the bank, which he'd always assumed meant she was devoted to the Delaneys.

"Lucky thing you two were on the road up to the cabin I rented for my vacation," Adele said. "Not sure what might have happened to you if I hadn't come along. Fate sure is a funny thing."

"You weren't scheduled for a vacation," Dylan said. Though Adele was technically in charge of creating the schedule, Dylan oversaw it. Knew it by heart. It was a habit he'd been taught by his father. *Always know who's in charge of what.* Dad did it to lord mistakes over people. Dylan had never been comfortable with that reason, but he made sure to know nonetheless. He never knew what that made him.

"Oh, I worked it out with your father," Adele said, her voice still overly cheerful. Not like her, and not at all appropriate for the situation.

Worse, as she drove she kept climbing the mountain. She didn't ask any questions about why they were wandering around the mountains lost, or why he had bruises on his face or why Vanessa had a bump on her head and needed a hospital.

Dylan realized far too late his worry over Vanessa's—and the baby's—health had caused him to make a very rash decision.

But this was Adele. He'd worked with Adele since he'd come back to Bent. It wasn't like they were best friends or anything, but he knew her. He and his dad had trusted her with all manner of bank business. Surely his instincts were going haywire because he was worried, because he was confused.

Because Vanessa Carson had dropped the bomb that

she was pregnant with his child minutes before they'd been kidnapped. Of course things didn't feel right. None of this was right.

But he couldn't convince himself this gnawing pit of doom opening up in his gut was something other than a premonition.

"Town's the opposite way," he noted. Not because he knew where they were, but because he knew going *up* the mountain definitely wasn't heading toward any town.

"Nowhere to turn around yet. Be patient." She flicked him a glance in the rearview mirror. "Isn't that what your father is always saying? 'Patience, Adele,'" she said, the last two words a low imitation of his father's voice.

Then she laughed.

Dylan didn't dare look at Vanessa, but with an unerringness that surprised even him, he found her hand and curled his around it. He could feel the tension radiating off her. She might not remember Adele with a portion of her memory missing, but she could feel how wrong this all was too.

And it was his fault. This whole thing from top to bottom. He couldn't even work up the righteous anger that Vanessa hadn't listened to him back at the bank and stayed in his office. He wouldn't have. How could he have expected her to?

Now they were in danger. No matter how he tried to convince himself he could handle Adele and that she wasn't out to get them, every cell of his being screamed otherwise.

She finally pulled up in front of a cabin. It looked like a fairly new construction and was completely isolated. It wasn't part of a cluster of cabins rented out to the odd tourist, and it wasn't like the Carson cabin, a ramshackle nod to the past.

"Adele. She needs a hospital," Dylan said calmly, clearly, keeping Vanessa's hand in his. He could overtake Adele. Drive Vanessa himself. He didn't want to hurt Adele, but he could, and he would if it meant getting Vanessa help. Getting their baby help.

Adele pushed the car into Park and then gave the horn a little honk. She looked over her shoulder at him, looking vaguely sympathetic. "I know. I really am sorry about this whole thing."

"Adele…"

But he trailed off when she pointed to the door of the cabin. His heart sank when the two men who'd kidnapped them stepped out. One still with his gun, the other bandaged and holding a rifle. Both unmasked this time around.

*Hell.*

# *Chapter Six*

Vanessa could only stare at the two burly men standing in the doorway. This was bad. Still, with Dylan holding her hand in his larger one, she felt safe.

*You are so very not safe, moron.*

Adele turned around to face them, and this time her expression was one of pure contrition. Vanessa didn't know why she didn't believe it, but she flat out didn't.

"I'm so sorry," Adele said, keeping her gaze on Dylan. "I had to," she whispered.

"You had to what?" Dylan demanded, his voice sharp as a blade. It made Vanessa shiver. No matter how uncharacteristic this was of the Dylan she knew, or thought she knew, she wouldn't cross *this* man.

Apparently, Adele had no problems doing so though. "They told me I had to find you, and I had to bring you back to them. They threatened my life. I didn't have a choice."

"A choice? You were in a car by yourself! You could have gone to town and—"

She shook her head sadly. "You don't understand, Dylan. I'm afraid you're going to have to go along with this. Now, don't worry. They assured me they won't hurt us. A ransom is all they're after. We just have to do what they say."

"Why didn't they hurt you?" Vanessa demanded. Both Dylan and Adele blinked over at her. But the fact of the matter was, Adele was unscathed and she and Dylan were not.

"I went along with everything they said," Adele replied, a slight edge to her voice. It softened with her next words though. "If we all do, we get out of this alive."

"How can you be so sure?"

"So far, so good. Come on, get out before they drag you out." Adele looked at Vanessa. "We wouldn't want that, would we?" As if she knew Vanessa was pregnant.

How would she know? Surely she couldn't divine that simply from Dylan saying she needed a hospital.

Adele got out of the driver's seat and held up her hands as she walked over to the two men, as if in surrender. Then all three of them watched Dylan and Vanessa climb out of the car.

"None of this adds up," Vanessa muttered as they stood, almost in a face-off with the men a few yards away.

"No. It doesn't," Dylan agreed. "But for the time being, Adele is right. If we play along, they won't hurt us." He nudged her gently forward.

Vanessa gave a pointed look at all the wounds on his face as they trudged their way toward the cabin.

He shrugged. "A few bruises won't kill me. They'll have food and water. Shelter. A ransom requires keeping us alive. Right now, since we can't get medical attention, getting you food and water is the most important thing. If this is dangerous, I'll find a way to get us out. For the time being, you'll get to rest and be cared for."

It was very strange to have someone looking out for her. Oh, she had a big brother and two cousins who'd lay down their lives for hers. But they weren't the fussy sort.

None of the Carsons were. They'd protect and defend, but they wouldn't think to put getting her rest above their other objectives.

"Good job delaying the inevitable," one of the men said with a happy grin. "Welcome home, friends." He was covered in bandages, clearly the man Dylan had "incapacitated."

Vanessa didn't like the gleam in his eye. Not out of fear for herself but fear for Dylan. It didn't matter that she *hated* Dylan, and she was sure she did. Once this was all over and her memory returned, the hate would come back and everything would make sense. She wouldn't care about Dylan's well-being at all.

But in that car he'd held her hand. In this short walk to the men waiting for them with gleaming smiles and guns, he'd expressed concern over her well-being.

Because she was pregnant. Allegedly. And the baby was his. Supposedly. That must have been why he felt the need to take care of her. If it was all true, he was only protecting what was his.

Vanessa was unaccountably tired all of a sudden. She even swayed on her feet against her will. But Dylan held her up.

A Delaney held her up. She couldn't believe what was happening.

"She needs a place to rest. Water. Food."

"Don't recall you being the one in charge here, friend," the man with the bandages said to Dylan. "Best you remember that before we do another number on your face."

"Seems like he did a number on you," Vanessa muttered before she thought better of it.

"Boss didn't say anything about you pulling in a hefty ransom. You might be useless to us."

Dylan stepped forward, even as the barrel of both

weapons pointed at him. "You lay one hand on her, you'll pay in every possible way for a man to pay. I don't care how many guns you point at me."

Something poked through the fog in her brain. That same image of Dylan facing down deadly weapons but in a different place.

Adele laughed nervously, and the image skittered away. "Wh-why don't we all calm down? No one wants to get hurt." Dylan spared her a glance that would have melted steel. Adele cleared her throat. "What do we need to do to get out of here?"

Vanessa didn't trust the way this woman spoke to men with guns. It wasn't placating. There was no fear. She seemed in perfect control. A mask, maybe, but it wasn't a mask that made Vanessa comfortable.

"Inside," the bandaged man said. He took Adele's arm and nudged her in, then did the same to Vanessa.

She jerked her arm away from his sweaty grasp, but he grabbed her again and gave her a shake that had her teeth rattling against each other.

"I ain't afraid to knock you around, tough girl."

Fury razed all the confusion and exhaustion. Knock her around? She'd like to see him try. She struggled to free herself from his meaty grip. "I—"

Dylan's hand rested at the small of her back, a quiet plea to stop fighting. Even with her heart racing and anger starting to fire through her blood beyond reason and control, the slight pressure of Dylan's big hand reminded her that she wanted to stay alive, no matter how much her temper strained.

She took a deep breath and let her arm go limp against the hand wrapped around it. The goon gave her a good shove inside the cabin, and though she stumbled, she managed to stay upright. She skidded to a stop next to

Adele, and noted with more suspicion that Adele didn't even try to stop her skidding slide. Just watched.

Too clinical. Too detached. She was no victim here. Vanessa was almost sure of it.

"Now you, *friend*." The bandaged man grabbed Dylan by the shirtfront and tossed him inside, hard. Dylan fell gracefully, an easy roll that nearly reminded her of a dancer.

*Seriously. Who is this guy?*

He was up on his feet in seconds.

"Now, before we get settled, let's get one thing straight. I'm in charge here." The man pointed his gun at Dylan's heart. "You do what I say, or they die." The gun moved to train on Vanessa, but the man's eyes stayed on Dylan. "You're the only one worth anything to me, with your rich daddy."

"You have no idea who you're messing with."

The butt of the weapon hit Dylan's face with a sickening crack. Vanessa cried out and rushed forward, but the second man shook his head and tsk-tsked, his gun pointed right at her chest.

Dylan got to his feet. "Takes a little more than a pathetic sucker shot to keep me down, you worthless piece of—"

The man raised his weapon again, and Vanessa couldn't just sit back and watch any longer. Heart pounding against her ribs, but with a clarity she hadn't felt since she'd woken up in that van, she jumped forward.

"Wait!"

Everyone looked at her. She didn't know what to say. She'd dealt with violence her whole life, but she'd never been any good at defusing a situation. She was more the stir-it-up type. But things changed. Life changed. She *had* to diffuse this one whether she was any good at it or not.

"We all want to live." She stepped forward again, though she was still behind Dylan. She watched the guns pointed at them warily as she did exactly what he'd done to her.

She lifted her hand and placed it gently if firmly against his back. It was rock hard, like iron. He was tense and ready to fight, but as much as she didn't trust Adele or this situation, she knew two armed men were dangerous. They all had to play this with smarts more than muscle. And she'd had a lifetime of experience doing that.

Though she wouldn't mind finding out a little more about Dylan's impressive muscle.

Where had *that* idiotic thought come from?

"Let's all calm down," she said in a low, controlled voice, far more for Dylan than the bad guys in front of them.

Dylan's chin jutted out, but he flashed a glance at her. Fury. An edgy flash of violence that should have seemed incongruous on Dylan Delaney's perfect face. In this moment, however, it just felt right.

DYLAN WANTED TO pound these two brain-dead barbarians to dust. He could too. They might be bigger, they might have weapons, but he had no doubt he could take them both out. He could even visualize it. A sweep kick here, use one goon's body to slam into the second. A quick gut punch, twist the rifle and use it to knock out the other. Blood. Bones cracking. Victory.

But what he could also visualize in his taking them out was them having an opportunity to hurt Vanessa or Adele. The two women were, very unfortunately, distractions and weaknesses he couldn't afford to ignore.

He let Vanessa's firm pressure on his back be a kind

of anchor. He had to think with his brain, not his temper. He even had to be careful not to let his instincts take over.

Because he wasn't surrounded by soldiers. He was surrounded by civilians. Their safety was paramount. Not his.

He turned to face Vanessa, ignoring the men with guns at his back. Her hand fell to her side and she looked at him with a whole slew of emotions in her dark eyes. Not the norm for her. Vanessa usually kept everything locked down.

But there were men with guns, a head injury, amnesia and the fact—whether she believed it or not—she was carrying his baby.

He couldn't lose his temper. He had to be methodical. Like he'd said to her outside, this was the best option right now. Get her taken care of, even if it was by hostage takers, and then he'd find a way for them to escape. No matter what they said or did, he had to be calm. He had to summon all that sniper calm he'd developed and use it here.

He glanced at Adele.

She stood a little behind both of them. He noted she was dressed in jeans and a long-sleeved T-shirt. Not what she would have been wearing at the bank last night. She watched Vanessa with a certain kind of speculation that made the hairs on the back of his neck tingle.

*Calculating* was the word that came to mind. Not exactly out of character for Adele. She was the calculating sort, but her high opinion of her intelligence often undermined her calculations.

Besides, maybe she was calculating how to get the heck out of the situation, same as he. As much as his instincts warned him something was off with Adele, his brain reasoned it away time and time again.

He was a man who'd spent a chunk of years living by his instincts and pure grit. Had that dulled in these last few years of doing what his father had demanded of him? Had all the fine edges he'd honed inside of himself—so he could live without suffocating in the box his name dictated—softened and been lost?

Now wasn't the time for an identity crisis. He had two women to save and two goons to fight.

He turned to the goons, calm now. Ready to *battle* rather than fight. Fight was instantaneous, with no real endgame. It was anger and revenge. A battle was all about winning. It was about getting these women safe, and making the world—even this tiny corner of it—a righted place.

He would win. Not just for himself, but for this future *child* that would somehow be a part of him. And Vanessa.

Who had to be taken care of at all costs.

"What's the plan, then?" he asked calmly. He'd treat it like a business meeting. They'd discuss what they wanted. He'd discuss what he wanted.

And when he had a good opening, he'd make them wish they'd never been born.

The two men looked at each other, and Dylan didn't have to be a mind reader to understand they weren't the designers of this little plot. They were here for muscle and muscle only.

But who was the boss?

"You two in that room," one said, pointing a gun at a door. "You—" he pointed to Adele "—in that one."

Dylan frowned. It was stupid to split them up. The glossy-looking doors to the rooms weren't at all intimidating, and surely there were windows in the room. He almost asked them if they were sure that's how they wanted to play it, then rolled his eyes at himself.

Adele shuffled off to her room, so Dylan took Vanessa's arm and led her to the other one. He pushed open the door to find what appeared to be an office. There were windows, but they were narrow and lined the very top of the wall. There was no way they could maneuver out of them, even if they could get up there.

One of the men had followed them inside. Dylan eyed him.

"Water. Food. You want me alive, I'll need both," he said, unable to soften the demand into something less abrasive.

"You'll get both. When I'm good and ready." The man slammed the door, the click of a lock echoing in the room.

It was clearly someone's office. Dylan wondered if they'd be able to figure out who if they snooped enough.

But first things first. He led Vanessa to the most comfortable-looking chair, a rolling, leather desk contraption that at least had some padding. He nudged her into it and, though she went willingly, he saw a flash of the old Vanessa in her expression.

She was still pale with exhaustion, and yet there was a clarity to her eyes that had been missing.

"Your employee is in on this," she said firmly.

Dylan hedged. *In on this* seemed a bit much, and yet... "Something is definitely fishy."

"It's her. All her. When I first stumbled onto her on the road, she didn't act worried or nervous at all. She was very calm and seemed to want me to leave you behind. I didn't know she knew me at first. Then you came and her tune totally changed. *'Oh, we've been worried sick,'*" she mimicked.

Dylan's jaw clenched. "It's off. But..."

"It's *her*," Vanessa insisted.

He nodded. "All right. She's mixed up in it somehow."

He could explain away almost everything. Except the change of clothes. If she was as much a victim as they, she'd be in her bank clothes just like he was.

He shrugged out of the now-tattered suit jacket and laid it across Vanessa's lap. "You need water, food and rest." What she really needed was a doctor. He'd find a way. He *would*. "We should look around. See if we can figure out who owns this place."

She looked up at the windows, and he could see her come to the same conclusion he had. There was no getting out that way. "We have to get out of here."

"We will. My father will pay—"

"The ransom business is crap. You know it and I know it. There's more to this than money, and even if Daddy Big Bucks would pay, I don't think Laurel and her precious police department would feel the same."

"I think the people we love would do anything to keep us safe."

"Keep *you* safe, goose."

Dylan wanted to laugh, but there was something vulnerable in the words no matter how sharply she said them. He crouched in front of her, took her hands in his and squeezed. He noted the surprise and suspicion in her eyes, and ignored both.

"No matter what you remember or don't, you know your brother would move heaven and earth to keep you safe. If he knows you're missing, he's out there looking for you. Noah and Ty too."

"They'd have to know I was missing."

"They will. Soon enough."

# *Chapter Seven*

*Back in Bent, Vanessa's mechanic shop*

"She wouldn't."

Laurel looked at the firm, furious line of her husband's mouth and rubbed at the headache pounding at her temples. As much as she agreed with Grady's estimation of Vanessa not leaving town on her own, his lack of cooperation was grating on her nerves.

Grady had let them into Vanessa's place to look around, and while there weren't any cut-and-dried clues, her motorcycle was missing. Everything else was where it should be. Hart's supposition that Vanessa had left of her own accord on said motorcycle had not gone over well with Laurel's husband.

"Hart isn't asking if she *did* skip town, since we don't know," Laurel said, keeping her voice calm and no-nonsense. "We're asking what you think it would take for Vanessa to leave without telling anyone."

"It wouldn't take anything, because Vanessa wouldn't take off without a word to anyone no matter what was up." He lifted the bill from an ob-gyn's office in Fremont they'd found when searching her above-the-shop apartment. "Pregnancy wouldn't be a reason. She knows we'd support her. No matter what. She wouldn't be *scared* or running from anything."

Laurel had to keep her mouth shut. Since she'd been dealing with her own, there'd been a few times in the past few weeks she'd looked at Vanessa and wondered. Yet Vanessa had been with no man, and showed no signs of telling her family about her condition. So, *obviously*, it wasn't totally clear-cut knowing she'd be supported.

But Grady continued to thunder his irritation. Luckily, Laurel knew enough about her husband to understand that was bluster covering up his fear. She couldn't afford to be soft, but it was hard when she was worried too.

"She sure as hell wouldn't have disappeared on her *motorcycle* and left her car at the Delaney Bank of all places," Grady continued furiously.

"Easy highway access," Hart countered, impressing Laurel with how even and calm he was being in the face of Grady's notable temper. "Kind of hidden. If she didn't want to be—"

Grady growled and Laurel pressed a hand to his chest. He was angry, but that anger hid a deep worry and fear. She felt it too. It had been a long time since she and Vanessa had been friends. Even marrying Grady hadn't smoothed things over from their teenage years, though it had softened some of the edge.

The Vanessa she knew—thought she knew anyway—wouldn't run away from anything. And if Laurel thought about *Vanessa*, she didn't have to think about the fact her brother was missing too. Without thinking the move through she pressed a hand to her stomach.

She heard Grady's sigh as his arm came around her shoulders. Despite her uniform, and the fact she was here in an official capacity, he pressed a kiss to her temple.

"What can we *do*?" he asked.

It helped ease a tiny fraction of tension in Laurel that he asked it of Hart, and helped her anxiety even more when Hart answered, plainly and certainly.

"You trust me to investigate." He smiled a little sheepishly. "And Laurel, of course. If you find any hints of what might be going on with Vanessa, you tell the police. Give the same instructions to any and all family members. Work with us. We want everyone home and safe, same as you."

Laurel's phone trilled. She would have ignored it, but the Delaney Ranch's number gave her stomach a little jolt. She answered, stepping away from Grady's arm.

"Laurel?"

She frowned at the grave tone in her father's greeting. "What is it?"

"I was catching up on my email," Dad began. "I hadn't had a chance to check since I'd been driving home from the airport, then I was distracted last night, obviously. I have one from Dylan dated yesterday that says he'll be gone for a while. No explanation. Just that he had to leave town."

"Forward it," Laurel said automatically, ending the call to wait for the email.

"Dad has an email from Dylan dated yesterday saying he'd be out of town for a while. He's forwarding it to me."

"Maybe they ran off together," Hart said, gesturing to Vanessa's place.

Grady snorted. "Sure. I mean, maybe to murder each other. But definitely not *together*."

"Erm…"

Laurel stared at Hart, noticing the odd flush to his cheeks. "Erm *what*?" she demanded.

"Well, it's just…" He cleared his throat. "They didn't

exactly look murderous at your wedding reception. Quite the opposite."

Both Grady and Laurel stared at Hart with matching dumbfounded expressions.

"You know, I left early because I had the early shift the next morning, and I happened to see them leave together."

Laurel rolled her eyes. "Maybe they left at the same time, but not *together*. They were probably arguing on their way out."

"Oh, no. They were very much together and very much not arguing. Hard to argue when you've got your tongues down each other's throats. I gave them a ride back to Vanessa's because they were far too drunk to drive." Hart nodded at the medical bill Grady had tossed back onto the desk earlier.

"No." Laurel and Grady gasped in unison.

Her upstanding, somewhat-inflexible brother would never... He'd never... She glanced at Grady. There'd been a time *she'd* have never, but she'd never cared about the feud the way Dylan did.

"Seriously though, they were drunk as skunks," Hart continued. "Believe you me. Definitely on the road to a bad decision. Maybe even one with consequences. Could be they ran off together to deal with them."

Laurel looked up at Grady. It made a strange kind of sense, even though she couldn't truly believe it. Vanessa and Dylan. It had to be impossible.

"Impossible," Grady confirmed, as if reading her thoughts.

Her phone's incoming-email sound dinged and Laurel shook her head. She had to focus on fact, not supposition.

She pulled up the forwarded email and read the words with a frown.

Be gone for a bit. Don't worry. Explain when I get back. Adele can cover at the bank for me. —Dylan

She showed Hart, then Grady.

"Except Adele is missing too," Hart pointed out.

"Nothing adds up," Laurel said, staring at the email. While she could see Vanessa skipping town on her motorcycle, she couldn't see her doing it without tying up loose ends at her shop. And Dylan would never leave the bank so abruptly—especially unlocked.

But she felt a niggle of concern over the possibility Dylan and Vanessa had hooked up drunkenly at her wedding, conceived a child and were now both missing. They'd be embarrassed. Probably horrified. Enough to skip town?

But Adele Oscar was the thing that threw a wrench into all this. Laurel and Hart had been by her house last night and this morning. She hadn't been home. Everything had been locked and secure, and her car hadn't been seen, though they'd put out an APB.

"We need to find Adele Oscar," Hart said. "Search warrant for her house?"

Laurel nodded. Adele was the key.

# Chapter Eight

A little while later, after watching Dylan meticulously search through everything in the room, then stalk around it, reminding her of a wolf—or some other dangerous predator—the door swung open.

The man she'd come to think of as Eyeballs, because his were the size of saucers, tossed a paper plate onto the desk. Then threw a bottle of water at Dylan. Hard.

Dylan caught it without a flinch, which made Eyeballs scowl. Without a word, Eyeballs closed the door and locked it again.

The heavy, almost chemical smell of the microwave pizza pocket made Vanessa dry heave, but she didn't throw up. That was a plus.

Dylan watched her with both concern and a kind of detached study. "You have to eat it," he said after a few seconds.

"Eating it won't help if I just throw it all up."

"You don't know that. Plus, vomit might be an excellent diversion."

She laughed against her will, but it died quickly when he crouched in front of her again, holding the plate with the offensive microwave meal in one hand. He held out the water bottle with the other.

"This atrocity is still frozen in the middle, but I'm

going to break off a small piece of the cooked edge. Eat. Drink. That should help keep it down."

"I don't need you to feed me." But she took the water, even as she eyed his movements warily.

He watched her with those steady brown eyes. Something in her chest fluttered—a light, airy feeling directly in contrast with their situation. With how she'd always felt about Dylan.

He disgusted her. He made her sneer. He made her *hate*. She had never had one positive feeling toward Dylan or one positive interaction with him.

But in the past twenty-four hours, he'd displayed a warmth she'd never seen and a resourceful strength she never would have believed. The man had fought off two armed men, and if not for her, and perhaps Adele, she had no doubt he'd be back in Bent, having happily dispatched all the bad guys.

Maybe it was just the beard that made her feel differently toward him. She was a sucker for beards, and his scruff was growing in fast and full and handsome.

She'd rather blame facial hair than her previous conclusions about him being wrong.

He broke off a piece of the gummy crust and held it up to her lips. Their eyes met, held. Something shuddered through her. She wanted to believe it was doom, gloom and hell, but it was lighter, sweeter, and some foreign part of her wanted to lean into it.

She could see him, clean-shaven and harsh-looking, in the dim light of another room. A flash of something. Hands on her face. He wasn't touching her, but she could feel him. She could remember the register of shock at—

"You have a tattoo."

He raised an eyebrow, slipped the food into her mouth.

She chewed and swallowed, so distracted by that odd flash of memory her stomach didn't even turn.

"Do I?"

"I couldn't make it out. It was dark. But you were shirtless. And you had a tattoo." It wasn't the first little burst of memory she'd had, but it was the clearest. And the most nonsensical. "Fill in the blanks for me."

He pulled off another piece of the crust, held it up to her mouth. "I don't know your blanks, Vanessa."

"Then fill in yours."

She could sense he didn't want to, but she could also tell he had taken responsibility for this mess. He thought it was his fault. He felt beholden to her.

She wasn't about to ignore the fact she could *use* that. She refused to take the bite and he sighed.

"Fine. You eat this, and I'll tell you as much as I can."

She nodded, letting him feed her small bites as she sipped water in between them. She realized he was picking off the heated pieces, and when he just had the frozen center left, he ate that himself.

It shouldn't surprise her he was noble. He *was* a Delaney, after all. Maybe the most condescending, high-horsed, snobbish Delaney of the bunch—next to his father—but noble tendencies ran in that clan.

What surprised her was that she was *moved* by the display of caretaking. She'd never wanted someone to take care of her. That made you beholden to them, and she would never let that happen to her. A Carson had to get by on their own wits. Sure, when she got in trouble Grady, Noah or Ty had stepped in and defended her. But no one had ever fed her and taken the crap ends for themselves.

*That you remember.*

"I have a tattoo," he said after his last swallow. "The only place you would have seen it is during our..."

She couldn't help the curve of her mouth. "Afraid to say the words, sweetheart?"

"See? You needed to eat. You're practically back to normal."

Except she didn't remember. Not really. Not in the way she needed to. She breathed through the panic that she might have lost thirteen years she'd never retrieve. At least she was alive to have more years.

"We had sex. I know that because I woke up naked next to you, also naked, the morning after Laurel and Grady's wedding. I don't—"

"Laurel and *Grady*?" she all but screeched.

He pressed his lips together, but his mouth curved anyway. "Don't worry. You made your outrage well known in the moment."

"My brother married... He couldn't have... *Married?*"

"Happily, even. Much as I'd like to deny it."

"But Laurel is such a do-gooder. She...she's a cop, isn't she?" Vanessa pressed fingers to her aching head. The food had helped her feel less shaky, but her brain hurt. "She always wanted to be. She'd have done it. She did. She helped..." But whatever fuzzy memory she'd been bringing to life faded. She swore.

"Easy," Dylan said quietly. "You're remembering bits and pieces. That makes me think it'll all come back, but we have some more important things at hand."

Vanessa scowled at the door. "Yes, we do. But tell me what happened. How we got here."

He recounted her coming to see him, the shooting from the front of the bank and their treacherous ride in the van. Vanessa didn't remember any of it, but she thought of Adele.

"She changed her clothes."

When she met Dylan's gaze, she knew he'd already put that together.

"And they separated us," Vanessa continued, working through all her suspicions, "because she's involved. If they had any sense at all, they'd put you alone since you're the money shot."

He winced at the term, which would have made her laugh if she wasn't so angry at Adele and her little farce.

"I bet a hundred bucks this is her place."

His mouth quirked. "A bet is what got you into this mess."

She racked her memory, but couldn't come up with it. So she focused on the here and now. "She works at the bank. For you and your father. She'd know your schedule." They had to figure out how Adele was connected, and if they did, maybe this would make more sense. Maybe they could find a way out.

"I would have been gone if not for you though."

"But you weren't gone. Your car was still there, right?"

"Right. But, she's worked for us for years. I can't believe—"

"What do you know about her?"

"She started as a teller. Moved from… I want to say Denver. Maybe Seattle. Some big city. She'd worked at a bank there and wanted the small-town life. Dad liked the idea of an outsider."

"That doesn't sound like your father."

"Better an outsider than a Carson or Carson sympathizer."

"Now, *that* sounds just like him."

"She had a kind of polish. She was a hard worker and moved up the ranks quickly. By the time I…came back home from college, she was second only to the assistant manager. A position Dad held for me."

"Came back. College. You say that so weird."

"Do I?"

"And you use that haughty tone to say 'do I' whenever something gets too close. Came back with your fancy finance degree."

"That's what they say."

Why was he talking in riddles about something so insignificant? It didn't make any sense. "What do *you* say?"

He shrugged. "Doesn't matter."

"Maybe it matters to me."

His eyes met hers, that same odd fluttering stirring in her breast, a little too close to her heart. But she didn't break his gaze, and she didn't back away. Maybe she'd lost her sense as well as her memory, but she couldn't bring herself to care.

POWER. THEY'D ALWAYS created powerful reactions in each other. Once hate. Now…the thing that crackled between them had altered. He wanted to touch her. His memories of that night were misty, probably like her memory of the past thirteen years, and yet he had images, odd feelings, like he could remember a rightness when their bodies joined.

He broke her gaze. He didn't believe in rightness or feelings. Reason mattered. Facts mattered.

Yet he was a man who'd shrugged off both and lived a lie for years, all so he could stand to live a different lie.

He stood, taking a few steps away from where he'd deposited her on that chair however long ago. It wasn't so much a retreat as a recentering. "We need to focus on—"

"No, don't brush me off. You're at the center of this. They weren't after me. I was a hapless bystander because we got drunk and stupid, apparently, if I believe that."

He raised an eyebrow and she huffed out a breath.

"Okay, *fine*. I believe we drunkenly hooked up, and I really hope I'm pregnant because I feel too much like crap to not have a reason. But, regardless, you're the center. Those men supposedly want a ransom for *you*."

"Supposedly." It didn't add up so clearly though, since he would have left the bank if Vanessa hadn't come. Since he didn't have a set schedule in the office that someone could have gleaned information from. Since it didn't seem like they'd taken any money from the bank—if money was what they were after.

Whoever those men were, whatever their purpose, it did have to do with him.

It would have been easy enough to see his car in the lot and act. But Adele had been there too.

*Only one.* But the men had three.

Adele had changed her clothes. He couldn't get past that one simple fact. He was still in his suit—dirty and tattered as it might be. Vanessa still had on the outfit she'd come to see him in. Yet Adele had changed into jeans and a clean shirt. And she didn't seem scared.

"If she's involved, the bank is involved."

"Which means money is involved," Vanessa supplied.

"I suppose."

"Did she have money troubles?"

"I don't know anything about Adele's personal life. Even if she didn't keep to herself, she's…"

"She's what?"

"It's hard to explain. She's perfectly nice, but underneath that is an abrasiveness. I wouldn't say anyone really *likes* Adele. Truth is, no matter how she tries to hide it—and I think she does try—she thinks she's smarter than everyone, a harder worker. She thinks she's better."

Vanessa snorted. "She must fit right in with the Delaneys."

He shot her a bland look. "But there's no tension. No

fights. She's never been demoted or scolded. She'd have no reason to hate me or the bank as an entity."

"What about your father? Would she have a reason to hate him?"

"I want to say it's the same, but…"

"But what?"

He rubbed the back of his neck. He didn't like parading his father's faults in front of anyone, let alone a Carson. "He isn't quite the stand-up guy I'd always assumed him to be." Dylan thought regretfully of what they'd found out last year about his father's extracurricular activities: an affair with a married woman. A *Carson* woman. It wasn't exactly murder or anything, but it had shaken Dylan's foundation of believing his father a good, if hard, man.

"So she could have had an issue with your father?"

"I suppose. But why not go after him?"

Vanessa rolled her eyes. "Don't you watch any movies? You don't go after the person you hate. You go after what they love."

It made sense. Uncomfortable sense, but sense nonetheless. "If that's the case—if this is some sort of revenge against my father—then I don't think she plans on me surviving. Get a ransom, kill me off?" He didn't shudder, didn't worry, because he'd like to see someone try to get rid of him. *Everyone* underestimated him. Even Adele.

Even Vanessa.

Vanessa watched him, consideration all over her face. "They made a big production about keeping you alive. Maybe it's to give weight to the ransom story, or maybe she's got something against you too."

"What would she have against me?"

"Same thing the rest of us peons do, Dylan. You're a jerk."

He puffed up, insulted even though he couldn't figure out why Vanessa's normal estimation of him would be insulting.

"Just like I'm a jerk. People hate us because we don't play nice. I say it like it is, and you ice out the world. Maybe it's not who we are underneath, but it's what people see."

"So what are you underneath, Vanessa Carson?" He hadn't meant that to come out sounding sexual, but it had. His body warmed, tightened. Because even if he couldn't remember the details of the act, there was a feeling he got when he thought about them being together. It was very nearly irresistible.

Nearly.

# *Chapter Nine*

Heat flooded through Vanessa, and worse, a beat of arousal she couldn't deny no matter how much she wanted to. Her skin prickled and her core hummed with need.

*Jeez.*

She tried to swallow through her dry throat. Then, realizing she still held the water bottle from before, unscrewed the cap and took an unsteady breath. She could not have sexual thoughts about Dylan, period, but most especially when they were abducted by goons. And yet there those sexual thoughts were.

"We should focus on you," she managed, hoping she sounded stabler than she felt. "I'm an incidental."

He made a noise, one she didn't know how to characterize, though she thought it had to do with guilt. But he didn't press. Which meant *she* had to press her one advantage.

"And since I'm here because of you, we need to figure this out. Which means focusing on Adele. And you."

"Yeah. I suppose it's possible she wanted my position."

"Wouldn't anyone? I mean anyone who worked in that bank. Certainly not *anyone*." She'd rather jump out a window than try her hand at staid, businessy bankerland.

"Everyone knew that position was mine. He held it for me while I was…away."

"You're going to have to explain that." Why he got so fidgety every time his years at college were mentioned.

But he ignored her. "It'd have been pointless and stupid to think she or anyone else would get that position. I don't think Adele is stupid."

"No, but people are oftentimes foolish even if you don't think they should be." *We slept together.* It seemed the height of pointless and stupid.

"Stupid enough to kidnap? To send armed men after me? I can't believe it, Vanessa. I really can't. She might be a hard lady, but she isn't a psychopath."

Vanessa thought of her father and her uncle. No one had considered them *psychopaths*. Jerks, sure. Alcoholics, maybe. But the fact they liked to use their fists on women went mostly ignored, no matter how incomprehensible that act was to a normal person.

Noah and Ty had considered their father a monster when he'd been alive. Grady didn't know much about what their father had done in his absence.

She sighed. Old wounds had no place here. *She* had no place here, and yet here she was.

She felt a little bit better, a little bit steadier, now that she'd had water and food. Her brain didn't feel so foggy and her body didn't feel as though the wrong move would send everything inside of her rushing out.

"It has to relate to the bank," she continued, trying to muse through the problem aloud. "Maybe not you. Maybe your father."

Dylan's eyebrows drew together. "But I'm here."

"Sure. You're daddy's pride and joy though. So it could be you. It could be him. It could be about both of you. Delaneys in general."

"You'd like that, wouldn't you?"

"Probably under any other circumstances, but not

when I'm tied to you and in this mess. But you said we were abducted at the bank. Adele is somehow weirdly mixed up in this. It has to connect to the bank."

"They said they wanted a ransom," Dylan said, taking her threads and adding some of his own thoughts to it. "Maybe it *is* just a ploy to get a bunch of money from my father." He shook his head. "Doesn't sit right though. There'd be easier, smarter ways to do that."

"Maybe. Maybe not. Adele wants money, needs money maybe? She pretends she's a victim and no one ever knows she has anything to do with it. She gets off scot-free. Biggest problem is I got in the way."

Dylan seemed to consider, *really* consider her words. She hadn't expected him to. She was used to dismissal from a Delaney, especially *him*.

"If it's about the money, I feel like there were better ways to get it than kidnapping. Adele has access to all sorts of things at the bank. She could have embezzled, stolen, cheated. Carefully."

"But not easily."

"I hear kidnapping is so easy."

Vanessa ignored his dry comment. "Everything she could have done at the bank would have been traced to her."

Dylan's mouth quirked, causing that weird, annoying, unwelcome feeling to flutter in her chest again.

"You've got a sharp mind, Vanessa."

"Imagine that," she returned dryly.

"Considered robbing a few banks now and again?"

She wanted to be offended, but mostly the tongue-in-cheek way he said it made her want to laugh. *With* him rather than *at* him. "Oh, I've considered all *sorts* of things, Delaney."

That flash of a grin had unwanted lust pooling low in

her belly. She'd always thought he was attractive. She'd just hated everything about him underneath the physical. Now everything was getting muddled.

Head injury. She'd blame the head injury. And change the subject. "You fail out of college or something?"

"Huh?"

"You're squirrelly every time it comes up. Something happened while you were away. I want to know what. Maybe it connects."

"It doesn't."

"Maybe it does."

"It doesn't."

She huffed out an annoyed breath.

"I didn't fail. I—"

The door burst open. The goon she'd decided to call No-Neck stood there, holding that gun like it was some proof of his epic power. Vanessa wanted to sneer, but she held back the nasty look at the last second.

Now that she was feeling more herself, it was going to be quite the fight not to be *too* much herself and piss off the men with guns.

"You." He pointed the gun at Dylan. "Out front."

Vanessa jumped to her feet, even as Dylan began to move to go with the man. "You can't separate us."

No-Neck laughed. "I can do whatever I want, little girl."

Dylan gave her a sharp look. "Stay here. Stay put." He gave a pointed look at her stomach.

She brought a hand to it without thinking. For the first time, she really, truly believed him without reservation. She was pregnant with his baby, and he'd protect her—and it—at all costs.

The knowledge, the acceptance, shook her to hell and back.

DYLAN FOLLOWED THE muscle-bound idiot into the living room, noting everything he saw. There was a phone on the table next to the couch. He filed it away. Furniture, art on the walls, windows. He took note which way the sun slanted outside the blinds when he could tell.

When he got them out of this mess, he'd know how to lead police or anyone else to this place and make sure these men—and their boss—paid for what they'd done. That was a promise he'd make to himself, and he was not in a habit of breaking those.

The gun-toting moron shoved him onto a plush leather couch. Expensive, Dylan noted. Whoever owned this cabin had money, which meant they weren't likely *after* money.

He filed that away too.

"You're going to make a phone call. One of those Face-Time deals."

Dylan tried not to let his excitement show. Were they *stupid*? Even if they didn't let him say anything of importance, a FaceTime call would show a background. It would give Dad some hints, some ideas. A damn *lead* to hand over to Laurel and the police.

He fixed a disgusted look on his face and put as much sarcasm into his voice as he could manage. "Lucky me."

The man raised the butt of his weapon and Dylan forced his body to relax so when he took the blow it didn't meet resistance. It'd hurt like hell, he knew, considering his face was already throbbing from all the blows, but it'd help downplay whatever injury he got in the long run.

But the second guy came out of what Dylan supposed was some kind of kitchen area off to the side of the living room. "Remember what Boss said."

The guy with the gun grunted, lowered the weapon with a lot of regret. Dylan smirked.

Which earned him a meaty fist to the gut. Dylan wheezed out a painful breath, doubling over and seeing stars.

The goon in the kitchen sighed.

The one who'd punched him laughed. "Boss said no more messing with his face. That wasn't his face."

"Your funeral," the other one said.

Dylan sure as hell hoped so.

Slowly, he sat back up. Even though just about everything on his body hurt at this point, he wouldn't let anyone see it. Goons or Vanessa or...

"Where's Adele?"

"She's in her room, just like you two were in yours. She gets the nicer digs because she cooperated."

"She wasn't in the van with us."

"So?"

"Changed her clothes too."

The guy in front of him flashed a look to the guy in the kitchen area. Dylan tried not to react, but that hesitation, that look, told him a lot. Because they hadn't expected him to question Adele's place in all this.

Then the man in front of him threw his head back and laughed. "Yeah, sure. The blonde's the real mastermind behind this whole thing. You figured us out. Maybe I'll go turn myself in now, since I got this sharp detective on my heels."

The other man laughed too. Uproariously.

Dylan didn't buy it. It might have planted a seed or two of doubt but barely. Still, he let that doubt show. He wasn't going to take the smarter-than-you tactic or the dumber-than-a-box-of-rocks one either. He had to mix it up. Keep them off-balance.

"Go get the blonde to unlock her phone," living-room

guy ordered of kitchen guy. "She's got the old man's number on her phone."

Even though Adele would of course have his father's number in her phone, Dylan thought it was an odd request. FaceTime. Adele's phone. There was a convenience to their plan Dylan didn't trust.

Or was it smart? Use her phone, then there'd be no way to trace it to anyone besides Adele. Adele had access to his father, and having that kind of insurance was smart if they thought he was going to be uncooperative.

Maybe this *was* simply about money, and Adele was unconnected.

But she had changed clothes, hadn't been hurt in the initial break-in, and the men had distinctly said they were only supposed to kidnap one person.

Either way, if someone knew Adele was missing and they used her phone, it could be pinged. It might take some time—Dylan knew from Laurel there were all sorts of legalities to jump through before the police could access that information—but it was a chance.

The second man brought Adele out. She still looked put together, but her eyes were a little wide. Dylan almost believed she was scared.

Almost.

"C-can't I just tell you the c-code?" she stuttered, as the man with the gun held it out to her. Her fingers fumbled with it and it fell to the floor.

One of the goons nudged it with his foot. "Pick it up and fix it up for us," he ordered, gesturing toward a little tripod they'd set up. "Get him in the shot, then make the call."

"You could just record a video and send it," Dylan suggested. He doubted they'd take the hook, but it was worth a shot. A video could be watched, studied. A FaceTime call... Dad would have to know how to take a screenshot and have the presence of mind to do so.

The man shook his head. "Boss's orders are clear, friend."

Adele was shaking as she set up the phone on the tripod. Convincing nerves, and yet Dylan didn't *feel* convinced.

Still, regardless of her innocence or guilt, she had a phone. That phone was the best shot he had, as long as people knew they were missing.

Surely Laurel knew at this point they were all missing in a capacity that required police involvement. *Surely.* His sister was a good cop and a damn smart detective. He had to trust she was on this.

"Th-there. I think it's all set up. I just have to click the movie icon."

"Sit next to him. Don't speak."

Adele nodded and took a seat next to Dylan on the couch. She seemed to vibrate, and his first thought was nerves, but there was a look in her eye, a lack of tension in her expression. He wanted to believe she was scared and that she was being forced to do this.

But Dylan couldn't shake all the strange little pieces of this mystery.

One of the men shoved a piece of paper at him.

"You'll say that, and nothing else, or things won't end well for your friend in there." He pointed his gun toward the room Vanessa was in. "Read when I say go. Even if he talks over you, you read it once and then I disconnect."

Dylan looked down at the paper. The statement was simple: I'm in grave danger. Instructions on how to deliver money. No mention of Vanessa. Or Adele, even though she was clearly going to be in the shot.

Dylan looked up at the man, then the phone. He didn't

allow himself a glance at the door where Vanessa was. Didn't allow himself to think about the fact they might hurt her. He had to focus on any possible way to figure out what was really going on here.

If he knew the facts, the players, he could get everyone out with minimum fuss. He believed that.

"All right, friend. The minute Daddy Money Bags answers, you read."

Dylan nodded. He could still feel the vibrations coming off Adele next to him, and yet he forced himself to focus on his core. The deep steadiness within his soul. He'd learned to compartmentalize as a soldier. Learned to live within the mission and nothing else as a sniper.

When his dad answered, the small rectangle of his face showing concern and fear and hope before he even managed a word, Dylan felt nothing.

He looked down and began to read.

# Chapter Ten

*Back in Bent, at the Delaney Ranch*

Laurel had her father go through it again. And again. She had him write down everything he remembered, and she wrote it down as he recounted his version of the phone call, as well.

She was worried for her brother, even for poor Adele, who seemed to be an innocent bystander now. Laurel believed she could save them though—had to believe it.

What made her sick to her stomach was that there was no mention or glimpse of Vanessa. She was going to have to go home to her husband and tell him that his sister may have run off without a word.

He wouldn't believe her.

*She* didn't believe her.

Vanessa's car in the bank parking lot was too much. If it had been found *anywhere* else, she'd feel the same as Hart—convinced Vanessa had run off to go have her baby far away from her family.

But even if Dylan was the father of Vanessa's baby—a theory Laurel had an even harder time believing—there was no reason, excuse or sensible explanation for Vanessa's car being in the Delaney Bank parking lot.

"It was new," Dad said, relaying that detail for the

fourth or fifth time. He sat at the Delaney kitchen table, looking pale and shaky and as disheveled as Laurel had ever seen him. He hadn't even been this upset when her mother had died or when he'd been mixed up in a threat to his life by Jesse Carson last year.

"I could tell the cabin around him was new. You could look at new cabins. Surely builders have records and…"

She tried to smile reassuringly at her father. "Hart's already on that from your first statement. We'll have the names of anyone who's built or bought a cabin in the county within the last year. It's a good place to start. And now we're trying to ping Adele's phone. We've got clues. Hard leads."

Dad looked at her imploringly. Apparently seeing Dylan on that video had eradicated his usual control. He was worried sick. It poked at Laurel's own sense of calm, but she was a cop. She had to be a cop now more than ever.

"What if they're not in the county?" Dad asked. "Or even the *state*?"

His words spoke to her own fears, but she couldn't show that to her father. "It's unlikely." A lie, but it was for the best for now.

Dad pushed back from the table and started pacing. "I need to send the money."

"You don't have the money. Besides, they'll only escalate and ask for more. You have to—"

He whirled. "I have the bank. I have access to all the money we need."

"Dad, you can't… That isn't legal. You know it and I know it."

"I could sell the cattle and pay it all back. I could sell everything if I had to. I could—"

"You could, but right now you have to sit down." She

took a breath and brought him back to his chair. She had to steady herself. If he'd been cold or demanding, it would have been easy. But Dad shaking, falling apart like this, made tears burn in the back of her eyes.

She wouldn't cry. She was a Delaney. Police officer. *Sister.* She swallowed at the lump in her throat. She could only be one thing here. The law. "You need to calm down, and let me and the rest of the police do our job."

"Laurel, your brother—"

Her heart cracked, but she didn't let it show. "I know. Trust me, I know. But we've called state, and they've got to look into this before I can let you pay off that ransom. It's rare a kidnapper gets the money and lets the abductee go. This whole thing is rare, but let's give state time to get caught up to speed."

"We should call the FBI."

"If there's a need, we will. State will. I can only do so much with my resources at county. But I'm doing everything I can."

Dad looked at her, and some of that cold disdain she'd grown used to since falling for Grady was back in his expression.

"Are you?" he asked coolly.

It hurt, even if she convinced herself it was his fear and temper talking.

She pressed her fingers to the table, taking a moment to steady herself when an unwanted wave of dizziness settled over her. She needed to eat. *Baby* needed to eat.

She glanced at her father, who still didn't know. And wouldn't approve. Bad enough to marry a Carson, but to procreate with one?

She almost smiled. If it was true Vanessa was pregnant with Dylan's baby, she'd get them home just to see the look on her father's face.

"Dylan is smart and resourceful. I don't know Adele that well, but she strikes me as someone who can keep her head in the midst of a crisis. I trust Hart to help me on this investigation, and I trust state to make the right call on when, if and how we should pay the ransom. You don't have to trust those things, Dad. You don't have to trust me. But it'd be a lot better for you, and Dylan, if you did."

"I'll never forgive you if anything happens to him," Dad said, cold and decisive. Yes, this was the father she'd known for the past year.

"Don't worry. I won't forgive myself either."

"You brought this on us. You've *cursed* us."

Her father's hatred of the Carsons had never shocked her, but this did. To the core. "Dad, you don't believe that."

"I absolutely believe this town has been in turmoil since you dared let that stain touch you. How many times has a Delaney been hurt since you—"

"I won't listen to this." She whirled away. It was too much. Too much blame when she was struggling with her own. "You'll sit tight," she ordered, striding away from him even as she barked out each word. "I've warned Jen to keep an eye on you. Don't make me bring in Cam." But she'd call her other brother nevertheless to make sure he kept an eye on the finances. If her father compounded this mess with a crime...

She couldn't think of it. She had a case to solve.

Dad said nothing else, and she let herself out. She stopped on the porch and took a deep breath of Wyoming air. The ranch was still, the quiet only interrupted by the breeze or an occasional cow lowing in the distance.

It was home, or had been. Now her home was with

Grady and this baby of theirs. The world was changing. Bent was changing.

Curses. She didn't believe in curses. She'd never believed in the Carson-Delaney feud that had kept two families sniping at each other for over a century. She wouldn't start now, and she'd never, ever allow anything to make her believe there was a curse when Grady was everything she'd ever needed.

But no matter how many certain, powerful words she told herself in her head, a flutter of fear beat against her gut.

## *Chapter Eleven*

Not having a clock was sending Vanessa into a low-level panic attack. How long had Dylan been out there? How long would she be in here alone?

She'd never had trouble being alone before. In fact, it was her preferred state of being. At least, when she was in charge of her own life. Turned out, kidnapping was wreaking havoc with her sense of the usual.

Plus, she'd drunk the entire bottle of water. Which meant she really, really needed to get out of here.

But something held her back. No, not something. She knew exactly what held her back. It was just hard to admit.

Fear. She was petrified of what existed outside those doors. What if they'd killed Dylan? Tortured him? He might be some kind of secret tough guy, but two men with guns were with him out there.

Ransom. They were after a ransom. They wouldn't kill their star in the ransom show.

Except they were morons. And whoever was the boss—and in Vanessa's mind that was Adele—had this cabin, which had to have cost a pretty penny. It wasn't about money.

Unless it was. Money could dry up. A person could always need more.

Where was Dylan?

Vanessa squeezed her eyes shut. She wasn't a coward, and since she was feeling mostly normal, she couldn't even blame it on a head injury or this...pregnancy thing. She couldn't be a coward. It wasn't allowed.

She moved forward to the door and started banging on it. She didn't stop until it opened—though just a crack.

"Knock it off," No-Neck growled, his beady little eye visible through the crack.

"I have to go to the bathroom."

There were murmurs, grumbles, then after a few minutes of shuffling, the door opened the rest of the way.

One big hand gripped her upper arm and gave her a jerk, and then he had her other arm in his grasp so that both arms were pulled behind her back and he could guide her.

She immediately searched the living area for Dylan, though it only took a second for her eyes to be drawn to the figure on the couch. He sat, ramrod straight, in the middle of it. They'd tied his hands and his feet, and she got the impression—though she couldn't see it—that something was making him have that absurdly straight posture.

Then there was the strip of duct tape across his mouth. He didn't look at her, kept his gaze straight ahead, which again she wondered if it had to do with how they'd tied him up.

But through it all, even as the goon pushed her to a bathroom, Dylan looked...bored. No fear. No worry. Just like he couldn't believe he was letting himself be subjected to this.

Such a Delaney. For the first time in her entire life, that made her smile. And the smile made her maybe a little too brave.

"Where's your chick boss?" Vanessa asked of the jerk holding her arms.

The man didn't answer. He just shoved her forward by his grasp on her arms. Vanessa supposed he was leading her to the bathroom. As she passed Dylan, he inclined his head slightly to the other room, still not making eye contact. Apparently, Adele was still in there.

The man pushed her through a door, and she stumbled forward, catching herself on the sink when he let her go. She glared at him. He smiled his smarmy smile. "Three minutes. Time starts now." And he shut the door.

Irritated and furious, Vanessa quickly did what her body demanded. Washing her hands, she looked at herself in the mirror. Her hair was a tangled mess. She was pale and dirty. There were shadows under her eyes.

"One minute left," the man outside called.

Indulging herself, she stuck her tongue out at the door before letting her gaze sweep the small half bath she was in.

Another narrow line of windows she couldn't possibly slither out of, high on the walls. She crouched and opened the cabinet underneath the sink, pushed through rolls of toilet paper and hand towels, searching for anything that could be a weapon or a clue.

Nothing.

"Time's up!"

Vanessa straightened just as the door swung open. He didn't immediately grab her. Instead, he watched her, leaning against the doorjamb.

"You're lucky, you know."

She rolled her eyes. "Yeah, I'm a regular fairy princess."

"If I was in charge?" He let his gaze take a tour of her

body that had her stomach roiling. "Things would be *very* different for you, *fairy princess*."

She wanted to tell him things would be very different because she would have cut off his balls, but she bit her tongue and held his disgusting stare with a bland one of her own.

"Who hired you two apes? You don't have one brain between you," Dylan called out.

Her own eyes widened, even as No-Neck's did. How was Dylan talking? He'd just had tape on his mouth and…

"How the hell'd he get out of the tape?" the man grumbled, turning his back on Vanessa.

Vanessa had a flash of attacking No-Neck. Just jumping on his back and going at it. He might be stronger, but she was strong herself. Wiry and quick. She knew how to punch a guy's lights out with the element of surprise.

But he had a gun, and she was apparently growing a baby.

Then the moment was over. No-Neck remembered himself, grabbed her by the arm and jerked her out into the living room.

Eyeballs was standing over Dylan, fury and something like bafflement written in every ugly line of his expression.

"How'd you get it off?" he demanded, nudging Dylan's side with the gun he never seemed to put down.

Dylan smiled up at him. "Magic."

The butt of Eyeballs's weapon struck Dylan's stomach. Hard. Dylan bent over, even gasped out a breath, but when he straightened into a sitting position on the couch again, his expression didn't radiate pain or fury. He was just grinning.

Maybe *he* was a psychopath.

"How'd you get it off?" Eyeballs demanded, holding the gun upward again, readying for another blow.

Vanessa desperately tried to think of a way to intercede, but No-Neck pushed her forward.

"Let's get them both in the room before you kill him and Boss kills *us*."

Eyeballs grunted, then muttered something as he yanked Dylan to his feet. "When it's time to kill you— and, oh, there will be a time—it'll be my pleasure."

"Nice fantasy life you've got there."

No-Neck cut the ties on Dylan's feet but left the hand ones on. Then Eyeballs practically lifted Dylan off his feet. Dylan was launched forward, falling into the room they'd been in, and with his hands tied he had no way to stop the forward momentum. He crashed into the wall, falling to the ground with a loud thud.

Vanessa struggled against No-Neck's grasp, and when he let her go she rushed to Dylan's side.

"God. *God.* Are you okay? Are you…?" She struggled to move him onto his back so she could see how hurt he was. She didn't even notice the door close or the loud thud of the lock, so intent she was on helping Dylan.

He didn't groan as she rolled him over, and she might have thought he'd passed out, but his eyes were open and on her. His mouth was quirked as if this were a joke. Gingerly, she touched all the bruises and scratches on his stubbled face.

She shouldn't have done it—somewhere in the back of her mind the real Vanessa was losing it over the fact she was gently caressing Dylan Delaney's face.

But her fingers brushed through his hair of their own accord. Gently, she cupped his wounded jaw. "Are you okay?"

His gaze, so direct and serious, did some strange

things to the spaces inside her heart. She wanted to look away, but her pride was at stake. That's what kept her gaze locked to his. Pride. Nothing else.

"If I say no, are you going to kiss it and make it better?"

She knew she should jerk away or cuss him out, but she couldn't bring her fingers away from the silky texture of his hair. "You've got to stop pissing them off. You won't survive."

He leaned into her touch, and something flopped in her chest. "I'll survive. And keep you safe while I do it."

"I can handle myself, Dylan."

He made a noncommittal noise, then pulled his hands out from behind his back.

"Hey, how'd you get out of that?" she demanded, staring openmouthed at the plastic bindings that had fallen to the floor.

He grinned at her, and she saw the red marks around his mouth where the tape had been did nothing to dim the potency of that grin. "Magic."

HE WANTED TO touch her. Hell, he wanted to kiss her. The pain in his stomach was nothing compared to the gentle comfort of her hands on him. On his face and in his hair. Her hair fell over him, a tangled dark mess, and nothing about her was different from how it had ever been—tattoos, wary eyes, hard mouth.

Except her touch was light, and in this strange kidnapped world, he didn't feel like Dylan Delaney, where the eyes of Bent and his father fit like a suit two sizes too small.

She, and he, felt right. Together they had the power to weather this odd storm. For a moment, brief and changing, he *knew* she felt that too.

And then she pulled away.

Which was fine. What could be done during a kidnapping? Not much. He was grateful she seemed more like herself. Sturdier and sharper, instead of lost and hazy. Maybe her memory was still fuzzy, but the blow to the head hopefully hadn't caused any problems with the pregnancy.

He sat up, not at all perturbed by the fact that she watched him with frustration simmering in her gaze.

"You have to tell me. The fighting. The getting out of duct tape and ties and…you have to tell me how *you* of all people know how to be—be—"

"Fiercely lethal?"

She rolled her eyes, but she didn't offer another term.

He sighed. Not more than forty-eight hours ago, revealing his secrets to anyone—let alone a Carson—would have felt like life and death. But now he understood life and death in a way he hadn't even as a sniper.

Because it wasn't facing death that had changed him, it was facing *life*. The moment she'd told him she was pregnant, he'd been handed new life and everything he thought he'd known had flipped. All the things he'd thought mattered dissolved. He didn't care what anyone thought of him. Not even his father. Because he'd created a life…and whether he fully grasped that yet, he knew this child would be the center of his life. Part of him. Always.

So it didn't matter if Vanessa knew. It didn't matter if she told everyone when they got back home—and it was *when* not *if* they got back home, in his mind.

"Well, all that college bragging my father did to you in that last memory of yours…"

She pushed a finger to her head, near the bump where

she'd fallen. Her eyebrows drew together and he got to his feet.

"You remember?"

"No. Not exactly. But it doesn't feel like… Even though I can't put it all on a clear timeline, that doesn't feel as close to now as it did. I still can't believe Laurel and Grady are *married*, but it doesn't seem… I feel like I remember them together. Being irritated at them together. She's a cop. I remember the uniform. I remember her holding a gun, I think. Maybe."

"There's been some trouble the past year or so. You'd likely have seen her draw her weapon a few times."

"Trouble? What kind of trouble? Is everyone…?"

He could see the fear and horror chase over her features as she realized she might not remember losing someone she loved.

"As far as I know, every Carson you care about is present and accounted for."

She swallowed. "Right." Then her eyes narrowed. "You're trying to distract me."

"You're distracting yourself. I don't even have to try." He folded his arms behind his head and smiled at her.

She growled. "*How* do you know how to fight and escape bonds? Jump out of vans and incapacitate dudes with guns?"

He figured he needed to be straight and simple, so they could move on to far more important matters. Like Adele's possible role and the small plan he had for escaping tonight once he got some more info.

"I didn't go to college. I made everyone think I did. Took the money for tuition, told Dad I wanted to handle all my bills to learn how to be responsible. I forged transcripts and report cards and enlisted in the army and became a sniper instead."

"You…" She gaped at him like a landed fish. "You… That's a lie. That… You couldn't have. Why? Why go through all the trouble?"

"I knew I had seven years. Graduate high school early, take five years for undergrad, claim the need for a masters for another two, maybe three if I could stretch it. So, that's what I made them think. I knew if I did what I wanted in that short period of time, I could come back and be everything he wanted me to be. I just had to go be *me* first."

"Dylan. That's crazy."

"No. It felt like that's what I had to do. Cam refused the bank, Laurel was always meant to be a cop, and Jen didn't have the patience for finance. She just wanted to run the store. I was the only one left."

"Considering your father's going to live to be three million since he's evil incarnate, I'd say he was enough left."

Dylan shook his head. "No. I was the only true Bent Delaney left to take the mantle. The bank has been in our family since it began. Direct eldest son to eldest son. I'm not the eldest, but Cam wouldn't take it. You have to understand family pressure, Vanessa. Carson and Delaney pressure. We are what our names are." And yet, wasn't he sitting here thinking none of it mattered anymore?

Maybe it didn't. Maybe it did. The *now* didn't matter in the story, because it was the choice he'd made. It was what he'd felt then.

"You went into the army, became a sniper, falsified your *life* for seven years. That's *insane*. You're talking like it was the only choice."

"For me, it was."

"You could have told your father what you wanted to do."

"No. It wasn't an option. I was coming back. I was going to take on my responsibility. But I needed a few years to..." It sounded stupid to say *find myself.* But that's what he'd needed. He'd needed to know who he was outside of Bent. Outside of numbers and appearances.

Cam had gone to the marines, and Dylan hadn't been allowed to follow. So he'd found a different way. Maybe he should have stood up to his father, but he'd been seventeen.

The bottom line was, he hadn't. "I needed it to be secret. I needed to be someone not connected to this place. I can't explain why I needed it, only that I did. And it shaped me, made me, gave me the time I needed to be able to come home and take that..." *Noose.* Following his father's footsteps felt like a noose he couldn't escape.

"I had my me time, then I came home to fulfill my role as a Delaney. It was a little out of the box, but it wasn't insane."

"Army. A *sniper.* I..." She shook her head and paced around the room. "That's a lot of work for risking your life for your country. You faked your life to sacrifice yourself, to protect. I don't understand that."

He cocked his head and studied her. She didn't realize it, but she'd put her hand over her stomach. He thought she was finally beginning to believe the pregnancy was real. That he was the father.

"I think you're starting to," he said gently.

She looked down at her hand, then dropped it. She kept her back to him, and he couldn't read her posture so he crossed to her. Gently, knowing she'd probably fight him off, he put his hands on her shoulders.

When she didn't move away and didn't even tense under his fingers, he turned her to face him.

Her eyes were direct, though there was something in

them he couldn't read. Suspicion maybe. Or possibly just confusion. She didn't understand him.

That didn't hurt his feelings though. She was a Carson. He was a Delaney. They'd never understand each other.

But, God, he wanted to. Understand her. Have her understand him. He wanted to chase this *power* that arced between them. But it wasn't the time or place. Maybe it'd never be, but definitely not now. "Right now, we'll focus on getting out of here."

When the tension crept into her shoulders, he squeezed. "Don't worry. I'll protect you. I'm an expert."

She didn't laugh or even crack a smile, but the moment held. And in that moment he needed her to believe that he'd protect her with everything he was.

He placed his own hand over her stomach, nerves and fear of the future jumping through every part of him. He didn't let it show in his expression though. "I'll protect you both."

She took a sharp breath in, then slowly let it out. Then her hand reached out and cupped his jaw, just as she had when he'd been sprawled on the floor after crashing into the wall. His chest clutched, a metal fist squeezing against his heart and then his lungs.

Her dark eyes were rich and deep and fathomless. He saw something he'd never seen in her before. Warmth. Care.

*You're losing it, Delaney.*

"Protect all three of us," she whispered and then pressed her mouth to his.

## Chapter Twelve

The kiss was a mistake. Out of place in every possible
way.

But Vanessa wrapped her arms around Dylan's neck
and took it deeper anyway. Her whole life had been built
on out-of-place mistakes. She *was* an out-of-place mistake. Her philosophy had always been, why not embrace
it?

So she lost herself in a kiss she shouldn't have allowed
herself, and figured that was vintage Vanessa.

Until Dylan took control, his hands sliding over her
cheeks and into her hair, fingers tangling there, changing the angle of the kiss as his tongue swept across her
lips, then invaded her mouth.

Now she understood why his hands were big and
rough and capable. Maybe it still didn't make sense to
her, a secret life, a secret self, but she understood all the
incongruous things about him now.

She knew something about him no one else did. In
this moment, they were experiencing something together
that no one would be able to share with them. They were
linked. Connected.

And she wanted him. So why not take?

Slowly, oh so slowly, he ended the kiss. Pulled away
just enough to keep their mouths apart, but her body was

still pressed to his. Their heartbeats thudded against each other as their gazes met.

She'd expected to see...*horror* wasn't the right word, but something close to it. Regret. Disgust. She was a Carson and he was a Delaney. He'd only ever see her as a mistake. Even without all her memory, she knew that.

She had the flash of him walking out of her apartment above her shop, looking rumpled and angry. Disgusted. At the time she'd thought it was with her, but somehow in this moment, she realized it was with himself. With his loss of control.

Because his image was the gift he'd given his family, even when it wasn't him at all.

"Dylan." She wanted to kiss him again. Comfort him for...something. Offer understanding, maybe, even though her understanding was limited.

But then she realized she could picture her apartment. She knew what color her sheets were and that she lived there.

"Wait. Wait." She could't analyze why he didn't look horrified now, only the fact that she knew... "I—I run the mechanic shop, not just help out. I run it. I live above it." She struggled to keep that thread of memory, holding tight to him as if he was her anchor, even as she looked blindly at his chest. "It's mine now, because—because Grady helped me buy it after Jim croaked." She swallowed. She could picture some of the cars she'd worked on. Could feel herself walking down the boardwalk from her shop to Rightful Claim.

Where Grady didn't live anymore. Because he'd married Laurel. They'd gotten together when their stepbrother had been accused of murder and Grady and Laurel had worked together to clear Clint's name. They'd fallen in love and pissed off a lot of people.

She looked up at Dylan's dark gaze, amazed parts of her memory had returned.

"You should probably kiss me again," Dylan suggested, pulling her closer.

At her sharp look, he shrugged, a grin flirting at the corner of his mouth. "What? It made you remember. Might jog some more pieces."

Her mouth curved, suggestive words about to tumble out of her mouth, no matter where they were or what they were facing.

But the door flung open, and afterward, Vanessa realized there was something telling about the fact she and Dylan didn't jump apart. She didn't know what, but it meant, well, something that they held on to each other instead.

But it was something they'd have to figure out later because Adele was pushed into the room. Her hair was disheveled, and there was a trickle of blood coming out of her nose.

Dylan immediately rushed to her side. Vanessa stayed put.

Blood or not, she didn't trust the woman with the icy eyes. Because though she made odd, almost crying noises, Vanessa didn't see any tears.

"Got a call with the boss," No-Neck growled. "You three stay in here. Plot your escape because I'd love to break your kneecaps in the process."

Dylan ignored No-Neck and Eyeballs as they cackled and shut the door.

"Are you all right?" he asked Adele, gentleness in his tone, in his touch.

Vanessa scowled.

"I just…" Adele swallowed, her hand shaking as she brought it up to her nose. "I did everything they said, but they're so rough." She made another little crying sound. Still no tears.

Vanessa went over to the box of tissues on the desk and handed it to Adele. Adele blinked at the proffered box and then daintily took one.

"Oh, I…" She dabbed it at her nose and squeezed her eyes shut. "I get a little faint when I see blood."

"It's all right," Dylan assured her.

Vanessa barely resisted the urge to roll her eyes. She wouldn't have cared for the fainting-damsel act in the best of circumstances, but considering Adele'd watched Dylan get slammed by the butt of a gun repeatedly with little reaction, Vanessa was having a hard time working up sympathy.

Of course, Dylan was trained to get beat up and keep fighting. A secret soldier. Dylan Delaney.

And she was the only one who knew. Something about that felt important, and it softened her enough to crouch down and clean up Adele's nose for her.

"There. Good as new. Just tilt your head forward and pinch it right at the bridge. Should be right as rain in a few."

Adele winced and did as Vanessa instructed.

Dylan raised an eyebrow at her. "Bloody-nose expert?"

"I'm a Carson. Of *course* I'm a bloody-nose expert. My own. My brother's. My cousins'. It's like a virtual parade of bloody noses from getting punched in the face." Vanessa turned her attention back to Adele. "You weren't punched in the face though, were you?"

"Oh, I…" Her hand fluttered restlessly in the air. "No. They pushed me around a bit and I…"

"Looks more like an elevation nosebleed to me," Vanessa observed, ignoring Dylan's censuring look.

"Oh, but I fell. They pushed me and I fell."

Vanessa got to her feet and shrugged. "If you say so."

"They said they have some meeting with their boss," Adele said, clearly trying to change the subject. "And they needed that room. Do you think whoever is behind this is coming here?" Her voice vibrated with concern.

Vanessa managed to swallow what she wanted to say: *I think their boss is already here, liar.*

She didn't want to believe Dylan was falling for Adele's flittering fragile-female crap, but he was so gentle when he helped Adele to her feet and then led her to the chair he'd put Vanessa in not that long ago. He picked up the suit jacket he'd placed over her lap earlier, and put it on Adele's.

"Just take it easy. Whoever their boss is can't be that dangerous, or he wouldn't have hired two muscle-bound goons to do his dirty work for him."

"Do you really think?" Adele replied, eyes big and something like adoring on Dylan.

He patted her shoulder. "Yes, I do. Trust me. The only thing we need to worry about is the fact those two have guns."

Vanessa didn't care for the oily black slick of jealousy running through her. She was starting to think Dylan's gentle caretaking wasn't because he cared about her or even their baby. No, this was just who he was. Vanessa wasn't special at all.

Well, except for that kiss.

"You also need to worry about the fact Eyeballs has a penchant for kicking your butt," Vanessa said to Dylan. Because it was its own kind of pain to see all the physical evidence of their brutal way with Dylan, even if he acted as though it was nothing.

Dylan sent Vanessa a sharp look. "I'm fine. We'll all

be fine." He turned his attention back to Adele. "I prom-ise you that."

Vanessa was not a jealous woman, or at least she hadn't been. But it burned in her now. Which pissed her off. At Dylan. At Adele. At No-Neck and Eyeballs out there. But mostly at herself.

Adele grasped for Dylan's hand, squeezing when she found it. "I feel so much better being in here with you two. It's awful being alone, not knowing what's going to happen."

"You don't have an idea or two of what they might be after?" Vanessa asked, hoping to sound innocent rather than sarcastic. "I mean, you've had more time with them. We escaped. Of course, you weren't in the back of the van with us." She smiled blandly.

"I was in the front," Adele said, letting Dylan's hand go and dabbing at her nose with the tissue again. "Tied up in the front seat. Only one person could fit, and they needed me to navigate. You were knocked out and Dylan was…uncooperative." She stumbled a bit over the words, and Vanessa thought it sounded rehearsed, but she had a practiced, simple excuse. Vanessa had to give Adele that.

"How'd you get in the van without us seeing you?" Dylan asked. There was speculation in his tone, but his voice was gentle.

"They took me out the front before they ever came into the back, at least that I can figure. I sat tied up in that van for I don't know how long before they returned and drove off."

It was a quick and plausible explanation. Vanessa scowled. This woman was a pro liar, that was for sure. Vanessa could tell Dylan was doubting her involvement, but Vanessa refused to entertain doubts. Sometimes you had to be hard and unyielding to get what you wanted.

She wanted her freedom and Dylan's safety.

*Maybe you just want Dylan.*

Well, maybe she did. But she couldn't get anything she wanted until they were home, safe in Bent, with only family curses to threaten them.

DYLAN WASN'T IMMUNE to Vanessa's speculative gaze. He understood it, even. The evidence pointed to Adele.

But was it too easy to put the blame on Adele? Dylan had the feeling something else had to be behind this. Maybe Adele really was being forced to cooperate, and since she was willing and not fighting, she was given certain things like a change of clothes.

Dylan knew Adele. He'd trusted her with the bank. He couldn't quite accept she was wholly behind this. Vanessa didn't know Adele personally, even if she was starting to remember more.

Something warm and very dangerous filled him at the thought of that kiss, of those memories. He wasn't foolish or romantic enough to think his kiss had unlocked her memories in a scientific sense, but it was nice to pretend.

Not the time or place though. Adele was shaking.

Well, if he sat back on his haunches and analyzed it the way Vanessa was, with some cynicism and suspicion, it was more that same vibration as when she'd sat next to him on the couch during the phone call. It reminded him more of excitement than nerves.

But people expressed nerves differently. He still had enough soldier in him to know he couldn't judge people's reactions by his own. Before he'd made sniper, there'd been a fellow soldier who'd giggled whenever they got into trouble in basic. Not because he was happy, but because nerves made him laugh.

That kid hadn't made it through, but remembering it

reminded Dylan that not everyone could control and hone their reactions to danger. More so, not everyone reacted in a way that made any sense.

Still, Adele's actions struck him as off, and he was still enough of a soldier to be wary of behavior that didn't make sense or follow a pattern.

Fear didn't always, of course. People didn't always. But he'd be wary until he found something concrete to believe in. Wary didn't mean cruel. It meant careful.

It wasn't like he could go by Vanessa's clear Adele-is-evil judgment. Vanessa had made a life out of distrusting people from the outset.

It irritated him that his own radar was compromised by knowing Adele for so long and not really ever *getting* to know her. She was Adele Oscar. Bank employee. He knew her attitudes about customers and the cleanliness of the teller station or her shared office, but nothing about how she'd act in crisis or what her background was that would inform her reactions.

Dylan couldn't let frustration lead him though. He had to focus on the task at hand, even if Adele was a wild card he couldn't pin down.

They needed an escape plan. And three against two was better than two against two. Especially when two on one side were armed, and one on the other side was pregnant.

"If they needed her to navigate, she knows where we are," Vanessa pointed out, not kindly. "We only need to find a way to have her make a phone call to get help up here." She sent Adele a challenging smirk.

Adele's eyes went wide. "I don't know where we are. Not really. Not enough to lead someone here." She grasped for Dylan's hand again, and he let her find it and squeeze.

"You could give them everything you know," Dylan said gently. "If we could get access to a phone, we can call my sister. Even with just some clues, the police would be able to track us down, if they haven't already pinged your phone."

"Pinged my...? Oh, maybe, but they made me turn it off. It's only been on when we made our phone call."

"Well, that doesn't mean we can't get a phone call in, and you can tell the police everything you remember seeing on the drive up here."

"It was dark," Adele said weakly.

"No. Not that dark," Dylan countered, extracting his hand from hers. She should be excited about the possibility of getting them out of here. Not shrinking away from it. No reaction to fear would make a person refuse to help them escape.

He stood and moved next to Vanessa.

"I don't know... I can't remember." She looked up at him pleadingly.

Dylan couldn't find compassion for her when she wouldn't even try to help. He narrowed his eyes at her. She swallowed audibly and even scooted back in the chair.

"Think," he ordered sharply. "Tell me everything you remember, no matter how insignificant it seems. But we'll start at the beginning. After they left the bank, which way out of Bent did they go?"

Adele blinked, her eyes darting everywhere. Her hands fluttered until she linked them over her lap. She took a deep breath. "I'm really not good under pressure," she whispered.

He'd seen her deal with difficult customers. Large, angry men who thought they deserved a loan, or a customer wanting a check to be cashed even if they didn't have the proper identification.

She'd never crumbled under pressure then. Either there was more to the story than she was telling them, or she was behind this. Either way, he'd be calm but firm. Until he knew for sure.

"All I'm asking you to do is describe what you saw, where you went. No one's going to blame you if you don't remember everything perfectly."

Adele nodded vigorously, twisting her fingers together. "Okay. Okay. I was afraid, Dylan. So afraid." She looked up at him, tears in her blue eyes.

They were meant to stir up sympathy, and it worked. He softened, even as he could all but feel Vanessa hardening next to him. Adele shrunk back in her seat, clearly intimidated by Vanessa's cold glare.

So Dylan stepped in front of Vanessa, a kind of shield. For both of them really. Vanessa could bore holes into his back, and he could hopefully find a way to get through to Adele. "You just take it easy and tell me what you remember."

Adele sniffled and nodded. "Okay. Okay. So. They started driving. Out of the front parking lot, but instead of getting on the highway, they drove down Ellington toward the back of town."

Dylan nodded. He'd figured that part out himself. He'd managed to pay attention to the turns in the back of the van, but measuring distance was harder since he hadn't been able to determine how fast they were going. He had a feeling he'd been lost the minute they'd gotten out of town.

"Then they went north, I think. I'm not good with direction."

"What road after Ellington?"

She pushed her fingers to her temples. "I-I'm not sure. I was just terrified. I wasn't paying attention. Those guns." She shuddered. "I never thought I was squeamish about guns, but they're so—so—"

"The roads, Adele. Let's focus on the roads. Ellington to the back of town then north?" He didn't think they'd gone north based on the sun's positioning when they'd escaped, but he'd draw out what she claimed to remember anyway.

"Country Road B maybe? Yes, I think that might be it. North toward the Tetons, maybe? It'd be isolated." She pressed her fist to her mouth. "We're *so* isolated," she whispered, a tear falling over and onto her cheek.

This time it didn't soften him. Everything she told him was the exact opposite of his own theories, his own gut reactions. He'd been paying attention. They'd gone to the back of town, then south. Not toward the national park.

Maybe he should trust the woman who'd seen it all, but Dylan couldn't bring himself to compromise what he *knew* in his gut to what someone he didn't trust claimed.

They *were* in the mountains though, and this nice cabin was more suited for Jackson Hole than anything south of Bent.

Maybe his instincts had been off. He had been beaten pretty badly. It could have messed up his sense of direction.

Hell. This was a mess. He didn't like second-guessing himself. Second-guessing got you killed in war, and this wasn't all that different from war.

"She's so full of it," Vanessa whispered into his ear.

Dylan gave Vanessa a sharp look. She returned it with a baleful one of her own. Because she'd been out of sorts—physically and in the memory department—and they were kidnapped and all, he'd somewhat forgotten her normal personality of doing the exact opposite of what anyone asked of her.

"Excuse us a second." He took Vanessa's arm and moved her to the far corner. They were all still in the same room, but if he kept his voice low, surely they could have a conversation Adele wouldn't overhear.

He huddled with Vanessa, lowering his mouth to her ear so he could whisper. "It isn't fair to hold her to our standards."

"What does *that* mean?" Vanessa retorted, crossing her arms over her chest. She kept her voice low, but she didn't whisper.

He kept whispering. "It means you grew up a Carson, and I was in the army. We're not exactly *normal*."

He could tell she took some offense to that, and probably wanted to argue with him that they weren't at all similar, but she didn't. She sucked in a breath and let it out, then glared over his shoulder at Adele. "She's fishy, one way or another." That one she definitely whispered.

He glanced over his shoulder at Adele. She was looking at them intently, but based on the confused line between her eyebrows, he didn't think she was getting most of the conversation.

"I agree with you on that, but that doesn't mean we can just leave her here. Any escape plan has to involve her, even if we don't trust her."

"There's too much goody-goody Delaney in you."

He managed a smile. "Some things you can't shake."

Her brown eyes met his, and he saw something venturing on soft there in the edges if he looked closely. Very, very closely. "Like feuds and curses?" she asked carefully.

He couldn't resist dropping his forehead to hers. "Like

who we are, underneath all that." And underneath all that, he thought they could maybe be something.

But first, they had to escape.

# Chapter Thirteen

*Back in Bent, Adele Oscar's house*

"Nothing." Laurel couldn't keep the disgust out of her voice. They'd gotten the search warrant to go through Adele Oscar's residence and so far had come up with nothing. Meanwhile, the seconds ticked down and Dylan, Vanessa and Adele were still missing.

She hadn't slept last night. She'd convinced herself it was because she was anxiously awaiting the search warrant to come through or something from the phone company about a location hit on Adele's cell. She was worried about her brother and sister-in-law, so tension and sleeplessness could only be wrapped up in work and fear.

Surely it wasn't over the silent, stilted dinner she'd shared with her husband last night. That was just anxiety. They were both worried about their siblings. It was natural there'd be this wall between them. Grady and his cousins were probably breaking laws trying to find Vanessa, while she was toeing the law's line trying to find them.

But they'd gone to bed and turned away from each other, and it had eaten at her all night.

She closed her eyes and rubbed her hands over her

face. On the job wasn't the time to think about her emotions or her marriage.

"You okay?" Hart asked, a note of gentleness in his voice. "You're looking a little, as my mother would say, peaked."

She opened her eyes to give Hart a sharp, fierce look. "I'm fine."

He shrugged. "If you say so, boss."

"I'm not your boss," she grumbled, closing Adele's hall-closet door, which contained nothing but meticulously organized coats and shoes.

"No, but you're grooming me," Hart said conversationally, taking off the latex gloves he'd used to poke through the trash.

"I'm not," she protested, probably stupidly. She was irritated he'd figured her out but also impressed. She'd been trying to be subtle, though that had never been her strong point.

"You've let me take the lead on almost everything. Laurel, I've worked with you enough years. You never let anyone take the lead without a very specific reason, and this is your *brother*. There's no way you'd let me take the lead without a reason. You're grooming me."

She let out a sigh. It would have been nice for him to keep thinking he was just her help, but he'd figured it out. That was good, all in all. "Okay, I'm grooming you."

"Leaving us?" he asked, his voice devoid of any tell. Also impressive. He'd grown a lot in the past few years. She felt a kind of older-sister pride in that.

"Temporarily."

Hart raised his eyebrows. "Never thought I'd see the day you'd..." He'd need to work on his poker face, because when he finally figured things out, his eyes got a little wide as it all clicked.

"Oh. *Oh.* Well, I guess congratulations are in order."

"We've got a ways to go till congratulations are in order. It's still early and no one at the department knows yet."

He frowned. "They should know, Laurel."

"You sound like my husband."

"And you're irritated I do because you know we're both right. They should know, and you shouldn't be running yourself so hard. Pretty sure you should be on desk duty."

She might have gotten bent out of shape about Hart of all people scolding her, but there was one simple truth to this case. "My brother and sister-in-law are missing and in danger. I can't step back. I'm taking care of myself. You're here, aren't you?"

"I'm here. It's wild though. You and a Carson. Your brother and another Carson." He shook his head.

"What? You think the whole town is going to fall down around our ears?" She asked it too sharply and with too much of her own baggage weighing the words down. *Idiot.* She needed to get ahold of her personal ties to this case. Pregnant or not, family or not, she had to be the detective this case needed.

But Hart didn't flinch or evade. He smiled kindly. "Nah. Just crumble at the edges a little bit. Maybe a few more kidnappings and fires. Mob might come through and get me shot again. But eventually Satan and hellfire will get bored. Bent doesn't die."

She laughed a little at the Satan-and-hellfire bit, but it hardly felt far off. They'd had a lot of trouble over the last year. It had started before her and Grady but not by much. Most of the trouble happened after.

She did *not* believe in curses. Or feuds. At all.

On a deep breath, she repeated Hart's words to herself. Bent didn't die. Through all the trouble, even the trouble they were knee-deep in, Bent kept living, and so did its people. Even if there were curses, Bent would weather them all.

*And so will we*, she thought to herself, twisting her wedding ring on her finger.

"Let's get ready to go." But first she'd send a text to Grady. She pulled out her phone, surprised to find one from him already there.

Taking care of yourself & co, princess?

She smiled at the & co, and what she knew was a tentative peace offering. She decided to offer one of her own.

Doing my best. I'm going to knock off early. Take a nap.

Real nap or metaphorical nap?

Depends. What time can you be home?

I'll beat you there.

Simple as that, she was settled again, centered. She'd married a good man. He'd married a good woman. And whoever was crazy enough to kidnap a Carson and Delaney together was definitely going to come out with the raw end of this deal.

"Ready?" Hart asked.

Laurel looked around the living room. "Yes. We've been through everything, and I think I'm going to take the afternoon off. You can handle things for a while— call the phone company again and again if you have to. We've got to get something on that ping, but my brain's mush. I need a few hours." She started for the door, but then she stopped at a little desk in the corner. They'd gone through it looking for clues and hadn't found any. But she realized, now that they'd been through the whole house, the little stack of paint samples and fabric swatches on top of the desk didn't actually match anything done inside the house.

"Hart. Look at this."

"Yeah." He picked them up. "Paint samples and fabric swatches. You think she's planning on coming into some ransom money to redecorate?"

"Could be, but things have been marked off. Chosen." She didn't say anything else and instead waited, wondering if he'd come to the same conclusion she was coming to.

"But..." He looked around the living room they stood in. He took the time to walk around the entire house again, studying fabrics and paints in contrast to the samples he held in his hand.

"This isn't for here," he finally said, certain.

"No. She has another residence. Or had one built. Recently."

"A new cabin, perhaps? Like the one your father described Dylan sitting in the middle of, with Adele Oscar silent and scared next to him?"

Laurel kept pulling the thread. "Surely she wouldn't be so stupid as to kidnap someone to a cabin in her own name. And we checked all the new constructs in the area. We didn't see her name."

"But she put herself on camera. Made herself look like a victim. We'll expand our search now that we've got a name and a reason to," Hart said, sounding suitably in charge. "But there are other options here."

"Like what? If she's redecorating, it's *her* place." Laurel began to think of all the ways that could be untrue, but she waited for Hart to explain his own theories.

"Two possibilities. First, it's her place but it's not under her name—at least the name we have. What if she bought it under another name? A name attached to a bank account where ransom money couldn't be detected."

"God, that's far-fetched." And possible. So completely possible.

"It could also be under a boyfriend's name. Or a family member's. She could have a stake in it without her name being on the papers."

A boyfriend. There was definitely no evidence of one, and the people at the bank they'd talked to couldn't list any friends she might have spent time with outside of banker hours.

But the bank.

"There's a third option."

Hart snapped his fingers. "She works at a bank and handles home loans."

Laurel nodded. "Let's see if we can subpoena some bank records."

# Chapter Fourteen

Vanessa wanted to escape this cabin because of the men with guns and whatnot, but at this point she also wanted to escape because she was going absolutely stir-crazy.

"Can't you just take them out?" she demanded irritably of Dylan as he went over the layout of the cabin with Adele again, trying to understand the full scale and find weak points for escape, or so he said.

Adele gave Vanessa a speculative look and Dylan gave her a censuring one. He still didn't want anyone to know about his secret. It made her want to scream. Partly because it was a stupid secret, and partly because they were kidnapped and who *cared*? Let everyone know that with a gun in his hand, Dylan Delaney could pick off anyone standing in their way.

"They have guns. We don't," Dylan said simply.

"We only need one," Vanessa returned.

"They'd still have one. We can't risk it."

Dylan's patient, indulgent tone pissed her off, even if he was right.

Right and protective and sweet somehow. It made no earthly sense that a part of her wanted him to bust into army-sniper mode, and another ached for the man who thought he had to hide himself because of his name and

Bent. She felt the second on a much deeper level than she wanted to.

She didn't have secrets. Bent and her family knew who she was...sort of. Maybe she'd cultivated a big-mouth, rough and dangerous, say-anything personality because she felt like she had to in order to survive being a Carson—especially a female Carson. You had to be hard and you had to be rough, or you had to leave. Hadn't her aunt disappeared and not talked to the family for years? She hadn't fit the mold—so instead of trying to fight that, she'd escaped.

Vanessa had done everything she could to fit the mold, even when she hadn't particularly felt as rough-and-tumble as she was supposed to be. She'd probably cut off some fingers before she'd willingly show any soft side to her family or to Bent in general.

"Maybe we should ask for food," Adele suggested brightly. "It might help everyone's mood."

Vanessa sent her the dirtiest look she had in her arsenal. Maybe she *was* hungry and irritable, but that didn't mean she appreciated Adele pointing it out.

"Good idea," Dylan said, striding over to the door. He began pounding on it until No-Neck appeared, growling and vicious.

"You need to feed us," Dylan demanded. "It'd be easier if you gave us some snacks and water to keep in here."

"Yeah, I'm real worried about your easy, pal," No-Neck returned with a snort, but he eyed Adele and then Vanessa. "Only because Boss's orders are to keep you alive and well. You'll come with me. I ain't your chef." He gripped Dylan's arm and yanked him out of the room.

Well, Dylan allowed himself to be yanked, Vanessa thought. He'd had that furious, violent look on his face, but then he'd tightened his jaw and banked it. She noted he couldn't seem to sweet-talk the guards, but he'd feign weakness for them.

She realized it was because he was used to one and not the other. He was always feigning weakness and never trying to sweet-talk anyone.

That flutter was back around her heart. Like she was impressed with him or something. Like he kind of amazed her and she wanted…

Well, it didn't matter what else she wanted right now. Just freedom. That was all that mattered at the moment.

Adele began to wander around the room in Dylan's absence. She touched a chair, poked at the wall. Her gaze went to the ceiling, the high, narrow windows.

It was dark, Vanessa noted. They'd been here two days now, with almost no sleep, and that was after their uncomfortable night in the woods.

She had to believe people were working to find them, but this was an awful long time not to be found.

"I didn't realize you and Dylan were so…chummy," Adele offered. A casual observation, or so Adele wanted Vanessa to believe.

Vanessa snorted from her seat in the desk chair. She was feeling a little queasy again, though not as weak. Adele walking in relative circles had her closing her eyes against the round of dizziness she could now remember was just one of her lucky pregnancy symptoms. "Chummy?"

"Is that not the word for it?" Adele chuckled. "There's certainly a connection between you two. An energy."

"Energy," Vanessa muttered with some disgust, opening one eye hesitantly.

Adele had stopped her prowling so she was standing in front of Vanessa. She leaned close, as if they were two girlfriends conspiring with each other. "It just crackles in the air."

"It's called hate," Vanessa returned flatly. Adele was fishing, and Vanessa wasn't about to be the trout she landed.

"You're pregnant," Adele said gently.

Vanessa gave Adele a steely look while she fought the urge to touch her stomach. "Not by a damn Delaney."

Adele rolled her eyes. "I never understood this town's obsession with Carsons and Delaneys. You're just people, like the rest of us."

Vanessa noticed she said *this town*. Maybe it was just the way she spoke, but it gave Vanessa a tingling jolt of excitement. Maybe they weren't that far outside of Bent if Adele was referring to *this town*.

"Besides, you two were wound around each other like vines when I was thrown in here. You can't tell me something isn't going on. Or maybe you just don't remember."

Still fishing for information. Assessing Vanessa's memory and relationship with Dylan with every question, every glance. Why would she need to know the nature of her relationship with Dylan or the state of her memory if she wasn't gathering information for something?

"It's an awful bump. Not recognizing people. Pregnancy. Quite a trauma."

"I'll live," Vanessa replied.

"Of course." Adele sighed gustily. "As soon as we get out of here."

"A shame you can't help that along."

"We can't all be like you, Vanessa. So strong and sure of ourselves. We can't all be Carsons and Delaneys in Bent. That would get a bit incestuous, wouldn't it?"

There was an edge to her voice and Vanessa wanted to smirk. She thought with the right attitude, the right throwaway comments, she might actually be able to break Adele into showing her true colors.

"And yet Carsons and Delaneys are all Bent seems to care about," Vanessa said with a sweet smile. "The world spins on and on, and all the citizens can seem to care about is Grady and Laurel getting married. Old man Delaney having an affair with a *married* Carson all those years ago."

Inspired, Vanessa blinked her wide eyes at Adele. "Oh, Mr. Delaney. I'd guess you worked more closely with him than Dylan, before Dylan came home."

Adele's face was perfectly blank, but everything about her was tense. Vanessa let her smile go sly and wide.

"I work with everyone at the bank," Adele said, in something like a robot voice. No inflection, no emotion.

"Sure, but Mr. Delaney is the boss. The head honcho. Surely there's some need to please the guy in charge?"

Adele's jaw twitched and her hand curled into a fist before she quickly released it. "I do my job. I've always done my job."

It was there, somewhere under the control—a breaking point. And it centered on that job. Vanessa only had to find it.

But Dylan returned just then with some food—more horrendous pizza pockets—and a few bottles of water.

Vanessa kept her attention on Adele. All that speculation, that intent staring and incessant questioning? Gone. The anger and tension melted away.

She was playing some kind of role, and Dylan was falling for it hook, line and sinker.

*Men.*

Vanessa couldn't even hate him for it because she knew it stemmed from that innate Delaney goodness.

He wanted there to be good in the world, and he wanted to believe the people in his life were that.

Vanessa wanted to blame it on arrogance and the fact he just couldn't believe someone who'd worked for his family for a decade was bad, because that would make his initial estimation about Adele wrong. A few days ago she *would* have blamed it on that.

But it wasn't that. He wanted her to be good because thinking people were bad was always his last resort. *Unless it has to do with Carsons.*

True enough, and yet he'd jumped to help Vanessa herself, taken care of her, protected her this whole time. Maybe at some point she'd convince herself it was just because of the accidental pregnancy.

But the kiss from earlier was too fresh in her mind. Dylan Delaney had fallen for *her* and was going to believe she was good regardless of all evidence to the contrary.

She swallowed, looking away from Adele to the man in question. He handed her a pizza pocket, wrapped up in a paper towel. This one was cooked through. He placed the bottle of water, already opened, on the desk next to her.

It was a gesture that, anywhere else, would have pissed her off. Why didn't it here?

"I think I have a plan," Dylan stated.

With that, Vanessa didn't have time to figure it out.

"Don't you think—"

Dylan already knew what Vanessa was going to say. Now, while he explained the plan, after the fact. She'd hate the plan simply by merit of her safety being paramount—and added to the fact he was going to tell Adele?

Yeah, he expected fireworks.

Hopefully, he'd learned how to deal with Vanessa's fireworks, because he was pretty sure he could pull this off.

"Those two idiots out there?" Dylan said, nodding his head toward the door and ignoring Vanessa's protests. "They *love* to talk to each other. They practically wrote down their evening routine for me."

"Just because we know their routine doesn't mean we could escape and then know where to go." Adele flicked a look at Vanessa. "I doubt a pregnant woman should be running around in the dark woods."

"You'd be surprised what a pregnant woman is capable of," Vanessa returned, her voice a low growl.

Dylan grinned at her. "*Very* surprised," Dylan agreed. "Plus, I'm not talking about escape exactly. I'm talking about diversions, redirection and calling for help." He gave Adele an encouraging smile. "With the information you gave me, I think I know where we are."

Adele nodded slowly. "Where is that?"

It bothered him she would ask that question. She should want to escape, not to check his theories. He could lie. He could tell her the truth, or he could avoid the question. He looked at Vanessa.

She was glowering at Adele, but she wasn't saying anything snarky. Dylan figured that was progress.

"Do you have any way to keep time, Adele?" he asked, ignoring her question completely.

She frowned. "Why are you asking me that?"

*I could ask the same of you.* Dylan held up his watch. "So we can make sure we act at the same time. Unless they let you stay with us all night, and I'm not sure that's going to happen. So we should have a way to act in the same moment. If you can tell time, we can decide on one."

"I don't think there's anything in the room, but I'm not sure."

Dylan shook his head. By trying to play it confused and uncertain, she was only proving herself to be in on the whole kidnapping. Still, he'd keep pretending that he trusted her, for the sake of his real plan. No matter how he could hear Vanessa seething behind him.

"That's okay. We share a wall. I'll come up with a signal. Two knocks, pause, two more knocks. That's how you'll know it's time to act."

Adele frowned. "Act on what?"

"The plan."

"We don't need to involve everyone in the plan," Vanessa said through clenched teeth.

Dylan looked back at her and held her gaze, trying to get across that he knew what he was doing. She remained scowling and infuriated.

"We'll wait until the middle of the night. Vanessa's going to ask to go to the bathroom. I'll knock on our shared wall right before she does. You'll listen for them to move around, open our door, lead her to the bathroom. Then it'll be your turn. You'll start banging on the door asking to go to the bathroom. Now, one of them sleeps on a cot in some room off the kitchen. So we'll have one guard confused by two women needing to use the bathroom. In the meantime, I'll slip out of our room and put in a 911 call off the landline."

"The door will be locked," Adele pointed out. "Even if you get around that, they'll hear you talking to the 911 operator."

He ignored the part about getting around a locked door. She didn't need to know everything he was capable of. "I won't say anything. I'll dial and leave the phone off the hook. By the time the guard notices, the dispatcher will already be tracing the call and sending someone our way. I'm sure of it."

"Well…" Adele chewed on her bottom lip. "Maybe it could work. But what if they realize the phone is off the hook because one of us dialed 911? Do we really want to risk them hurting Vanessa?"

It was a question that might have struck fear into him a few minutes ago and given him another reason to believe Adele had nothing to do with this. But he'd seen the evidence. Thank God for pizza pockets.

"No. We don't want to risk *anyone* getting hurt, but the fact of the matter is Vanessa isn't getting the care she needs here. We need to get her out of here. As soon as possible."

"I am right here and fully capable of speaking for myself," Vanessa said, a warning quietness to her tone that he knew well enough. Soon she'd go nuclear. He almost wanted to see it.

Instead, he chose to ignore her, because her being furious worked into his plans well enough for now. "I can handle anything those guards can dish out."

"Yeah, I bet a bullet to the brain would be *real* easy to handle," Vanessa muttered.

"Vanessa has a point. They don't want to kill you, Dylan. You're the one with the rich family. Vanessa and I? They could kill us with no compunction. Why don't we just wait until the ransom is delivered? I'd feel better. They've threatened my family, you know."

Dylan kept himself relaxed even though he wanted to tense. "No, that's not information you chose to share."

She shook her head and closed her eyes. "I've been so scared, so confused. Every step is a potential misstep and then my family is dead."

"I didn't realize you still had living family back in

San Francisco." He'd chosen the city because he knew she wasn't from there. He wanted to see if he could catch her in another lie.

"We're not close, but I don't want them to die." Her voice trembled, and she produced more tears.

Dylan felt no softening this time. Adele was a believable actress, and he could think of enough scenarios where she might have been forced or threatened into cooperating. Blackmailed into helping rather than violently intimidated into keeping quiet like the tactic the goons had taken with him and Vanessa.

But her family *didn't* live in San Francisco. He might not know everything about her, but she'd never spoken of family. She had spoken of going to Seattle or Denver on occasion over holidays, and the assumption had been for family visits. She never mentioned San Francisco.

So it was the final nail in the Adele-has-always-been-against-us coffin.

Dylan couldn't let her know there were nails or coffins. Somehow, despite his rage and disappointment, he had to keep it all under wraps. And he had to make sure Vanessa didn't blow their cover either.

So he whirled to face her, giving her the most murderous look he could manage while she sputtered and opened her mouth to certainly ask Adele why she hadn't mentioned this earlier.

She gave him a murderous look right back, but she didn't ask the question.

"Do you have a better plan, Adele?" Dylan asked calmly.

"Yes. We wait until the ransom comes and they let us go. They'll have to let us go."

"If you believe that, you're the dumbest human on the face of the planet," Vanessa spat.

Adele straightened and glared right back at her. "I beg your pardon."

"Do you?" Vanessa asked sweetly.

Adele returned the look. "I do beg your pardon. Because getting mad at such a trashy whore who doesn't even know the father of their baby is beneath me. So very, very far beneath me."

Vanessa straightened slowly, her hands clenching into fists and giving Dylan no doubt she'd throw a punch if given the chance. Dylan slid in between the two angry women and focused on Adele.

"Don't speak to her that way again, Adele."

"Hmm." She looked him up and down, cold, calculating disdain in her gaze. "Did that hurt your feelings?" she asked in a baby voice. "Because maybe she *does* know who the baby daddy is, and maybe it's you?" She pretended to gasp. "What would *your* daddy say?"

He took a step toward her before he remembered he was playing a dangerous game here. If Adele was the mastermind, he had to play it cool. He could wring her neck, and what would it do? He still didn't know what she was after, and the men out there with guns could easily kill them without Adele to play her little games.

No matter how his temper boiled, he needed to understand this better. More importantly, he had to get Vanessa out of the crossfire range before he attempted anything.

"You're starting to sound jealous, Adele," Vanessa offered from behind Dylan's back.

God, she wasn't helping.

"Let's all calm down. We're tired. We're hungry. We're lashing out at each other at the worst possible moment. We need to band together." Or at least he needed Adele to believe they had.

Adele took in a deep breath and let it out. She nodded.

"You're right, Dylan. Let's eat these awful things. We'll all feel better after."

Vanessa kept glaring, but she took a big bite of pizza pocket and chewed instead of arguing any more.

# *Chapter Fifteen*

Vanessa hated to admit she felt better after eating. Too bad eating didn't cure the fact Adele was evil.

Was Dylan *really* this stupid? she wondered incredulously. She hadn't thought so. But he was going over the plan with Adele again as if he trusted her. As if he didn't see all the holes in her story.

Vanessa had stopped listening, stopped getting angry, because it was pointless. He was the dumbest man alive, and he'd deserve what he got when Adele turned on him and shot him through the heart.

Even in anger, that thought made her blood run cold, and she had to remind herself Adele clearly wanted Dylan alive for some reason. She'd had too many chances to kill him or have him killed.

It could be money. People had done less for money, but Vanessa didn't buy it. There was something bigger at stake here. If only she could figure out *what* before Dylan got his dumb self killed.

The door flung open to the sight of Eyeballs waving that butt of his gun around like it made him important. Vanessa barely resisted the urge to roll her eyes. He hadn't acted particularly quickly to use it as anything other than a battering ram against Dylan. Should they really be scared?

He grabbed Adele roughly by the arm. Adele whimpered and resisted, but Eyeballs squeezed hard enough to have Adele gasping.

Vanessa watched the whole thing as dispassionately as she might a play. Eyeballs could rough up Adele all he wanted, but unless he used even half the force against Adele that he'd used against Dylan, Vanessa wasn't buying this as anything more than a farce.

"Ransom time, and you're insurance, sweetheart." He pulled Adele toward the door. "I'd stop making all that noise before we start hurting that family of yours. We've got a man in San Fran ready to go."

"P-please. Don't…" Adele stopped struggling and let Eyeballs lead her out of the room, the door slamming shut and the lock clicking into place behind them.

"What a load of—"

Dylan held up a hand. Vanessa was tempted to punch it, but he put a finger to his lips. Quieting against her will, she watched him as he moved stealthily to the desk and began clicking keys on the computer.

He'd tried to get past the password protection earlier and failed, so she didn't know what he thought he was doing *now*. But after a few clicks where he seemed to just fiddle with the volume directly from the keyboard, he started to rummage through the desk.

He pulled out a piece of paper and a pen. Then he wrote in big fat letters: BUG.

She didn't understand what on earth he was doing. He'd seen a spider or a cockroach. Who gave a crap? "I'm supposed to be scared there's a b—"

His hand clamped over her mouth, sending the pen, paper and chair between them clattering to the ground. He gave her face a gentle squeeze, opening his eyes wider as if willing her to catch on. It took a minute, but then she finally got it.

Bug. Listening device. Had she fallen into some bizarre movie?

"They won't know what's coming," Dylan said cheerfully, slowly letting go of her face. "This 911 plan of mine is genius, and Adele helping us is huge."

Vanessa frowned at him. He didn't sound like himself, and wasn't he talking a little too loudly? But she couldn't exactly mount objections if they were being listened to.

He righted the chair and picked the pen and paper off the floor. He scribbled on it as he repeated the plan he'd made with Adele.

It was only now that there was a listening device and he was still going on about his 911 plan that Vanessa fully understood. He didn't trust Adele. He was setting her up.

She read the note he'd written.

*I think the mic is in the computer. I didn't find anything earlier. Going to try to disable it.*

Vanessa looked around the room. She tried not to think about the things Adele or her goons might have listened to or heard. Even though she hadn't revealed anything particularly telling, Dylan had. Because she'd made him.

A wave of regret washed over her. Whoever was listening knew who and what he was now. They wouldn't underestimate him anymore. They knew about the baby and that it was Dylan's. There were no secrets.

*That* was scary. Money could maybe buy silence but not forever, and Vanessa still didn't think this was about money.

"Dylan…" Except she couldn't talk because they were

being listened to, and he kept trying to hack into the computer to turn off whatever was listening to them.

Vanessa glanced at the wires coming out of the desk and snaking their way to a power strip. She walked over, studied it. One of them had to power the computer, and without power to the computer...

She stepped on the thick main cord that hooked into the outlet, dislodging it. The computer went off with a *pop.* She looked up at Dylan and shrugged. "Oops."

He shook his head. "I was going for something a little less noticeable. If they notice the feed just die, they'll come fix it. Or put in a new listening device."

"I doubt they have backup listening devices. Besides, this looks like an accident—not that we knew they were listening. If they come and plug it back in, we know. And we can keep doing it as long as we need to."

Dylan looked around the room. "*If* that was the only listening device. I searched before, but Adele could have added one."

Exhaustion washed over her. *Another* listening device? How were they ever going to escape if someone could hear every word?

"They could be recording to play later too," Dylan said as if thinking it all through aloud. "So it might not be getting to them immediately, whatever we say. I certainly haven't heard them listening to anything when I've gone to get food, and you didn't hear anything when you went to the bathroom, did you?"

"No. But Adele's door was closed. *She* could be the listener."

Dylan nodded. "Adele wouldn't do that," Dylan said, but he made a big production of rolling his eyes and mouthing, *"She darn well would."*

Vanessa couldn't help but grin at him. He wasn't stupid after all. He was simply covering his tracks, throwing Adele off the scent. Thank God.

"Still, we need to be careful," he said. Then he wrote something down on a piece of paper and handed it to her.

*I'm going to search the room one more time with a better idea of what I'm looking for.*

It felt like he took hours. He left no stone unturned. She almost nodded off on the chair, but then he made her get up so he could search the chair.

"You're tired," he said as he poked at folds in the fabric and pushed on the cushion—presumably looking for something hard inside.

"Exhausted," she returned.

"I'm tempted to demand some kind of bed, but if they're off pretending to collect ransom, maybe the best thing is to keep a low profile. I'm about ninety-nine percent sure there's no other listening device, and the fact they haven't busted in to turn the computer back on or tell us we'll never call 911 makes me think they're just recording, not listening in. So we'll take a few hours to sleep."

"I want to go home." She did, desperately. So much so her eyes were starting to sting.

He crossed the room to her, sliding his hands over her shoulders. That touch, the simple *care* in his gaze, just about had the tears spilling over.

"I know. I know. I'm going to get you home." A promise. A vow.

She hated that tears spilled, that something like a sob escaped her throat. But instead of being horrified or letting her wiggle out of his grasp, he simply pulled her to him. He held her there, putting gentle pressure on her head until she rested it on his shoulder.

He didn't say anything—nothing to try to make her feel better or stop crying. He simply let her cry there on his shoulder, rubbing his hand up and down her spine.

So she wept. In a way she'd never, *ever* done in someone's presence before. She let it all out, like she was alone in the shower or something. But she wasn't alone. She had Dylan. And he was holding her like he always would.

She really had to get ahold of herself. Crying was ridiculous, but thinking about *always* was the height of ridiculousness. She pulled away from his grasp, wiping at her face with the palms of her hands.

"I'm—"

"I know you're not about to apologize for crying after you've been kidnapped and had a major head injury that caused temporary memory loss, all while pregnant I might add. Because that kind of apology would just be stupid."

She sniffled, glaring at him, which she assumed had been his intent. Get her back up and a little irritated with him so she wouldn't start blubbering again.

"You need to rest up," he said gently. "We have to see what comes of this ransom thing." He looked at his clock. "I want the second guard fast asleep before…" He trailed off, still worried about the prospect of being recorded or heard.

"They won't be able to hear a sound if they're still recording," she whispered. She was too tired to wait around for him to write notes and then keep her eyes open to read them.

"We're not going to call 911. Well, we are, but we're going to escape in the process. We will not spend another twenty-four hours in this cabin, I promise you that."

"You really think we can escape?" she whispered.

"I'm going to get you home. It's a promise."

She frowned at the way he worded that—so it was about her, not them—but he walked away and started chattering on about finding a makeshift bed.

IT WOULDN'T BE a comfortable nap, but it was sleep and that's what was important. Dylan had stacked two rugs on top of each other, tilted the chair on the ground so the headrest could act as a pillow of sorts and found a drop cloth in the closet that could act like a blanket.

She watched him the whole time he worked, wary and speculative.

He ignored all those things in her because the quiet worked. He needed to slightly reformulate his plan, and being able to do it without her questioning or arguing was easier. "Here. It's not luxury, but it'll do." He gestured her toward the makeshift bed.

"You think I'm used to luxury?" She stood where she was, eyebrow raised at the sad attempt at a bed. "Where are you going to sleep?"

He gestured toward the door. "Against it. That way, if they come in, we're ready. I can sleep against anything." He forced himself to smile. "All that army training."

She walked over to the pretend bed and scrunched up her face, but eventually lowered herself into it. She leaned her head against the headrest acting as a pillow, and then studied him.

He didn't mind being studied by her. Didn't mind *her*. Life had changed in a blink. He was still trying to wade through what that meant, but he couldn't get a handle on it until he knew she was safe.

Everything else could be dealt with once that happened.

Eventually, Vanessa patted the spot next to her. "Come here. There's room."

It was amazing how much he wanted to—a physical need he had to beat back. "Better to be ready." Sleep on the door so they couldn't be taken unawares.

"Come here, I said. Aren't soldiers supposed to follow orders?"

There was enough steel in her tone to have him smiling. "I haven't been a soldier in years."

"You've done an impressive impression of one these past two days. Now, do as Captain Vanessa says and get over here."

"Captain, huh?"

"You're right. I'm really better suited to general."

He chuckled, and really, what was the point in resisting? He'd protect her whether he slept next to her or against the door. Besides, he probably wouldn't sleep at all. Though getting an hour or two would keep him sharp, and he was pretty good at sleeping when he needed to, he'd never been in the position before of protecting so much that was valuable to him.

On a sigh, he crawled into the fake bed, facing her. They were close enough he could feel her warmth, count each faint freckle on her nose and the long inky lashes of her eyes.

"When did you figure it out?" she whispered.

He didn't have to ask her what she meant. "I've been suspicious the whole time, but Adele's a good actress and I... It's hard to believe someone you've trusted is willing to hurt you."

Something in her expression shuttered. "Not for everyone."

He didn't know much about her childhood, but he knew enough. The Carson generation that had raised the current one was full of hard men, mean men. Violent men. He'd used that as an excuse to hate all Carsons, but the truth was…

Hell, Grady was an okay guy. Dylan had never had a problem with Noah. Ty…well, sometimes he'd like to knock that guy's block off, but none of them were like their fathers.

"No. I guess you're right." Unable to stop himself, he reached out and brushed some hair off her face. "But no one ever gave you a reason to trust them not to hurt you."

She shrugged jerkily. "Grady. Noah and Ty."

"That's different. Believe me. When it's just kids it's different. You need an adult who has your back. You guys never had that."

"You softening to Carsons, Delaney?"

"I'm going to be a father to half of one. I figure I better."

She held his gaze, and he saw everything he felt reflected there. Fear. Hope. Care.

"So, what sealed the deal? Regarding Adele?" she asked, her voice thick. He told himself it was exhaustion, but part of him wondered if it was emotion.

"When they took me to the kitchen to make the pizza pockets, I was trying to look around. See out windows, anything that might give me an idea where we are, and the door to the room she'd been in was open. There were two perfectly normal-sized windows. A computer. She's running the show, and the guys she hired to be the muscle don't have two brain cells between them."

Vanessa blew out a breath, sliding closer to him. Like this was their normal life. Nightly conversations in bed together where they weren't kidnapped and trying to sleep on the floor with office materials as bedding.

"I think it centers on the bank and on her job. When

you were out there, she was getting so angry with me. I kept poking at the bank, at your dad. It's something about that."

"Well, the bank is an endless source of money."

Vanessa shook her head. "It isn't about money." He noted she kept her voice at the lowest whisper yet. "I know it's not about money. You have to find the connection to the bank."

"She's off getting the ransom."

"It's a ploy or a lie." Her lips all but brushed his ear, and it was the absolute wrong time to feel the wave of lust and want coming over him.

"What's a bigger motivation than money?" he asked, trying to keep his brain focused on the task at hand instead of being distracted by the way she shifted closer, so their bodies pressed together.

"I'm not sure I can come up with anything," she said, rubbing her cheek against his jaw. "If you've got money, which it seems like she does, at least enough to get by on, why would you go through all this for more? It has to be something else. Too bad we can't ask your dad."

Dylan smirked. "He'd always take more."

"Sure. We all would, but this is about what you'd risk. Why risk everything for money if you've got it?"

"Secret gambling habit? A family member's bills for an illness? This cabin?"

"No. It doesn't add up. This is something personal."

"Or she's mentally unstable. Also a thought we should consider."

Vanessa closed her eyes. "I'm so tired of considering."

He brushed his mouth over her temple, wanting to soothe both her and himself. He wanted them out of this too. Wanted her checked out and safe and sound at home.

Home. Something they'd have to talk about, because

he'd be damned if she raised their baby over her greasy deathtrap of a mechanic shop, and he had no doubt she'd fight tooth and nail to make sure their baby wasn't raised anywhere near Delaney property.

He rested his cheek on top of her head and held her close. They had all sorts of challenges ahead. The predicament they were currently in. The baby. But something in this quiet moment resisted all need to figure it out. He wanted to breathe, and he wanted peace.

Vanessa sighed against his neck. "I know it doesn't make any sense," she whispered, and this time he didn't think it was because of the potential of being overheard. "But we fit."

"Yeah, we do."

She pressed her mouth to his neck and then his jaw, sliding her body sinuously against his.

"Well." He had to clear his throat since it was suddenly dry as dust.

This time her mouth touched his, light and teasing, and then she nipped, causing his grip on her to tighten, just like the rest of his body.

"And for about five minutes," she murmured, right against his lips, "I'd like to pretend that's the most important thing in my life."

"Five minutes?" he scoffed. "Really?"

She chuckled against his mouth, maneuvering herself on top of him. "I don't need more."

Dylan slid his hands down her sides, enjoying the sweet pleasure of the friction between their bodies, even with clothes on. "I do."

She flashed him a grin. "Wanna bet?"

## Chapter Sixteen

Even though bets were what had gotten them into this mess—something she remembered around the time her clothes were quickly being removed from her body—this one felt right. He felt right. They fit together.

Maybe when they were back in the real world, she'd have to deal with that a little more head-on, but the real world wasn't here.

She took a moment to trace her finger over the small tattoo on his chest. She recognized it as the Delaney brand. It touched her. She had a quite a few tattoos herself, and some had heavy meanings, but she'd never branded herself with her family's legacy. It seemed both noble and a little sad that Dylan of all people had.

But she couldn't hold on to sad when Dylan slid into her. There was no world at the moment except them together. It was peace, and it was bliss. It didn't matter he was a Delaney, only that his body moving with hers felt perfectly right.

"Van," he murmured as she arched against him. He spoke her shortened name as if it was a precious, solemn prayer. He touched her like she was his to care for, and everything in her shimmered with a life she didn't know how to control or put her own impenetrable shell over.

"I want you. Us." *Us.* She wanted there to be a *them.*

Her brain couldn't wrap itself around that simple fact, but her heart had already made the leap. Maybe even before this whole mess. Maybe on that fuzzy night they'd conceived a child together.

She sighed into her release, holding him close as he found his own. When she drifted off, the sleep was deep, long and perfectly happy.

When she woke up—she wasn't sure how much later—she was somehow dressed and curled up in the makeshift bed Dylan had made. He was curled up behind her, arms wrapped protectively around her stomach.

She closed her eyes again, wanting to sink into this feeling of utter safety, no matter how uncomfortable the bed was.

But Dylan shifted, tightening then loosening his grip. She could feel him coming awake next to her, and the real world crashing back into them. She could tell his brain immediately clicked into gear, working out what the next step was.

Fear washed through her. Bone-deep fear that she'd lose him somehow.

"Are you sure it isn't safe to just wait? Surely someone's looking for you." A tension she didn't know how to label crept into her shoulders, and suddenly she felt... insignificant. "Do you think anyone knows where I am? I'm sure all of Wyoming has been rallied to look for Dylan Delaney, but does anyone know I'm a part of this?"

"Your car was in the bank parking lot. I'd wager there's an army of Carsons convinced *I* kidnapped *you*. They're probably roaming the mountains looking to take me down."

Vanessa laughed, snuggling into him. It was a nice feeling. Definitely new. She'd never considered herself a cuddler or a hugger. She got to sneak some cuddle time in with Noah and Addie's kid, but he was quickly turning into a toddler who squirmed and wiggled away.

She slid a hand over her stomach, and Dylan did the same. Their fingers brushed, both palms resting over the life they'd made.

"I know it's not the time to discuss it since we have to survive this all first, but how are we going to do this?" she asked, swamped with so much emotion she had to get it all out lest she fall apart again.

"I notice you've switched to *we* instead of cutting me out completely."

She turned in the circle of his arms to face him. "I guess you saving my butt a few times here and there during this whole ordeal softened me up."

"It's my fault you're even—"

"No, it's Adele's fault." Vanessa sat up and rubbed her eyes. There was a low-level queasiness in her stomach, but it wasn't as bad as usual. They could and probably should talk about not cutting him out of the future, but the reminder of Adele brought back the fact they had to survive first.

"Do you think she's back?"

Dylan pointed up to the windows. "It's still dark, but you can see dawn creeping in. She'd have to be back, wouldn't she?"

"There's one way to find out." Vanessa pushed to her feet and started for the door.

"Van—"

She looked over her shoulder at Dylan and winked. "Sorry, Charlie, pregnant women gotta pee and you aren't invited." She started pounding on the door even as he glared at her grumpily.

It took longer than usual for No-Neck to answer the

door. He looked a little rumpled, like he'd been asleep. Vanessa raised an eyebrow at him.

"Go to the bathroom. Try anything funny and I'll shoot." He led her out but didn't grab her by both arms. Before she even got to the bathroom, he let her go and trudged over to the kitchen area and began fumbling with a coffee machine.

Vanessa walked slowly toward the bathroom door, looking around the living room for signs of Adele. She didn't see the evil mastermind, but she did note that where there had once been a landline phone, there was now an empty end table.

*Evil witch.*

"Get on with it," No-Neck grumbled, waving his coffee mug at her.

She did as she was told and went to the bathroom. Since No-Neck was preoccupied, she took her time to paw through the cabinet under the sink, but there was nothing weapon worthy or helpful.

On a grunt of frustration she stood, just as No-Neck jerked the door open.

"Hey!" Vanessa protested.

"You're taking too long."

She sailed out of the bathroom past him. "You're cheery in the morning."

He gave her a shove, and only quick reflexes kept her stomach from slamming into the back of the couch. She turned to glare at him, but he was too busy gulping down his coffee and wincing, presumably at the scalding heat.

"Where's your buddy?" she asked.

"None of your business. You want another shove or you going to go back to your room on your own two feet?"

It was *so* tempting to say something snarky in return.

She briefly considered smacking the coffee mug so that it spilled on him. It would be enough of a distraction to...

*What? Get to the door and be shot in the back?*

Scowling, she sailed back to the room. She was going to grab the door herself, see if she could con him into forgetting to lock it behind her, but No-Neck was there in a flash, opening the door and pushing her inside.

She whirled and glared at him, which was good because she didn't look at Dylan standing right next to the door, pressed to the wall so he was out of sight from No-Neck.

As No-Neck grinned snidely at her scowl, he pulled the door closed. While he did it, Dylan soundlessly slipped something between the door and the frame.

"What—"

Dylan held a finger to his lips and shook his head. He led her over to the far corner of the room and then leaned down to whisper in her ear.

"Tape on the lock. Found some when I was looking for the bug. Not sure I got it on like I needed to, or that it's strong enough to keep the lock from engaging, but it was worth a shot." He shrugged. "We'll test it later. See anything out there? Adele?"

"Just No-Neck, but the phone that was on that table is gone."

Dylan didn't panic or frown or do anything she expected. He grinned.

"Why are you *happy* about that? It means we can't call 911! Our plan is shot to hell."

"Babe, that was never the plan."

She scowled at him. "Take your *babe* and shove it where the sun don't shine."

He grinned more broadly. "*And* it proves Adele is behind this."

"Yeah, because the giant window you saw in her room didn't," she returned sarcastically. "So, now what?"

"Now—" he took her by the shoulders, holding her gaze "—we plan *our* escape."

LAUREL COULD HAVE used a jumbo coffee. Instead she had to settle for water, because she'd inhaled her caffeine intake for the day by approximately 7 a.m. Now it was well after noon and she had been summoned to the Delaney Ranch to deal with her father.

She'd left Hart poring over the bank records they'd finally managed to get under subpoena. Still no cell phone ping to help them.

With a headache drumming at her temples, she knocked on the door and then stepped inside.

"Dad?"

"He's upstairs." Jen stepped out from the kitchen, where she usually was if she was home. "No word?"

Laurel shook her head and exchanged a quick hug with her sister. "State is setting up for a potential ransom drop-off, but they're having trouble getting details from the kidnapper. Apparently she's fallen off the face of the planet after her demand for money."

"Her?" Jen asked with a raised eyebrow.

"That's my theory." Which, much as she loved her sister, Laurel wasn't going to share more of. "Do you have any idea why Dad wanted me to come by?"

Jen shook her head. "He's been holed up in his office since he woke up. He wouldn't even talk to Cam when he stopped in." Jen looked up at the ceiling, worry lines creasing her forehead.

"Did Cam go out looking again?"

Jen nodded, wringing her hands. "I wish there was something *I* could do."

"Watching Dad is what I need you to do, okay? It's not fun, I know, but it's important."

"He's a mess."

Laurel nodded. "I'll head up. Thanks for staying with him while we work on this."

"You know you don't have to thank me."

"Yeah." Laurel thought briefly of telling Jen about the baby. She'd agreed with Grady not to tell anyone until she was further along, but Jen was her sister and her closest friend. Not to mention she'd had to tell Hart. "Listen…" Laurel chewed on her bottom lip. "You didn't see anything going on between Vanessa and Dylan at my wedding, did you?"

"Dylan and Vanessa?" Jen laughed. Hard. "You mean other than pure, unfiltered hatred?"

"Yeah, other than that."

"No. I mean… I don't remember really seeing them that much." Jen got a weird look on her face and then shook it away. "Do you really think they're together?"

"In more ways than one."

"That can't be," Jen said, surprisingly adamant.

"All evidence points to—"

"I don't care what all evidence points to. You and Grady are bad enough but Dyl…" She trailed off, squeezing her eyes shut. "I don't mean it like *that*."

"Yes, you do," Laurel said. Normally, it didn't bother her. Her family was set in their feuding ways, except Cam. She'd accepted that, moved on. But with being pregnant and Dylan missing, it stirred up…

Well, feelings she didn't have time for. "I'll be back," she murmured, heading away from Jen and her apologies and toward the stairs. She trudged up them, tired and dreading any discussion with her father while Dylan remained missing.

She knocked on the closed office door, only stepping inside once her father said come in.

"You wanted to see me."

"I've been sent another correspondence."

"What? And you didn't forward—"

"It was on the porch this morning," he interrupted, nodding to a manila envelope on the desk.

"How long ago?"

Dad shrugged.

"Dad. What's wrong with you? Why didn't you call me sooner? Why didn't you tell me you found a lead?" She was already pulling her latex gloves out of the pouch on her utility belt as Dad pulled a photograph out of the envelope. "You've got your prints on it."

It was grainy, but very clearly showed Dylan and Vanessa in a room that seemed to be a kind of office, arms around each other.

"Put it down. We could get prints off of it. We could—"

"Do you see what is happening in this picture?" Dad demanded, shoving it into her face. "And it isn't just this picture. The envelope is full of evidence my son has been lying to me for years. About everything. His education. His entire *life*, and now there's some nonsense about that *Carson* woman being pregnant and..." The rage on his face went cold. "You don't seem surprised."

"I knew Vanessa was pregnant as part of the course of the investigation," Laurel returned coolly. "Whatever other lies you're referring to, I'm in the dark on."

"And the baby being Dylan's?" Dad all but spat.

"It was a theory."

"How could you both be so—"

"No. No. We're not doing this. We're trying to find Dylan and Vanessa. You... How could you jeopardize them this way? You should have called me the second you got these. You never should have… How can you do this? All over something so insignificant."

"Insignificant? If he dared impregnate that scum—"

"What is wrong with you?" she demanded, temper bubbling over. "Dylan could be *dead* because of you."

He paled at that, but he still grasped the picture. "He's dead to me if this is true."

Laurel reached out and slapped him across the face before she'd even thought the action through. She expected regret to wash through her, but there was none. Dylan was in danger and an innocent bystander—a pregnant woman—was in trouble, and all Dad cared about was the family reputation.

"You're sick and twisted," she managed, though her voice cracked along with her heart. She ignored the tears of hot rage that spilled over. "Your son is in grave danger and all you care about is a *name*. A dusty old feud. You still talk to me and Cam, but this is somehow unforgivable?"

"You and Cam are not creating *children* with those mongrels. It goes against all our history. It goes against the very nature of Bent, Laurel. Carsons and Delaneys were not meant to be. Have you noticed what hell has gone on since you started your thing with Grady?"

She ignored the last part. She wouldn't let him put this on her. She wouldn't let him put this on *love*. "I am. I *am* creating children."

"I know you think that, but Carson will show his true colors before you—"

"No, Dad. I'm pregnant."

The picture in his hands fluttered to the ground and he sat with an audible thump.

"Your future grandchildren are all part Carson thus

far. I hope they all will be. And I hope to God you get it through your head that's something to be proud of."

Laurel refused to look at her father. She had a job to do. She pulled on the gloves so she could touch the pictures and envelope without adding her own prints.

"I don't know where I went so wrong with you children," Dad said, his voice faint and thready. "I taught you what was right, and this is how you've all repaid me."

"You did. You taught us the difference between right and wrong, justice and injustice." Hadn't he? Hadn't his four children grown up to be upstanding members of the community because he'd instilled in them a responsibility to do what was right? But the past year had shown her over and over again that her father didn't know what right was. "I don't know what happened to you that you can't see it."

"You're cursing us," Dad said, his voice sounding brittle and desperate.

Through this whole ordeal she'd wondered, no matter how stupid or utterly fantastical, if she hadn't cursed the town by loving the wrong man.

Except the man she loved was not wrong, in any way, shape or form.

"No. The curse all these years is this." She gestured at him. "This pointless, relentless hate. It's what you've all gotten wrong for over a hundred years. Hate doesn't solve a damn thing. It never has. It never will." She looked at her father, unbearably hurt. "But love will."

She'd believed in right and wrong, truth and justice, her entire life. She'd built her career and her soul on that very foundation, but the truth of the matter was that underneath that foundation was a base of love.

"I hope you change your mind in time to be the grandfather our children deserve." Because with love came hope and, hopefully at some point, forgiveness. "Now, while I'm busting my butt to get my brother home safe and sound, I hope you'll take some time to think about what you want to be the center of your life. Some stupid, pointless feud or your family."

She took the picture and the envelope and left her father silent and brooding. She sucked in a breath and let it out, compartmentalizing the hurt so she could do her job.

She left without saying goodbye to Jen, got to her car and bagged up the evidence. As she was backing up, her cell rang. She answered.

"I think I found it," Hart said, sounding breathless. "I called backup. We're heading out now."

"Address," Laurel barked.

"No way, Laurel."

"It's my brother."

"Exactly. I've got the manpower to handle it myself, and you've got the manpower to sit at a desk and wait."

She hated that he was right. She couldn't risk herself and her baby. She had to believe Hart could handle it. Which burned—enough that she said something she thought she'd never say.

"Fine, but I'm sending in my own backup."

"Laurel, I don't need Carsons."

"But you're going to get them." She always played by the rules, but if she couldn't be there to save her brother, she'd darn well send in a bunch of guys who would break every rule possible to save the people they and she loved.

# Chapter Seventeen

Dylan could wait with the best of them. He was a trained sniper. He could sit in one uncomfortable position for hours on end, gun at the ready. It had been his life for a couple years, and his capacity for patience and control hadn't just evaporated the moment he'd reentered civilian life.

But waiting with an impatient pregnant woman who couldn't sit still to save her life was driving him insane.

"Babe, you've got to sit."

She glared at him. "This whole *babe* crap is getting real old, real fast."

He grinned. "Okay, no babe. Honey, you've got to sit."

She crossed her arms over her chest. "Real cute."

"I know." But because he knew her glares and irritation were really nerves, he crossed to her and put his hands on her shoulders. He gave them a reassuring squeeze. "Waiting is the hardest part, but it's the most crucial. Timing is everything."

"We don't even know if the tape worked. Shouldn't we check?"

"We have to wait."

She groaned and tried to wiggle away from his grasp, but he only wound his arms around her waist and pulled her close, dropping a kiss to her neck. "I could distract you," he murmured, enjoying the way her resistance slowly melted into him.

But she didn't relax fully, and she kept her palms on his chest for distance. She looked up at him, some attempt at skepticism keeping her mouth from curving, but her eyes gave her away. He was tempted to tell her how easily they did, but he figured she'd only make sure they didn't anymore.

The slight humor there faded though, and she grew serious. "If this works—"

"*When* this works," he corrected.

She blew out a breath. "Fine. *When* this works, and we're back home, we sure have a whole hell of a lot to figure out."

"Maybe. Maybe that's all just details. Bottom line, when we're back home, you and I do everything to build the best life for our baby."

Her eyebrows drew together. "We'll never agree on the best life."

Dylan shrugged. "I think you'll be surprised by how much we'll agree on. But, first and foremost, we need to get out of here. So let's go over it one more time."

She groaned again, and again he held tight when she tried to push him away. "Lay it out for me," he instructed.

She glared at him, but did as she was told. "We wait until four, which is when they start their evening switch-off. No-Neck takes his little nap, and Eyeballs makes his dinner. We see if the tape worked, and if it did, we slip out. Me first. Then you."

"And if Eyeballs sees, or Adele pops up from wherever she's hiding?"

"I say I had to go to the bathroom and they forgot to lock the door. If pressed, I admit you picked the lock and forced me as a sacrifice to try to leave. If they start moving for your door, I scream and say I saw a spider. You'll create a diversion, and I'll run." She looked up at him, and this time he was pretty sure she let him see all the emotion on her face on purpose. "I don't like that part, Dylan."

He rested his forehead on hers. "I know, but we have to get you out of here, and the bottom line is if you're not in firing range, I can take out those two nimrods."

He wasn't scared of sacrificing himself. The way he saw it, unless there was some big surprise waiting for him, he had an 85 percent chance of survival. As long as she didn't try to interfere.

Which meant he had to make sure she didn't. No easy feat when the woman in question was as contrary as they came. But they had more at stake than each other.

"Van, it only works if you run no matter what. No looking back. No trying to save me. It only works if you're off like a shot and leave me to deal with them."

"Dylan—"

"You have to run. You have more than just yourself to think of. Besides, I can handle myself."

"I'm not just going to—"

"Promise me."

"I want it to be clear the only damn reason I'm doing this is because I'm pregnant, and I promised myself a long time ago I would do whatever it took to be the mother my mom wasn't and put my baby first. That's it. The *only* reason I'm letting you do this. Carsons don't run. They protect what's theirs."

He smiled. "So protect what's yours."

"You're both mine," she said fiercely. And she didn't take it back or look away. She held his gaze, serious and determined.

It rippled through him, all that it meant, all that he felt.

The thing was, feelings were dangerous. They led to mistakes, and he couldn't afford any. His first instinct was to compartmentalize, put them away for later.

But he needed Vanessa to understand, to do what he asked. Which meant he'd use those feelings, *then* put them away.

He pulled back enough to frame her face with his hands, ignoring the fact they might have trembled just a little. "I never thought I'd fall in love with a Carson."

He ignored her sharp intake of breath and kept talking. "Or during a kidnapping. Or after I'd already gotten someone pregnant. But maybe it's fitting, all in all."

He felt the tremble in her own body, watched the way she swallowed. Hard. "Well," she managed on a shaky breath. "I'm pretty sure even a week ago I would have told you I'd rather drink bleach than fall in love with a Delaney."

"Lovely."

"But I think I felt that way because…well, not because I hate Delaneys."

"You sure about that?"

"I hate your dad. And sometimes I just want to punch Cam in his perfect face for no real reason. I've never hated Laurel. I…" Her shoulders slumped and she pressed a few fingers right under the bump on her head that was slowly lessening in swelling. "We were friends. We didn't stop being friends because I *hated* her. It's complicated. And with Jen I'm mostly just ambivalent."

"That's my father and my siblings, but so far nothing about me."

She took a deep breath and pushed it out. "There's been something between us for a long time."

"Yeah, there has." Something undeniable in so many ways.

"I wanted it to be hate, but maybe it never really was."

He pushed some hair behind her ears. So many pieces inside of him that he'd hidden or locked away or tensed eased suddenly. "Yeah, maybe."

"Maybe that's always what's gone wrong. People have seen hate where there was really love and…well, anyway. I guess what I'm saying is I love you too, and I'd say I don't know why, but I know. You're good, and underneath all that polish you're as tough as any Carson. You care and I… This isn't some goodbye, is it? Because I'm not letting you out of this. We're riding back into Bent together. Screw their curse."

He smiled, because it was so her. Because he hoped they could make that happen. "No goodbyes. I just want you to know what's at stake. So you can promise me you'll run. You'll run and you'll protect that baby. And if you get a chance to call your brother and cousins to help me out here, I wouldn't say no."

"You don't want me to call Laurel and the police?"

He eyed the door, considered that. "I'd take both."

She took his wrist, tilted the watch to her gaze. "Looks like it's show time."

But he didn't release her. He held her tighter. "Promise me."

She shook her head, but she looked him in the eye. "I promise. I'll run. And I'll trust you to fight your own battle." She took his hand and placed it over her stomach. "But remember what you're fighting for."

He nodded. Kissed her once, hard, and then put it all away. Tied it up and shoved it out of his brain. It was a shame he couldn't, just for the next few minutes, shove it out of his heart.

He released her and a breath. "All right. Here goes nothing." He moved to the door. With care and patience he could all but feel made her bristle, Dylan twisted the knob. It gave, slowly and silently, and he ignored the excitement pounding in his chest.

He twisted the full way, then pulled. The door gave for a second, but then caught. He wanted to swear, but instead he kept his mind clear, calm.

"I need something to wiggle in here. Something thin enough to fit through the door crack. Like a credit card or a hair pin. Find me something." He held the doorknob turned all the way, ignoring the impulse to jerk the door open. They needed quiet.

And a metric ton of luck.

Vanessa hopped to work, pawing through the things on the desk. She found a spiral notebook and ripped the cover off. She held it up to him and when he nodded, she ripped it in half.

"Smaller," he instructed. She ripped it again and again until it was the size he wanted. She handed it to him, and he slid it into the space between door and frame. He wiggled the light but firm cardboard cover against the lock partially engaged by the tape.

It worked. He eased the door open.

The living room was empty, and as suspected, he could hear someone moving around in the kitchen.

He motioned Vanessa out, and she followed the plan, moving quickly and quietly to the front door while Dylan scanned the room for weapons he could use if they were caught. There wasn't really anything, but he trusted his fists—and his wits.

He didn't dare watch Vanessa since he had to observe the opening to the kitchen to make sure no one popped out. At one point he heard the faintest squeak of the front door and winced, then readied his body to attack.

But no one came.

Heart thudding with too much hope to contain, Dylan

began to back away from the living-room opening and toward the door. It couldn't be this easy. It couldn't be, and yet...

He made it to the door where Vanessa was poised in the opening she'd made, just big enough for her body. He nodded to her, then took the doorknob from her grasp.

He'd need to make the opening a little bigger to fit himself out. As he did, the door squeaked. It was faint, but he knew they would hear it.

Dylan gave himself one precious moment to look Vanessa in the eye. "Run." He gave her a little shove, shut the door and prayed to God she listened.

VANESSA RAN.

Tears threatened, some mix of anger and fear. What an idiot he was, shoving the door closed so he had to handle it all himself. That was not going to fly if they got back to Bent and got to plan their lives together.

"When. *When* we get back to Bent," she whispered to herself, running for the trees. Dylan had instructed her to run there first. Deep enough she couldn't see the house. Then she was supposed to stop and listen. If she didn't hear anyone coming after her, she was supposed to slowly inch her way back, using as much cover as she could, then follow the road back down the mountain.

If anyone came out of the cabin, she was supposed to run as deep into the woods as she could, and trust he'd be able to find her once he took care of everyone.

It was a desperate, stupid plan and she wanted to punch herself in the face for ever listening to it. But she stopped, deep enough she could just barely make out the faint color of the cabin far off in the distance through the trees.

They didn't come after her. For as long as that was true, Dylan was alive.

*Unless you don't matter and they only wanted him.*

She choked on a sob, but she got out of the crouch and slid slowly and carefully between trees, getting closer and closer to the tree line until she could make out the road.

She noticed there were two cars in front of the cabin and tried not to let that worry her. Nothing could worry her except getting the baby inside of her back to safety.

Another sob escaped her mouth, but she bit her lip to keep the rest in. She kept behind trees, moving forward quietly and carefully through the woods parallel to the road.

After a while, the sobs stopped and tears dried, and all she had was a grim determination to keep walking no matter how badly her feet hurt or her head throbbed.

When she reached a fork in the road, tears threatened again. She didn't know where she was. Should she try to cross the road and follow the opposite path? Or follow this one under cover? What if it wrapped back up into the mountain? What if she crossed the road and someone started shooting?

She couldn't take the risk of stepping into the open. One way or another, either fork would lead her somewhere eventually. She stayed on the fork that allowed her to keep in the tree line and trudged on.

On and on, until she had to stop and lean against trees for support every few minutes. Her head was spinning and her mouth was too dry. She was wrung out and dead on her feet.

But Dylan was back there somewhere fighting two armed men, and she had to save him. Somehow, she had to save him. She needed to get to a town, to a—

She stopped abruptly at the sight of a car parked on

the other side of the road. Someone was leaning against the hood.

Vanessa held very still, squinting through the trees. It was a tan car, with some kind of logo on the side. A logo she knew. And the person in baggy clothes and a puffy coat leaning against the hood was—

"Laurel." When Laurel didn't move, Vanessa realized she hadn't really said it. She'd gasped it, afraid it was a mirage. But as she weakly stepped forward, the police cruiser didn't waver and disappear. Laurel's serious profile didn't morph or change. She wasn't hallucinating. She wasn't.

Vanessa kept moving for open air and the road, still waiting for the image to disappear. "Laurel," she said as she stumbled through the tree line.

Laurel's head whipped around, and it didn't escape Vanessa's notice that her hand went straight for her weapon, though she didn't draw.

"Oh, my God. Oh, my God." Laurel dropped her hand from the weapon and immediately rushed across the road.

She was at Vanessa's side in a flash, and for a moment all Vanessa could think to do was hug her and sob. It was real. Laurel was here, and Dylan had gotten her out. She leaned against Laurel's shorter frame, squeezed her as tight as the strength she had in her body allowed and sobbed.

Laurel pulled away, though she held Vanessa upright, which was about the only thing doing the job at the moment.

"Dylan," Laurel said, eyes searching and scared. "Where's Dylan?"

"He's still there. He needs help." Vanessa swallowed, summoning her strength. "He's back there. He's back there. Come on." She grabbed Laurel's arm. "You've got a gun and a badge. I'll lead you."

But Laurel didn't budge. "We're not going back there, Van."

Panic and fear skittered up her spine. "What the hell is wrong with you? He's back there fighting off two goons with guns and a crazy woman. You have to get to him."

Laurel closed her eyes as if against some great pain, but still she didn't let Vanessa pull her toward the trees. "My men are handling it."

"Your *men*? Since when do you let a bunch of Podunk deputies save your flesh and blood?"

"Vanessa. Calm down." Laurel used her free arm to pull Vanessa's hand into hers. "Are you all right? I should call you an ambulance. Come on." She started leading Vanessa a few steps toward the police cruiser before Vanessa skidded them to a halt.

"No! I'm not going anywhere until Dylan is safe and sound. You have to find him, Laurel. You have to save him."

Laurel nodded. "We are. They're surrounding the cabin as we speak."

"It should be you."

Again, Laurel looked incredibly pained, but her voice was level and calm. Her cop voice. "It can't be me. For the same reason Dylan got you out of there."

"You…" It took a moment, or a few, to connect all the dots. Laurel knew. And she was… "You know."

"We had to search your place. Hold on." She lifted the radio on her uniform to her mouth and started using codes and police blabber to explain Vanessa was with her. "Two men with guns, and one woman? Adele Oscar?"

"Yes. You knew?"

Laurel led her to the passenger's side of the cruiser

and opened the door. "We figured some things out." Gently, Laurel nudged her into the passenger seat. "So, it's true. Dylan is..."

"The father of my baby? Yes. I surely hope Grady is the father of yours."

Laurel gave her a baleful look, then gently closed the door. She marched around the front of the car, then took her seat behind the steering wheel.

"We can't just sit here."

"We have to." Laurel shook her head. "You have to know it's killing me too, but...sometimes a woman has to make a sacrifice a man never has to make. We're making it. If it makes you feel any better, I gave Grady the address. It's not just my deputies up there."

Vanessa relaxed into the seat. "Thank God. Someone with some brains." And all the people she loved were in danger. "There has to be something I can do," she whispered to Laurel.

"There is. You're going to tell me everything you know about who's in there, what the layout is and what dumb plan got you out and is no doubt about to get my brother hurt, while I drive you to the hospital to get checked out."

Vanessa's eyes flew open and she reached out and grabbed Laurel's arm. "I'm not going anywhere until Dylan's out. I'll tell you everything right here, and once they get him out safe and sound we go up there. He's hurt too. Not bad, or at least it wasn't bad before. I'm not going anywhere without him."

"You love him," Laurel murmured. There was shock in her voice, but not censure. Then again, of all the Delaneys to censure it, Laurel didn't have a leg to stand on.

"Maybe I always did," she muttered.

Laurel smiled gently, taking Vanessa's hand off her

arm and then squeezing it and interlocking their fingers. "I know the feeling. Now, tell me everything."

So Vanessa did.

# *Chapter Eighteen*

The fight was a brutal marathon, but Dylan was still alive. He figured that was something. Now, if he could just get his hands on one of their guns, he'd be home free.

But he'd knocked No-Neck's across the room and, considering the man currently had his meaty paws around Dylan's throat, there wasn't much hope of getting to it.

Luckily, Eyeballs hadn't fared so well. He'd been the first on the scene, so to speak. When he'd lunged at Dylan as he was closing the door, Dylan had decided to use the door as his best weapon. He'd swung it open as Eyeballs lunged at him. The corner of the door had cracked right against Eyeballs's forehead, and the man had dropped like a deadweight. He was bleeding and moaning now.

But then No-Neck had come out to see what the commotion was. Dylan had considered running, almost sure he could outrun him. But he might lead the guy straight to Vanessa, and he couldn't risk that. Especially if No-Neck had some kind of vehicle.

So he'd fought instead. He'd managed to land a few decent kicks and get the gun away from him, but it had clattered out of reach. Then No-Neck had used his considerable girth to knock Dylan off his feet.

There'd been a moment of panic, which was why Dylan was in his current predicament of having the air slowly choked out of him. If he'd held it together like he had when he'd been a sniper, he would have been able to break the hold.

*Still can. Still can.* He chanted that to himself even as his vision grayed. He tested the mobility of his legs, feeling the pressure build and build in his head without the ability to take in new air.

One slip of his hand in the right place and he'd—

A gunshot rang out, and No-Neck's body jerked, eyes going wide and then blank as he lurched to the side, lifeless.

Gasping for air, relief coursed through him. Enough that he even closed his eyes. He'd been saved. Saved in the nick of damn time too. His throat ached, his head pounded, but God, he could breathe again and someone...

He opened his eyes, ready to be pissed as hell if Vanessa had come back.

But it wasn't Vanessa.

And he certainly hadn't been saved.

Adele gestured with the gun. "Get up."

Dylan couldn't follow orders because he couldn't make sense of this. "You killed him."

Adele glanced at the lifeless body. "Wasn't as hard as I thought it might be." She glanced at Eyeballs, who was still groaning. Then, before Dylan could even move, she shot him too. Not very cleanly, so she pulled the trigger again. This time, Eyeballs went still.

She turned the gun onto Dylan. She paused there though, not shooting like she had the other two. She watched him, consideration all over her expression.

Dylan didn't let fear enter. He focused on what he could do. She was just a little too far out of reach to knock off her feet, and it would take him a few seconds to regain his clear vision.

"Why are you killing your own men?" he asked incredulously. Surely she wasn't actually saving him.

"My own men are stupid and useless. How many times can they be overpowered by some second-rate unarmed soldier saddled with a pregnant woman?" She cocked her head, still studying him. "You're rather stupid, but you aren't useless yet. Get up."

Slowly, gauging every move she made, every potential action to grab her weapon, Dylan moved to his feet, but before he could fully straighten from his crouch—which was from where he'd planned to lunge and dislodge the weapon—the gun fired.

The searing stab of pain in his gut had him falling back to his knees. He bit back a howl, his body involuntarily shaking at the unbearable pain in his stomach.

He could feel blood seeping into his shirt, his pants, gushing out of the wound. Gritting his teeth, he sat back on his butt and pushed his hand over the hole. He needed a bandage. Hell, he needed a miracle.

"Sorry. Men with bullets in them are less likely to overpower a poor little woman like me." She shrugged. "Hope I didn't hit one of those internal organs."

Dylan could only hold his hands to the wound, hoping to God she was right. But the blood…

His vision grayed again, so he pressed hard and focused on the pain.

"This would have been easy, Dylan. Simple. But you had to complicate things," Adele said, walking in a circle around him. "No one would be dead if you'd done what you were supposed to. You certainly wouldn't be shot. Don't you always do what you're supposed to?"

"Guess not always," he managed to say between gritted teeth. He needed to get the gun away from her. Preferably before he passed out from blood loss.

"Your perfect daddy knows. About all of it. The sniper nonsense. Vanessa." Adele laughed. "God, I wish I could have seen his face. His precious prince knocking up a Carson. I never *dreamed* I'd get something that good, but you keep *ruining it*."

"Adele. Please, I—"

"Oh, don't patronize me. Don't try to mansplain my life to me."

She waved the gun around, enough to make him nervous. He could maybe survive this bullet wound. He wasn't so sure about another one.

"I'm smarter than you," she said, her knuckles going white on the handle of the gun. "I've always been smarter than you, but somehow you keep ending up on top. Not this time. I'm better. I've always been better."

Dylan fought off a wave of nausea. "If you kill me… Adele, it's over. You don't get any job, any life. *Yours* is over just as much as mine."

"Because you ruined it! I had a plan and you ruined *everything*!" She huffed out a breath and Dylan realized that in this moment in particular she'd lost it. Before, she'd been controlled. She'd had a plan, and he actually believed it hadn't been to kill him.

Now? All bets were off.

"That woman wasn't supposed to be there," she muttered, tapping the gun against the palm of her hand. "You weren't supposed to know how to fight. I rolled with the punches as well as I could, but these two fools were the last straw."

"You can't kill me, Adele."

She raised an eyebrow, and cold, bone-deep fear settled itself in his soul.

He cleared his throat, tried to focus his vision, his brain on anything except the constant wall of pain assaulting him. "Of course you *can* kill me. I'm suggesting it wouldn't be in your best interest."

"And you, of course, would know my best interest. Being a man and all."

He tried to make an argument, but the words sounded jumbled in his head. Everything around him was dim. Had someone turned off a light?

He tightened his grip on his stomach, but he was fading fast.

"I could let you bleed out." She pretended to consider it. "Killing you wasn't in the plans, Dylan. But plans change. Your father told me to be patient. He told me if I proved myself, the job would be mine. And you know what I did? I proved myself. Again and again. Above and beyond, and still *you* got everything."

"What does that have to do with me?"

"You got it. Killing you means you don't have it anymore. And your father suffers. Though I was hoping you'd suffer right along with him when he realized you were a lying, Carson-impregnating disappointment and kicked you out. But death works too."

"You'll miss out on your satisfaction," he managed to slur.

"Maybe. I didn't plan to kill you, Dylan. I just wanted to ruin you." She held the gun up again, this time at his head. "Turns out, I get to do both."

"Like hell." Though he knew it was just as likely to get him killed, he let go of the bullet wound and used his hands to push himself off the ground in the most fluid movement he could manage.

He'd thought to grab the gun, but mostly he just crashed into her. She fell backward, and he fell on top of her. They howled in pain at the same time, the gun clattering to the floor.

Dylan tried to fight, to think, but everything was going black. Pain. So much pain. It was so hard to remember what he was doing or what he was fighting for.

"I'm going to kill her too," Adele screamed, narrowly missing kneeing him in the crotch.

Her. *Them.* Van and his baby. He summoned all his strength, all his focus, shoved the pain away and made a grab for her arms.

His hands were slick with blood from pressing on his wound, and he couldn't manage to hold on to her wrists as she landed blows against his face and then—worse—right where the bullet wound was.

His body went weak and everything became a particular kind of black. Adele made some sound of triumph as she managed to slither away from him.

Dylan couldn't let her win. Couldn't. He struggled to his feet, his balance wavering as Adele rushed over to where the gun had fallen. Using his side that didn't have a bullet wound weakening it, Dylan grabbed the lamp off the table he was standing next to and heaved it at her as hard as he could.

It crashed against her, and she wailed in pain. She began to sway and fall. Or was that him?

A few seconds later, he realized he was on the floor. And someone stood over him.

It wasn't Adele.

It was Grady. And Ty. Carsons. "Am I dead?" Dylan managed to ask. "And in hell?"

Grady swore viciously. "He needs an ambulance. Yesterday." He nodded at Ty, who disappeared from Dylan's wavering vision.

"Adele?"

"If you're talking about the blonde, you knocked her out with that lamp business."

"Where are the police?"

"Setting up they said. They told us to wait. Aren't you lucky we didn't?"

"Grady." He could make out the man's face. Sort of. "Van?"

"Laurel's got her. They're probably on their way up."

"No. Don't let her…" He groaned at the wave of pain, the threat of pure oblivion—or was that death? "Help me up. Get me a clean shirt."

"You need a hospital, moron."

"Yeah. That too. Don't want her to know it's this bad, okay? Just help me… She can't know. Not until a doctor looks at her, okay?"

Dylan didn't really hear Grady's response, but then there were cops running this way and that. Someone ripped off his shirt and pressed a bandage to the wound. He wavered in and out of consciousness, but fought back every time.

He thought he heard Adele screaming, but the most important thing was Vanessa. She needed…

"Come on, tough guy," Grady muttered, pulling a T-shirt over Dylan's head.

"Get me on my feet."

"Ambulance will be here soon. Just sit ti—"

Whatever the cop was saying was cut off by Grady hefting him to his feet. "She's not going to buy this," Grady muttered.

Dylan breathed, letting his body lean against Grady's. "She'll believe it." One way or another. "I want her checked out and good to go before she knows how bad this is."

Grady shook his head, looping his arm around Dylan's waist. Dylan felt another arm helping him move forward. Ty.

"You're going to be dead before she knows how bad this is," Ty said disgustedly.

"Well, you just make sure she doesn't find that out either until she's talked to a doctor."

"He's got it bad," Grady said.

"Bad? He's got it terminal," Ty replied.

If he lived, yeah, it was damn well going to be terminal.

THE RADIO CALL for an ambulance made Laurel's blood run cold, but she forced herself to smile reassuringly at Vanessa. "They're out." She flicked off the radio, because if they started describing things… Well, as much as she wanted to know what had happened, it was more important to keep Vanessa calm.

She was too pale and even shaking, though Laurel had a sneaking suspicion Vanessa didn't realize her body was reacting to the shock and worry.

"Can we go? I need to see him. I need to be sure…"

"We'll drive up, just as soon as someone gives me an all clear."

"Laurel. If they called an ambulance, doesn't that mean there's an all clear?"

"Not necessarily. Listen—"

She was interrupted by the sound of her phone chiming. She pulled up the text and frowned at Grady's words.

I don't suppose you'd just take Van to a hospital and let us handle all this?

"We're going up," Laurel said. She kept her voice detached and her expression calm, but dread pooled in her stomach.

Surely if Dylan was dead someone would just come

out and say it. Surely. She swallowed at the bile that rose in her throat. She'd been a cop long enough to know how to deal with being sick with fear and appear untouched.

She drove too fast up the road toward the cabin Hart had told her about. Two police cruisers, one motorcycle and Grady's truck were parked along the road out of sight, but Laurel drove right up to the cabin.

There were two officers with a handcuffed Adele Oscar. She was bleeding from her head, but clearly yelling at everyone around her. Laurel hoped like hell the cut on her head was the only reason they'd called for an ambulance.

Laurel pulled to a stop. Hart, Grady, Ty and the other deputy Hart would have taken were nowhere to be seen.

"Stay here and—"

The cabin door opened and, before Laurel could stop her, Vanessa was out like a shot. Grady and Ty appeared, Dylan between them.

Vanessa rushed to him, but Laurel held herself back. There were a few things she noted about her brother. His face was a mess, but underneath bleeding cuts and blooming bruises, he was deathly pale. He was wearing what he'd probably worn to the bank the other morning, except for the shirt, which she recognized as one of Grady's T-shirts he often left strewn about the back seat of his truck. Lastly, Ty was all but holding him up.

But if Vanessa noticed any of those things, it didn't stop her. She flung her arms around Dylan and clung tight.

Laurel tried to get ahold of herself as tears stung her eyes and she felt the weakness in her muscles. Dylan's eyes weren't focused, even as he wrapped an arm around Vanessa and murmured something into her ear.

Slowly, Laurel approached, trying to gauge anything from Grady's expression, but it was infuriatingly blank.

"He's hurt. Let's give him some room," Laurel managed to say gently.

Vanessa sniffled and unwound herself from Dylan. "You need an ambulance."

"Getting one," he said, his mouth curving.

But everything about Dylan was wrong. Faded and weak.

"Van, let me take you down to the hospital. You've got your own knock on the head," Grady said.

He moved away from Dylan, who now leaned even harder on Ty.

"Why can't I just ride in the ambulance with him?" she demanded, pulling her arm out of Grady's grasp.

"You'll have a smoother ride with Grady," Dylan said. His voice was thready.

He was hurt way worse than he was acting, and no one wanted Vanessa to know. Laurel thought about demanding they stop, but Vanessa was a mess herself. Added stress wouldn't help.

"I'm afraid it's procedure," Laurel improvised. "We'll want your statements separately and without the other's perceptions clouding it. We want to make sure Adele goes away for a long time." She touched Vanessa's arm. "You go with Grady and get to the hospital. I'll follow in a minute to get your statement, and Hart will ride with Dylan in the ambulance to get his. Once we've done that, you'll be free to see each other as much as you want."

Vanessa frowned, but Laurel had a sinking suspicion time was of the essence.

"Go on now. We'll get this all sorted ASAP."

Grady managed to lead Vanessa away, though she kept

looking back. Dylan managed a smile, but Laurel didn't see anything other than a blankness in it.

"What is it?" Laurel hissed.

"Just wait," Dylan muttered.

His gaze stayed on Vanessa's retreating form until it disappeared around the corner, then his whole face went slack. He swore weakly.

"What *is* it?"

Since Dylan looked like he was in the middle of passing out, she turned her glare to Ty.

"He was shot. In the gut. That ambulance of yours better be quick."

"Get him on the ground," Laurel barked. "What the hell is wrong with you? Letting him stand up? Are you stupid?" Her voice cracked on the last word, and she helped Ty lower Dylan to the ground.

Laurel kneeled next to him, berating him the whole way. "How can you be this stupid?"

"Don't cry, sis."

"I'm not crying," she retorted, even though the tears were rolling big and fat down her face. "What are you doing getting yourself shot? That's my job," she managed, hoping to keep him talking, keep him awake. As long as he was awake…

"I'll be okay. Probably. Tradition, right? You, then Cam. Now me. Someone better get Jen a bulletproof vest."

"Not funny. Stay with me, okay? Stay with me." She took his hand and squeezed it. "You've got an awful lot of explaining to do, so you can't go."

He didn't squeeze back and his eyes were closed, but he kept talking. "Damnedest thing, Laurel. I love her. I don't know how it happened. It was like…there. Just there."

"Yeah, I get that." *Keep him talking. Keep him talk-*

*ing.* "One minute you think they're the bane of your existence and then you realize they were just…meant to be part of your existence."

"Meant to be. I never believed in meant to be, but I believed in a feud. How backward is that?"

"Nothing's backward if you right the ship." She could hear the faint sound of sirens and prayed they'd hurry. She pressed Dylan's palm to her cheek. It was bloody and beat up, and she couldn't hold back the sob that escaped her mouth.

"Laurel. Don't worry so much. It's going to take more than a bullet to stop me from being a father. Better one than ours."

It shocked her to hear Dylan say that. He'd been Dad's staunchest supporter, and he certainly didn't know about Dad's outburst earlier.

"Better than ours," Laurel agreed. "And you'll have to work on your uncle skills too, okay?"

"Uncle. You too?" He chuckled, though it sounded more like a wet wheeze that had Laurel crying all over again. "That's a trip. That's a—"

"All right." Laurel looked up, relief almost making her pass out as the ambulance came into view. "Time to show us how strong you are."

"I'll be okay. I'll be okay. Tell Van I'll be okay, yeah?"

Laurel got out of the way of the paramedics and turned away from watching them work. When she felt a hand squeeze her shoulder, she turned to see it was Ty.

"Come on. Let's get to the hospital."

She nodded, pulling herself together bit by bit. There was still a lot of work to do.

*Chapter Nineteen*

"Definitely a nasty bump, and the short-term amnesia is concerning, but it's probably more a response to trauma than head injury. Though you'll want to pay specific attention to headaches, vision problems, anything that might point to an underlying issue."

Vanessa nodded at the doctor and bit her tongue so she didn't say something like, *"I don't give a damn about me. Tell me about the baby."*

"Baby's heartbeat is strong. I don't think you'll have anything to worry about there, though I'd make a follow-up appointment with your ob just to be sure they don't have any concerns."

"So the baby's okay?"

"Seems to be."

Vanessa slid off the exam table. "So I can go?"

"Your blood pressure is high. I'd like to keep you here and see if it levels. So let's have a seat and relax."

Vanessa glared at Grady. "Did he just tell me to relax?"

"Come on, Van." Grady nodded the doctor to the door, and the doctor did the first intelligent thing since he'd opened it—he left without a word.

Grady ushered her back to the exam bed. "Listen to the doctor," he said gently, urging her back onto the bed.

She went, but she folded her arms across her chest and glared. "I want to see Dylan."

"He's getting checked out, same as you."

Now that she had time to think, there'd been something very wrong in that whole scene outside the cabin. Dylan hadn't been himself. But he'd been standing there, talking to her.

She *hated* this feeling that she was missing a piece. Laurel had questioned her earlier, looking pale and distracted, and informed her Adele was being treated for her injuries and then would be released into police custody.

But she couldn't tell her Dylan's condition or what he'd said in his statement or what would happen to that awful woman.

"Where's Laurel?"

"She told you. She went to check on Dylan."

"*I* want to check on Dylan."

Grady gave her his patented raised-eyebrow look. "Funny thing, that."

Vanessa looked away. She wasn't embarrassed. Not after everything she and Dylan had been through, but there was a certain discomfort over the fact she'd given Grady such a hard time about getting together with Laurel and now she... "How did it happen?"

"How did what happen?" Grady asked, scooting the too-small chair he was balanced on closer to her bed.

"Us. How did we... How are they...?" She shook her head, feeling overwhelmed and emotional. "I love him. I don't know how. I don't know what did it, but I love him. So much it's scary. A *Delaney*."

"Yeah, kinda hits you over the head like that." He took her hand in his and gave it a squeeze. "I couldn't tell you why. I can only tell you if it feels right, it is."

Vanessa nodded, blinking back unruly tears. "I need him to be okay."

"Then he'll be okay."

"Because I have such a great track record of getting what I need?"

"Because he's a Delaney, and they do." He touched her hair gently. "You gave us quite the scare."

"You should have known I'd kick my way out of it." All those emotions inside her wanted to lean into her big brother and just sob them away, but she felt trapped. Until she knew for sure Dylan was okay...

"Something's wrong."

"It only feels that way because you've been through this crazy thing. Time's only going slow because you're waiting. But you aren't getting out of here until that blood pressure comes down, so why don't you try to rest?"

Because she wouldn't be able to. She couldn't *rest* until she was out of this claustrophobic room and she could hold Dylan again.

Something wasn't right. Something hadn't been right for a while, but she wasn't going to get answers until that doctor let her out of here, so she closed her eyes and breathed.

She was more than grateful Grady didn't drop her hand. He held it the whole time, and it became an anchor.

Time passed interminably, but no matter how many times she asked, Grady didn't have any information. When the doctor returned what felt like a million years later, her blood pressure had gone down enough that he felt comfortable releasing her.

Which took another million years, with paperwork and instructions, warnings of headaches and blah, blah, blah. Her baby was fine and she needed to know why the hell she hadn't seen Dylan yet.

"I just need to use the bathroom. You want to wait here?" she asked, pointing at some chairs in the lobby.

Luckily, Grady was distracted enough by texting with Ty that he didn't look at her to see the lie.

"Sure." He took a seat and kept typing on his phone.

Vanessa walked casually toward the restrooms but then kept going. She found a map, tried to decide where Dylan would be. He'd come in an ambulance, so Emergency probably. She started backtracking to where she'd been treated in Emergency, but before she made it there she saw a cop going in the opposite direction. She knew him. Something Hart. He worked with Laurel a lot.

He didn't see her, and she made sure he didn't. She turned, waited, then casually started tailing him at a reasonable pace.

At one point he looked back, but there was a large gentleman in front of her who blocked his view.

When he pushed open the doors for the surgery wing, Vanessa's heart dropped and she didn't bother to keep her pace slow or calm herself. She ran forward, then came to a stumbling stop at the row of chairs occupied by Delaneys.

"Oh, my God."

Laurel jumped to her feet, swearing under her breath as she came up to Vanessa. "Don't jump to the worst conclusion."

"You're all here."

Jen's face was blotchy, and so was Laurel's. Hilly, Vanessa's long-lost cousin and Cam's girlfriend, was dabbing her eyes with a Kleenex.

"You're all crying," Vanessa accused, pointing wildly. *God, no. No.*

"Not all of us. Cam isn't crying," Laurel offered hopefully. When Vanessa only looked at her in horror, Laurel hooked arms with her and continued. "Look, Dylan's in surgery."

"For *what*?" Vanessa demanded, wrestling her arm away from Laurel's grasp.

Grady stormed through the doors, face etched in furious lines. "Damn it, Van. You told me you were going to the bathroom."

"And you told me everything was fine!" She whirled back to Laurel. "Why is he in surgery?"

"He was...shot."

"Shot? *Shot?* When? How could he have been...?" She swayed on her feet but Grady grabbed her and pushed her into a seat next to Hilly. It dawned on Vanessa why everything had been wrong since that moment. "He was shot before we got there. He was *hiding* it from me."

"Yes," Laurel agreed.

"Why?" She looked up helplessly at Laurel, then Grady. She'd give Dylan a piece of her mind once he was out of surgery. Oh, boy, would she. "How long? What are they— Tell me what you know."

"Let's just—"

"Tell me what you know." She grabbed Laurel's arms, trying to get it through the woman's thick skull. "I don't care what he wanted kept from me. I don't care about anything except knowing what's going on. I *need* to know what he's going through."

Laurel softened, but her eyes filled again. She ruthlessly blinked those tears away, putting on that cop face Vanessa had to admit she envied.

"He was shot in the stomach," Laurel said, and she might have sounded like some detached cop if her voice wasn't so scratchy. "Unfortunately, it did hit some organs, which means he could be in surgery for a while. Right now, all we can do is wait for the surgeon to do his job and then let us know how it went."

"He might die." It slammed through her, the understanding. Why he'd been trying to shield her from knowing. He might legitimately *die*.

"Van, listen—"

She looked up at Laurel, fury and fear causing her to shake. "He might *die*. Don't *'listen'* me. It's true. He might die."

"It's true," she said, though her voice was an unsteady whisper.

"But he might not," Hilly said, taking Vanessa's hand in hers. Her voice was calm and collected. Soothing. Not detached like Laurel's. "No use focusing on the worst-case scenario when it's not the only option. Focus on—on—"

"Healing thoughts," Jen supplied. "Prayers, vibes, whatever you got."

Vibes. Prayers. Thoughts. Vanessa wanted to scream. None of it mattered. None of it helped. "It's a curse. It's true. I didn't believe in curses, but here we are."

Grady crouched in front of her. Her brother who'd happily talked about feuds and being better than Delaneys for most of his life. He took her hands in his, looked right at her, certain and sure.

"There is no curse. Love is never a curse. New life is no curse. This is a challenge, but not a curse. And if we beat all these challenges, can you imagine what we'll have?"

No feud? Carsons and Delaneys all intermingled? Not so long ago she would have told anyone who listened that that was her worst nightmare.

But somehow it had become her brightest dream, so she did what Jen said. She prayed. She thought about healing. She sent all the energy she could muster into the universe.

And in a waiting room full of Carsons and Delaneys holding hands and murmuring encouragement to each other, Vanessa waited.

THE DESERT WAS never ending. And why was he wearing all these clothes? A cowboy hat, of all damn things? He was riding a horse through the desert and all he wanted was a drink of water.

His body hurt everywhere, rivers of fiery pain. He looked down. Bullet holes, but no blood.

He tried to make the image go away, since it couldn't possibly be real, but the scene just kept playing out. He could see it, like a movie, and yet it was him. He could feel the cowboy hat. The weird scratchy pants and boots that fit like a second skin.

But he was full of bullet holes.

When he looked up, there was another horse. Another rider. He was in white. She was in black.

She.

"Vanessa?"

The black flowed around her as she rode toward him—the fabric of her clothes, the long strands of her hair. The wind whipped her skirts and scarves and she had a hat. A bright, shiny skull glinted on her hat. It looked just about perfect.

Her horse pounded through the sand, closer and closer and yet not close enough.

A choice. Somehow he knew that somewhere, there was a choice. Take the bullet holes and go to her. Doomed.

Turn away and everything would be fine. He could turn his horse in the opposite direction and the bullet holes would heal and all would be well.

Except she wouldn't be his. He was alive, maybe? Bullet holes and all, but no blood. Pain, yes, but you had to be alive to feel pain.

Why would he turn away?

He fell off the horse into the sand, but it didn't feel like sand. It felt like a bed.

He blinked his eyes open and…the desert was gone. He still needed a drink of water, desperately. But everything was dim instead of blinding. All he could think was she was gone. The horse and her swirling black costume.

"Van."

"There you are."

Her voice. God, he thought he might cry. But he didn't. He couldn't seem to move his head toward her voice. "You were all dressed up," he muttered, realizing somewhat belatedly it had been a dream. Just a silly, weird-as-hell dream.

"Can't even have a sex dream right?"

"I can't…move."

"That's okay." He felt her hand on one shoulder, then she moved into his line of sight. "They said you'll be out of sorts and they've got you hooked up to all sorts of things. Just lie still."

He drank her in. She looked good. Healthy and sturdy. Not pale. She wasn't swathed in black layers, but instead wore jeans and a T-shirt. Still, she looked so good and so *his*, he didn't think it could be real. "Am I dead?"

"Not unless the dead can speak. And all those doctors and nurses prodding at you day and night seem to think you'll recover. I guess you don't remember waking up? You've been in and out."

"I don't remember much of anything since Adele shot me. Except that I felt dead there for a while."

"Yes, well, speaking of that. You're lucky you're laid

up because I'd like to kick your butt to Toledo." She slid onto the edge of his bed, studying his face intently. Her dark eyes were hard to read, but he thought he saw relief.

"I don't have much interest in going to Ohio, so I guess that works, all in all." He closed his eyes, feeling unbearably exhausted. "Are you going to touch me or what?"

She made a sound that was almost a laugh, and then he felt her shift next to him, stretching out in the small amount of bed space available. "They're going to come in and yell at me, but I don't care."

"Good, I don't either."

"Dylan Delaney, you always care about the rules and what's right."

"Nah, that's just what people think." He nuzzled into her. "I want to hold you."

"Well, you'll have to settle for me holding you for now." Her arms came around him and he sighed into her. Because one arm was close to her, he managed to inch it toward her belly. He touched her stomach, fitting his hand over the softest swell.

"Baby's fine," she murmured, her fingers feeling like heaven against his hair.

"What about mama?"

"Mama." He felt her whoosh of breath against his face. It felt like heaven. "You know, it's funny, I hadn't really thought in terms of *mama* yet."

"Well, you've got some time to get used to that. And the fact you're going to have to marry me."

She was quiet for a while. He worked up the energy to open his eyes. She was looking at the IV hooked up to him, and all the other machines that seemed to keep beeping at him unnecessarily.

She met his gaze. "Never really figured I'd get married. I'm not much of a traditionalist."

"I am. But I can be flexible. We'll hyphenate our names."

Vanessa snorted. "You want our child to walk around Bent, Wyoming, with the names Delaney and Carson together?"

"I do," he returned. "You can keep your name. I'll keep mine. Baby will have both. You'll keep your shop. I—I don't know what my position is at the bank, but I can get a job at Cam's security business if I have to."

"Mr. Secret Sniper."

"I was thinking more along the lines of accounting. I think my sniper days are behind me." He gestured helplessly. "I don't know if you noticed, but I got beat to hell back there."

She closed her eyes, an expression of pain taking over her face. "Yeah, I noticed." She held him a little tighter, though he could tell she was being exceptionally gentle. He wished he didn't feel like he needed it.

"So, your plan is...you're going to marry me?"

"Damn straight."

"In front of your father and the rest of your family, in front of Bent citizens, you're going to promise to love and cherish a Carson?"

Though it felt like flaming hot needles in his side and shoulder, he lifted her hand to his mouth and pressed a kiss to her palm. "Till death do us part."

"Are you sure you don't have a head injury?"

"I might have several for all I know." He sighed, letting his arm fall back down, his eyes drifting closed. "But I'm sure I'm going to marry you. If you want to wait to decide until we make sure my body's in working order again, that's fine. But I can tell you right here, right now, I love you. And we're going to get married. Bullet holes or no."

"Holes? Pretty sure you were only shot once."

"I dreamed there were bullet holes all over the place. But I had a choice. Live through them with you, or walk away. I didn't walk then. I'm not going to, ever."

"You aren't making any sense."

He muttered something and slid back into dreams. There weren't bullet holes this time. No horses or desert. Just a quiet porch.

He awoke a few times, mostly to nurses poking and prodding him. Once Laurel was there with Grady. Twice it was Jen. A few times it was Cam and Hilly. And always, every single time, Vanessa was there too.

The next day when he woke it was dark, and it wasn't to a nurse poking at him. He just surfaced naturally. Vanessa was curled against him, fast asleep.

Unable to resist, he brushed some hair off her face. She hadn't left him. Maybe a hospital wasn't the real world yet, but it was real enough. This wasn't going to evaporate. They were going to make it work.

She stirred, blinked open her eyes and yawned. "You're still too weak for sex, buddy."

He didn't laugh because he knew it would hurt his side, but he smiled. "Noted. They let you stay in here?"

"Tried to kick me out. Even threatened to call security. I just snuck back in."

"Mmm, have I mentioned I love you?"

She snuggled closer. "Not enough."

He managed to move more than he had yet. He turned his head and kissed her temple. "Decided to marry me yet?"

She shook her head. "You're relentless. I thought the bullet hole and massive blood loss might slow you down."

"Your family and mine both donated blood. I'm just filled to the brim with relentless now."

She laughed at that, and he couldn't get over being

able to lie with her, make her laugh. The pain didn't matter. The circumstances. She was his. And they'd made it through.

"You going to move in to my shop?"

"No."

"You think I'm going to move onto the Delaney ranch?"

This time he laughed, then winced at the wave of pain. "No. Not in a million years." He frowned, realizing something he hadn't quite put together till she'd mentioned the ranch. "My father. Everyone has been in here except…"

Vanessa stiffened, then slowly exhaled. "Well, you know he has a lot to clean up at the bank."

Dylan maneuvered so he could look down incredulously at her, but it hurt so he ended up just kind of flopping around. "Are you defending my father?"

"No. I think he's a dirty rotten bastard." Vanessa blew out a breath, rubbing her hand over his shoulder. "Let's not talk about your dad."

"He really hasn't been by, has he? He…" Dylan couldn't wrap his head around it. He'd almost died.

Well, he supposed it told him all he needed to know. No matter how much it hurt, his father wasn't the man Dylan had thought him to be. Dylan closed his eyes. His body hurt. His head hurt. His *heart* hurt.

"So where are we going to live if I marry you?" Vanessa prodded. "My answer depends on that."

She was trying to distract him. Why not let her? "Well, I'd consider your shop except I'm pretty sure there's no way on earth to baby proof it. We need some room. A house to build our family in." He thought about the cabin they'd been stuck in, then chuckled a little to himself at the fact it'd likely be on the market eventually. "I know a cabin that's going to be up for sale."

She laughed. "Yeah, let's buy Adele's cabin and live there. How much of your blood are we going to have to scrub out of the floorboards?"

"It *is* where we fell in love," he said, warming to the idea. "Isolated and away from Bent. Even if we didn't live there full-time, it could be our vacation home. I'd miss ranch life, but being outside of town would be good enough."

"It's only a twenty-minute drive to town. We'd both be able to get to work." She gently slapped his chest. "No. What am I saying?" She laughed again, and it was like heaven to hear her laugh. Soothed all the rough edges, the pain and the disappointment.

Maybe he didn't have his father anymore, but he had something bigger. Greater. A family who cared. *Family.* Love. No more feud nonsense or pointless bitterness. He was going to embrace the good.

"We're not buying Adele's cabin," Vanessa said firmly.

"I don't know. Something to think about."

"You go back to sleep. Wake up with an ounce of sense in your head."

He kissed her temple again, since he could, and then decided he would go back to sleep. But he wouldn't make any promises about sense.

# Chapter Twenty

Vanessa was exhausted. Sleeping in a hospital wasn't exactly restful, fighting with nurses and doctors even less so. But Dylan was getting released tomorrow and...

He'd have to go back to the Delaney Ranch for a while. She couldn't take care of him in her shop, much as she wanted to.

She'd made a promise to herself back in her teenage years that she'd never, ever step foot on the Delaney Ranch again, but she was going to have to break that promise to herself. For Dylan. For their future.

Which meant she had to clear some air. She'd left Dylan after his meeting with the doctor to discuss rehabilitation. Jen had planned on spending the day with him while Vanessa did what she had to do.

First up? Something long overdue.

She knocked on the door to Laurel and Grady's house, knowing Grady would be at Rightful Claim getting ready for opening.

Laurel opened the door looking bleary-eyed and miserable.

"Oh, so I see it's hit you too."

Laurel groaned. "I felt fine. Maybe a little tired. Dizzy sometimes. Then this morning? Barf city."

"I'd love to tell you it gets better."

Laurel groaned again, motioning Vanessa inside.

Weirdly, the shared morning sickness both put her at ease and somehow made this harder. "So, um."

Laurel waited patiently, but all Vanessa could do was stutter. Irritated with herself, she decided some things didn't need to change. Including her *go-for-it* attitude.

"We used to be best friends," she blurted.

Laurel blinked, then nodded slowly. "Yeah, we were."

"I haven't really had one since. A best friend."

Laurel's confused expression softened. "Me neither. I mean, there's your brother, but his eyes glaze over when I want to discuss the romantic overtures in a movie."

Vanessa managed a weak laugh. "Hey, my eyes used to glaze over too."

"No, you pretended, but you watched all those rom-coms right along with me."

Years ago. Something like a lifetime. How was Vanessa expecting to go back to that? Of course, how was she expecting to marry Dylan Delaney? Life just didn't make sense. "I guess I was hoping we could be friends again."

Laurel grinned. "Van. We aren't friends."

Vanessa frowned. Why was she grinning at that? Laurel wasn't *mean*. But that was a mean thing to say. "Well, screw y—"

Laurel rolled her eyes and stepped forward. "We're *sisters*." She held out her hands like it was as simple as that.

For Laurel, it was. And Vanessa was beginning to realize, after coming through the hardest, scariest, most complicated moment in her life, that sometimes simple was the best way to go.

"Do you really believe all that stuff Grady said in the waiting room about no curses, just challenges? Do you really believe that?"

"I do. I'll admit when you and Dylan were both missing, I wondered. I doubted. But…" She shook her head, then placed both hands over her stomach. "How could I ever think this was wrong? Cursed?"

Vanessa put her hands over her own stomach. It wasn't a curse. The baby had never, ever felt like one, even when she'd been certain she'd write Dylan out of their lives forever. "Us both pregnant at the same time? Kinda feels more like fate than a curse."

This time, Laurel gave her a hug. "Fate," she said, squeezing tight. "I like that a lot."

Vanessa squeezed her back, uncomfortable with all this baring of her soul and whatnot, but she wasn't quite done. "Listen." She pulled away. "There's something else I wanted to talk to you about. Your dad hasn't been by to visit Dylan."

Laurel blew out a breath then made her way over to the couch and sank into it. She gestured for Vanessa to do the same. "No, he hasn't."

"Dylan wants to go see him when he's released tomorrow. I don't want him to go if your dad's going to be a jerk."

"Then you'll have to stop him, because the bottom line is my dad's going to be a jerk."

"I don't get it. I mean, I always hated your dad but he didn't whale on you. I figured…you know, that meant he was a good dad at least, even if he was a snobby jerk."

"I don't get it either. That's not the man I knew. Sure, the feud was important to him, but his family was the *most* important thing. But…"

"He came to your wedding."

"Yeah. I thought that meant something. Turns out he thought I'd come to my senses before I started popping out babies."

"That's awful."

"It's sad. He's sad." Laurel reached over and took Vanessa's hand. "I know you want to protect Dylan. I do too. But he's going to need to face him. Talk to him. If it ends badly, you'll be there to support him. Trust me. It won't make it not hurt, but it helps."

"You know, I think you're good for Grady."

Laurel raised her eyes. "Are you sneaking Dylan's painkillers?"

Vanessa rolled her eyes. "He needed someone to depend on but not another Carson dude. You. You're... I've been awful and I think it's because I knew..." Vanessa pulled a face. "I'm about to be barf city too."

"Yeah, because you're talking about your feelings, not because you're having morning sickness."

"I guess you've still got my number."

"Well enough, anyway."

"It's just... I knew you were better for him. I resented that. I resented you and him both getting over all that crap they've been feeding us since we were babies. The feud was safe. No one got hurt with it."

"And no one got any better either."

"Yeah, I'm figuring that out. I don't want your father to hurt him."

"I know. He probably will. You won't be able to shield Dylan from that hurt any more than he'll be able to, say, give birth to that baby for you, though I know he'd take all that pain on himself if he could. Love, I've discovered, doesn't really solve all our problems."

"So what *does* it do?"

"Gives us a hand to hold to get through the problems with. Which actually works out a lot better than just avoiding pain."

"If you say so," Vanessa muttered. But much as it

sounded like a load of crock, Vanessa had no reason not to trust Laurel. And that felt pretty damn good.

DYLAN MIGHT HAVE kissed the ground if he wasn't in a world of pain. Still, he was free. Free. Walking of his own accord out of the hospital, not to return.

Except for rehabilitation and checkups and blah, blah, blah. But he'd focus on his freedom.

And what he had to do. The sun was shining and the sky was a vibrant blue. It felt like a fresh new start.

It would be, once he dealt with this one cloud over his head. First, he had to get rid of Vanessa and preferably one sister. In an ideal world, he'd get rid of all of them, but he wasn't cleared to drive just yet.

"I've never had so many females fluttering over me in my life. Remind me never to get shot again."

"Remind yourself, hotshot. I wasn't the one playing Mr. Hero and shoving me out the door, then pretending like you hadn't been shot. You'd probably be in better shape if you'd owned up to it."

"The ambulance would have gotten there at the same time either way. Besides, your blood pressure was high enough."

Vanessa crossed her arms over her chest as they stopped outside the hospital doors. "I can't believe Grady blabbed to you about that. Besides, I was *fine*."

"We'll go get the car. You two sit tight." Laurel smiled and pulled Jen away.

"They're giving us privacy to argue."

Dylan tilted his face up to the sun. "Yeah. Or themselves privacy to gossip."

"I want to go with you," Vanessa said firmly.

He didn't need a translator to figure out her abrupt subject change. "It's just not a great idea."

"I'm not afraid of your father."

"I'm not afraid of him either. That's why I'm going to talk to him, but you being there is only going to irritate him."

She glared. "Good. A man can't visit his on-death's-door son in the hospital, he can stand to be a little irritated."

Dylan tried to hold on to the contentment he felt over being out of the hospital, but tension was creeping into his shoulders. "It'll be better for all of us—"

"No. We're done with that. I'll let you handle the crazy lunatics with guns since you know how to handle yourself, but you're not deciding what's right for us. That's not how this goes."

"You're exhausting."

"Get used to it."

"You have to know some of the things he's going to say, and I don't really want an audience for how awful he can be. I don't want you to feel—"

"What? You're not really afraid I'll have second thoughts?"

Laurel pulled the car to the curb and Dylan started to move for it, but Vanessa stopped him.

"Babe, I ain't ever cared what this town or your father thought, and I'm not about to start now. In fact, I think I'm going to take out an ad in the paper and make a big old banner that says 'PREGNANT WITH DYLAN DELANEY'S BABY AND PROUD OF IT.' I'll hang it above Rightful Claim so everyone can see."

He took her hand, brought it to his mouth and brushed a kiss across her knuckles. "I love you."

"And I love you. Which means I'm not leaving your side no matter how many Delilah references your father makes."

Dylan looked at her. Really looked at her. He'd accepted he'd fallen in love with her despite previous incidents. She was strong and brave and awe-inspiring. He wanted to build a life with her because she fit, perfectly, like she'd always belonged at his side.

But he'd never fully grasped the simple fact that Vanessa Carson would be *good* for him. He'd spent far too long caring what people thought—not enough to capitulate always, but enough to lie or cover it up when he didn't.

Vanessa wouldn't do that, and he didn't think she'd let him do it either. He knew she wouldn't let their kid grow up feeling like they had to be something they weren't.

"Why are you looking at me like that? Your sisters are waiting."

"You're right."

Her eyebrows rose. "Well, I know I am. So, you're not going to fight me coming with you?"

He linked his fingers with hers and moved to the car. "No. No, you're right. We're a team. No more lone-wolf stuff."

They climbed in the back seat of Jen's car and chatted casually on the way over to the Delaney Ranch, but the tension that crept into the car the closer they got didn't escape Dylan's notice.

"Can you guys let me and Van do this on our own?"

Jen nodded. "Of course. We'll go down to Hilly's, and you just holler if you need anything."

"Appreciate it."

Much as it grated, he had to let Vanessa help him out of the car. Even though it had been a mostly smooth ride, he felt jostled and achy. This whole recovery thing was not going to be a walk in the park.

But walking up to the door with Vanessa's hand in his

was a soothing balm to that pain, and he had to believe that would always be the case.

He opened the door and led her inside. He called out for his father once, but it was soon clear he wasn't on the main floor. Must be upstairs in his office.

Dylan was exhausted. He lowered himself onto the living-room couch. "Need a minute before we head upstairs," he muttered.

"I'll go get him," Vanessa said, already striding toward the stairs.

"Van."

She gave him an arch look.

"Teamwork, remember?" He patted the spot on the couch next to him.

She wrinkled her nose then huffed out a breath before she plopped herself next to him on the couch.

"Man, you got some fancy digs, Delaney."

"It's no above-business apartment, but it'll do in a pinch."

She smiled at him, then brushed her fingers over his hair. "You're wiped."

"Yeah. I'll live though."

"I'll make sure of it." She kissed his cheek. Her random acts of gentleness never failed to move him.

"I love you, Van."

"I love you too."

Footsteps sounded on the stairs that led into the living room. "Gird your loins," Dylan muttered.

Dad appeared at the base of the stairs. There was a moment of shock in his expression, then something more like pain. He cleared his throat. He looked…rough, Dylan decided. There was no wave of sympathy though, because he'd been in the hospital for *days*, and not once had Dad been by.

Didn't that tell him everything?

He'd had a plan to ask his dad how things were. To be calm and kind when he asked where they stood. But that plan evaporated.

"I'm only here to get my things," Dylan announced. A man who'd made the mistakes his father had and still refused to see his son in the hospital wasn't worth an attempt at civility.

"Dylan."

"No. No, I can't stay here. Not under this roof. I thought I could be reasonable, but I just keep thinking of Adele telling me she'd been promised my job and—"

"She was a good employee, but she needed motivation. My handling of the situation hardly made her kidnap you and—"

"Shoot me? Try to kill me? Maybe it didn't *make* her do that, but it certainly didn't help. Your manipulations and lies...all the hurt they caused." He pushed himself into a standing position. "I won't be a part of it. *We* won't be a part of it. I'll get my things and we'll find somewhere else to—"

"Perhaps we can come to an agreement where you both stay here," Dad interrupted, his businessman-negotiation tone of voice firmly in place.

Dylan sank right back onto the couch, all his energy whooshing out of him with that bombshell. "Excuse me?"

"You certainly don't *have* to, but the offer is open if it might help your rehabilitation. I'm sure you could make room for Vanessa in your room. She'd be welcome."

"Okay, we'll take you up on that."

Dylan looked incredulously at the woman who'd once said something like she'd rather drink bleach than live at the Delaney ranch. "We will?"

"Temporarily. Until you're recovered enough to do it

all on your own." Vanessa looked imperiously at his father. "Thank you."

"It's settled, then."

Vanessa nodded firmly. "Settled."

Dylan pushed his fingers to his temple. "I think I'm hallucinating."

"No. Your sister said some things to me that…" Dad blew out a breath. He was clearly flummoxed and irritated, but instead of retreating or putting on his usual cool disdain, Dad ran a hand through his hair. "I've made mistakes. I don't regret all of them. But I've been…wrong a time or two. It isn't comfortable or joyful for me that you've all decided to…"

Dad shook his head, trailing off and then pacing. He stopped, looking at Dylan and Vanessa. He drew into that ramrod posture that Dylan was used to seeing precede a lecture. "I've been working with some lawyers about setting up trusts."

"Trusts?"

"For your child, and Laurel's. That's simple fact, and regardless of circumstances they will be my grandchildren. My grandchildren will have the best."

"Your grandchildren will have a choice," Vanessa replied.

Dad clearly wanted to say something to that. But he didn't.

Dylan was pretty sure he was hallucinating. Maybe Vanessa had slipped him one of those painkillers that made him loopy.

"Family is the most important thing. Which isn't the same as our name, I suppose."

The *"I suppose"* almost made Dylan smile. But he wouldn't put Vanessa through his father's behavior. "There will be rules."

"Of course. As long as Vanessa is the mother of your child, I'll treat her with the amount of respect that entails."

"Now I think *I'm* hallucinating," Vanessa muttered.

"I've made some mistakes and things have gotten out of hand these past few years. Everything, really. Well, that won't do. We're still Delaneys. So instead of falling apart, we'll—" Dad made a face, but Dylan gave him some credit for continuing "—work together. Make adjustments and a few compromises. Maybe…maybe Laurel was right and that's been the answer for this town all along."

Vanessa's hand curled around Dylan's and squeezed. "I think working together is just what we need."

Dylan squeezed her hand back. He'd spent most of his life hating Carsons and everything they stood for. He'd never imagined himself here…being part of a linking of the Delaney and Carson names.

But he'd never been prouder of anything in his life.

# *Epilogue*

### *Two months later*

"You guys know this is the most insane thing possible?"

Vanessa swung on the porch swing Dylan had installed yesterday, while their families helped move furniture and boxes so neither Vanessa nor Dylan would overexert themselves in their move from the Delaney Ranch to their new place.

"Are you talking about *us* or the cabin?"

Laurel eased onto the spot next to Vanessa. They'd both gotten much bigger recently. Once Vanessa and Dylan were all moved in, they were going to have a joint baby shower. Then in no time at all, their babies would be born just two months apart.

It felt like it was taking forever.

"I suppose you heard about Adele's insanity plea," Laurel said softly.

Vanessa shrugged. She'd had to let some things go in her life. Anger toward Adele was one of them. She'd never forgive that woman for the hell she'd put them through, but she wouldn't waste her energy being angry over it. "Long as she's locked up, I don't care if it's a jail or an asylum."

Laurel looked at the cabin again and shook her head.

"I can't believe you want to live in the house you were basically held prisoner in."

Van smiled at the gleaming wood, her brother and cousins hefting in couches and bed frames while Dylan's brothers surreptitiously handed him only the lightest of boxes.

"I fell in love with your brother here. Why wouldn't we want to raise our family here?"

Laurel only shook her head again. "If you say so."

Dylan crossed the porch, eased himself next to Vanessa. "I think that's it."

Vanessa studied his face. She'd been worried he'd overexert himself. He was mostly back to normal, but still working on endurance and range of motion, and he tended to push himself.

But she didn't see signs of extra fatigue or that awful gray note to his complexion he sometimes got. He'd held up well, and it allowed her to relax.

"Cam and Hilly are going to get the pizza. They treated me like a damn toddler when I suggested I could get it myself."

Van patted his shoulder. "You get toddler status a little while longer."

Dylan rested his hand on the rounded mound of her belly, and they both sighed contentedly. Home. They were home. And about to be a family. Whatever hell they'd been through, it had been worth this moment right here. Them. Their families. A future.

Vanessa nodded at Ty, who was standing by the moving van looking standoffish and moody. Then Jen, who was all but hiding behind Grady as she chatted with her cousin, Gracie. "Have you guys noticed those two act like they have a magnet repelling them at all times?"

"No," Dylan replied, frowning.

"Oh, totally," Laurel said. "I'm almost *certain* they had a thing in high school."

"Jen and Ty?" Dylan demanded incredulously. "No way."

"Way. Then he went off into the army. I don't think I've seen them exchange more than two words in the year he's been back."

"Maybe they just don't like each other." Dylan patted Vanessa's belly. "Not everyone falls in love with the enemy," he said with a wink.

Vanessa shook her head. "There's something there, and at some point? It's going to explode. Happened to us. Don't know why it wouldn't happen to them."

Dylan studied his sister, and then Vanessa's cousin. He shook his head. "No way."

Laurel got up off the swing as Grady sauntered over. "Mark me down in the *something-is-there* column," she offered, walking to meet her husband.

Vanessa looked at *her* husband—a term she surprisingly loved, as much as she had their simple courthouse wedding and raucous after-party at the Carson ranch—and grinned. "How much you want to bet those two hook up by the end of the year?" she said, nodding back toward Jen.

Dylan rubbed his hand over his chin, studying Ty, then Jen again. He named the same astronomical sum he'd named at Laurel and Grady's wedding. The night that had changed both their lives for the absolute best.

She leaned over and kissed the scar on his eyebrow, a parting gift from No-Neck, he liked to say. "Delaneys always love to flaunt their money," she murmured.

He linked his hand with hers. "These days, I hear tell, Delaney-Carsons love to flaunt their love."

She rolled her eyes, but she leaned into him, content to

swing on the porch swing with her husband, watching their family—all those intertwined Carsons and Delaneys—interact and love and laugh.

Yeah, that was definitely something to flaunt, enjoy and nurture.

Forever.

* * * * *

# PROTECTIVE OPERATION

## DANICA WINTERS

To those who serve in silence both at home
and on the battlefield.

Your sacrifices do not go unappreciated.

Your dedication makes the world a better place.

# Chapter One

In a world filled with diamonds and pearls, Shaye Griest had never really thought about what she didn't have—the staff would take care of such things for her. She'd never found herself lacking tangible things. No, not when her father was the prime minister of Algeria, the head of state in the oil-and-gas-rich country. When she had been merely five years old, she had been given a gold-plated Rolls-Royce by the president of Nigeria with the flippant comment "for when you can drive."

Fifteen years later, the car sat in a garage in the underbelly of her father's lair in Algiers—where she would never see it, or her father, ever again.

Truth be told, she had never been a fan of the car, the man who had given it to her or her father who now held it in his keep. Good riddance.

She pulled up the collar of her coat around her neck as she made her way to the Combine Diner in the heart of Mystery, Montana. The wind had started to kick up, making the bite of the December cold even more vicious. It was ten degrees outside, but it felt like she had stepped onto the dark side of the moon. She may as well be on the moon—her father would sooner look for her there than Mystery, Montana.

Or at least she hoped. The bastard always had a way of finding her.

The diner's wooden sign rattled as the wind pulled it against its chains, making a sound like the Ghost of Christmas Past. The sound echoed off the glittering snow that lined the edges of the road and sidewalks, reminding her of her abject loneliness.

She thought she had known frigid temperatures, thanks to all of her travels, but she had failed to calculate the level of desolation that came with the icy grip.

She should have run away to somewhere warmer; Tahiti was nice this time of year. And yet, the thought of Chad Martin and all he had done for her had pulled her in his direction.

She owed him and his family so much, yet instead of paying him back, here she was showing up in his last known location in a feeble attempt to find him, with nothing but her hat in her hands and a request for shelter. He and his family were hiding out and were probably long gone, but she had to try and catch him here. He was her only hope.

She should have texted before she flew to the middle of nowhere, but no.

A sane person would have texted, not dropped her family, been ostracized by her friends and then caught the next flight to a man who barely knew her.

*What had she been thinking?*

This was exactly the kind of pattern of actions and reactions her father had always criticized her for. She could hear his voice now. "Child, you will go nowhere, be no one. The weight of your imprudent decisions will always pin you down."

Well, damn it, she was going places and living her life as best she could—pins or no pins.

She walked to the door of the diner and grabbed the handle. It made a dull thump as she pulled against the bolt. The blue-and-red neon Open sign was glowing, its light casting a purple shadow on the snow. Apparently, *open* meant something different in Montana. Maybe it was more a suggestion of what could be if the conditions were just right…kind of like marriage.

The thought made the harsh taste of sadness rise in her mouth.

It had been nearly a year since Raj had been killed, but sometimes thoughts of his death struck her like a bolt of lightning.

She tried the door one more time, but it was just as locked as it had been before.

*Ugh.* She sighed.

The words *hot mess* clanked in tandem with the sounds of the sign's chains.

"If you're looking for a hot meal, you came to the wrong place," a man said from behind her, making her jump.

She reached into her purse and grabbed her pepper spray. She clicked open the safety, but didn't take it out as she turned to face the man.

"If you want food, Missoula is about twenty miles that way," the man said, jabbing his thumb toward a pink cloud of light pollution in the sky behind him. "And as safe as Mystery normally is, as of late, this ain't a real good place for a woman like you to be walkin' around alone."

The way he spoke was ambiguous. He was skirting the line between a threat and a warning. He was tall and lanky, and he stood with his feet apart and perched on his toes—the style of protectors. He must have been military, or perhaps law enforcement of some kind. Or maybe, just maybe, he was here as one of her father's minions.

It wouldn't surprise her if her father had someone posted at her heels.

He'd sent his people after her before.

She slowly pulled her hand from her purse, palming the pepper spray but keeping her finger on the trigger as she checked the direction of the wind.

It would send a clear message to her father if she took out his man.

"I'm not homeless, or needy. Thank you very much," she said, but as she spoke, she knew those words were a lie. She gripped the canister harder. "And if you are truly concerned for my safety, I think it best if you leave."

The man in front of her frowned and his hand slipped down to something at his waist. Before he could draw a gun, she pulled her pepper spray. It misted, throwing a cloud of capsaicin into the air. The yellow liquid hit him straight in the face and over his open palm as he tried to stop the spray from reaching his eyes.

"What the hell? No. Stop." He waved at her as he was overtaken by a coughing fit. As he gagged and spat on the ground, he stepped toward her blindly.

"You can go back to whatever hole you crawled out of." She emptied the can, wishing she had bought something bigger instead of just the tiny one she had picked up at the gas station. Dropping the glittery can to the ground, she rushed toward the man who was gagging and spitting.

"Stop. Right. There," he said, dabbing his eyes frantically with the sleeve of his jacket.

She circled around him, careful to stay upwind from the spray. "Tell my father that I'm not his little plaything. I'm not coming home."

She had to get out of this one-horse town. If anyone knew she was here, and if her father was looking for her, then she would be putting Chad and his family in danger. Her father was capable of anything. In a different world, her father would have been the perfect hitman—he was cold, calculating and devoid of anything resembling remorse.

"Wait," the guy said as he staggered toward the pickup that was parked a few slots down from her car on the street. The truck was a banged-up old white Ford that had seen better days.

This hillbilly had another think coming if he thought she was going to listen to him.

She opened her car door, then paused and stared over at the staggering mess she had created. The man's eyes were red and puffy and tears streamed down his cheeks. But even as a slobbering, sweating mess, he wasn't bad-looking, even though he wasn't her type. And the ring on his finger was the nail in the coffin.

*And he was no Chad.*

As she stared at him, the man didn't even look in her direction—not that he really could—but something about his helplessness made her call into question whether or not he was truly one of her father's men. Her father usually employed only the best of the best, and this fumbling and spitting man was definitely not that.

A tiny bit of guilt wiggled up from her core. Maybe she'd been a little too defensive. Maybe she should have waited another second between seeing the threat and acting—but if Raj's death had taught her anything, it was that a single nanosecond was all it took to decide which way the sickle would fall.

The man grabbed a bottle of water from inside the cab of his truck and started flushing his eyes. As he worked, she glanced back at the ring on his finger—it was one of those newer black silicone ones and it appeared to be devoid of any normal wear and tear.

Most hitmen weren't married. It didn't fit the lifestyle—in fact, it was about as far from the lifestyle as a person could get. All of the henchmen she had ever met were made up of three things: muscle, too much testosterone and a machismo complex. But hitmen weren't all terrible. Chad Martin, for example, was built like a lumberjack—complete with the flannel shirt—with arms the size of small tree trunks, but when he spoke there was a hint of another kind of strength within him, as well. And it was likely that it was this charm and down-to-earth likability that made him even more efficient and deadly when pulling the trigger.

*Damn it.*

Even now, facing down a possible threat, she was haunted by Chad.

She got into her car and slammed her door shut. She shifted into Reverse and hit the gas without looking back.

There was a large thud as her car struck something. She gasped as she stopped. "Holy. Crap."

Glancing in the rearview mirror, the man was lying on top of her trunk, facedown.

It was one thing to pepper-spray the man, but she hadn't meant to kill him. Oh, God, what if he was dead? And what would happen if someone had just witnessed her hitting him? What if she got arrested? How would it look if she did prison time for killing an American in the first days she was stateside?

Her father would have a diplomatic mess on his hands. And that was to say nothing about what she would do...or if she would even be able to walk away without prison time.

The blood rushed from her face and down into her toes as she stepped out of the car. "Are you okay? I'm so sorry."

He groaned.

*Good. At least he is still alive.*

Now to keep him that way.

She stepped closer and as she moved near, the breeze turned toward her and with it came the residue from her pepper spray. Her eyes started to water and her nose ran, and as she took another breath, trying to free herself from the spray, she only inhaled it further.

She gagged and laughed at what she had done to herself and to the poor man she had tried to take down.

"Laughing at me now, too?" the man said with a groan. "You know, there are a lot of easier ways to kill a man."

She tried to open her eyes, but she could only squint, thanks to the pain.

"There's more water." She heard the sound of the man standing and moving toward her.

He kneeled down beside her and pushed a bottle into her hands. "Just pour it right on."

"I'm sorry," she said through wheezing breaths.

"Me, too." The man dropped down on the ground beside her as she opened the bottle and started pouring it over her face. The water was ice-cold, but it did little for her burning face and eyes. Instead, all it seemed to be doing was freezing to her eyelashes. "I didn't mean to scare you. I just thought with it being so cold and all, you might have needed a little help."

He wasn't helping the swell of guilt growing within her.

"This really is the backside of hell, isn't it?" she said, chuckling at where she had suddenly found herself.

"You ain't seen nothing yet," the man said. "If you want *real* cold, you should head up to the Hi-Line sometime."

"Hi-Line?" she asked.

"Clearly, you aren't from around here. The arctic fronts run through there like a shiver running down the Devil's spine, freezing cows where they stand," the man said. He groaned as he tried to put weight on his leg, then he pulled up his pant leg. "Crap, there goes my dancing tonight."

Even through blurry eyes, she could make out the blood that twisted down his leg from a gash on his shin. "Seriously, I'm so sorry. I didn't see you back there. I just—"

"Wanted to get the hell out of Dodge," he said, finishing her sentence. "You're hardly the first person to step foot in this town and immediately want to head for the hills."

"That's not it... It's just—"

"I scared you...and you thought your father sent me," he said.

"Are you in the habit of always finishing other people's sentences?" she asked, slightly annoyed.

"Ha, it's sad, but you aren't the first woman to tell me that. My wife loves to constantly remind me." He rolled down his pant leg. "Now, what was all this nonsense about your father? Clearly, you're on the run—I'm assuming from him. But where you running to?"

Regardless of his ability to piece together the puzzle of her life, she wasn't sure she wanted to tell him anything. Considering the fact that she had pepper-sprayed and then nearly killed him, he was being remarkably nice.

He stared at her as she dumped the last bit of water on her face and gasped from the cold.

"You gonna tell me, or will I have to play twenty questions to get it out of you?" he persisted.

"Actually," she began, "I'm here looking for a man. His name is Chad Martin. Do you happen to know where I can find him?"

The man stood up, then reached behind his back and pulled out a set of handcuffs. Before she could even react, he had her arms behind her back and the cuffs flipped over her wrists. "Lady, I don't know who the hell you are or what the hell you are doing here, but if you're looking for Chad, you ain't gonna find nothing but trouble."

# Chapter Two

Chad Martin looked around his cousin's barn. It was the quintessential guest-ranch barn, designed to charm their visitors. Everything hung from the wall in neat order. On each halter was a shiny little badge with a horse's name. On the top shelf of the tack room was an assortment of different-size helmets, and there were at least twice as many stalls as at the Martins' place, the Widow Maker Ranch. Ever since Gwen had sold the Widow Maker property to his family, it was almost a ghost town—they had a few pieces of necessary equipment and a saddle or two, but that was about it. They only had Sergeant, the black gelding, who was more of his sister's pasture ornament than anything else.

After Gwen sold them their ranch and moved in with her husband, she'd turned her sites to fixing up the Dunrovin Ranch. Atop the normal trappings of the barn, the ranch's crew had strewn up string after string of Christmas lights, wreaths, pine boughs and bows, making the place look like something from a Hallmark movie.

At the front of the barn they had set up a makeshift dance floor and the band was just setting up and plucking the strings as they tuned their instruments.

Though he had never been to a Yule Night Festival before, he was sure this was going to be one hell of a shindig.

His sister, Zoey, walked into the barn. Her hair was a bright red color that matched her Christmas gnome sweater. He laughed, glancing down at her gnome leggings as she walked toward him.

"Laugh it up, chuckles," she said, giving him a wink. In her arms was another sweater, which she thrust at him. "Guess what you're wearing."

He groaned. "No. I'm not wearing some ludicrous, ugly sweater."

"If we had a choice, do you think I would be wearing this marvel of modern fashion?" she asked, waving at her so-ugly-it's-cute outfit.

He chuckled as he unfurled the sweater, revealing a goofy reindeer with too-large eyes and a bit of hay sticking from its mouth. "Wow, this is *something*. Please tell me this isn't one of the new bulletproof numbers you and Mindy have been working on."

She raised an eyebrow. "Come on now, you have to know that we have better taste than that." She smiled. "If our tactical-gear team came up with something like this, we would only use them as target practice."

"Are you telling me you want to use me as target practice?" he asked, teasing his sister.

"Just put it on before Mrs. Fitzgerald comes out here and sees you aren't dressed for tonight's event." She nudged him. "Their ranch depends on this night to cover most of their yearly overhead."

"Don't you think this is a bad idea?" he pressed. "We're in hiding, remember?"

"I've done the legwork, everyone attending has been

cleared," Zoey said with an exacerbated sigh. "Dunrovin needs our help to make ends meet. Family does for family."

"Family or not, you do realize that if our CIA liaison saw me wearing this, I would be a laughingstock for decades." He slipped on the sweater over his T-shirt.

"You already are." Zoey stuck out her tongue, reminding him that even though she was team leader, she'd always be his older sister.

He snorted. "Where's Eli? Is he wearing something to match with you?"

"He was called to the Pentagon. For what, I don't know." Her face pinched. "But Jarrod is here and he has a gnome on his sweater. I'm not surprised you haven't seen him around. I'm sure he's hiding out in the ranch's main office, watching the game or something."

"There's a game on?" He perked up.

"Don't you even think about it," she said, wagging her finger at him. "You volunteered to help out as bartender tonight. Don't think you're getting out of it now."

"You better hope no one orders anything other than a Budweiser or they are going to be in trouble." He nudged his chin in the direction of the bar, which was set up in front of the barn under a heat lamp.

"I thought you might say something like that," she said, reaching into her back pocket and pulling out a bartender's guide. "Just remember, heavy-handed pouring makes for a short night."

"But bigger tips."

"If *we* were after the money, I could think of a thousand better ways to get it. To start, we could have let someone act on the contract that was out on you."

"*Was*. That ship has sailed, sister. Now, I'm a free

man." They both knew he was full of it. None of them were *free,* not with the Gray Wolves—the terrorist organization responsible for killing his twin sister, Trish—trying to hunt them down. But now wasn't the time to point out such nagging threats. Now was the time to put up their feet, take a little break from life and have some damn fun. For the last few months it had been nothing but a constant barrage of life's curve-balls, all attempting to strike them out. For once, he wasn't going to let any drama ruin his fun.

He took the red book.

"Regardless," she said, passing over his little white lie, "we are here to help Dunrovin, not act like jerks. Don't make an idiot of yourself tonight. *You*, on your best behavior." Zoey pointed at him like he was still a five-year-old boy.

Zoey turned on her heel, then tore off to go after some other poor, unwitting soul.

As he made his way out of the barn and to the bar, he thought about the last time he'd really felt at ease—the days he'd spent with Shaye after they had gotten out of Spain. She had helped him find his center, thanks to the quiet days they had spent together in France, sitting at the wrought-iron bistro tables, listening to street performers and just staring out at the Mediterranean Sea. In a life as manic and dangerous as his had been for…well, *years*, it had been nice to breathe.

Though there were definite sparks, nothing had materialized between them. He had been there to avenge the death of her fiancé, who was also his best friend, not to make a move on Raj's widow. Chad took out his phone and scanned through the couple of photos he had taken of Shaye when they had been together.

Even though he shouldn't have been thinking about her, given who she was, he missed her. Hopefully she was doing okay.

He and Raj had met in the battlefield of Syria three years ago. Raj had come from a modest background, where hard work and determination were the name of the game and it had served him well in his work as a protective ops team member of STEALTH. He would do anything that was asked of him without needing micromanaging. He was like the unicorn of employees. Right up until he had fallen in love. After meeting Shaye, Raj told them he was leaving STEALTH and intended on going back to work for his father in the fishing industry—all so he could marry the woman of his dreams.

Chad had tried to convince him to stay, told him that no woman was worth giving up the good life—a life with no boundaries and a world just a keystroke away.

Shaye's father had hired a hitman to kill the man his daughter wanted to marry. Chad still found that unbelievable. And yet, from all he had learned, Raj had been aware of the danger. His friend had made a choice—one that had ended up costing him his life and Shaye her family and her childhood home.

However, after Raj died—and Chad met Shaye—he could finally understand why Raj had made such a crazy choice. Shaye had a way of smiling, with one corner of her lips, and the simple action made the world brighten around her. She was just like the sliver of moon on an otherwise dark night—her presence made those near her feel not quite so alone.

He slipped his phone back in his pocket as Mrs.

Fitzgerald, the sweet and powerful matron of Dunr-ovin Ranch, came roaring through the front doors of the barn. Her gray hair was just a touch purple, but it was perfectly coiffed, and even as she breezed by him, not a single piece moved. "Places, everyone!" she called. "Our guests are beginning to arrive and the limos from the hotels will be here in just a few minutes." She fluffed up her hair as she spoke. "Don't forget to be kind, considerate, thoughtful! These are our friends, family and esteemed guests!"

Chad chuckled as he watched the nerves take over the normally steady woman. The way she lit up at the talk of the party and all her guests reminded him of Trish and how she had had always looked when they found out that they were being sent on a new mission.

It was almost the same look that she'd had on her face when they had gone to Turkey for the gun trade with the Gray Wolves.

*The Gray Wolves... Trish...*

Some of his joy slipped away at the memories of his twin sister.

He couldn't wait to say goodbye to this year, and all the heartbreak that had come with it.

He heard the sounds of chatter and laughter coming from the parking lot as a bus arrived with their first round of guests. Thank goodness they were here, so he no longer had to deal with the thoughts of all he had lost.

Some losses were too great to think about, too large, too all-encompassing and dangerous in their capacity to bring him to his knees. It was just so much easier to shove them away and lock them up in the area of his mind that he rarely allowed himself to wander.

Screw healing. Hopefully time would make him forget.

The first group breezed into the barn and a line formed at his bar. Most people were asking for spritzers, wine or beer—thankfully. But soon he found himself making up the night's signature drink—the drunk cowboy, his take on an old-fashioned. It quickly became a hit and the guests kept buying him shots in thanks.

A man sauntered up to the bar, an empty tumbler in his hand and a sneer on his lips. Chad recognized the man—he was an off-duty sheriff's deputy, Kash Calvert. "Oh, how the mighty have fallen."

*Crap.*

It had been years since he'd seen him, and time had done Kash no favors. He was only a few years older than Chad, but the crow's feet at the corners of his eyes and the gray at his temples made him look at least a decade older. For a split second, Chad wondered what had happened in this man's life that had aged him so prematurely.

On the other hand, the last time he had seen this man, Kash had been calling him a rotten son of a b—

*Not that he hadn't had it coming.*

"Kash, what can I get you?" he asked, hoping to get him moving along so he could stay out of his direct line of fire.

He thrust the tumbler at him. "Let's start with a drink, then we will go from there."

As Kash stared at him, a woman walked into the barn. Her dark hair was down, covering her face from his angle, but as she walked there was an air of breeding and plutocracy in the way her hips swayed from side to side, the action smooth and graceful but hinting at sexual prowess. It reminded him of Shaye and he went spiraling to thoughts of her as he poured the whiskey into Kash's drink.

He stopped pouring when the glass was three quarters of the way full.

Maybe the guy would take the heavy pour as an apology.

He splashed a bit of orange in the drink and handed it over. "This one's on the house."

Kash gave him a look of surprise as the next person in line pushed past him and gave his order. Kash started to say something, but stopped as Chad went to work. He was relieved as Kash turned and sucked away at Chad's best attempt to mollify him.

He worked quickly until the line finally dwindled and the band moved into full swing, playing old George Strait songs. As he wiped down his work space, he looked out at the dance floor. Shaye was standing there, her arms crossed over her chest and an expression on her face that made it clear she wished she was anywhere other than standing at the edge of a crowded dance floor in the middle of Montana.

He stopped wiping as he stared at her.

*What was she doing here?*

Maybe it was her doppelgänger. Shaye didn't know he lived anywhere near here. At least he didn't think she did. Was it possible that the Fates had brought them together at this place and this time, or was she here looking for him? The odds seemed long that she was still thinking about him, too, after all that had happened in Spain.

She was wearing a thick coat and black leggings, and stood out against the rest of the crowd, who were all wearing this season's best ugly sweaters—several complete with colorful Santa jokes. Maybe she was just like him and hesitated to participate in the nonsense, or maybe she wasn't here of her own volition. He knew all about that.

He closed down the bar for a moment, then walked across the barn toward Shaye as the band started to play "Honky Tonk Christmas." She glanced around at the two-stepping couples and suddenly looked about as comfortable as a ballerina at an MMA fight.

"Shaye?" he asked, rubbing his hands together in a feeble attempt to stave off his nerves as he walked toward her from across the room.

As she saw him, her eyes lit up and a smile took over her entire face. "Oh, my goodness, Chad!" she said, her voice taking on a high-pitched excited sound. "I'm so glad you are here."

Her eyes were red, as though she had been crying. "Are you okay? What's wrong?"

She rubbed at her wrists. "It's a long story and I may have been nearly arrested, but I'm here and I'm fine."

"Arrested? It must be a whopper."

"You have no idea." She gripped her hands in front of her, looking sheepishly up at him like she was about to ask for one helluva favor. "To be honest, I came here looking for you. You once said if I needed anything, you'd help."

"Absolutely," he said, surprised by her candor. Shaye had more connections than he and his family combined. If she was here, standing in front of him, asking for his help... Well, it could have meant any number of things, but first and foremost she must have been desperate. "What do you need me to do?"

If her request was that he was to kill a man, he was going to need an hour to finish his shift, then they could hit the road.

A look of discomfort washed over her features.

He glanced around at the crowd and saw a few people looking in their direction. "If you don't want to tell me here—"

He was cut off as Kash stumbled toward him, his empty tumbler in his hand. "Hey, man, you gonna get back to work or you just gonna hit on poor, defenseless women all night in hopes they'll take your sorry butt to bed?"

Heat rushed through his body and his cheeks felt as though they were on fire. He instantly regretted giving Kash the extra pour.

"Excuse me, I'll be right back," he said to Shaye, hoping to save himself at least a small amount of embarrassment—even if he had it coming.

He took Kash by the arm and made to move him, but Kash jerked out of his grip. "Come on now, *Chadie boy*," he said, spitting his name out like it was watermelon seeds. "What? You don't want to look bad in front of your new love interest? What is this, number five this week?"

Chad gritted his teeth as he attempted to check his anger. "Kash, if you want to take your anger out on me for what happened with your sister, then let's take this outside."

"Chad?" Shaye shot him a look as though she was

trying to figure out if he was really guilty of the philandering the man was accusing him of or not.

"He is blowing a mistake out of proportion. Seriously, it's just a misunderstanding." He turned back to Kash. "Isn't that right, Kash?"

The man expanded like an angry puffer fish, and like the fish, his words were poisonous. Chad stepped back but Kash teetered toward him. "Is that what you call my sister—a *mistake*?"

Dating Kash's sister was a mistake, and he hadn't meant for anything to head to the bedroom, but Kayla had been lonely an emotional basket case. If he had been thinking straight, the nights they had spent together would have ended with a game of spades and a cup of coffee, but… "No. Kayla's a nice woman… I didn't want—"

Kash swung, his fist connecting with Chad's cheek. The pain was muted by the shots the patrons of the bar had bought him throughout the night. Until now, with the world spinning around him and the throbbing in his head, he hadn't realized how much he'd had to drink.

As he ran the back of his hand over his cheek, he stumbled. Kash was coming at him, his fist pulled back, and Chad watched as it came down upon him. Kash connected with his left cheek and he could feel the bones crack against each other. The dull thud of the hit reverberated through his skull.

He saw a swirl of stars as he felt his body hit the floor. A boot connected with his ribs as he crumpled into a fetal position.

As he struggled to remain conscious, he let the man deal his blows. No matter what physical damage this man did to him, it wouldn't hurt half as much as the pain in Chad's heart as he recalled all those he had done wrong.

He opened his eyes. Shaye stood a few feet away, watching in horror as the man delivered his beating.

Maybe that was why she was here—maybe she was his saving grace. Or maybe she was here to witness his final humiliation.

# Chapter Three

She may have known how to make an entrance, but Chad sure knew how to make an exit.

*Had he always been this much trouble?*

Kneeling beside him on the floor, she pressed her fingers against his neck, checking for a pulse. His face was covered in blood and it streaked down his neck. When she finally felt the familiar thump of his heartbeat, she pulled back her fingers.

Not for the first time in the last few months, she found herself with blood on her hands. At least this time the sticky, hot blood was literal and not figurative.

She sucked in a harsh breath as she thought of Raj. She wasn't the cause of this fight between Chad and the man he had called Kash, but that didn't mean she wasn't to blame. It seemed like anytime she got close to someone, they always found themselves in trouble.

Chad mumbled something unintelligible as she brushed the front of his hair out of a cut just above his eye.

"Chad?" she asked, the crowd around her starting to abate as everyone must have realized that he was still alive. "Are you okay? You need to wake up."

He needed to be okay. She couldn't stand seeing him hurt.

An older woman came hustling out of the crowd. She was well dressed, with a wide, muscular physique that spoke of years working on a ranch. She carried herself with a matronly air—this was her domain. The woman's hair was thoroughly hair-sprayed, but as she moved the wind caught an edge of it near her face and made a blade of hair fly up. For a moment, she could have sworn that the woman's silver hair looked like an axe just waiting to fall. And she had a sinking suspicion that Chad was the chicken at the woman's mercy.

"Get up, Chad," Shaye said out of the side of her mouth as she watched the woman descend upon them. At her heels was Chad's sister, Zoey.

Both women wore matching scowls.

She reached over and nudged him. Chad grumbled something and as he tried to speak there was a whisper of drink on his breath. Looking to the crowd, she searched for a friendly face. All she spotted was Kash, sneering down at the man he had just left bloodied and battered—he would have to do.

"Kash, come here and give me a hand," Shaye said, motioning toward Chad.

"To hell with that," Kash scoffed.

"If you don't get down here, I will personally ensure that you spend the rest of your days cleaning latrines at an army training camp in Algiers, in the summer." It wasn't completely an idle threat. In the past her father had made similar threats and followed through on them. Though she didn't have her father's authority, it didn't mean she didn't still carry his confidence in administering justice.

Not that Chad was innocent.

No, her friend was far from that if he had done as Kash had said, but that hadn't given the man the right to dishonor her friend in a public place.

Kash stepped in and lifted Chad off the ground like a limp mannequin, just as Zoey and the older woman reached them through the crowd.

"What did Chad do?" Zoey asked, giving the older woman a side-eyed glance as she tried to hide her embarrassment. "Aunt Eloise, I'm so sorry about my brother and this scene he's created at your event. You know how he can be."

*How he can be?* What did that mean? From the time Shaye had spent with him, he had seemed like a good man. Sure, he had the culinary tastes of a five-year-old, loving macaroni and cheese and hot dogs, but that seemed to be his most glaring fault.

But now wasn't the time to ask Zoey for specifics about Chad's character.

"Does this have something to do with you?" Zoey asked, pointing at her.

She stepped back as if Zoey's finger was a dagger thrust straight toward her gut. "No. I—I just arrived. I have no idea—"

"Wait, *what* are you doing here?" Zoey asked, her eyes widening as she must have realized how out of place Shaye was. "Never mind," she said, once again turning her attention to the woman she'd called Aunt Eloise and the reddened state of her face. "I'll take care of this." She grabbed Chad's other arm and threw it over her shoulder.

Shaye wasn't exactly sure what she should do. She didn't really belong anywhere, especially not at this party, standing in front of its host, looking like she had caused a scene.

"Ms. Eloise, I offer you my most sincere apologies," she said, with a slight supplicating bow. "It was not my intention for such events to occur."

Her frown disappeared as she looked at her. "None of this was your doing. Oh, I'm sorry," the woman said, extending her hand in welcome. "I believe we weren't introduced. And please just call me Eloise—Eloise Fitzgerald."

The woman's manners were the best she had found since she had come here, and they made her feel as if she was at one of her galas. She immediately took to the woman. She'd always liked a woman who was driven to lead instead of taking a back seat to a man—just another reason Shaye had to leave her father's control.

"It is a pleasure," Shaye said, taking the woman's hand in a demure shake. "I'm Shaye Griest, a friend of Chad and his family."

"Well, Ms. Griest, the honor is all mine. I'm glad you could attend tonight, and please pardon my nephew's manners. He was raised like a worm in the Big Apple."

"Thank you for having me. I must admit this day has turned out to be far more *interesting* than I had anticipated." She chuckled as she glanced over her shoulder and checked on Zoey as she and Kash dragged Chad from the barn. "If you don't mind, I must excuse myself. I want to make sure Chad is okay."

Eloise waved her away. "Why don't you all make yourselves right at home in the main house, all the guest rooms are booked for the night and there is no sense in you going anywhere."

This woman was full of surprises, and was nothing like the iron horse she seemed to be when she'd come steaming in.

Shaye hurried after Kash and Zoey, and caught up to them just as they were making their way into the parking lot.

Chad moaned, and his head flopped to the side. He looked as though he'd had too much to drink on top of the beating. Maybe that was part of it. Maybe he had been taking shots between pouring people drinks. From what she'd gleaned from his family, he could be the type. When they had been together, he had been so kind and caring, and he didn't seem like the man he was being portrayed as tonight.

Raj had always liked him. That had to say something, didn't it?

The thought of Raj made her belly do a little flop. Hopefully, if he was watching down upon her, he understood exactly why she was doing what she was doing.

"What should we do about him?" Kash grumbled.

It took a second for Shaye to realize they were talking about Chad and not Raj.

"Eloise said we would have to put him in one of the rooms of the main house—everything else is booked for the night." Shaye walked up beside Kash.

"If it was up to me, I'd drop him right here and be done with him," Kash grumbled. "He got what he had coming, and he knows it just as well as I do."

"Did he really?" Shaye asked, sounding far more naive than she would have liked.

Kash smirked. "I told you what he did. I ain't gonna repeat it." For a brief moment, he just looked at her, taking her in as he helped her friend. His gaze slid over her like a set of hands, but surprisingly it didn't make her uncomfortable. Actually, as she really looked at the man, he was someone she could have considered classically handsome, but in a Western way. He had Cary Grant features, with dark eyes and a pronounced jaw, and when he smiled—like he was doing right now— there was a single dimple that adorned his cheek.

If Shaye had to guess, this man could probably have any single woman at the party, and probably several of the married ones if he was so inclined. But perhaps he wasn't that type. He'd judged his sister and Chad harshly.

"I'm sure if Chad acted as you say he did, there was a reason. So be careful what you say—few things are ever as erroneous and detrimental as our presumptions about others." Shaye stepped closer to Zoey, who was studying them but staying quiet.

She didn't need Zoey presuming anything about her being there aside from her needing a safe place to land—which was in the *entire* Martin family's hands, and it was up to all of them if they would allow it.

And she certainly didn't need any man looking at her like Kash was doing right now.

Shaye cleared her throat. "We probably need to make sure Chad doesn't need a doctor. Don't you think, Zoey?"

"Uh, yeah," Zoey said, smirking at her as she glanced over at Kash. "Let's take him in, to the back bedroom. I don't think anyone is staying in there. We can check him over there. Kash, do you have your squad car or your truck tonight?"

*Squad car?* Was Kash a police officer? The idea

caught her completely off-guard. It wasn't that she didn't think it possible of the drunk, surly, but well-built man, but it seemed strange that his revenge wasn't handled in a more *political* manner. If someone had acted against her father, they would have ended up dead in a matter of hours.

America was strange, but there was something to love about this Western, cowboy-style justice. At least all the things could be put on the table and dealt with in the open. Sure, it wasn't particularly civilized when blood dripped on the floor and they were forced to drag a man out of a party, but at least everyone knew where everyone else stood. And, to Kash's credit, he had picked up his enemy after the fight and was helping him—even if he was doing so begrudgingly.

Even Raj would have been more likely to kick dirt on his enemy instead of carrying him to his sick bed.

Maybe there was something to cowboys after all.

Yet, as handsome and drawling as Kash was, he paled in comparison to the enigmatic Chad. There was something about Chad that made her feel sorry for him. Well, not sorry exactly. She was more *curious*. Or perhaps it was mystifying. Chad wasn't like anyone she had ever known before. He was a mixture of all the things she found incredibly beguiling in a man. Whenever he was near, she found herself wanting to see more. But, for the most part, she could say the same thing about a car accident.

And, right now, getting involved any more than she already was would be the personal life equivalent of a four-car pileup.

As they made their way into the main house, she couldn't say she had ever been anywhere quite like it.

It looked like something out of a John Wayne movie, with animal skins mounted on the walls and a roaring fireplace at the center of the room flanked by leather couches and chairs. A buffalo plaid quilt was folded neatly and hung over the back of the couch as though the entire room was just waiting for someone to come in and make themselves comfortable.

At the far side, standing tall, its gold angel touching the ceiling, was a Christmas tree decked out in white and gold, all except one bright pink Dora the Explorer ornament hanging at a little girl's eye level—the effect was breathtaking. Shaye peeked around her, half expecting to see a little one running down the hall that led to the room or laughing from inside the kitchen, which wasn't far from where they stood.

*This* was a home.

It was nothing like where she had grown up, where staffers constantly waited on her hand and foot. Sure, everything was spotless and in perfect order, but with that austerity came a certain distance—it was like the sterility of their palatial surroundings stripped the soul from the building and kept it from ever truly becoming a home. Compared to this place, Shaye had grown up in a museum.

Kash readjusted Chad, making him moan. "Can't we just dump him on the couch?" Kash asked.

Zoey shook her head. "You don't get to complain. You're the reason we're here. If you had half a brain, you'd have stopped at one punch."

Kash mumbled unintelligibly, but Shaye heard something about honor.

So even Zoey agreed Chad had this beating coming. She found herself shaking her head. This definitely was an entirely different world.

As they made their way down the hall, Chad started muttering as though he was coming back to his senses. "Do you think we should take him to the hospital, get him checked and make sure he doesn't have a concussion?" Shaye asked as she spotted the steadily growing lump on Chad's forehead.

"He doesn't have a concussion—he's just a drunk bastard," Kash growled.

Kash dropped Chad on the bed in the back room. His body was half off the mattress, but Kash didn't bother moving him as he left the room mumbling obscenities under his breath.

Zoey closed the door behind him and turned to Shaye. "Why are you here? Did you have something to do with this fight—with his drinking?"

Shaye tried to control her face, but she couldn't stop her jaw from dropping. Was that what Zoey really thought? That she had come here and immediately gotten Chad into trouble?

"No, I…" She panicked. "I had to get away from my father."

Zoey nodded and tried to roll the rest of Chad onto the bed. Shaye hurried over, grabbed hold of Chad's sweater and pushed the rest of him onto the bed. He was bent at an uncomfortable angle, but at least he was in one piece.

Zoey turned and there was a pinched look on her face. "But why are you *here*? I mean, I'm glad to see you. You know I like you, but we had no idea you were coming. And…as for how you found us…"

The blood drained from her face as she realized

what Zoey was thinking. Zoey was probably concerned that she had managed to find this family in hiding. If she could find them, who else could?

"It's okay, Zoey. I didn't tell anyone where I was going. I only knew the town where I could find you because Chad once mentioned something about it. He knew I could keep it a secret. Don't worry," Shaye said, nearly stumbling over her words.

The worried expression on Zoey's face didn't lessen. "How did you find this party?"

Shaye couldn't help but bite at the corner of her mouth as she felt a new sense of shame. "Um, actually the deputy, Wyatt, brought me here after we had a bit of a *misunderstanding*." She thanked her lucky stars that she had been able to convince him that she had no intention of causing trouble for the Martins, and he had accepted her apology for accidentally pepper-spraying him.

Zoey scowled and seemed to study her for a moment before she finally relaxed. "And you are sure that none of your father's men followed you here?"

"My father and I are done. After he tried to kill Chad, and what he did to Raj, I'm no longer his daughter." The words felt like pebbles as they rolled over her tongue and slipped from her lips.

And that was to say nothing of how her mother had died under mysterious circumstances when she was only nine. Her nanny had told her that her mother had experienced a heart attack, but had refused to answer any further questions. When she was older, she had heard whispers about her mother filing for divorce mere days before she died. Looking back now, she re-

alized that her father likely had a hand in her death...
and its cover-up.

The moment he lost control over someone, they always ended up dead.

The only thing she had left from her mother now
was the ring she'd worn—a ring that had been worn
by her grandmother, and now was stuffed in her bag.

She nibbled at her lip, as her thoughts moved to the
rest of her family, all of whom had chosen to stand behind her father and left her with nowhere to go—even
though they all knew what kind of man he really was.

"I don't blame you after all you've been through.
But I guess I didn't realize that you and Chad...well,
*you know*, that you were a thing or whatever."

Shaye flushed. "Oh. No. That's not it. We're just
friends. He's like a brother to me. He just told me that
if I ever needed a place to go that your door was open."
Her body was rigid as the awkwardness of the entire
situation hobbled her. "I didn't mean to intrude, or
bring any sort of danger into your lives. If you would
like, I'm happy to leave."

Zoey paused for a moment, like she was thinking
over their options. "No, you're fine. In fact, it will be
nice having another woman around. Jarrod is here with
Mindy, but they're in a honeymoon phase. And, well,
Trevor is *Trevor* especially since Sabrina is away at
Quantico in training."

"What about you and Eli? Chad told me that you
two got engaged, as well?"

Zoey laughed, the sound high and filled with joy.
"Yeah, I guess this getting-married thing is contagious.
But, I gotta admit, I'm not in a huge hurry to pull on
the white gown just yet. I'm loving this whole engaged

thing. But I miss Eli. He's currently off the grid, but should be back before Christmas. At least I have this— Look at this thing." She flipped out her hand so Shaye could take a look at the rock on her finger. It was a beautiful ring with a sapphire at its center and around it was a ring of diamonds.

A wiggle of sadness and jealousy twisted through her. She had taken off the gold band that Raj had given her, but sometimes she could have sworn she still felt the weight of it on her finger. She missed the security of knowing that just like the circle of the ring, Raj's love was unending—that was, until his death.

A lump formed in her throat.

"You know," Zoey said, almost as if she could feel Shaye's sadness, "Chad is going to be all right on his own. Why don't you go back to the party and just enjoy the night?"

Shaye took a look over at Chad, who had started to snore. She should stay with him, take care of him throughout the night and ice his bruises. And yet, if she stayed here with him, she feared what could come of it. If he woke up and saw her taking care of him, the sexual tension that already pulsed between them would intensify. And if he asked her why she had stayed, she would have to tell him the truth—that she cared about him, that he was the only person she had wanted to run to and when she had been all alone, he was the man who had consumed her every thought. And it was this, all this *attraction*, that made it impossible. *They* couldn't be.

# Chapter Four

One drink had been a mistake, but the sixth had been beyond absurd. Chad groaned as he rolled over in the bed and found his feet. He recalled Kash's fist, the sound it made when it crushed against his face and the copper taste of his blood mixing with the whiskey he'd been drinking before the fight.

And he remembered Shaye. Her turning and seeing him. The light in her face as she caught his eye. And the excitement he felt when he realized it was really her standing before him.

And then he had gone and made an absolute fool of himself.

He had to get to her. Explain what had really happened. Explain everything so he didn't look like a blithering, drunken idiot. He wasn't *that* guy. No, and hopefully Shaye knew it.

He stood up, but as he made his way to the mirror, the world swayed and pitched under his feet. Drinking wasn't a solution, he knew. And he made a mental note to stop using it as a crutch—but damn, last night… Seeing Kash and Shaye. Watching the world bounce around him like it was nothing but a party… In the last year he'd lost his sister, gotten wrapped up in a kidnapping plot and seen more than his fair share of people die, even for his profession. And yet, people were out there dancing like it never happened.

It had been overwhelming—that level of oblivion.

If only he could go back in time and do things over. Raj would be alive, Trish would be alive and his family wouldn't be at the top of everyone's goddamn hit list.

They would go back to the shadows, doing a job where all they had to worry about was the task at hand and the targets that needed neutralizing—a world where they themselves weren't the targets.

He ran his hands over his face, and after doing a quick breath check, he found a trip to the restroom to be in order. As he walked in to the bathroom, he sniffed his shirt—it smelled like the barn mixed with the pungent sweetness of cheap liquor. Yeah, the schnapps at the end there had probably been the kicker he really hadn't needed. And yet, perhaps it was the elixir that had helped him take an uppercut to the face, one that had effectively ended his night.

He glanced around the foreign bathroom. There was a collection of toothbrushes in the stand by the sink. For a split second, he considered using one of them, but he stopped himself. This wasn't Camp You-Got-Nothing. Instead, he opened up the linen closet and extracted a new one that was still in the box.

As he caught sight of himself, he couldn't help but notice the welt on his cheek. Luckily, his eye wasn't too black and blue, but there was a faint purple line where Kash must have been wearing a ring. If nothing else, at least the guy packed a mediocre punch—if it had been someone else swinging, it was likely he would have found himself with a broken nose and a pair of raccoon eyes to match.

After a quick freshening up and brushing of his pearly whites, he stuffed his newly acquired purple toothbrush into his pocket. Aunt Eloise wouldn't mind him taking home a souvenir—it would be nice to have some daily reminder of the ass-kicking he had received. If nothing else, maybe it would help him make decisions that kept him between the lines.

He chuckled as he left the room. He and Trish used to always say that they needed to keep their lives like sandwiches—keep their asses between the mustard and the mayonnaise and out of trouble. Damn, he missed her.

He made his way toward the sound of voices wafting out of the kitchen along with the smoky scent of bacon. A woman was giggling, the sound so high that he wondered if it was the sound of someone truly enjoying themselves or if they were forcing themselves to laugh. Either way, the sound rang in his ears like empty cans dragged behind a beat-up car.

*Tylenol. He needed Tylenol.*

He opened the kitchen door and saw Shaye and Kash sitting at the antique wood table. He stopped and just stood there, unsure of how exactly he should proceed.

What in the hell had happened after he had left the party last night?

Shaye looked up at him and her face flushed. "Oh, hey. Good morning." She rushed to stand up and she made her way over to the frying pan, which was sizzling away on the stove. "We were just having eggs—want some?" She grabbed a plate out of the cupboard as if she had lived in the house for a million years, and not simply showed up on the doorstep last night.

"Uh, no." His stomach growled in protest of his refusal. "I—I was just going to get a cup of coffee and then head out."

Kash started to turn, like he was considering whether or not he wanted to face him, but he stopped. Instead he lifted his coffee cup in acknowledgment of all the things that could, should and likely wouldn't be said.

"Kash," Chad said, the man's name barely audible thanks to the embarrassment that weighed it down.

Shaye grabbed a travel mug and sloshed a bit of coffee on the counter as she poured.

*At least he wasn't the only one who was nervous.*

There was only one way to handle this situation.

He tried to think of something funny to say, but only one joke—the joke he'd learned for Anya, his niece who had Down syndrome—came to mind. "Why did the cowboy adopt a wiener dog?"

Shaye groaned, but he could see her relax as she handed him his cup. "Why?" she said, a smile peeking out on the corner of her lips.

"Because he wanted to *get a long little doggie*." He chuckled at his own inanity, and his feeble attempt to mollify the man whose sister he owed more than a simple apology.

Kash chuffed, but Chad didn't doubt that he was probably storing it away to tell his little cousins later.

Shaye arched an eyebrow and chuckled. "Seriously? That was awful."

"But I made you laugh. Job done." He tipped his head and made to leave the kitchen and the two of them. He didn't know what he had walked into this morning, but a few eggs and a cup of coffee wasn't enough for him to ignore his feeling of not being welcome.

"Wait," Shaye called after him.

She said something to Kash, but he couldn't quite make out her words from the other side of the door.

The door swung shut behind her as she made her way out to him. She grabbed her coat and purse, which were sitting beside the front door, then dangled a set of keys in front of him. "Zoey asked me to drive you home when you got up." She pointed to the parking area, where his white pickup sat waiting for them.

He ran his hands down the back of his neck and stretched out his chest, as if doing so would rid him of all the pent-up anxiety he was feeling. Unfortunately, it failed to do the trick.

He nodded, following her outside and getting into the truck without a word, though he had a bevy of questions about last night running through his mind. First and foremost, why were Shaye and Kash buddied up this morning?

And yet, he couldn't find an excuse that would give him a reason to ask her anything about it. He was already on thin ice, and he had no doubt that if he kept pressing her, Shaye would undoubtedly crack and he would lose having her in his life forever. It was best if they stuck together—they both needed a friend. He couldn't give her much, but he could give her a sense of safety if nothing else—it had been his job for a long time now, and it was the only thing he was half good at…*usually.*

He gave her directions as they made their way toward the Widow Maker Ranch. The nearer they got, the stronger the gnawing in his gut became. Though he had gotten out of Dunrovin with little fanfare and a crappy joke, he wasn't sure his family would forgive him quite so easily. Zoey was probably chomping at the bit to lay into him for making a scene. She had told him to keep himself in check, that they were there for the Fitzgeralds and to make it a seamless event.

He'd never been good at taking directions.

The snow had started to melt on the roads, and as they crested the hill that led to the house, the black gelding, Sergeant, greeted them with the throw of his head and a whinny he could hear even over the rattling of the truck's tired cylinders.

"Looks like someone is glad you are home," Shaye said, a tiny lilt to her words from her boarding-school upbringing.

"At least there is one," he said, half under his breath.

She gave him a look as though she was considering saying something to contradict him, but instead a muscle twitched in her cheek as she clenched her mouth shut.

What would she have said?

Unlike at Dunrovin, their house wasn't bustling with the sounds of morning when they walked in. Instead, they were met with the stench of overflowing garbage cans and dirty dishes. If Shaye was going to be here for any amount of time, he was going to have to get everyone on board with making more of an effort. Their life was a major contrast to her palatial estate. They really did need a housekeeper.

"You sure they said they were coming home?" Chad

asked, dumping the keys for the truck on the table near the door.

Shaye shrugged, then took off her coat and placed it over her purse on the table beside his keys.

Zoey's car was in the driveway, the tires free from snow or slush, so she hadn't gone anywhere lately. "Zoey?" he called, half hoping that she wouldn't answer.

It was quiet.

The back door slammed. Out of instinct, Chad put his finger up to his lips to shush Shaye and he moved in front of her. He could hear her breathing, faster than normal, behind him.

No harm could come to her. Not under his watch.

He tried to tell himself that the door slamming was only Zoey coming inside, but nothing felt right. He moved toward the back of the house and the kitchen. From just behind the door, he could hear the sounds of Zoey cursing and he relaxed; if she was sounding like a sailor, everything was fine. It was when Zoey was silent that he needed to worry. He stood up a bit straighter and cleared his throat.

"Is everything okay?" Shaye asked.

He sent her a comforting smile. "Yeah, it's gonna be fine." He turned back. "Zoey, everything okay?"

She came storming out of the kitchen, her hair wrapped in a towel and her mascara running down her face. "So, you made it home? Good," she said, the words all nearly in the same breath. "The damn water heater went out. I went down to the mechanical room to see if I could figure the stupid thing out, and as wonderful as YouTube tutorials are... Yeah, we are going to have to call a plumber."

"You got something just there," Chad said, pointing to a blob of black streaking down under her left eye.

"Thank you, smarty-pants. I'm aware." She ran her hand under her eye, but instead of wiping it away it only made the inky mess worse, as she smeared it over her cheek and almost to her nose.

He bit his tongue. As fun as it was to harass his sister, the glare she was giving him right now said it wasn't time to tease—a cold shower had that effect on people.

"I'll go take a look at it, see what I can do," he said, though he was abundantly aware that plumbing wasn't exactly in his wheelhouse. "Shaye, do you mind hanging out with the banshee... I mean Zoey, while I go down in the crawl space and check things out?"

"No, that's fine," Shaye said, stepping over to Zoey. "And, hey, I think I have makeup remover." She got her purse as Chad headed to the mechanical room.

He could only imagine what Zoey and Shaye would talk about while he was out of earshot. He had a better chance of making it out unscathed from a battle with the broken water heater. Hopefully Zoey would set her straight about Kayla. After what had happened last night, no amount of apologies or insisting that it was all a misunderstanding would help him. People were going to think what they were going to think.

The heavy wooden door leading to the mechanical room had been swept clear of snow by the wind, and as he moved to lift the cellar-type door, it groaned loudly in protest, as though it wanted him there as little as he wanted to be there.

The wooden stairs creaked as he made his way down to the crawl space. The sump pump kicked on, sending a blast of mold-scented air in his direction. Of all the things that had failed, it was a wonder the sump pump hadn't gone first. With its black cast-iron parts and rusted joints, it looked like it belonged in the early 1900s rather than the current century. If they continued to live here, no doubt he would be back down here a hundred more times fooling around with all the things that could, and probably would, break down.

All the glories of homeownership.

The thought of domesticated life made his entire body clench. There was a lot to be said for being the kind who was always on the road. He definitely missed parts of his old life. Maybe, once things died down with Bayural and his henchmen within the Gray Wolves organization, he could go back to living out of a suitcase, taking assignments and getting reacquainted with his firearms. He looked down at his palms. The calluses he had built up over years spent at the firing range had started to diminish. With their disappearance came a surprising sadness.

He tried to shake off the feeling. Feelings were ludicrous. They were nonsensical, and rarely actually did any good. In his experience, feelings were a temporary problem that, if allowed to seep into his consciousness, always led to disaster. If he pushed them down, and just dealt with them on a need-by-need basis, he would be far more successful in keeping the disasters to a minimum.

And yet, here he was *feeling* all the things he really didn't want to feel.

On the topic of irrational fantasies, he had no idea what he was going to do about the situation with Shaye. On the one hand, he was so glad she was here so they could run away from their problems together, but at the same time her presence made him incredibly nervous. Whenever she was close to him, tension seemed to vibrate in the space between them. He wasn't quite sure what was causing it, or if he should even acknowledge the fleeting sensation. Maybe it was nothing more than his own mind playing tricks on him. If she was feeling in any way uncomfortable, no doubt she would've said something to him by now.

She wasn't the type who was going to sit by and be quiet about anything. When she felt that there were things that needed to be said, she definitely didn't hesitate to speak her mind.

She was a round peg in a square world. And he had always been a square peg in a round world, never taking things as seriously as he should have, or doing exactly what he had been ordered to.

The water heater was a silent sentinel standing at the center of the room. He opened up the side panel and peered inside. It was a collection of wires, circuit boards and thermostats. As he stared inside, footsteps moved on the floor above him. The women stopped walking, and as they shifted their weight, the floorboards creaked ever so slightly. As their movements stopped, he could make out the sound of his sister's voice.

"He's still hurting," Zoey said.

He didn't know if he should knock on the floor above him to let them know he could hear them talking, or if he should just shut up, listen and learn what his sister really thought about him.

"Aside from last night's performance, he's seemed

okay around me," Shaye said. "In fact, he seems to be his normal joking self."

Zoey mumbled something and Shaye laughed—no doubt it was some comment on his character, but he didn't really mind. It was better to be laughed at and mocked than the target of everyone else's wrath. Being the family jester was far easier than being the family monolith.

"Losing Trish was hard on him. And I think being back here is making it a little harder on him," Zoey continued. "Being with you, and away from the family, he didn't have to face the loss every day."

"Do you think I should convince him to leave? I'm sure he and I can disappear, be safe," Shaye said.

There was the creak of the floorboards as Zoey must have walked toward the kitchen sink. "One thing you will come to learn about our family is that we are fiercely loyal creatures. We aren't like most families, who scatter their children like seeds. We have learned, through entirely too much pain and loss, that when we are divided, we are at our weakest."

Chad inwardly groaned. Zoey needed to be quiet. Shaye was already hurting, she didn't need Zoey rubbing their strong family unit in her face...not when Shaye had just walked away from the family, the country and the people with whom she had spent most of her life. Zoey's words had to be a knife piercing Shaye's already shattered heart.

He grabbed a broom that was sitting by the door and moved to bang it on the ceiling of the mechanical room, but as he moved, Shaye spoke up.

"If you're worried about me taking him away from you, from this place, or from your team, you needn't be. I'm just offering him safe passage to wherever he needs to go, if he needs to seek refuge. I have no intention for anything more than that." Shaye paused and Chad lowered the broom. "Chad is a friend. A *good* friend. I won't deny it. But there is nothing else that could ever happen between us."

The broom slipped from his fingers and it clattered on the concrete floor, announcing his presence.

Zoey called down to him, quietly at first, but then louder.

He pretended not to hear, and instead slammed the metal panel shut and made his way out of the belly of the beast. Zoey had been right—he must be hurting. There was no other excuse for the way anger burst inside him at Shaye's words.

She didn't want him. That was fine. Better, even.

He stomped up the wooden steps and let the door boom shut behind him as he closed up the cellar. For once, he wished he hadn't stayed quiet.

# Chapter Five

Ever since Chad had come back, he seemed to be in a sour mood. When Shaye caught him looking at her, he quickly looked away, and when she had asked him what was wrong, he had simply mumbled something and then disappeared into the back bedroom.

Not for the first time, Shaye questioned her choice in coming here. She tapped on her phone, looking for an Uber to take her to the airport, but the closest Uber was forty minutes away.

For now, she would stay put. Maybe call a taxi or get an airport shuttle.

She didn't know where she would go, or to whom, but anywhere had to be better than here. Chad had been a mess, emotionally and physically, since she had gotten here and she had a sinking feeling that his downward spiral was her fault. For both their sakes, she needed to go.

It was just... Well, she had thought he felt something for her. Especially when he had looked at her last night, when he'd first seen her across the room at the dance. All the distance that had been between them over the last few weeks had disappeared. He had been standing across the room from her, but it was as though they were pressed against each other. She had nearly been able to feel his breath on her skin and smell the sweet scent of his cologne and the heady aroma of his sweat.

But that feeling had been an illusion. He had made it clear with his actions last night that he wasn't the man she had thought him to be, and he was certainly not interested in her for anything more than a simple tryst.

If she wanted to get laid, she could have had any number of men. Sex and lust were easy to find, and truthfully she wanted neither. She wanted more. She wanted something like she had with Raj. She wanted to come home to her husband at night and find him happy to see her. She wanted someone to travel the world with, who had the same wanderlust that beckoned for them to keep moving, experiencing, finding adventures and perhaps a bit of trouble. She wanted to live with someone she loved, a man who could be her partner for life. Someone who wouldn't leave her bereft.

Not that Raj had wanted to die—no, he had died to be with her. And yet, he could have handled things so many other ways and instead he had pitted himself against her father, taunting him instead of playing the political games that could have kept him safe. He had known the risks, but he had refused to listen to her advice to make himself invaluable to her father. Things could have been different if he had listened to her; instead he stayed stuck in his ways. He had gone against her father after she had begged him to go along with him. In the end, he had been killed for his failings— but he had stayed true to who he really was.

She should have never let Raj into her heart. She should have known he wouldn't change to please her father. And if she had been smarter, she would have learned the same lesson sooner. If she had, perhaps she could have saved Raj. He had sacrificed himself by falling upon her father's contemptuous sword, all to stay true to who he really was.

If only she had been braver sooner.

Tears started to well in her eyes.

And here she was again, starting to feel something for a man—a man her father had already deemed unworthy. If she stayed, if she allowed herself to feel anything beyond friendly for him, then she would be repeating her mistakes all over again.

She had to be brave.

Chad walked into the living room, slipping his leather wallet into his back pocket. The truck keys jingled in his hand. "I need to run into town, go to the hardware store and pick up some parts for the water heater. You want to go with me? If you're going to stay, I'm sure you're going to need a few things."

She glanced over at him and at the purple toothbrush still poking out of his pocket like a businessman's pen. "Actually, I forgot my toothbrush," she lied, as she tried to come up with any reason to be nearer to Chad.

Sure, she needed to be brave. She also needed to prove to herself that what she had said to Zoey was true—she didn't want anything more than a friendship with Chad. And besides, he could give her a ride to the airport. It couldn't be too far from the hardware store. And then she wouldn't simply run out on him.

Though, if she did run out on him, would he follow her?

Would he even care that she had left?

He probably wouldn't even bat an eye when she

asked him to drop her off and would likely drive away as soon as her feet touched the curb.

How had she misread this situation so badly? All she had wanted was...well, to see *him*.

*Mission accomplished.* And failed.

*Ugh.*

It was painfully quiet as they rode toward the small town. The deeper he drove into the town, passing the late 1800s redbrick buildings with Western fronts and chipping and fading paintings on the sidewalls advertising long-gone pharmacies and bars, the more she started to wonder exactly where he was taking her.

She pulled her purse harder against her chest. If only he would just talk to her, tell her what he was thinking about, what he was feeling. She just needed some kind of sign for what she needed to do with the feelings in her heart.

She glanced out the window and watched as they passed by a hardware store. That had to be the shop he was looking for, but he hadn't even slowed down. "Hey," she said, motioning toward the store.

He looked over and slammed on the brakes. "Damn it."

Here she figured she was the only one who had been lost in thoughts of what could be, but there he was just as lost as her.

"Chad?" she said, his name barely a whisper.

"It's fine. I'm fine," Chad said, pulling into a parking spot right in front of the building. He slammed his hand against the steering wheel. "Actually, that's crap. I need to know why you really came here. Is it for me, or did you just need a place where your father couldn't reach you? If that's why you're here—"

"Chad, stop."

"I heard you talking to Zoey."

She gulped. "So that's why you've been in such a foul mood," she said. "Just so you know—"

"You don't need to recant what you told her. It's fine if you don't have feelings for me. It's probably easier that way."

Anger charged through her. Zoey had told her that he was hurting, and she was seeing it firsthand, but that didn't mean she didn't have her own feelings, too. "I'm sorry, Chad, that you overheard us and took it at face value. But please understand that there were things happening in that room that you may not have been privy to."

"Like what?" he asked, looking over at her with the raise of an eyebrow. In fact, he looked a slight bit hopeful, like somehow, somewhere deep within him, he wanted her to tell her that there was something more between them than just a simple friendship.

But she was probably misreading everything. And, even if she wasn't, she had already decided that it was best that she leave. This wasn't the right place for her. Nothing had gone the way she had imagined since the moment she had set foot in this stupid town.

"I think that maybe you and I...maybe neither of us really fit in the other's real lives." The words carried the sting of truth. "We are friends. We will always be friends. And, to be totally honest with you, I thought maybe we could have been something more. But I don't think we really know each other. You know?"

He tapped his fingers on the steering wheel. "You and I have a lot more in common than you think." He sighed. "What happened since you got here, it's not how things normally are with me. Kash… Well, Kash has me pegged wrong, and no matter how much I want him to know the truth, sometimes not all truths are meant to be told."

*Just like the fact that she still cared for him…no matter how poorly they fit.*

"I get it," she said, looking into her bag. Lying on top of her pocketbook was a set of keys— Oh, her rental. How had she forgotten about the car? "Crap."

"What?"

She twisted her purse closed, afraid that if Chad saw the keys he might somehow figure out that she was planning on running away. It didn't make sense, all that she was feeling. Why did being around Chad always make her feel like she was totally out of control and that nothing made sense anymore?

With Raj, her feelings had been so much easier to understand…at least when they had first met. Things between them had been *uncomplicated*. And yet now, the only thing she seemed to have in spades was complications.

"Nothing," she said, faking a smile. "Why don't we run inside and grab the parts you need." She hurried out of the truck before Chad could say anything. Talking would only make her leaving that much more difficult. If she left now, at least she would do so knowing that it was the right thing, but if he said one more thing about truths, she would undoubtedly lose her nerve.

She glanced down the road, where she saw only a smattering of parked cars. Snow had started to drift down from the sky, reminding her of last night. So much had changed in such a little amount of time. A chain creaked in the breeze, and she caught sight of the same little wooden sign she had seen when she had arrived. Just a few feet away was her magenta rental car.

She could just send Chad inside and disappear.

There was a little bell as Chad opened the door to the hardware store. He stood waiting for her.

"You coming?" he asked. "You're gonna freeze out here." He pulled his jacket tighter around him.

It was the perfect weather to sit beside a warm fire, wrapped in a quilt, and sip hot cocoa with someone she loved. She glanced over at Chad.

*Not that she loved him. Attracted to him?* Definitely. *But love?*

Her body didn't shout *no*.

She hurried inside, brushing past him but careful to keep from touching him. As if touching him would weaken her resolve about leaving and the truths she was afraid of facing would bubble to the surface.

For now, they would worry about one simple water heater.

That was about as uncomplicated as life could get. Right?

She didn't even really know what a water heater looked like, but she was sure she had a better chance of fixing it than she did in setting things right with her life.

The hardware store smelled of grease and, oddly, popcorn. And aside from the elevator music playing from the sound system, the place was eerily quiet.

Was this what it was normally like, living in a small town?

A man came walking down the white-tiled aisle in front of her and gave her a nod. "Good morning, folks.

Can I help you with anything?" he asked with a strong Canadian accent.

"Actually, we need some parts for our water heater," Chad said, standing beside her as he addressed the man. "Could you tell me what aisle we can find them?"

The guy led them toward the back of the store, asking questions about the model and what seemed to be the problem. It was a wonder that one person could know, or rather would want to know, so much about a single item in this store.

And then she felt like a jerk. Just because this man didn't have the weight of a country on his shoulders didn't mean that he didn't have passion for his job. In fact, maybe if she'd been more like him, with his clear love of all things tool-related, then maybe she wouldn't be in the position she was in now.

She chuckled as she thought about how her life was filled with tools, but not the same kind.

Chad's brow furrowed as he looked at her, and she stifled her laughter as she realized that it must seem as if she was laughing at the man.

"That is amazing," she said, as the man stopped walking and turned toward a long row of free-standing cylinder-shaped devices. On the other side of the aisle was what Shaye assumed were all the things necessary to install a water heater, including a menagerie of cords and doodads and a few different kinds of tubing.

Maybe she was wrong in thinking she could understand and fix water heaters better than she could her own life. Each had a thousand different options.

"I know, right?" the man continued, completely oblivious, or perhaps choosing to be oblivious, to her total lack of knowledge on the subject.

"We certainly do appreciate your time," Chad said.

"Don't be afraid to ask me if you need any more help. As you can see, it's pretty quiet in here." The man waved around the nearly empty store. As he dropped his hand, the bell rang as someone else made their way inside.

"Absolutely," Shaye said, equal parts nervous and relieved when the man headed down the aisle and toward the sound of the front bell. It was nice to have another person there, filling the silence that rose up again between them.

She felt a leave-it-alone attitude coming off Chad, different from the need to talk that had burst from him in the parking lot.

She walked across the aisle and ran her finger over the steel boxes. Their edges were razor-sharp and the metal was cold on her fingers, reminding her that this really was her life. She really was here.

Maybe what she needed more than anything was a minute to just *breathe*. She had been going nonstop ever since Raj's death. That had to be part of what was going on within her. This was nothing more than a bit of anxiety with everything that had changed in her life. Chad was her friend, and even if she was attracted to him, there couldn't be anything between them. Maybe he was right to clam up. If they talked about it, there was a large probability that it wouldn't end well.

Though she was tempted to run, maybe the best thing she could possibly do was just stay put for a week, at the very least a few days. Get some rest, and let her body recover from the stresses of travel before she started moving again. In the meantime, she and Chad… Well, maybe it was best just to leave that whole *idea* alone.

Or maybe she really should run.

"I have to admit," Chad began, "I have no idea what I'm looking at. Did you get anything that guy tried to explain to us?" he asked.

She laughed and some of her anxiety slipped away. "No, thank goodness you admitted it. I felt utterly daft for not understanding a single word that came out of his mouth."

Though they were only talking about water heaters, it felt good to get her mind off the swirling enigmatic torture she was putting herself through.

"I think I'm just gonna order a whole new water heater." Chad opened up his phone and pulled up a picture he must've taken. "It seems like this one is the same size." He pointed to a random tan-colored water heater, which to her eyes looked like every other one there.

"Do you think we need anything else to go with it?" she asked.

Chad tapped on his phone some more and stepped over beside her, pulling a random set of tubes off the wall. "According to YouTube and Google, I'm going to need one of these tubes." He lifted them like they were prize ribbons he had won for being the manliest man standing in the aisle.

"You know Google can be wrong sometimes, right?" she teased.

"Which is why I got corroboration on YouTube." He whirled the tubes around in the air victoriously.

She giggled at him. He was such a dork sometimes. Maybe that was one of the things she had missed most about him—his ability to walk into any snake pit of emotion and make a joke that changed the entire mood of the room. In fact, he was one of the few people she had ever met who had that ability. He could take her from raging bull to demure house cat in twenty words or less.

"Are you sure you grabbed the right size?" she asked, raising an eyebrow at the number of different kinds of hoses and tubes that were still on the wall. "And what about like clamps and stuff?"

He huffed and grabbed a box of clamps from the wall, acting like he was almost doing her a favor by getting parts that she was sure he would need by the time this entire thing was over. She could see that they were going to be spending more than their fair share of time in this hardware store before he was done completely fixing what was broken.

"Hey, now," she said, holding up her hands in mock surrender, "if you don't think we need the hose clamps, be my guest and leave them behind. You don't have to do anything because I think it's a good idea." She could barely hold back her smile as she wondered how long he would go before he admitted that he had missed something.

He chuckled as though he was aware of the game she was trying to play with him. "We'll see if we need hose clamps or not. Really, I was just thinking about recycling. I'm sure that whatever parts we need are already on the water heater that's down there. Why replace good parts? I just care about the environment. Reduce, reuse, recycle—am I right?"

She rolled her eyes, the simple gesture making her feel like a teenager. But if he was going to act like a petulant teen, then she could, too. "Recycling, my ass." She laughed, the sound bouncing around the empty aisle like a rubber ball. "You and I both know that you need that part."

"Oh, you want to make a bet?"

"Okay, mister, but be prepared to lose." She crossed her arms over her chest. "What are you prepared to lose if you do end up needing those clamps?"

He tapped the box of metal clamps against his chin, making like he was thinking. He made a show of it, taking his time, but she had no doubt he had something in mind before he had even offered to make a deal. He was far too smart a man not to always have some kind of endgame.

"If I don't need the clamps, you have to—"

There was a loud thump, making her jump. "What was that?"

"Wait here." The playful edge left Chad's voice, instantly replaced by the cold sound of a trained member of a black-ops crew.

"No," she said, but as soon as she spoke, she realized how weak she sounded. "I should go get the salesman." She jabbed her thumb in the direction the man had disappeared.

Chad held up his fist, stopping her. He was already at the end of the aisle, clearing the area. Chad edged toward the front of the store. They were being jumpy, and as the song shifted to "Santa Baby," she felt even more neurotic because of their response.

Opening her mouth to say something to Chad, she stopped. He was nowhere in sight. She tried to laugh at herself, but as her body grew rigid, the sound came out as nothing more than a rasping wheeze. "Chad?" she called, her voice strangled.

There was no answer.

*Had the Gray Wolves found them?*

She started to rush in Chad's direction, but there was a loud *thwack* and pain screamed up from the back of her thighs as she plunged toward the ground. She turned and saw the two-by-four coming down, this time striking her in the calf as she tried to crawl away. Pain tore up her leg as the person hit her in the lower back, dropping her flat to the ground.

"Chad!" she screamed, covering her head with her arms.

She rolled to her right just as the board came cracking against the tile floor. The hit sent splinters careening at her face, one striking her just below her left eye.

There was the sound of footfalls as someone ran toward her. Chad. The box of clamps fell to the ground and the metal brackets skittered around her.

It was going to be okay.

She tried to move and stand up, but as she did, a fiery, brutal pain pinned her to the ground.

She rolled on her back, the action taking more strength than she thought she possessed.

Chad was standing at her feet, with his back turned to her. Pressed against him, with a black hose wrapped around his neck, was a man. She wiped away her tears. As they struggled, she caught a glimpse of the attacker's face. The long horse-face and bulbous nose belonged to someone she had never thought she would see again. A face she could never forget—it was her father's chief security officer.

She wanted to yell at Chad and tell him to stop

as he pulled the hose tighter around the man's neck. There was a *pop* as the hose tightened against the man's esophagus. And, as the man struggled, he turned slightly and their eyes met. His face was red and sweaty, and his eyes bulged under the pressure of Chad's hold.

The man deserved to die. And yet, this could be their only opportunity to ask questions about her father and why he'd sent the man here. Did her father hire a hitman to kill her, just like he likely had killed her mother?

The thought sickened her. And yet, she had a sinking feeling that she was probably right.

"Chad," she said. "Don't kill him."

Chad's hold on the tubing remained the same. "He killed the guy working here. The poor man is lying over there by the front door with a knife in his chest. And you want me to not kill this guy?"

"I didn't say he doesn't deserve it." Shaye pushed herself up to a sitting position. As she moved, the fire from her thighs rattled up and she was forced to bite back a yelp of pain. The man certainly deserved to die, but they had to play this smart. "Chad...please."

She was tempted to tell Chad she knew the man. But if she did, what would Chad think? He would probably hate her for bringing more trouble to his life. What if he realized that she may have just brought all of his enemies straight to them because she had needed to be closer to him?

Even if she left now, her father knew about the Martins—and likely knew about the contract Bayural had out on their heads. She had just put everyone at risk. No wonder everyone had seemed put out by her arrival. Maybe they had known exactly what a security breach she was.

Chad tightened his grip on the hose, and her father's man dropped to his knees, grasping at his throat.

"Who sent you?" Chad screamed, kicking him and loosening his grip so he could answer.

The man looked over at her and gave her a sickening grin. He reached downward and pulled a knife from an ankle sheath.

"Screw you," the man said, scrambling to his feet and jabbing the knife in Chad's direction.

Chad picked up the piece of lumber the man had dropped to the ground. "Put down the knife," he ordered.

"Give me the girl and no one has to get hurt," the man said, slashing the blade in her direction. "Shaye, do you even know what this man is dragging you into?"

What was he talking about? She jerked as she peered over at Chad. This wasn't the first time someone had hinted that he wasn't the man she had assumed he was. She needed the truth from him—the complete truth and not this whisking around it that he always seemed to do.

Chad looked over at her and then back to the man, like he was assessing for a split second whether or not he should do as the man commanded. "Tell me who sent you, and maybe I won't kill you."

The man laughed, the sound rattling off the metal shelving in the store. "Whether or not you kill me, it's not going to make a difference. Your family is going to die, but you shouldn't make this girl die with you, as well."

"Chad, don't listen to him." Shaye moved beside

him, stumbling as she tried to walk. "My father sent this man. They must've been following me or something, but I doubt your family is really in any danger."

"You know this guy?" Chad asked, pointing at him with the beam of lumber.

She nodded, a foreboding sensation congealing within her. "He works for my father."

"I thought you said that you had split ways with your family. Didn't he know you were leaving?" Chad asked.

"I'm never going to be free of my father's grasp. I was foolish to think that he wouldn't have me followed." Or kill her… But she couldn't tell Chad about her suspicions. She put her hand on Chad's shoulder. "Maybe it would be best if I go somewhere else. If I leave, at least you wouldn't have to worry about my familial drama making things harder for you and your family."

"You don't have to go back and be your father's prisoner. Not on my watch," Chad said. "If we kill this man right now, no one would be the wiser." He pointed up at the ceiling, where the white drop-down tiles were conspicuously missing any black, round eyes-in-the-sky cameras.

Just because they weren't being recorded didn't mean that someone in this little town wouldn't figure out that they had killed someone. And even if someone didn't figure it out, she would still know the truth.

On the other hand, this man had attacked her. If he'd been willing to harm her in order to do her father's bidding, what was going to stop him from killing her if they let him go?

"I am under direct orders to take you back to Algeria, no matter what." The man kept his knife raised, like a silvery rendition of her father's pointed finger. He would always be there, standing over her shoulder, commanding even if he wasn't present.

"You're only to take me back, nothing more?" she asked.

The man smiled again, his teeth stained dark brown, thanks to his many years of drinking black tea and smoking hand-rolled cigarettes. "As long as you behave yourself, everything should go fine."

"What does my father have planned for me upon my return?" she asked.

"Your father has plans, I'm sure." The man sneered at her, making chills run down her spine.

"Do you want to go back?" Chad asked with a sweet softness to his voice. He almost sounded like he was pleading, asking her to stay, without saying those words.

All of her wanted to stay with Chad. And yet, they were nothing more than friends.

If she stayed, things would only get more complicated.

She should've known. Nothing in their lives had ever been simple. No matter who was after them, or what evil was lurking.

She shook her head as she looked at Chad. "I don't trust him."

"Your father or this man?" Chad asked.

"Both."

Before she had the chance to tell him to stop, Chad swung the two-by-four, hitting the side of the man's head with a sickening thump. He hit the ground and blood oozed from the dent in his temple. Chad hit him again, this time a few inches to the right. There was a crunch, and she was sure his skull was fractured—likely beyond repair.

Part of her wanted to tell Chad to stop, and yet she knew that, given the right circumstances, this man would stop at nothing to kill her.

As Chad hit the man again and again, she finally reached over and touched his arm. "He's gone. And we need to go, too. If someone finds us here, we're going to go to jail."

He dropped the board and turned away from the man, but she noticed his hands were shaking. He had saved her life by taking another.

She would have to return the favor.

# Chapter Six

She had already been through so much, and then this had to happen. Chad was glad he had killed the bastard.

As he drove, he looked over at her. She was pale and her hair was disheveled, but she didn't bother to right it and neither did he. Simply being shaken up wasn't even the start of it. From the way her face seemed to have momentarily aged and her eyes had darkened, she looked terrorized.

"Are you okay? Do I need to take you to the hospital? A hit like that to the back of the legs can cause clots, could move straight into your lungs. Dead in an instant."

*Shut up, Chad*, he told himself. *I need to work on making her feel better. Not worse. And seriously, telling her she could die? What in the actual hell is wrong with me?*

Shaye didn't answer, instead she turned her face away.

*She thinks I'm stupid, too.*

"I told Zoey that we are going to need a cleanup crew in the hardware store. She already sent someone out." He tried to sound reassuring, like he was talking about someone taking out the trash and not disposing of a dead body.

"You can't tell me that no one is going to report a murder. What about the guy who worked there?" she asked, her voice tired and drawn.

"He'll stay where he is. No one needs to know who the assailant was. We should be in the clear." He nodded like it was the perfect plan.

She finally looked his way and gave him a disbelieving look. "If I've learned any lesson, too well as of late, it's that nothing ever goes according to plan."

He couldn't help the chortle that escaped him. She had that right. "Yeah, but in this town, with my cousin as one of the few deputies, I think if we were forced to let him in on everything that was going on...well, Wyatt might see things our way."

"He may not entirely be on my side after what I did to him," she said with a guilty smile.

"Don't worry. I can get him to forgive you. He's family," Chad said. But as he spoke, he wasn't entirely sure if Wyatt would come to their rescue or not.

"And what about Kash? He seemed hell-bent on revenge."

He twitched. He had forgotten about Kash. "Well, yeah, Deputy Calvert may be a bit of a hassle, but even he won't be able to trace this one back to us." He paused. "And besides, I think he has a bit of a thing for you. It may be our saving grace."

A hint of redness rose up in her cheeks. "He has no interest in me."

And yet, from the way her body responded to the sound of Kash's name and the mention of his potential interest, her naivety seemed dishonest.

Until now, he wasn't entirely sure what was going on between them, and unfortunately, he had gotten his answer. A strange sensation of jealousy penetrated his shell as he drove the truck toward Missoula.

"Where are we going?" she asked, her hand gripping the truck's door as if she was one step away from opening it, then tucking and rolling out onto the highway.

"It's okay," he said, reaching over and touching her thigh. "I just need to go and buy a water heater."

She seemed to relax under his touch, surprising him.

"There is no way in the world that I'm going to step another foot into a hardware store." Her hand slackened on the door. "I've already relived enough of *The Equalizer* to last me a lifetime."

He laughed out loud. "Okay, that was a good movie."

"A movie that I didn't think I was ever going to re-create in my actual life." She smirked.

"You have no idea. I was like one step away from grabbing a chainsaw and going all Denzel Washington on that guy's ass."

"Ha." She snorted. "Yeah right, *Denzel*. And, I have to say that if you moved here to have a quiet life, like he did in the movie, then you are failing miserably."

He shrugged. *Failure* was the word of the hour.

"I know, it's bad…" He laughed. "Over the last few months Zoey's been on me about reducing my kill-rate."

Shaye's mouth dropped open. "You have to be kidding me."

He laughed. "What if I'm not? What if the man you have befriended is the biggest badass ever?"

"Wow," she said, shaking her head at his complete

nonsense. "Apparently adrenaline kicks your ego into high gear."

He flexed his arm. He wasn't exactly jacked right now, but there was a bit of burliness to his arms. Even if she wasn't completely impressed with his physique, he hoped he had her attention.

She laughed at him, the sound high and almost free of the tension that bounced between them in the car.

"Wow, you are the most ridiculous man I have ever met. Has anyone ever told you that?" she teased.

"I'll take that. I would much rather be ridiculous than anything else. At least I won't die of boredom anytime soon." He put his hand down on her leg and she moved slightly closer to him. "You know who might?"

"Hmm?"

"Kash Calvert," he said with a wry grin. "From what I hear, that man is about as much fun as a walrus on an iceberg."

She frowned. "A walrus on an iceberg? That's one I've never heard before. Is that really the best you can come up with?" she mocked.

"Hey, now," he said, glad she was feeling good enough to tease him in retaliation. "I kick asses, I'm not a wordsmith."

Her sparkling laugh returned. "You didn't need to tell me that!"

He gave her knee a squeeze, silently thanking the Fates for the change in their moods. It felt so good moving back into the friendship that he knew was at the core of their relationship.

She reached into her purse, took out her phone and clicked on a few buttons.

"What are you doing?" he asked, trying to peek while keeping his eyes on the road.

She smiled. "I'm ordering a water heater and I just hired someone to install it. Hello, Home Depot." She hit another button with a flourish. "They'll be at your place tomorrow morning to handle everything."

He opened his mouth to protest. She couldn't have thought putting their address in connection with her name was a good idea. He gulped back his assumptions. "You didn't really just do that, did you?"

She frowned. "Come on now," she said, showing him the confirmation of their appointment on her phone. "It is a gift. And we both know you're going to need a professional, even with the internet's help." She stuffed her phone in her pocket. "And besides, if I'm staying at your place, I think getting your family a new water heater as a thank you is the least I can do."

Before he went into full panic mode, he took a breath. "Um, you didn't tell them to deliver it to our house, or give them our address, did you?"

She gave him a look like she wasn't following his logic. "How else are they going to do the install?"

"And you used your name and credit card number?" he asked, his voice a nervous growl.

She opened her mouth to speak, but then stopped and a tiny squeak escaped her. She threw her hands over her mouth and the color that had just returned to her features disappeared. "Oh."

He pulled his truck over to the side of the road and took out his phone. He dialed Zoey.

They had all agreed to stay at the ranch and face whatever came their way, but there was no way that they were going to survive this faux pas without a major fight. They had no choice—he and his family would have to leave the ranch.

"Oh, Chad, I'm so sorry." She spoke from the spaces between her fingers. "I wasn't thinking. I just thought I'd do something nice, and…" She choked on her tears as a few twisted down her cheek. "I… I'll cancel."

He waved her off. No matter what she did now, it didn't matter.

Zoey answered his call. "Another dead guy?"

"No. But we are going to have to hole up for a bit. Get everything you need out of the ranch house."

Zoey sighed. "What happened?"

"Nothing," he said, afraid that if he told Zoey about what Shaye had done that Zoey would take it out on her. "Our location may have been compromised. Is Anya there with Mindy?"

"Yeah," Zoey said. In the background he could hear her heavy footsteps, as though she was running through their house.

"Get them out—take them and Sarge over to Dunrovin. And you're going to need to pull our entire team to the ranch for backup."

The footfalls came to a stop, as though Zoey had stopped in order to think about the idea. "It will take a bit of work to pull them in from around the globe—and they're all working on contracts."

Their STEALTH team was currently strewn around the world, providing security for their clients. It was silly to think that using them for their personal security team was even an option. Sure, they could pull a few, but with so many people pointing in their direction now, that wasn't really an option. Their only choice was to leave.

*Damn.* He had really started to like living in one place for more than a month. Montana's state motto was The Last Best Place, which, for Chad, was the truth. The mountains that huddled around their small town and abutted the ranch were his fortress, his safety net.

He would miss this place.

"Send me the address of the new safe house," he said.

"For now, I'm thinking we stay in the valley," Zoey said. "It's a good defensible position."

The idea surprised him. Maybe she was as reluctant to leave their home as he was.

"You think that's the best option? You think you should talk to Jarrod first? You know, before we come up with a plan?"

He could almost hear Zoey bristle. "You don't worry about anything other than getting your butt home, and fast. Jarrod will go along with whatever I think is best. And right now, I think the best thing we can do is focus on our family, lure these bastards into one place and then strike down with the force of Thor's hammer. I want to be free of this weight. And the only way this is ever going to happen is if we kill them all."

He looked over to Shaye and thought about their conversation.

STEALTH was more than capable of cleaning up a dead guy here and there, but an entire menagerie of dead Turkish mercenaries and Algerian Special Forces was another story. And he wasn't sure he wanted to test Wyatt's familial bond or his willingness to sweep the Martin family's dirty deeds under the rug.

With the growing body count, he would need to

work fast in order to protect not only the people he loved, but the town that offered them solace. No more innocents could die.

## Chapter Seven

How could she make such an imprudent mistake? Shaye criticized herself the entire ride back to the ranch. She thought she was doing something nice, helping the family out, and instead she had made everything so much worse. Once again, she only had herself to blame.

Chad reached over and took her hand, like he could almost read her mind. "Don't worry about it, Shaye."

That was easy for him to say. All she could do was worry about her stupid mistakes and stupid decisions. Her entire life had been nothing but a mistake. If she didn't make it out alive, she had it coming.

And what if her father came here, looking for her?

"I can see you're beating yourself up, but you need to stop." Chad squeezed her hand. "Everyone makes mistakes, but you can't dwell on it. If we did, nothing would ever get done." His hand went slack on hers, as if he was thinking about all the mistakes he had made throughout his life—mistakes she wasn't sure she wanted to know about. Was he thinking about Kash's sister? More women like her?

His being secretive was both a comfort and a hindrance. She wanted to know him on a deeper level, but with that deeper level they would both have to unearth their skeletons.

And yet, with his hand on hers it was hard not to want more from him. He had just saved her. What had she done in return?

She groaned. "Tell me how I can make this right. I can leave." There had to be something they needed that she could provide, something other than the water heater and a spontaneous evacuation.

Based on her latest faux pas, he'd probably be smart if he told her to catch the next flight out.

He paused for a long moment, as though he was trying to think of something nontaxing and especially harmless that she could do to assuage her guilt.

He tapped on the steering wheel of the truck. "I know it's selfish, but I really enjoy having you around. With my siblings all coupled up, I sometimes feel like the odd duck." He glanced over at her as if he was gauging her reaction. "Not that we are a couple or, like, dating or anything, but well…if you don't have anywhere to go, it's nice to have a friend."

That wasn't the most romantic thing she had ever heard, but it still melted her heart. Truth be told, she was enjoying being around him just as much. It was nice to think about something besides her own family dynamics—even as her father's constant torment was still raining upon her.

"You're only saying that to be nice. I would totally understand if you thought it best if I left. From the moment I got here, I've brought nothing but misery and hardship." She touched her cheek lightly, motioning at the bruises on his face.

"Oh, you don't get to feel bad for these bruises," he

said. "Are there any new ones? If there are, yeah, you can claim those." He sent her a wilting smile.

She laughed. "Well, I'm sorry about that guy trying to kick your butt back at the hardware store."

"As you should be." They rolled up to the ranch's parking lot, where Sarge was currently being loaded into the horse trailer.

She shouldn't have been surprised that this family would be quick to mobilize and would refuse to leave a man—or animal—behind.

Zoey stepped out of the horse trailer and latched the door behind her. Wiping her hands on her jeans, she made her way over to them. "We found a rental in the area, cash only, no names. It's about ten miles from here on the frontage road. We set up a series of cameras around here, so we can keep an eye on the place after we bug out. At least that way, we can see who our enemies are and act fast."

Shaye couldn't help but notice the way Zoey's gaze slid over to her.

"I'm sorry—" Shaye began.

"I'm sorry we were so slow in getting home. Roads are a mess, lots of snow," he interrupted, shooting her a look that told her she was to remain silent.

It only made her feel worse.

"I want you to stay and button up the last things after the rest of us leave." Zoey handed him a piece of paper. "Make sure nothing happens that could compromise us again when you come to our new place. I'll have new phones ready for you after you arrive." She motioned to the slip of paper, and gave Shaye a look, not even bothering to hide her disdain.

Without thinking, Shaye stepped behind Chad like

he could deflect the hatred in Zoey's eyes. The worst part was she couldn't blame her for being mad.

"I promise nothing," Chad said. "As the boots on the ground say, life sucks and whether you want to or not everyone has to take a ride in the blue canoe."

Zoey looked like she was trying to hold back a laugh. "Well, brother, we're not talking about just a few people who were impacted. Now, when we have to move out, we have Anya and our fiancées and the horse to think about."

"And whose fault is that?"

Zoey raised an eyebrow. "Really, Chad, are you going to begrudge any of us for finding happiness in our lives?" She nudged her chin in Shaye's direction. "Besides, we've had enough crap happen in our lives that it was about damn time for us to finally get a break."

According to Zoey's logic, Shaye should be getting her big break and finding happiness anytime now. And yet, with each passing minute, it was like happiness was drifting further and further out of her reach.

Chad reached behind his back and took hold of her hand. It was a simple action, and he had done it before, but this time it felt different. It wasn't just about comforting her. It felt protective and possessive, as though he would allow no one—not even his sister—to hurt her. Had something changed back there when they had come under attack?

She looked at the back of him. Before now, she had never noticed that he had a small brown birthmark at the base of his neck where it met the top of his shoulders. She could barely see it, as it was mostly covered by his jacket, and it made her wonder about all the other mysterious things he hid under his many layers.

"I'm sorry, Zoey," Chad said, finally taking a breath. His hand slackened slightly. "It's been a long day. And I appreciate everything you've done to pull this together. What all do you need us to do?"

Zoey nodded, seeming satisfied with her brother's attempt to mollify. "Just make sure that we leave nothing behind that can give us away. Then make sure the barn is locked up."

Chad nodded. They followed her over to her truck, where Sarge was stomping loudly in the horse trailer. Zoey got into the pickup.

They watched as the caravan pulled out and Anya, Chad's niece, gave her a big, toothy smile and a joyous wave. Out of all of them, she was the only one who had a smile, as if her life was just becoming one bigger adventure and more wondrous things waited for them out there on the road.

She couldn't wait for a chance to get to know Anya better. So far, she'd only seen the girl in passing, and it hardly seemed like enough. Shaye had always loved children, but had rarely spent time with any. What little time she had spent with children had been like reliving her childhood. It was as if children had a magical power to, for at least a short amount of time, bring a sense of innocence to an otherwise burdened life.

She and Raj had talked about having children someday, but they hadn't had enough time together to make any sort of concrete plans. It was simply one of those things they had discussed superficially, almost as if they were talking about each other's favorite foods and not about bringing another human being into the world. How naive she had been.

Thinking back about Raj's favorite food, she couldn't even remember.

Just when she thought she couldn't feel any worse, his ghost came back to remind her of all she had lost—and, most importantly, time and memories that were slipping away.

If she wasn't careful, she would lose Raj entirely and be left with nothing more than a place in her heart reserved for the first man she had ever loved.

Maybe now she was doomed to live a lonely life as her penance for not being able to stop Raj from picking a fight with her father.

As they walked through the house, turning off lights and eating half a box of chocolate-chip cookies that someone had left on the kitchen counter, she and Chad barely spoke. It was like in the space between them, the echo of his sister's words circled—the family couldn't be compromised again.

Chad stuffed the last bite of chocolate-chip cookie into his mouth, and a crumb caught in the corner of his lips. She was tempted to reach up and brush it away, but she didn't trust her feelings enough to get that close to him. Right now, she couldn't trust anything she was feeling, least of all when it came to Chad.

"You've got something right there," she said, pointing at his mouth.

Of course, he wiped away at the opposite side, leaving behind the little stowaway. It made her laugh. He was so *normal* and she liked him even more for it. If she brainstormed about her ideal mate, *normal* wouldn't have been anywhere on her list—it would've been comprised of qualities like *ambition, self-motivation* and *a sense of humor*. But after getting to know Chad, *normal* was going on the list.

It was nice to see a man unburdened by the constraints of high society—he was free to be himself.

He wiped at the other side when she smiled and yet still missed the crumb, making her laugh out loud.

"If you're going to laugh at me, the least you can do is help a man out." He gave her a pouting look.

She stepped closer to him and brushed the crumb from his lip with her thumb. His lips were soft and warm, which made her wonder what it would be like to kiss those lips. They would be such a contrast to the strong, deadly man they belonged to.

*Not that she could kiss him.*

As she stood there thinking about him, she realized that her hand was still on his face, holding this unexpected moment longer than she had intended. And yet, she didn't pull away. Instead, she envisioned him pulling her into his arms and taking her lips with his in a moment of heated passion. It had been so long since somebody truly held her, kissed her, wanted her. She dropped her hand to his shoulder and he reached up and took it.

He placed his fingers between hers, only further reminding her of her carnal desire—the entangling of bodies and the heat of embrace. Her breathing quickened and a part of her she had nearly forgotten came to life.

Though she could think of a thousand reasons not to, she wanted him.

He moved in closer to her, his breath caressing her

skin and she didn't have to wonder whether or not he was feeling the same way.

He reached around her with his free hand, wrapping his arm around her waist, drawing her closer to him. Their lips were mere millimeters apart, and she could've taken the helm and kissed him, but she held back. She wanted this stolen moment, and she wanted to know what it felt like to kiss his lips, but she also wanted him to make the first move.

She knew it was somewhat archaic, for a woman to yield her sexual power to a man, but in a moment like this, she wanted her lover to relieve her of her need to control.

"Have I ever told you how beautiful I think you are?" he asked, the warmth of his words brushing like secrets over her skin.

She gave him a lust-drunk smile. "Keep talking."

He exhaled, long and hard, like he was releasing the pressure of being so near to her, so close to…

He kissed her. His lips were as soft and pliable as she had expected, but beneath their softness was a hard urgency, as if he needed to taste her…all of her.

Her body was electrified by his kiss, sparks of lust mixing with the flames of desire.

His kiss. Oh, his kiss. She put her arms around his neck, running her fingers through his soft, thick hair.

He roamed over her curves with his hands. Teasing her as his fingers slipped under the edges of her shirt, playing with the waist of her pants, making her body ache for all the places they could go.

Desire didn't even begin to describe what she felt for him—it was closer to a wild, unchecked primal *need* to be one with him, to be possessed by him, both body and soul.

"Chad," she whispered against his lips, wanting to draw him in even closer, but he leaned back.

*Damn it.*

She moved after him, hungry with the need to continue their kiss.

But the look on his face stopped her.

"Did you hear that?" he asked, suddenly on guard even though just milliseconds before he had seemed so vulnerable.

She strained to listen, but all she could hear was her own blood thundering throughout her body.

"Hmm?" she asked, the only word she could think of other than *more*.

"I think I hear a car outside," he said, but this time his words were slow, like he was somewhat legless after their kiss. "I bet Zoey forgot something."

She forced her body to move back from his. She'd already been castigated by Zoey, so she didn't need another browbeating.

If it wasn't for Zoey's arrival, Shaye had little doubt that things would have quickly escalated and they would've ended up making love right here on the kitchen floor, rolling in cookie crumbs.

The silliness of the cookies made her smile.

"You better go check on things," she said, smoothing her ruffled clothing and hair as though they really had made love. Zoey couldn't see anything that would give away their budding romance.

Not that she didn't already know that there were feelings between them. But hopefully she just assumed that it was merely friendship and nothing more. Their changing friendship didn't need a witness, at least not now. Not when things were so new and fresh between them.

He pulled down, straightening his shirt and cleared his throat. And as he turned away from her, she could see his body had been reacting in nearly the same way as hers.

She rubbed the back of her neck, about to comment, but then again she was sure that he was aware of his body's current state.

A sense of accomplishment filled her, though she knew it was somewhat ridiculous. But it had felt good to turn him on. She still had *it*.

She followed him out of the kitchen and toward the front door as Chad took his time, no doubt trying to right his state of affairs.

As they drew nearer to the door, they heard the sound of a car careening from the house. Outside, a gray Ford Escape was slipping and sliding as the driver, a woman, must have been slamming on the gas pedal hoping for a speedy retreat.

"That's not Zoey," she said, chastising herself for stating the obvious. Of course, they both knew that it wasn't Zoey. "You have any idea who it is?"

He shook his head, and there was a puckered expression on his face.

"You don't think it's somebody looking for us, do you?" she asked, fully back in their current reality.

It had been foolish to think they could steal a moment and kiss.

She had Chad, and if they were smart, they would make it out of this mostly unscathed. And if she had her way, maybe things between them could continue to progress.

Although, she wasn't entirely sure she was ready for anything more than a love affair. Anything else was far too dangerous for her heart.

The expression "dancing too close to the flames" came to her mind, but she pushed away the thought.

Chad stepped to the front door, moving like he was going to take off after the car. As he opened the door, he stopped. From where he was standing, she couldn't tell what he was looking at, but she could hear a long line of expletives.

"What is it?" she asked, hoping against all hopes that whoever had come hadn't left them with any sort of explosive surprise.

"I... You—you aren't going to believe this." He let the door move farther open as he squatted down to something on the porch.

*Oh, please be a puppy,* she silently pleaded, though she was more than aware that the odds of her wish coming true were slim to none.

She stepped over to him and stopped. There, sitting just outside the door, fast asleep in a black car seat, was a baby.

"Oh," she said, the wind nearly knocked out of her.

What in the actual hell was a baby doing sitting on their doorstep? Who would have done such a thing? Why?

Her world spun out of control as she tried to fit together the pieces of a puzzle that had no edges. Apparently, nothing was outside of the realm of possibility when it came to this family.

"Whose baby is it?" she asked.

"I have no clue." Chad lifted the baby inside, closing the door as he brought the bundle over to the warmth near the dwindling fire.

"Does one of your brothers have a baby?" she asked, hoping that perhaps the drop and run was nothing more than a bedraggled babysitter in a rush and not something more.

Chad shook his head. "There's only Anya, at least so far as I know."

Ever so carefully, she kneeled down and shuffled around the tattered gray blanket that rested over the sleeping baby, in search of some sort of note or anything that would give away the identity of the child. She found nothing.

The baby rustled slightly, putting its little red fists over its face as it yawned. The baby's breath smelled of milk and newness.

Though Shaye didn't have much experience with babies, she guessed this little one was no more than a month or two old—far too young to be left out in the cold on some stranger's doorstep.

"How long have you guys lived here?" she asked, looking up and over her shoulder at Chad.

"Just a few months." He stared down at the baby, like he was trying to figure out exactly what it was.

*Not long enough for this baby to have been his.*

Though, if the baby was his, it didn't make her feel any less attracted to him. In fact, a dude holding a baby could be one hell of a sight to see—even swoonworthy.

"Go look outside—did they drop off a bag with the baby or anything?" she said, pointing toward the door as she tried to keep her panic and excitement in check.

He stepped out the front door and returned with a

small blue diaper bag. He handed it to her like it might carry some communicable disease. His scrunched expression made her laugh. "Babies and dirty diapers aren't contagious."

The look on his face disappeared and was quickly replaced by mock annoyance. "I believe I know how babies are made. And dirty diapers, for that matter."

She laughed. "At least there are a couple of things I don't have to worry about explaining to you."

She could feel the warmth rise in her cheeks even though she was a damn adult. Why couldn't she just be a bit cooler under pressure...or in this case, when flirting?

Opening the bag, she pulled out a handful of store-brand diapers, generic formula, a little boy's onesie and a dirty burp cloth. There was nothing in the side pockets, or anywhere else, to indicate the baby's name, or where he had come from.

"What do you think we should do?" she asked, looking up at Chad with a diaper in her hand.

"First, don't look at me like that when you have a diaper in your hands," he teased.

She smirked as she dropped it back in the diaper bag. "Okay, does that make you feel better?"

He nodded, but his face had tightened, almost as if his teasing had simply been a mechanism he'd employed to give himself a moment to process her question. "I... We can't call anyone. At least not yet. First, we need to get out of here." He bit at the side of his cheek. "And I hate to say this, but it may be best if we simply drop him off at the hospital. They can contact the police and figure out where the kiddo came from."

"We're not dropping this kid off like he's some kind of orphan." She ran her fingers gently over the edge of the baby's car seat. He rustled in his sleep, letting out a sweet baby sigh. Though this baby was not really her problem, it didn't feel right to just abandon him for what would be the second time today.

Chad sighed. "I know he's cute. But what will we do with him? We're one step away from being on the run. In fact, we're literally in the middle of running away from hitmen. Now isn't the time to bring a baby into any of it. Not only for his safety, but for our own."

Everything Chad said made absolute sense. But that didn't change the feeling that there was a reason he had been brought to their doorstep, a reason that neither of them understood.

"Chad, you're right." She searched for an excuse for them not to give up the child, at least not yet. "But all hospitals have cameras, even hospitals in little tiny towns like this. If we drop him off, we'll be on the radar."

"We are already on the radar, Shaye." He crossed his arms over his chest and leaned against the couch. He didn't need to finish his statement for her to know what he was thinking—that their being in danger was all her fault. She didn't need to be reminded.

"Chad, I know that you may think that I'm being crazy, but I think that for right now we should keep him." She gave Chad a pleading look, and as she did, she could see some of his resolve melt away.

Hopefully she wasn't making another mistake by begging for this child's reprieve.

There was just something about the baby's cherubic,

chubby cheeks and plump little wrists that drew her.
Perhaps it was her motherly instincts, but she had to protect this little one—at least until they found his mother,
or learned why he had been left on their doorstep.

# Chapter Eight

Chad locked the door of the ranch behind them and checked the cameras as he pulled the car seat higher up on his arm until the bar sat nestled in the crook of his elbow. Snow was sputtering down from the heavens, and as they walked toward the truck, he could see his breath. Gently, he pulled the blanket up higher around the baby, making sure that none of his delicate skin was exposed to the chill.

He still stood by what he'd said—the baby had no place in their life right now. But somehow, and he wasn't exactly sure how it had happened, they were now the proud caretakers of a mystery baby. He had one crazy life.

He strapped the car seat into the back seat of the pickup, which was way harder than dismantling and putting back together a rifle. As he sat back and inspected his work, he wasn't quite sure if he had put the belt in the right spot, and there were some random hooks that he had absolutely no idea about, but he was satisfied. He gave the car seat one more wiggle to make sure it was tight, and as he did, the baby jostled awake. His blue eyes were the color of the shallow Caribbean Sea. He had never seen a blue so pure and bright.

As the baby stared at him, a wide toothless grin appeared on his face. The little boy cooed and gurgled and then stuffed his tiny fist into his mouth, covering it with saliva.

Shaye stood beside him and smiled as the baby smacked and cooed. She had a soft, motherly look on her face as she peered at the baby, and he couldn't deny that she had never looked more beautiful to him.

He had not been the kind of man who dreamed of having a family, but standing here with Shaye at his side and a baby in the back seat, he couldn't deny that something about it just felt *right*. It was like Shaye was correct in assuming that whatever force, or culmination of events, that had put this baby in their lives had been right in doing so. It felt good to have this little carefree munchkin as part of their journey.

Unfortunately, it wouldn't last. But that didn't mean he couldn't enjoy the moment.

He took a long look at the baby and then walked around to the passenger side of the truck and opened the door for Shaye. She gave the little one a tiny wave and blew him a kiss before making her way into the pickup and letting Chad close the door behind her.

As soon as he got in and started the pickup, Shaye turned to him. "Do you ever think about having a family?"

His entire body seized up. Though not a moment earlier he had imagined *them* as a family, he wasn't sure whether or not he dared to admit such a thought to her. Sure, there had definitely been some flirting, and, well…that kiss… But he wasn't quite ready to have the conversation about children. If they did, it was almost like they were taking their relationship to another level.

And, truth be told, he was a bit relieved that the thing in the kitchen hadn't gone too much further.

If she had touched him one more time, he couldn't have resisted lifting her to the counter and showing her exactly how much he wanted her. He could almost imagine it now—her hair falling down over her shoulders as she leaned back and pressed herself against him. Her hands on the button of his pants, roaming downward until… And he could only dream of how good it would feel to experience all of her.

His body stirred to life.

Nope. He couldn't have those kinds of thoughts.

They were on the run. Not only that, but they were also now on the run with a baby. Everything in his life was a bad idea, and yet it seemed to be careening toward even more bad ideas around every curve. That said, just because something was a bad idea, it didn't mean he couldn't enjoy the hell out of it.

"Chad?" she asked, pulling his attention back to the snow-covered road in front of them and the question she had raised.

"Kids?" he said, his voice half-choked. "I like them."

*Good. Vague. Noncommittal.* He gave himself an imaginary pat on the back.

"I figured that much, Chad," Shaye said with a wave of her hand. "But what about having ones of your own?"

He gulped.

"What about you and Raj? Were you guys thinking about having kids?"

*Avoidance. The second-best tool in his arsenal when dodging a question.*

He was so nailing this.

And then he glanced over at Shaye. The glowing happiness that had taken over her features since the baby arrived seemed to seep out of her, replaced by a simmering unease.

*Damn it*. He shouldn't have brought up Raj. No doubt she had taken the mention of his name as a blow.

As he opened his mouth to offer an apology, she started to speak.

"Actually, Raj and I had talked about it. But we were together such a short time."

He collected himself. Okay, she wanted to talk about Raj and he hadn't hurt her feelings by mentioning his name. But now he wasn't entirely sure he had done the right thing in opening up this can of worms. After their kiss in the kitchen, talking about Raj made him deeply uncomfortable.

He would have never even met Shaye if it hadn't been for Raj and his love of her. If his friend was looking out at them from whatever beyond, would Raj even approve?

He shook off his thoughts. "You don't have to be married to start having kids. Or even if you wanted to wait, you have options." He stopped. It felt so weird talking about her getting knocked up by another man.

He inwardly groaned.

They *definitely* couldn't take things to a more intimate level again. Nope. No way. Not now. Not ever.

She gave a slight grimace, making him wonder if she felt just as uncomfortable with all this. "I understand that we *could* have decided to start having children, it's just that it never felt quite right. You know?"

No. He didn't really understand. The closest he had ever come to getting married was when he was… He tried to think of a time he had been tempted to ask a woman for her hand, but none of his former girlfriends had ever made the cut. Not that they weren't all amazing women—they were great. It was just that he had never met a woman who had fit into his crazy, erratic life.

That was, until he had met Shaye.

*No.* He reminded himself.

But if Shaye and Raj hadn't really felt the push to have kids, then why was she talking to him about having kids now?

"So what about you?" she persisted.

He rubbed the back of his neck, checking in the rearview mirror and catching a glimpse of the car seat. "I... Well, it's never been on the docket for me."

"How is that?"

"You know...never met the right woman. Never had a life that would lead to family living." He could feel his pulse quickening, thanks to her interrogation.

"Raj once told me that you were somewhat of a serial dater. How could you date all the time and never talk to one of your girlfriends about having kids?" she asked, giving him a pinched look, as if he had to be lying to her.

He didn't want to tell her that he normally didn't date the kind of women that were interested in having anything serious. He tended to be drawn to women who, just like him, didn't have a long-term commitment in mind—women who had just gotten out of serious relationships and were just looking for a rebound, or women who were young and unencumbered.

His last girlfriend had been thirty-two and recently divorced. They'd seen each other off and on for a few months while he had been bouncing between countries, but as soon as he left her apartment, she never really seemed to ask him where he was going. He would text her when he was back in town—they would go to dinner and occasionally things moved to the bedroom. But beyond laughing and telling stories about their day, their relationship really hadn't taken steps toward anything more. In fact, the only reason he had known her last name was because he did a background check before giving her his phone number.

They never really broke up, but then they had never really dictated the limitations or boundaries of the relationship. That was the way he had liked it. Until recently, he hadn't really considered he was the kind of guy who would be interested in anything more than a companion. And yet when he spent time with Shaye, he wanted something more than a dinner date. He wanted someone who was beyond a companion. He wanted someone who was a partner, but also a person who made him want to be a better man.

But he couldn't tell her any of that. Trying to explain how his former relationships worked seemed more dangerous than climbing Mount Kilimanjaro. The last thing he wanted was for Shaye to think any less of him, especially after what happened with Kash back at the party. But if he didn't open up to her, and tell her who he really was—imperfections and all—then he was making a conscious choice to wall her out. And if he wasn't going to open up to her, there was no chance there would ever be anything more between them. And he wouldn't be happy keeping her as a shirttail friend.

Come hell or high water, she needed to know him for who he really was.

"To be honest, Shaye, I don't recall ever talking to a woman about having children. I don't typically find myself in relationships that were anything like what you and Raj had—you really loved each other."

She started picking at her fingernail as she looked down into her lap. "Things weren't perfect between us, but we did love each other. I miss him a lot."

He nodded. "I miss him, too. He was a good friend and a good man. You would have to search high and low to find a man worthy of you—a man as good as Raj will be hard to find."

He could feel her glance at him, but he kept his eyes firmly planted on the snow-covered road in front of them as he edged out onto the frontage road.

There was a long awkward silence between them. And he wished he could have taken back all of his talk of Raj and they could somehow have a conversation without so many land mines.

He glanced in his rearview mirror as a silver Suburban came racing down the road behind them and nearly attached itself to his rear bumper. He gritted his teeth as he tried to focus on the road and not the guy behind him.

"I didn't mean to upset you," Shaye said, having likely misinterpreted his anger.

"No, it's not that," he said, jabbing his thumb toward the car behind them. "The jerk behind us is in a big hurry, and doesn't seem to want to pass."

She turned around and looked out the back window toward the offending driver. "Just slow down—they'll eventually take a hint."

He eased off the gas, hoping that she was right. But instead of going around him, the dude driving crept closer to the back of their truck. How he was not actually scraping his bumper was a mystery.

Up ahead, on the left, was the road that led to the address that Zoey had stuffed in his hand. Once again, Chad checked the rearview, hoping somehow the guy had backed off, but the man was still right behind them. He was wearing dark sunglasses and a baseball cap pulled tight, hiding his face.

He didn't like the looks of the man. Instead of turning left, Chad didn't even slow down and stepped on the gas, causing the truck to fishtail slightly as he put space between them and the Suburban.

"What are you doing?" Shaye asked, clinching her hands in her lap nervously.

"This place is a small town," Chad said. "There are crappy drivers anywhere you go, but this is the kind of town where everybody knows everybody. You know, the it's kind of the place where if high-school Johnny is pulled over by the cops, his mom and dad are both gonna get phone calls long before the cop even leaves the driver-side window. And forget what will happen when he gets home." He forced a smile.

She gave a nervous laugh.

"I don't know who the guy is behind me, but if he was from around here, he wouldn't be driving like a complete ass." He readjusted the rearview mirror, hoping to get a glimpse of the guy's license plate, but it was covered with snow.

"I didn't know you had turned all country boy," Shaye said with a tight grin.

"Well, ma'am, I've always been country," he said,

doing his best John Wayne impression. "A horse is a horse, it ain't gonna make a difference what color it is," he said.

"No. You, sir, are turning more country by the minute. You're not careful, the next thing I know is that you will be driving cattle and singing 'Git Along, Little Dogies.'"

"Ah, shucks, them's some high hopes for this little ol' cowpoke," he teased as he glanced back in the mirror. The Suburban was speeding up again. Chad sped up until he was doing seventy-five in a forty-five, but he wasn't putting much additional space between them and their tail. "Crap."

There was somebody in the back of the Suburban, and as he watched they climbed into the passenger seat. He wasn't completely sure, but he could have sworn he saw the glint of a rifle barrel as the man had moved.

They couldn't get into a shoot-out, not with Shaye and the baby in the truck. He hit the gas. The speedometer shot toward ninety miles an hour—far too fast for the road conditions.

"Chad, don't drive so fast," Shaye said, her voice tight.

"You need to grab the baby and get on the floor." The road blurred by as they screamed down the straight road that led to more and more ranch land and little else.

"Are you kidding me?" She gave him a disbelieving look. "There's no way I'm going to take that baby out of his car seat. What happens if we get in an accident? I couldn't live with myself if something happened to this little one."

"Those guys behind us have a gun. If they take a

shot, the metal back there isn't thick enough to stop a bullet from penetrating and…" He didn't dare finish his sentence.

She unbuckled, turned around and reached back, quickly unfastening the baby from the car seat. "Be careful, Chad. Please."

He was known for his driving skills, having gotten his various STEALTH members out of some extremely hairy situations, but that didn't mean accidents didn't happen—especially when the conditions were treacherous and icy.

She lifted the baby over the back of the seat and crouched down on the floorboard in front of the passenger seat, encircling the child with her body. She looked up and her eyes were filled with terror.

"It'll be okay, Shaye," he said, hoping to make her feel better. "I'm just being extra cautious."

She nodded, but remained silent.

He had no idea who these bastards were, but he had to get Shaye and the baby to safety and as far away as humanly possible. The road stretched out in front of them like a white snake, making slow bends right and left toward the mountains in the distance. To their right, ahead was the highway. It ran parallel to the frontage road just for a few miles and then the two roads forked apart. Between this brief pairing of snakes was a thin, barbed-wire fence.

He was tempted, but did he dare go through it, hit the highway and get the hell out of there? If they managed to make it onto the highway without popping a tire, getting stuck, or spinning out on the ice and snow between the roads, maybe the plan would work. But just *maybe*. He wasn't sure it was worth the risk.

If something happened, they would be sitting ducks. All the bastards would have to do is get close and pull the trigger, and everything would be lost.

He silently reminded himself that he had been through worse and made it to the other side. This was far better than the firefight he had been caught up in Aleppo. He and Raj had been taking rounds from all sides while escaping after a contract hit. They had thought their team had neutralized their opposition, but as soon as they hit the streets, hellfire had started raining down on them, as tracer rounds had zipped by, inches from their heads.

But then he hadn't had a baby and a woman he cared for in tow. He and Raj had known what they were getting themselves into. And though Shaye may have had a clue about how dangerous his world could be, he was sure she hadn't come here thinking she'd be attacked around every corner. Between this and the hardware store, it almost seemed like the entire world had it out for them.

He had promised Raj that if anything happened to him he would keep the woman Raj loved safe.

That was one promise that, now more than ever, he couldn't break.

# Chapter Nine

Over the years, Shaye had been tied up, held hostage and had her life threatened, but she had never been more frightened than she was in this moment. She hugged the baby tighter against her chest, cooing in his ear in hopes of keeping him calm.

His eyes were wide open and he shifted restlessly, pushing against her hold like she was the one who wished him harm. The baby let out an ear-piercing wail. "Shh, little one, it's going to be okay." Shaye rocked the child as much as the tight space would allow. "I'm here. I've got you." But as she said the words, she couldn't help the sense of impotence that overtook her.

As it was, she couldn't even keep herself safe. Everything about their situation screamed of their inability to adequately take care of this baby. Though she had wanted to keep him, at least until things were straightened out, she couldn't deny that they had made the wrong choice. If only she had called the police and had them come and pick up the baby.

Why did the choices always seem so much clearer in retrospect? Not for the first time, she wished life came with a manual.

The truck lurched violently with the crunch of metal on metal as they were struck from behind.

"Son of a…" Chad said, reaching out his arm toward them as if to press them down into the footwell.

Though she was more than aware that his arm wouldn't stop any real injury, his closeness made her feel safer.

"Are you okay?" Chad asked, his words fast.

She nodded and looked down at the baby, who was still squealing in her arms. The little one's wails turned into a drone of crying. "Screw this," she said, getting up off the floor and into the passenger seat. She tucked the baby's blanket tightly around him, protecting him from the cold air, and then opened up the passenger-side window.

"What are you doing?" Chad asked.

"Hand me your gun. I'm not going to sit down there and do nothing. We're in this together. Together, we are going to fight."

He unclipped the gun on his ankle and handed it over.

She leaned out the window, tucking the baby under one arm and bracing herself against the back of the seat. She pointed in the general direction of the Suburban.

The man in the passenger seat started to move, as if he was raising his gun, but before he could do anything, she fired. The gunshot ripped through the air, the sound booming around her like an invisible mushroom cloud.

The Suburban swerved, but it was too late. Steam poured out of the radiator.

Pride welled within her. Though she had never shot a gun before, she had hit her target.

And yet, they didn't stop.

"I think I got him," she cried.

Chad stared up at the mirror. "It looks like you struck the radiator. It won't be long before their car overheats. But they can still go a couple miles before they'll be forced to stop."

She moved to lean out the window and take another shot, but Chad stopped her.

"No," he said. "I don't want you getting hurt. Whoever these guys are, they aren't inexperienced. I don't want you getting shot."

She sank down in her seat and rolled up the truck's window. She pulled the baby against her chest and gently ran her fingers over his head as she shushed him. As she looked up from the helpless child in her arms, the Suburban rammed them. The force of the hit sent them into a full fishtail. The world blurred around her, and as Chad tried to regain control, the truck skidded off the road and screeched against the barbed-wire fence, which collapsed under them. The front tires hit the side of the highway and the rumble strip before Chad had a chance to recover and he jerked, overcorrecting. Even with the snow on the ground, their tires squealed on the highway as they spun in a half circle.

The baby went silent and she wasn't sure if she should be relieved or concerned. She glanced down, and he had gone rigid in her arms, his eyes wide open and his little mouth a perfect *O*.

"My feelings exactly, little guy," she said, as Chad regained control of the truck.

They hurtled back toward Mystery, having done a

complete 180. Thankfully, the highway appeared to be empty of traffic.

Behind them, working through the snow and downed fence, was the Suburban. It was pouring steam from the front of its grille, but as the driver merged onto the highway, the vehicle didn't appear to have lost any power.

Chad had the gas pedal pressed to the floor, but even with that, the Suburban was gaining on them. The man in the passenger seat leaned out the window. In his arms was a large, long gun. She didn't know much about weapons, but it looked like a rifle that the military would use—one with automatic shooting capabilities.

She wasn't wrong.

Chad reached over and pressed her downward, so she was completely covering the baby just as a smattering of gunfire rang out. She heard the ping as bullets struck the tailgate and then the shattering of glass as a round pierced the back window.

The shooting stopped.

She looked up at the windshield. It had been hit from behind several times, one just mere inches away from Chad's head.

Her breath caught in her throat.

"Chad," she said, breathlessly staring at the bullet hole.

"I know," Chad said, "but I'm okay. Everything's gonna be okay. It looks like they're slowing down." He jabbed his thumb in the direction behind them.

"Do you want me to call the police?" she yelled over the whistle of the wind through their open-air truck.

Chad chewed on the inside of his cheek. He glanced

up at the mirror, like he was assessing just exactly how much trouble they were in. "No, we just need to give them a few miles for their vehicle to overheat and stay out of their line of fire. Then we can call Wyatt."

"But don't you think that by now Wyatt has his hands full with the incident at the hardware store?"

Chad sighed. "It would look awful strange if first they have a murder, and now they have a high-speed car chase and shoot-out. I'd rather we not be tied to any of it."

She nodded, but thought about their earlier mistake in not calling the police about the baby. "I think you're right about this guy," she said, nodding toward the child. "It would've been better if we had turned him over to someone else."

She looked in the side mirror at the Suburban as they roared down the highway. The cloud of steam pouring out of the engine had grown, obscuring the driver from her view. Finally, she and Chad seemed to be putting a bit of distance between them.

"See that road sign there?" Chad asked, pointing toward a turnoff they had passed on the frontage road.

The sign read Mockingbird Heights.

"What about it?" she asked, staring out at the road as they passed it by.

"That's the road where the other bug-out cabin is. I think it's tucked back in there a couple of miles."

A sense of excitement crept up inside her belly. "Do you think your family saw the chase? Maybe your brothers are on the way to help?"

Chad shook his head. "I don't know. Why don't you give Zoey a call and let her know that we have some bogies."

"Bogies? As in *Top Gun* bogies?" She let out a nervous, scared laugh.

"Are you really going to make fun of my eighties reference at a time like this?" he teased, giving her a half grin as he checked the mirror.

Their assailants were falling farther and farther behind and now the steam was completely enveloping the car.

He passed her his unlocked cell phone, Zoey's name highlighting the screen like he had already pressed the call button.

Was he handing her the phone to avoid talking to his sister?

"Oh, no... You're not going to make me the fall guy on this one," she said, pressing the speaker button as the phone rang.

"What? No. I—" Chad said.

"Where the hell are you guys? Are you Flintstoning your way over here or what?"

Apparently dated pop-culture references ran in the family. It only made her like them more.

She gave Chad a look to tell him that he needed to deal with this.

"Uh, I'll take the or-what option," Chad said, chuckling nervously.

"What in the hell is that supposed to mean?" Zoey grumbled.

"It means that we met up with a couple of guys in a Suburban who seemed hell-bent on filling us up with holes." Chad shifted in the driver's seat like it was getting hot underneath him. "The last thing I want to do right now is lead them, or anyone else who may be with them, straight to our bug-out location."

There was a long moment of silence on the other end of the line. "Did you neutralize the threat?" Zoey finally asked.

"Kinda," he said, wiggling again.

The baby let out a wail.

"What? And what was that sound?" Zoey asked.

She and Chad looked at each other and a stone dropped in her belly. She had forgotten that Zoey didn't know about the baby just yet.

"Well, um…" Chad began, as Shaye leaned back and rifled around in the diaper bag until she found a pacifier and plopped it into the baby's mouth.

He took the blue plastic nub and sucked at it greedily, making Shaye wonder if the baby wasn't so much frightened as he was hungry, or maybe just reacting to the terror around him.

"Someone dropped a baby off on the doorstep of the ranch," Shaye said, helping out Chad.

"You have to be kidding me." Zoey was the one who now sounded breathless. "And you have this baby with you, why?"

"Seriously? You wouldn't expect us to leave a baby on the doorstep of a house that was about to be under siege, would you?" Chad asked, his voice tight and rigid with anger.

"Of course not," Zoey said, and Chad appeared to relax ever so slightly in his seat. "But you don't think bringing a baby over here is a good idea, do you? And what about the dudes shooting at you? What about the baby?"

Finally, it sounded as if Zoey was putting all the pieces together.

"Jeez," Zoey said, letting out a long exhale. "Where are you guys now?"

"We are by mile marker seventeen, heading north toward Mystery," Chad said.

"And the guys who were following you?" Zoey asked.

"Well…that's the other part." Chad ran his hand over his face. "They broke down. Shaye shot out their radiator and they overheated. I was hoping you could catch up to them and finish what we started."

Shaye hated to think about what exactly Chad meant by that, but at the same time, the men had shot at them and a child—whatever they got, they deserved.

"And where are they now?" Zoey asked.

"Unfortunately, they are near mile marker nineteen." Chad cleared his throat.

"But that's… Are you kidding me right now?" Zoey spat. "Were you trying to lead them straight to us? What the hell, Chad?"

"It wasn't like we were trying to do anything other than get away. Just go take care of it, Zoey."

Shaye turned around and took one last look at the Suburban that was growing smaller and smaller as they drove away. She'd been so proud of her shot, and now once again, she'd screwed things up. When was she ever going to do anything right?

No, she wasn't going to feel bad about this. They had saved the baby from any harm, gotten away from their enemies and delivered the men almost straight into STEALTH's hands. In her book that could be counted as a win.

# Chapter Ten

When they made it back to Mystery, the town was abuzz with people coming and going as they left work and went about their shopping. But outside the hardware store, on Main Street, was a coroner's van and two police cars. Chad cringed.

Though he was nearly positive no one had seen them at the hardware store, he couldn't say the same about what had just happened on the highway. The odds were stacked against them that with all of the nonsense that had happened today, they had gone unnoticed.

Hopefully the cleanup crew had done their job and wiped the place clean of anything that could have put him and Shaye at the scene. If not, well…he couldn't think about that.

"I think the baby needs a change," she said, rubbing at her nose like she was trying to waft away some foul odor.

As he spoke, the stale air invaded his senses. "Whew," he said with a nod, "you are right about that one. It shouldn't take us too long to get to the new place, but do you think he can wait that long?"

There was a ripple of small explosions inside the boy's diaper.

Shaye laughed. "If that sound is any indication, I think he's not quite done yet. A few minutes or so won't make a huge difference. But I don't want him going too long." She nuzzled the baby's cheek with her nose. "We don't want you getting diaper rash, now do we?"

Checking to make sure that no one else was following them and their six was clear, he turned toward the road leading to their new hideout. He glanced back at the end of pickup bed. Even from where he sat, he could make out a series of dents where the Suburban had crashed into them. Hopefully no one in town had noticed the damage—or the bullet holes that riddled the cab.

The more he thought about how many loose ends were out there, the deeper the pit in his stomach became. There was no way, with everything stacked against them, that they weren't going to attract attention .

If only he knew who the men in the Suburban were.

He was tired of sitting idly by, waiting for the attack. He wanted to go on the offensive.

He had been in on the meeting when they had all decided to face whatever came their way, but now, with so many people depending on him to provide protection and safety, he wasn't sure that they had done the right thing. He couldn't help feeling like they were sitting ducks. Now that the world was crashing down on them, their idea to stay and face their enemies seemed naive.

But he wasn't sure he could convince Zoey to change their strategy.

"What are you thinking about?" Shaye asked.

Whenever one of his former girlfriends had asked

him that question, he had always hated it. But hearing
the question from Shaye, he didn't feel the same way.

"I was thinking about dumping this truck. The guys
back there, they can identify it now—especially with
it being all shot up." He reached over and put his arm
behind her, pulling her and the baby closer. "And, more
importantly, I was thinking about how we're going to
keep everybody safe."

She tucked into him. She didn't say anything, which
surprised him. And yet he appreciated that she wasn't
offering any sort of platitude, or trying to convince
him that everything would be all right. As of right
now, their future was up in the air. It would only be a
matter of time until the men and women gunning for
them would be upon their doorstep.

"You know," Shaye said, sitting up with a start as
she reached down into her purse and pulled out a set
of car keys, "my rental is parked just up the street. We
could take it. Maybe dump the truck?"

He reached over and gave her a peck on the head
as a sense of relief welled in him. "You are a real life-
saver, you know that?"

"I don't know if I agree with that," she said. "I'm
part of the reason you're in this mess."

He shook his head. "Don't talk like that. One way
or another, hellfire was going to come raining down
on us. Maybe it was a day sooner than we expected,
but it was coming. I don't want you to feel bad. For all
we know, your being here may have saved us in the
long run. I've always believed that there's a reason for
everything."

Shaye looked out the window, and he wondered if he
had said the wrong thing—though it had been a while

since she had lost Raj, she would likely never be entirely over his death.

"I usually hate when people say that," she said. "At Raj's funeral, people kept telling me that there was some sort of plan, a reason for his death. Every time someone spoke those words, I wanted to scream." She sucked in a breath and held it for a long moment before slowly exhaling. "But here, now, with you... I'm wondering if they were right."

He held her tight, nuzzling his nose in her hair, taking in the sweet perfume of her honest vulnerability.

"Whatever happens, we're in this thing together." He smoothed her hair behind her ear as he pulled the truck down the alley behind the buildings on Main Street and parked.

He grabbed the gun and all their personal items, then threw them in the diaper bag before flinging the bag over his shoulder and helping Shaye and the baby down from the cab of the truck. "Be careful, there's a big step," he said, holding her hand.

Shaye smiled at him, and some of the sadness that was always in her eyes seemed to lighten. If nothing else, their time together could finally complete her healing. He may not have been her hero, but at least he could provide her with something.

They made their way over to the rental car, carefully steering clear of the hardware store and the crowd that had gathered to watch the coroner and police as they removed the innocent man's body. He wasn't sure whose squad car sat outside the building, but he hoped it was Wyatt's. More importantly, he hoped that they had deemed the man's death nothing more than an accident—and that Zoey and their team had set it up so that the man's family would be taken care of. If he had his way, his family would be receiving a large, unexpected life insurance check from a strange company.

It was a quiet ride to their new place. As they were about to turn down the snow-covered lane, he spotted the deserted Suburban sitting on the side of the highway. The men from inside were nowhere to be seen. Hopefully Zoey and his brothers had gotten to them before they got away. If they had, and if they had left them alive, maybe they could get some much-needed information.

As they slowed down to turn, she looked up at him. "Do you think...?"

She didn't have to finish her sentence for him to know what she was asking.

He shrugged.

She didn't complete her thought. And as they drove deeper into the enclave of mountains, a towering log cabin came into view. Around the outside of the house was a wraparound deck complete with a railing comprised of plasma cut steel panels shaped into moose, bear and elk. The black steel stood in deep contrast to the white snow that drifted around the deck as the wind blew down off the mountains.

Chad had no idea to whom the home belonged, but whoever built it must have been affluent, and around here, it wouldn't have surprised him if it was some ski house for a Hollywood star.

He glanced over at Shaye and caught her smiling as she looked toward the house and gave an approving nod. Though the house was beautiful, he didn't really care about its aesthetic qualities. More importantly, everyone he loved was inside and protected.

As they ascended the driveway leading to the house, he was relieved to find that the house itself was perched on a knoll, giving those inside a better vantage than those on the ground. No doubt, Zoey had taken it into consideration when she had chosen this spot. Though he and Zoey didn't always see eye-to-eye, she was incredibly intelligent. Maybe he had been wrong in questioning her plan, after all.

As they grabbed their gear and walked up the steps leading to the front door, it opened. Jarrod looked down on them as they approached. "Glad to see you both could finally join us."

"You can't be half as relieved as we are." Chad gave his brother a smack on the arm as he waited for him to move out of the way.

Jarrod took the diaper bag from Chad and dropped it inside the door. "Is that the baby everyone is talking about?" Jarrod asked, opening up his arms and motioning to take a child. "You know his name?"

Shaye's smile reappeared. "No idea. We really haven't been calling him anything."

"If this little guy's gonna hang out here, he's gotta have a name," Jarrod said, taking the baby. He made a pinched face as the smell reached his nose. "Little one, you are one stinky dude." He laughed, running his finger down the baby's cheek. "I think for now, we should call you Pig-Pen."

She shook her head. "That's a terrible name."

"Nothing from *Peanuts* is terrible," Jarrod teased. "By the way, Shaye, it's nice to officially meet you. I'm glad you're here."

Shaye looked slightly taken aback at Jarrod's warm reception, but Chad was grateful for his brother's gesture.

"Thanks, Jarrod," Shaye said with a nod. "Though, I must say, I'm sorry for all the upheaval I've caused."

"Upheaval is the name of the game in this family." Jarrod waved her off. He looked down at the baby as he rocked him gently. "And as for this little guy, I think we should call him Peanut for now. We can't have a nameless baby on our hands."

"Regardless of his name, we shouldn't have a baby on our hands. Period," Zoey said, walking down the hall that led to the great room. Her voice echoed out from the corridor like she was speaking down upon them, commanding them from high. "We need to protect the innocent. Anya is staying at Dunrovin with our cousins—I fear there may be more danger coming our way."

"Did you catch the men who were chasing us?" Chad asked.

Zoey nodded, giving Jarrod a knowing look. "The men are currently here. Trevor is with them."

"Here," Jarrod said, reaching for the diaper bag. "I'll take Peanut and get him changed. I'm sure that Mindy will want to see this little one. She has a major case of baby fever going on right now." He cooed at the baby as he walked off in the direction that Zoey had come from.

Just talking about sending the baby away filled him with a strange loneliness. It was kind of nice having a little one around. Babies took a huge amount of work and attention, and in this case added more fear to an already fraught situation, but there was no question about the love he had started to feel for the little one.

It would likely nearly kill him when they returned him.

But he couldn't deny that his life was no place for a child.

As if validating his thoughts, a man's yell rippled out from deep in the house, the sound filled with rage and hate. Shaye moved closer to him, and he could feel her body tense beside him.

"Have you found out who sent them?"

Zoey nodded. "They're not talking but they both have the Gray Wolves brand on their arms, so I have little doubt that they were sent here by Bayural. And, from what I've been able to pull from the cell phones, they were in direct contact with someone from Turkey while they were in pursuit of you." She paused, looking down at the floor for a moment like she was trying to summon the strength to say what Chad was already thinking. "It is only a matter of time now."

He reached down and took Shaye's hand, giving his sister an acknowledging nod. There were no words for the sense of foreboding that filled him. And all he could think about was whether this acceptance was what Trish had felt in the moments before her death, when the sickle rested upon her soul and darkness loomed.

They could fight against the Gray Wolves, but even with their resources, there was little chance they could win. Bayural's men and women didn't wear uniforms. They didn't fight by rules. They didn't have a certain look. They weren't driven by morals or obligations— only money. And money was the one thing that Bayural seemed to have an endless supply of.

"But there is some good news," Zoey said. "I've called in our operatives and taken on a few new employees. Our teams should be arriving throughout the next couple of days. So far, I've assigned about twenty guards to the perimeter of the house. As of now, the family is on lockdown. No one is to come or go from this compound."

Shaye grabbed his hand harder, leaned in and whispered, "It suddenly feels as if I'm back with my father at the palace. I can't say that I like it."

He couldn't deny that suddenly it felt as though they were a country under fire.

He turned to her. "Shaye, I think you should consider either finding another place to go, or at least going to Dunrovin with Anya and Sarge, until this is all over. I don't want to put you in any more danger than you are already in."

She let go of his hand. She looked to Zoey and then back at him like she wanted to say something but was afraid of speaking freely in front of his sister.

Zoey cleared her throat. "Excuse me, I need to go and check on things with Trevor. In the meantime, Chad—I'm serious. I don't want you going anywhere."

The expression *sitting duck* came to mind. He had only just arrived at this place, and yet he already felt as if he was going stir-crazy. He'd never been one to accept boundaries well. But he understood why Zoey was acting the way she was. They couldn't keep running. Come hell or high water, being constantly on the run had to come to an end. They couldn't keep letting Bayural and his teams of mercenaries dictate what they were or weren't going to do with their lives. Bayural had already taken Trish—he couldn't have the rest of them.

As Zoey retreated, he suddenly couldn't stop looking at his hands. "It's not that I don't want you here. I hope you know that," he said. The sharp expression on Shaye's face stopped him.

"But it's convenient to push me away, I get it." She slipped her hands into his. "I told you, Chad, I'm not going anywhere. We are a team and we are in this together. Whatever happens to you, happens to me. Like it or not, I'm a part of this now. From the sound of things, you are going to need as many hands as possible to fight this battle."

"I made a promise to Raj. I told him that I would always protect you." He reached up and pushed a stray hair out of her face and away from her beautiful chocolate-colored eyes. "I already lost my sister to this enemy. I know what he and his people are capable of. They won't think anything about killing you. And I think even your father knows it—that's why he sent his men to retrieve you."

"So you agree with my father?" There was an edge of antagonism in her voice.

*Crap.* There was no way he could get out of this situation without making her even angrier.

"I guess, if it means keeping you safe."

She swiveled on her heel. As she moved to walk away, she looked back at him. "It's been a long day. If you need me, I'm going to find myself a bed and take a nap before I say something that I'll regret. I recommend you do the same."

*Chapter Eleven*

It was a long night, and early the next morning, Shaye heard footsteps outside her bedroom door. She prayed for it to be Chad.

*Just knock. Tell me you're sorry. That you want me.*

But it remained silent. For a moment, she considered calling out and telling him to come in. But she couldn't make the first move. He had made it clear exactly how he felt—he cared about her, but he was Raj's friend, first and foremost. And as such, he would never be anything more to her.

And she couldn't begrudge him for it. On so many fronts, she understood. The betrayal of Raj's memory sat like a bitter pill on the tip of her tongue. But she couldn't help her growing feelings for Chad. If anything, having him around was like having a piece of Raj with her all the time. Though they were very different men, they had the same heroic spirit at their core. Each would have done nearly anything to keep her safe, and what they felt was right—even if doing the right thing was at odds with their own feelings.

At least, she assumed Chad was at odds with his own feelings.

She had hoped that their kiss was real. It had certainly felt oh, so real. There was an undeniable attraction between them, and yet maybe he considered it a mistake. Maybe he was simply swept up in the moment, and his other brain had taken over his thinking for a moment. Maybe once he came back to his senses, guilt had taken the place of desire.

And as much as she cared for him, she didn't want to be the reason he felt like he was betraying his friend, nor did she want to be a reason for him to feel guilty... or to agree with her father.

Maybe she should go away. She could build a different life. She could pretend she wasn't the daughter of a tyrant. She could pretend she hadn't lost all those she loved. She could pretend she hadn't fallen for a man who should have been strictly out of bounds.

But that was all it could be—nothing but pretend.

She opened her mouth to call out, but stopped as the footsteps moved away from her door.

He must have been as confused by this as she was. Maybe it was better that they just stayed apart. Maybe she was the one who needed to clear her mind and start thinking with her head instead of her heart.

A sickening sadness filled her at the sound of his retreating.

She got out of bed and walked to the door. She pressed her hands against the cold wood and dropped her forehead to the paneling. It didn't make sense, but she missed him...and she wanted him here.

There was a knock from the other side of the panel, the vibration against her skin making her jump.

"Uh, yes?" she asked, moving back from the door.

Had Chad come back? Had he changed his mind?

Did that mean that he wanted to make things right between them?

"You awake?" a woman said from the other side of the door.

Her stomach sank as the excitement seeped from her. "Uh, yeah, come in." She grabbed a sweater and threw it on over her pajamas as the door opened and Mindy walked in carrying the sleeping baby.

Shaye smiled at the sweet sight of the cherubic baby, his arms akimbo and a smile trembling at the corners of his dreaming lips.

How easy it was to love a child.

Maybe someday she would have one of her own, one who would look as peaceful and serene as he did.

"How is he doing?" she asked in a whisper as she moved to the bed and patted it for Mindy to sit down.

"Oh, he's the easiest baby. Once we got him changed and fed, he went right to sleep. He slept most of the night. I think he was a tired little Peanut."

"Oh, so the name stuck, did it?" Shaye asked, gently stroking the baby's head as Mindy gently rocked him.

Mindy inhaled the baby's scent, like she was soaking in all the baby she could. "For now, but I wonder what his real name is. He looks like he could be a Gavin or maybe a Lincoln. He's just so darn cute." She hugged him closer.

"He is such a beautiful boy," Shaye said.

"In truth, I wouldn't mind adding him to our family." Mindy looked up and gave her a conspiratorial grin. "You know, Jarrod and I are talking about starting a family. I think he's still on the fence, but this little guy may give him the push he needs." She looked down at the baby. "In fact, I think he wouldn't even mind if we adopted this one—if the stars aligned."

Shaye had been doing her best to try and not get overly attached to the baby, but she could see that she wasn't the only one struggling. "I hear you. It's hard not to want to take him in your arms and never let him go."

As she said it, it dawned on her that she could say the same thing about Chad—and the reality was, just like the baby, she was going to have to let Chad go.

"The men we love have a way of doing that to us, don't they?" Mindy asked, sending her a knowing smile.

"Is it that obvious?" Shaye asked, her cheeks warming with embarrassment.

"A woman like you doesn't travel halfway across the world just so she can hang out." Mindy smiled down at the baby like she was telling him a secret. "You can try and tell us that you just needed a safe place, but with your connections around the globe, we all know that there were at least a thousand other places that you could have landed...not that we aren't glad to have you here," she added.

"I don't think the entire family is happy with my being here, but thank you." She ran her hands over her fleece pajama bottoms. "You would be surprised how people drift away when you ostracize yourself from the prime minister of a country. I didn't have a lot of options."

"Was the man from the hardware store involved with your father?" Mindy asked.

She nodded. "I'm assuming that was obvious, as well?"

Mindy gave her a soft smile. "It wasn't a big leap.

Your father is a tyrant, but he cares about you—which is admirable—even if he does go about showing it in entirely the wrong ways."

"Yes, killing my husband was the wrong way to show he cared." Her words came out sharper and more accurate than she had intended. But thoughts of her mother collided with Mindy's words. "That's just one of the reasons I can't be with Chad, now or ever. Clearly my father's still singularly focused on controlling my life." And maybe killing her. "I can't put Chad in danger."

"I don't think you can stop falling for Chad, or he can stop falling for you, no matter what the danger. It's obvious you have feelings for each other, so denying them you isolate yourself and only diminish your capabilities to stand up against your father. United you stand…" Mindy stood up with the baby and walked toward the window. "One thing I've learned about the Martins is that the source of their power isn't Zoey, or Chad, or Jarrod, or Trevor, or in any individual within their STEALTH team. Rather, their power lies in the fact that regardless of what life throws at them, they stand united. Trish's death could have torn them apart, and for a while it looked like it might, and yet they've struggled through, more powerful than ever."

"Do you really think that Chad is over her death?" Shaye asked.

"You would know more than I about how Chad is feeling. But I think he's had a harder time than the others because of his unique bond with Trish. Jarrod said that Chad and Trish were so close as babies that they even had a secret language. There's a bond between twins. And I'm sure, no matter how much time goes by, Chad will always have a void."

But was that void too big for him to love her?

"I hate to say it, but do you think two people can be too broken to love?"

Mindy shook her head. "I think love is like a bone. It can be broken, it can be cut, it can grow weak and brittle, but if you give it everything it needs it can recover and become stronger than it ever had been before."

She didn't want to be a cynic, but she couldn't help herself. "What about when we grow old and our bones weaken?"

"They may have changed, but just like love, they are the foundation of our being. Without them, we would be nothing."

Now there Mindy had a point.

They sat there in silence for a long moment as Shaye digested all that Mindy had told her. Her mind kept swirling back to love and relationships. Chad was scarred by his past, but so was she. It would be unwise and hypocritical for her to begrudge him when she herself had baggage. In fact, every person had baggage—hers was just in the form of her past and her family. Where Chad's family's love strengthened and built him up, her father's was like a cancer that threatened to bring her down.

But she would fight.

There was another knock on the door.

*What was this place, a meeting room?*

She laughed at herself as she walked over and opened the door.

Chad and Zoey were standing side by side, and Chad looked like the cat who had swallowed the canary. The look on his face made her wonder what kind of verbal condemnation Zoey had administered before they had arrived.

"What's wrong?" Shaye asked. His gaze refused to meet hers as she stared at him.

Zoey lifted her cell phone up like it was going on public display. "I pulled the video surveillance files from the Widow Maker Ranch's eyes-in-the-sky." Zoey clicked on a few buttons and sat down on the hope chest at the end of the bed. "After you told me about someone dropping off the baby, I thought I might be able to identify the person who had left him."

Had Zoey identified the baby's mother or guardian? Is that why Chad looked so upset? Did he have something to do with this baby? Something he wasn't telling her? She tried to stomp out the panic that rose within her.

No matter what, if the baby was Chad's, or if he knew the mother, or whatever…it was going to be okay. They could get through this. If he was the baby's father, they could even talk about incorporating the little one into their lives as they moved forward. That was *if* they ever truly had a relationship.

Or maybe he wouldn't want more encumbrances in his life. A baby and a new girlfriend… Maybe it would all be too much for him.

And what if he didn't know if he wanted to keep the baby? What if he put it up for adoption?

She glared at him, but as she did, she realized she was being ridiculous. She took a deep breath. She was getting ahead of herself.

Shaye paced around the room as Zoey tapped away on her phone.

*It's going to be okay*, she repeated to herself over and over with every quick step she took.

"Here, I got it." Zoey held up her phone for all to see.

There, standing beneath the lens of the camera, was a dark-haired woman with olive-hued skin and enormous black sunglasses covering most of her face. Her lips were the color of ripe blackberries and by all measures she was beautiful.

Was she one of Chad's exes?

If she was, it made Shaye wonder why he would ever be interested in a woman like herself. She wasn't ugly by any means, but in comparison to the virtual supermodel on Zoey's screen…well, she was at best a two out of ten.

No, she couldn't be so hard on herself. Maybe she wasn't a two. When she dressed up and squeezed her butt into her Spanx, she was at least a solid four… maybe even a five. And a good pair of heels could turn her up maybe even another point on the hotness scale.

Chad stared at the women in the image, but he said nothing.

Zoey pressed the phone toward him. "Do you know who she is?" she asked, as if she also wondered if he was somehow connected to the woman and the baby.

Chad swallowed hard.

Shaye wasn't entirely sure, but her heart may have actually seized in her chest.

Was he afraid of making her feel bad by admitting he knew the woman—that he may have been the baby's father?

She had to sit down, so she stepped over to the hope chest and flopped down beside Zoey.

"Well?" Zoey persisted.

"I... I'm not sure," Chad started. "But I don't think I know her."

Shaye let out a long exhale.

"Have you seen her before?" Zoey asked.

Chad shook his head. "It's hard to tell with the sunglasses, but she doesn't look familiar."

Zoey glared at him. "If you don't know her, then why in the hell would she leave a baby on your doorstep?"

Chad bristled. "First, it's not just *my* doorstep. It's *ours*. Did anyone even stop and think about that for a freaking moment?" His voice boomed as his anger exploded into rage.

Shaye instantly felt guilty. With the thing with Kash's sister, Kayla, and the fistfight, she had jumped to the conclusion that there were probably other skeletons in his closet, as well. Based on the facial expressions of his sister and his sister-in-law, they must have been following the same line of thinking.

Which didn't make her feel any better.

Here she had been consumed with whether or not she had feelings for this man, but at the same time she was making him out to be a person he wasn't.

She had been foolish.

And now he was the one paying the price, a victim of their assumptions. She wanted to pull him into her arms and tell him that she was sorry, that she had him all wrong. And yet, he would likely never grant her forgiveness for her stupidity.

After this, she could never be his...no matter how badly she wanted him.

## Chapter Twelve

Had they all thought him capable of doing something like fathering a child and keeping it a secret? Or perhaps not knowing about the baby?

Sure, he had made his fair share of mistakes, but none was bigger than what had happened with Kayla. And in his defense, it wasn't like had been alone in the bed. She had been searching for a companion, a one-night stand as luck had it, just as badly as he had.

It had blossomed into something more for her, but to him it was only physical. The more they talked, the more Kayla had wanted more from him—and emotional attachment wasn't something he could provide then...maybe not even now.

He looked over at Shaye, who was giving him an apologetic look. He wanted to forgive her for assuming the worst of him, but the damage was already done. Like the rest of his family, she must have thought he was just a player. Didn't she know him better than that?

He was surprised by how much her incorrect judgment of him hurt.

Zoey tapped on her phone. "I'll look deeper into the woman's identity, but so far I've not been able to pull anything up. I'm thinking those sunglasses were no accident. But sunglasses or no, give me time and I'm sure I can get something."

"In the meantime," Chad began, "maybe you should go talk to Trevor and Jarrod. Maybe they have an idea who the woman may be."

Mindy looked slightly hurt at his suggestion and she started to make her way toward the door.

Before she could escape, he had to say something—something that didn't make him come off like he was totally insensitive, or worse, making assumptions about his brothers that were only too much like those about him.

"Not that the baby is one of theirs," he said, but it sounded weak coming from his lips. He stepped in Mindy's way and looked down at the baby.

Peanut looked like most babies, with round little cheeks and ruddy, long fingers. He had never understood why, upon a new baby's birth, everyone always insisted that the baby "had their father's nose" or "their mother's eyes." To him, all babies looked cute, but one step up from a chimpanzee's offspring when they were born.

As he searched the baby's features for anything familiar, a giveaway of some sort that would definitively tie him to their lineage, he found nothing. He was a baby. A sweet, cuddly baby who beckoned to be held and played with, but a baby nonetheless.

Mindy looked up at him with a thin-lipped expression. "You know as well as I do that anything is possible—just look at the situation with Anya."

He swallowed back his guilt as he thought about how thoughtless he had been in condemning anyone for having a secret baby.

His niece had been introduced into their life as a child that no one had known existed. And for all Chad knew, perhaps he was the boy's biological father. Just because he didn't recognize the woman who had left the baby, didn't mean he didn't know the baby's mother. Maybe she was someone's sister, or even just the person who had been given the child to deliver to their feet.

Some of his animosity toward the women in the room slipped away. Though he had a right to be angry at them, it would be stupid to continue with his indignation—what would he say if their assumptions turned out to be correct?

He hadn't followed up on every one-night stand or chance encounter with women he'd been with—not that there had been that many. But anything was possible... and sometimes what seemed obvious was far from it.

He took a long, deep breath and slowly exhaled, like the simple motion could relieve him of the rest of his pent-up anxiety.

"Regardless of whose baby this is, he needs us. And for right now, I think we should focus on his safety and find him a safer place to live until we have everything sorted out with the Gray Wolves." He kneeled down and sniffed the boy's head as he gave him a soft peck. He smelled like the powdery scent of a fresh diaper.

Though he knew it was silly, and perhaps an invitation to be hurt, he couldn't resist the feelings of love that welled up within him as he drew the aroma deep into his lungs.

He loved this boy. No matter what came of the future, he would love this boy and make sure he was safe—even if that meant he was far away from their family.

Shaye stepped closer and put her hand on his arm,

the simple action tender and affectionate. "I agree. I think we should call Wyatt. Maybe he can come out and we can tell him some of the situation."

He stiffened as he tried to think of a way for the local deputy to get only part of the story.

"It's okay," Zoey said, nodding. "If there's one thing I know about our cousin it's that he doesn't ask too many questions." She gave him a knowing look.

*Good.* He relaxed slightly. At the very least, some of the pressure was off since they had an ally in local law enforcement.

But they weren't in the clear.

"And what about the men we have tucked away here?" Chad asked.

Zoey sighed, like his question somehow annoyed her. "Don't worry about them. As of right now, they're with Jarrod and Trevor. They've had a long night." A wicked smile crossed her lips.

"Did they give us any new information?" Shaye asked, sounding the tiniest bit nervous. She was probably still worried that they'd been sent by her father.

He reached up and touched her hand, which was still resting on his arm. "They are with the Gray Wolves, right?" he asked, hoping that it would make her feel more at ease.

"They each had the brands on the inside of their arms," Zoey said. "They were made members, not just some hired guns."

Chad gave Shaye an it's-going-to-be-okay look and wrapped his arm behind her back like he could support her body as well as her soul. She gave him a weak smile, as though she was as exhausted as he was by all this.

"As for Wyatt," Zoey continued, "he's on his way. I haven't told him anything, but hopefully he won't have too many questions. If he does, well…let me be the one to handle it."

"Can I see your phone one more time?" Shaye asked, motioning for it.

Zoey frowned, clutching the phone to her chest. "Um, why?"

"Oh," Shaye said, like she must have realized what she had asked of his sister. "No, I just want to see the video of the woman again."

He looked at her. "Why? Do you think you recognized her?"

She shook her head. "I don't know. I just… Maybe there is something in it we are missing." She sounded somewhat defeated.

Zoey lifted her phone and pulled up the video. "The more eyes, the better." She sent Shaye a smile, the first he had seen his sister give his friend since Shaye had set foot on American soil. Maybe some good had come of them both assuming he was a total jackass.

Maybe she was finally starting to warm to Shaye. He would have to be sure not to give Zoey any other reasons to relegate her back to the land of the unwelcome.

The video started, grainy at first, but quickly clearing. They watched as the woman walked up to the porch, the car seat in her hand and the diaper bag on her shoulder. She lugged the baby as though he and the seat weighed a ton, and as she moved, the diaper bag slipped down from her shoulder and she was forced to keep pushing it in place. As she put down the baby, she said something that looked like "be gone" from the movement of her lips.

She turned and walked away without looking back at the baby she had left in their care—the baby who was now sleeping peacefully in Mindy's cradling arms.

The woman slipped slightly in the snow as she walked toward a waiting car. The video stopped.

"There has to be more," he said, wishing that it would keep going.

"All of our cameras are motion-activated," Zoey said with a slight shrug. "If she came back though, we would know it."

Shaye gasped as though she had an idea. "Wait… rewind it."

He didn't have the heart to remind her that this wasn't the nineties and they weren't watching a VHS tape, but a smile moved over his lips as he silently corrected her. He must have been spending entirely too much time with his techie sister, who would have called him out for saying something like that.

"Huh?" Zoey asked.

"Go back. Did you see she was walking toward a car? Let's zoom in, see if we can get an ID on the car." Shaye sounded excited.

Zoey skipped back in the recording. Zooming in on the car, there was little to see. It was just a normal Ford Escape.

But as he squinted, he noticed a small white sticker in the car's front window. "Look, right there," he said, pointing at the sticker. "Can you make that legible?"

Zoey clicked away, pulling and cleaning up the sticker until they could read the word: *Alamo* in blue-and-yellow writing.

"It's a rental," Shaye said, excitement in her voice.

The rental car told them with almost complete certainty that the woman wasn't from Montana. And it gave them a place to start digging. Maybe if they could get the woman's identity nailed down, then they could figure out why she had dropped off the baby.

"I got it," Zoey said, her voice high with excitement. "Good job, Shaye, Chad. I'll go see what I can pull up from this. It shouldn't take me too long to hack into the rental car company's system and pull up their recent rental agreements."

He nodded. "I'd love to get a solid ID on this woman, as well."

"That makes two of us," Zoey said, smiling at him as she jogged down the hallway toward her office.

Mindy walked toward the door, Peanut still asleep in her arms. "I'm going to try and get him snuggled into bed so he can sleep a bit longer. If you need me, I'm in my room." She closed the door gently behind her, giving Shaye a wink as she left.

And suddenly they were alone. Very. Alone.

The room sat silent, but there was the vibration of unspoken words buzzing between them.

"I'd better go check on Trevor and Jarrod. I bet they're ready to take a break from their interrogation." Not that he had the stomach for some of the face-to-face methods his brothers used to get information from their enemies, but interrogations had be to easier than being here with Shaye.

"I'm sorry, Chad," Shaye said. "I shouldn't have—"

He shook his head, quieting her. "I know what you thought... And clearly you weren't the only one. But don't worry about it." He shrugged like it wasn't still bothering him that she thought he was capable of abandoning a baby.

"After the fistfight, and what everyone was saying?"

"What?" he said, jerking his head. He knew people assumed the worst about him, but why would anyone tell Shaye anything about him? Or had it been Kash? "Who said something?"

She looked down at her hands. "It doesn't matter who said what, I was the one who made a mistake in listening to them. I should have known what they were saying was wrong."

"I thought you knew me. My family saved your life. And yet, you think I'm some kind of sleaze?"

She stepped toward him, but he moved away from her reach. "Chad, no... I don't think anything like that about you. I appreciate all that you and your family have done for me, but—"

"But you still thought I had fathered a baby and kept it a secret," he said, finishing her sentence.

"You can't act like it was out of the question," she countered. "You alluded to the fact that your past isn't without blemishes."

He wanted to tell her that neither was hers, but he didn't want to stoop to that level. He was mad and hurt by her suppositions, and though it would have been easier to push her away and maybe drive her from his life, he didn't want to hurt her. He just wanted to go back to the way things were before the baby came along and she had made it clear exactly what she thought of him.

"I've had women in my life, you're right," he said, but as he spoke the words it was like she had been slapped across the face.

She looked up at him with pain in her eyes.

"Damn it. That's not what I meant. I just mean—"

"It's okay, we all have a past, Chad." She sucked in a long breath, as if she was trying to control her anger, or was it the tears that were starting to well in her eyes?

"This is all coming out wrong," he said. "I'm not really upset with you. I get how you could assume what you did. And I'm sorry that I have a reputation that would lend itself to a rush to judgment. But I'm telling you, Shaye, I don't want to keep secrets from you, of all people—"

Before he could finish his thought, there was a knock at their door. "Wyatt's here," Zoey said and stomped quickly down the hall.

"The queen is beckoning," he said, wondering if Zoey had talked about him.

Shaye gave him a look that made him question his irritation toward his sister. "I know your sister can be...*tough.*"

"She hasn't been kind to you, and for that I'm sorry." He put his hand on the doorknob as he moved to go out.

"That's not entirely true," Shaye said, shaking her head. "I think she just wants the best for your family and isn't afraid to upset others to keep everyone safe. Her love is fierce."

"And so is her attitude." He could hear how angry he sounded.

"Her ferocity is something to be admired, and she is a natural-born leader. If my father was anything like her, I think my life would have been far different."

"What do you mean?"

Shaye shook her head. "Just that he doesn't put his family first. For him, everything and everyone is fair game when it comes to getting himself ahead. My back carries many of his footprints."

He let go of the doorknob and wrapped her in his arms. As he hugged her, he drew in the scent of her lavender shampoo and the sweet smell of sleep that still lingered on her skin.

They both carried wounds deeper than time could completely heal, but that didn't mean they couldn't keep trying to learn and move past the pain inflicted by others.

"Do you accept my apology?" she asked, her breath warming his chest through the thin cotton of his T-shirt.

"I couldn't stay mad at you if I tried." And, oh, how he had tried. Pushing her away would have been so much easier than trying to make sense of what was going on inside him.

But when she was in his arms and pressed against him, she felt like she was a part of him—like just maybe she was the part of him that he'd been missing.

# *Chapter Thirteen*

Chad and Shaye walked out of the back bedroom holding hands. As they entered the great room and Shaye looked out the front window, she let her hand slip from his. Wyatt was out in the driveway talking with Jarrod. Though it was barely a secret that they had feelings for one another, it didn't feel like the time or the place to advertise their growing relationship.

Shaye watched as Jarrod and Wyatt started walking toward the front door. Wyatt laughed, making her wonder if Jarrod had told him anything that even resembled the truth of their precarious situation.

Zoey walked out from the kitchen and flopped down on the couch. She was eating a banana and scrolling through something on her phone, almost as if it was just any other day and they weren't holding two men hostage with a stranger's baby in their midst.

It made her wonder what else this family had faced. How could they be so nonchalant when law enforcement showed up on their doorstep and so much was at stake?

Or maybe it was just that they knew they were safe with Wyatt.

Even assuming the latter, her hands were sweating

and she kept rubbing them on her pants in an attempt to rid herself of her nerves. She could only imagine what would happen if Wyatt caught wind of the men in the basement. Would he arrest them all and take the men? Or would he join the family in their craziness? And if he did, would he be as kind as Mindy and Chad had been about her role in the upheaval?

And that was to say nothing of the baby.

She tried to swallow back the rest of her nervousness, but it was a losing battle.

Chad opened the door for Wyatt and Jarrod. Jarrod walked in and Wyatt took off his hat and slapped it against his leg, bumping off the snow before he stepped inside.

"This is a nice place you got yourselves here," Wyatt said, looking around the room with animal hides decorating the walls and a large river-rock fireplace at its heart. He whistled through his teeth as his gaze came to rest on the oil painting of a waterfall that sat over the hearth. "You know who this place belongs to?"

"No," Zoey said, shoving the last bit of the banana into her mouth and her phone in her pocket.

"Well, it's a nice place," Wyatt said, moving from one foot to the other as he gripped the corners of his bulletproof vest.

Chad cleared his throat as a long, awkward silence permeated through the room. "So I'm not sure exactly what my sister told you, but I'm glad you're here."

Zoey shot him a look that told him to shut up in every language. The silent edict made Shaye chuckle inwardly. *Fierce* had been an understatement. Zoey was an inspiration.

Chad stopped talking.

"Jarrod, do you want to go get the package while I talk to Wyatt here?" Zoey said, motioning her toward the back bedrooms, where the baby was sleeping.

Jarrod nodded as Zoey turned to face the deputy. "We meant to call you sooner, but hearing all that you were facing the last few days, we didn't want to burden you." Zoey sounded far softer and more supplicating than Shaye had ever heard before.

"Yes, things have been running amok here lately," Wyatt said, frowning at them. "Though I must admit, I'm not sure I want to know exactly how you all know what's going on. By chance, you and your brothers wouldn't have any knowledge about a strange series of events that occurred at the local hardware store, would you?"

Zoey shook her head and smiled. "No idea what you're talking about," she said. "All I'd heard was that there was something going on downtown, something that involved the coroner. What happened?" She gave Wyatt a concerned look.

The woman could've been up for an award with that kind of performance.

"Apparently, one of the store's employees tripped and landed on a knife." Wyatt gave them a disbelieving look. "Though there was no evidence of foul play, and everything seems to add up to a brutal accident, if you ask me... It looked a bit *forced*." He looked over at Chad as if he could smell the guilt and fear emanating from him.

Without thinking, Shaye reached down to touch the welts on the back of her legs where she had been struck by their attacker. Did Wyatt have an idea about what had really happened?

Zoey's smile grew ever larger, and she looked more and more like the Cheshire cat. "Was there any kind of recording, anything that could help make sense of his death?"

She sounded so innocent.

Wyatt turned to her. "Unfortunately, here in Mystery, you'll find that most everyone thinks of that as an invasion of privacy. Now and again you find somebody with cameras," he said, eyeing Zoey knowingly. "However, I find that people who run high-tech gadgets around their places always have something to hide."

"Cousin, come on. What would we have to hide from you?" Zoey laughed. "Besides, I have to disagree. In our case, we find our surveillance helps keep us safe. In fact, from what I know about your family, it may not be a bad idea for you all to get a little more security."

"You've got me there," Wyatt said with a chuckle. "Maybe our two families are more alike than I ever thought possible. And if that's the case, we'll be lucky if this town is left standing."

Shaye laughed—he was more on point than he even knew.

Zoey wrapped her arm in Wyatt's. "Now, cousin, you know that whatever we take down, we'll do our best to rebuild."

"Just make sure you don't go about taking down my career—got it?" Wyatt said, raising an eyebrow.

Shaye wasn't sure, given the circumstances, that was a promise that Zoey could make.

Zoey walked Wyatt back toward the kitchen and she and Chad followed behind.

Chad leaned down to her ear and whispered, "I have a bad feeling that this isn't going to go as well as Zoey was hoping. We are going to need to watch for the fallout."

"Hey, trust your sister. She knows what she's about." Shaye patted him on the arm, though she had a sneaking suspicion that Chad was right.

Zoey handed Wyatt a steaming cup of coffee and motioned for him to sit down at the bar that stood at the center of the room. "Yesterday, we became the proud caregivers of a little boy."

"Oh, yeah?" Wyatt said, taking a long draw from his coffee. He glanced over at Chad, and Shaye could feel Chad grow tense. "And whose baby would this be?"

Zoey smiled and took out her phone. "Well, we are currently working on trying to find the identity of the woman who left him on our porch."

"Whoa, she *left him on your porch*?" Wyatt said, dropping the mug to the counter with a ping as it struck the glass. "What have you guys gotten yourselves into?"

"Nothing we can't get ourselves out of," Zoey said, her voice hard and unwavering and leaving no room for Wyatt to argue or question.

He shifted like he was trying to prepare himself for the weight of the situation that had been presented to him. "Do you know the baby's name? Birthdate?"

"As of right now," Zoey said, "all we know is that he's a little boy and we're guessing he's about two months old. I've been searching missing children's databases, and nothing has matched his description."

"Sounds like you've put in your paces," Wyatt said, inspecting her. "In fact, it sounds like you've done hours of research. So how long has this baby been in your care?"

Zoey's face twitched, as though she intended to say something, but checked herself. "Less than twenty-four hours."

Mindy walked out from the hallway carrying the baby and Jarrod followed after her with the baby's things. The sight made a deep, inexplicable pool of sadness within her. The feeling made her question herself. The baby wasn't theirs, so why did she feel as she did? From the very moment she had set eyes on the child, she had known that he was only going to be in their lives temporarily. And yet, watching this unfold, she couldn't help the feeling that he was being ripped out of her arms.

Glancing up, Mindy stopped as she stared at Wyatt, then back down at the baby. She looked like she was just a second away from making a run for it, baby in tow.

"Is this the dude?" Wyatt asked gently, as he walked over and pulled down the boy's blanket just enough to look on his face. As he moved the blanket, Peanut squirmed and let out a high-pitched wail, as if he was experiencing the same panic Shaye was. "Whoa, little guy, it's okay. Shh… Shh…" Wyatt said, trying to quiet the baby, but instead of quieting down, his cries became louder and more piercing.

"I think he needs a quick change and a bottle," Mindy said, her voice cracking as she headed out of the room. As she moved away, the sounds of her cooing to the baby echoed out toward them.

Jarrod stood there staring like he wasn't quite sure what he should do. He finally turned and followed his fiancée out of the room.

"I'm assuming that there's a hell of a good reason

you didn't tell me about this baby earlier," Wyatt said, glaring at all of them. "You do know, that if the baby's parents wanted, they could actually charge all of you with kidnapping if they played their cards right."

Shaye hadn't thought of that and a sickening sense of dread crept up within her. "But we didn't kidnap the baby—we have video of the mom dropping him off."

Zoey jerked and almost imperceptibly shook her head, reminding Shaye to be quiet.

"You have what?" Wyatt said, looking directly at Zoey. "I can't believe this family." He put his hands up in submission. "I'm sure you think you have your reasons for not getting me involved, but not telling me right away was stupid. It's almost like you guys are trying to get yourselves in trouble."

Once again, she couldn't disagree with the deputy. But she was right alongside the rest of the Martins, in this constant blurring between right and wrong.

"We called you now." Chad stepped between her and Wyatt, like he could somehow protect her from his cousin's fiery glare. "And we know that you're the best option that we have right now."

"What do you want me to do?" Wyatt asked, rubbing the back of his hand over his nose in a huff.

Chad stretched his neck like he had a nervous tic. "We want you to help us keep him safe."

"I notice that you didn't say you wanted me to help find his parents," Wyatt countered.

She wasn't sure why, but somehow this family fight—even in its explosive possibilities—made it clear what a real family would do for one another. Though Wyatt had been angry about the prospect of getting this baby, and hiding it, he hadn't overtly said no. Instead, he was just angered that they'd left him out.

This family, regardless of what they could lose, were bound together by something so much more than blood.

She envied that. Moreover, she wished she could be a part of this forever.

"Of course, we want you to try and find this little boy's family, but if you don't, I know that I would be more than happy to take him under my care." As the words came from Shaye's mouth, they surprised even her. "I have the means, and I'm happy to supply you with whatever else in the way of paperwork you should need to get the adoption started."

Chad turned on his heel, staring at her as she spoke. "Do you really mean that?" he whispered, so that only she could hear.

She nodded. For the first time since she'd gotten here, she was actually certain about something. Though she was scared witless, and though she was likely nearly the last person that anyone would entrust with the baby—given her current circumstances—she would do anything to make sure that he was protected and well-loved.

Wyatt rubbed his hands over his face, exasperated. "Whoa now. We're getting ahead of ourselves. A lot of things need to happen before we can even talk about long-term care options for this child. For now, we need to get him into the care of CPS."

"No, that's not an option." Zoey sounded angry at the proposition. "We're not putting this kid in some foster home while your department comes to the same dead ends I've been facing. While I know that there are some great foster-home options out there, there are also some that I wouldn't wish upon my worst enemies. If you're gonna stick him in some hellhole, I am not giving you this baby. It may be a little bit dangerous here, but it's better than whatever he might face out there."

Shaye walked over and stood at Zoey's side, making a show of a united front.

Wyatt sank down, resting on the sofa as he dropped his head into his hands.

"There has to be another option. If not, we can keep working to figure out who the baby's biological parents are, and maybe even get his name." Zoey crossed her arms over her chest. "If I find something I don't like or if I can't get the information I need, I'm more than capable of getting my hands on the appropriate paperwork to make it seem like he was born into this family."

Wyatt looked up at her. "If you're hell-bent on breaking the law, why did you call me here? Did you want some moral support, someone to tell you that it was okay to steal a baby just because someone left him on your porch? We don't understand or know the circumstances behind this baby's arrival at the ranch, but I'm more than certain that we need to follow the law with this one." Wyatt's hands flew around as he spoke. "It can't just be circumstantial that this baby randomly arrives on your doorstep the day a man turns up dead by some freak accident and I also get reports of a high-speed chase on the highway. You guys are up to something, and I know it. You're lucky you're family, or I would be dragging all of your butts to jail."

She had heard the expression "so angry a person could spit" but until now she hadn't experienced a moment that quite fit that idiom. Yet as she watched Wyatt's face redden with anger and little bits of spittle fly from his lips, she finally understood.

But she couldn't be upset with him for his reaction. He was a man with honor, a man bound by the oath of his office to do what was right...a man who cared about this nameless baby and his welfare just as much as they did, and he'd only met the child for a few seconds.

Shaye walked around Chad and sat down beside Wyatt on the sofa, hoping against all hope that she could do something to help instead of further strain the situation. "Wyatt, we all understand how you're feeling. And we are sorry for putting you in such a terrible position. If we didn't feel as though it was absolutely necessary, we wouldn't have called you here."

Zoey nodded, but she still appeared reticent at Shaye's intrusion into her plan. "And just so you know, Wyatt, while we aren't here to cause trouble, we are hoping to stay off the radar."

"Does that mean what I think it does?" Wyatt asked, giving Zoey a tired look.

"It means that if you don't want to put your career in jeopardy, it is best if you don't ask too many questions. And we will do our best to keep you out of our trouble," Zoey said.

Wyatt swore under his breath.

Shaye dropped her hands into a prayer position between her knees as she turned toward him, hoping that he would see that she was speaking to him in all earnestness. "For now, there has to be something you can do with this child. Something that will ensure his safety until the danger sweeping through this community is resolved."

A lump swelled in her throat as she thought about

the truth she had just danced around. The *community* wasn't the problem nearly as much as *she* was.

"There is another option," Wyatt said, but his face paled slightly as he spoke. "My mother, Eloise Fitzgerald, has always had a soft spot for taking in kids who are in need. She would box my ears if she heard I had gone against you guys and put this baby in foster care."

"Yes, and Anya will love having him over there. She loves babies," Zoey said, supporting her with a hand on her shoulder. "And if you need to write up a report or something, you can say we're working as consultants on the case, helping to find the child's parents. And maybe, when things cool down, we could come and see him. Help your mom out, or whatever you need."

"Whoa, I'm not putting any of this in writing," Wyatt said, shaking his head. "If I do, I'll be out on my ass. I've been walking a fine line at the department for the last year or two. If they find out I didn't follow the departmental policy on this one... Well, we're not going to talk about what would happen."

Chad sighed. "Wyatt, you can't put your job at risk for us. That's not right, either."

Zoey shot him a look, but Shaye couldn't disagree with him.

Wyatt stood up and looked down the hall in the direction Mindy and Jarrod had fled with the child, then turned back. "The way I see it, none of this discussion ever happened. For now, I'll take him over to my mom's place. He can stay there for a bit, but I want you to look into the whereabouts of this boy's family. When you find them, you tell me."

"And if we don't?" Shaye asked, a sliver of hope curling around her dreams of having a child.

Wyatt looked at her with a deadly seriousness. "I don't advocate breakin' any laws just so you all can play house. When it comes to this boy, we are going to do what's best."

As Wyatt disappeared down the hall, so did her hope and dreams of a future with this baby.

# *Chapter Fourteen*

Holy crap, Shaye had to have lost her mind. He couldn't believe that she'd actually offered to adopt the baby. With everything going on, he hadn't really considered the long-term prospects of the child. But she must've put all kinds of thought into it. And if she had, then why hadn't she talked to him about it? Which brought him back to the place where he questioned what exactly was going on between them.

There was no doubt in his mind that she had feelings for him and vice versa, but now he questioned her intentions. There was no way that he would have agreed to something so life-changing without consulting her.

Clearly, he must've been reading more into the situation and what was there.

They spent the rest of the day sifting through online records and photo banks and any lead that they thought could provide them with more information. Surprisingly, the car-rental website had proved more of a hassle than Zoey had anticipated, but she let out a loud whoop when she finally made it past their safeguards and opened up access to their servers.

"I'm in," Zoey said, showing them all her tablet's screen like it was a major award.

Shaye was sitting beside him on the sofa, but since Wyatt had left with Peanut, they had barely said a word to one another. He glanced over at her, hoping that this little bit of good news would help raise her spirits, but she seemed unchanged.

He stuffed his phone in his pocket, frustrated both with his lack of headway and his inability to say the words that needed to be said to Shaye. Part of him wished he could go back in time and tell Zoey that they would keep the baby and that Wyatt needed to stay away, but it was too late now.

They sat in silence, nervously watching as Zoey worked to nail down the identity of the boy's guardian, until he couldn't take the silence another moment. He couldn't sit here idly and watch—he had to move.

He got up off the couch, went to the kitchen and decided to make himself and the rest of the family tuna salad for lunch. As he stumbled around the kitchen, looking through the drawers for spoons and knives, the door opened and Shaye came inside.

He stopped as the door closed behind her, and they stood staring at one another. It was as if neither of them knew exactly what to say, or how to proceed.

"Hungry?" he asked, finally breaking the tense silence between them.

She nodded, walked to the fridge and pulled out a bottle of sparkling water. "Can I help you do something?"

So this was how it was going to be—they were both going to delicately dance around all the things they were thinking and feeling instead of actually heading them off. He didn't mind the footwork involved in this dance. He was nearly an expert in avoiding everything that involved actual emotions. He'd been practicing this his whole life, and until recently, doing a damn good job of it... That was, until she had reappeared in his life.

Or maybe now things could go back to the way they had been—comfortable and completely repressed.

He handed her a sharp knife and a jar of pickles. Without a word, she pulled out a pickle and started slicing away.

As they worked in silence, their bodies seem to take on each other's rhythm, as if they were also weaving around the invisible bombs of stress and trauma that littered the space between them. As they moved, he couldn't deny that there was something beautiful about it—the way they could eloquently avoid the other's emotional triggers, yet still want to be so physically close. It was as if their hearts yearned to speak the words that their mouths refused.

He wished that being with her was easy and carefree—if it had been, perhaps they would be chatting away, dreaming of their futures together. He could almost envision what it would be like had everything been less stressful. By now perhaps they would've been sharing a bed and whispering their secrets. She could have been ready to move forward, and he the same.

At least they were stuck in this weird emotional place, and a life full of drama, together. He could think of no one he would rather be with.

He shook the thoughts from his head as he pulled out two slices of bread from the bag and rested them on the cutting board near Shaye.

Yes, repression was far easier than having to feel the

sparks in his fingertips when he gently brushed against Shaye's arm, or the way he felt when he leaned in so close to her that he could smell the sweet scent of lavender on her hair. Everything about her drew him in. It was like she was his own personal drug—and being with her, or contemplating being with her, was nearly as dangerous.

"What's that for?" she asked, pointing her knife toward the bread.

"Gonna make tuna sandwiches for the crew," he said, like the answer was obvious.

"Okay…" She sounded a tad confused by the meal, but continued chopping until she had a nice little stack of pickles.

"Haven't you had a tuna-salad sandwich before?" He gave her a disapproving look.

"I've had tuna, and sandwiches, but not a tuna sandwich." She gave him a little grin, and some of the tension he was feeling lifted. He was sure she hadn't meant to smile, but it made him feel better nonetheless. More than anything, it gave him hope that with enough time they could get past the initial shock of handing over the baby.

She had to have known it was the right thing to do. Maybe that was why she was finally coming around.

She walked over to the fridge and opened the door, peering inside. "Where's the tuna?"

"Here, we only have the best—the kind in a can. I know, so much swankier than what you are used to," he said, walking over to the pantry and pulling out a can of Chicken of the Sea.

She covered her mouth as she gave a little squeak of a laugh. "Oh, yeah… I…"

"Have you seen tuna in a can before?"

"Only at the store," she admitted, looking even more chagrined.

"Dang, lady, you are in for a real treat. There's *tuna* and then there is *tuna*," he said, slapping down a couple of cans on the counter like they were the gold standard for lunch boxes everywhere.

"Has anyone ever told you that there is likely something really wrong with you?"

He winked at her in a sexy, sideways glance. "Just because I love a good sandwich."

"That among many other things. Namely, that you can't take anything too seriously."

That wasn't entirely true, but he was relieved to have her think such a thing of him. Taking anything too seriously was just a quicker way to age oneself.

As he set about putting together the ingredients, it felt good to be setting around the kitchen, puttering away and getting the opportunity to do something that was just *normal*.

He was really going to have to focus on enjoying the small things in life. If they kept coming under attack it was hard to say how many more of these tiny diamonds of time would come his way.

He handed Shaye a sandwich and she daintily picked at the crust, pulling it off and setting it on a napkin before taking on the food.

In truth, tuna salad was far from his favorite lunch, but it was the only thing that had come to mind when he had set foot in the kitchen, but now it was too late to tell her that it wasn't the best American food out there. Now, hot dogs…that was another story entirely.

She took a tentative bite, and she nodded as she took

another bite. As she looked up from her sandwich, she gave him a thumbs-up. "This is good," she said, her words muffled as she spoke with her mouth full.

It was good to see her being less than perfect. And as silly as it was, it made him like her more...and the thought made him realize that every second he spent with her, he liked her more. Given time, he could only imagine what he would feel for her in five, ten or even twenty years.

From a single second to twenty years, being with her was one journey that he wanted to take.

He ate a sandwich, downing it with a glass of milk, and then made a few more. After putting some veggies beside the sandwiches on the platter, they carried it out to the living room. Jarrod was sitting with Mindy and whispering. They both looked up and stopped talking as he walked into the room, making Chad wonder what they had been talking about.

He set the plate on the table in front of the couch. "We thought you guys might be needing a little bite."

Jarrod reached over, grabbed a sandwich and started stuffing it in his mouth as he looked over at Zoey, like she was the only one who could answer any questions.

Zoey didn't even look up, and seemed completely unaware that anyone else was even in the room.

"So she hasn't found anything yet?" Shaye asked Jarrod, motioning in Zoey's direction.

Jarrod shook his head, bread crumbs tumbling from his mouth.

Mindy opened a box. Inside was a stack of black T-shirts. She threw each one of them a shirt, and as Chad caught his, he felt its heaviness. He twisted the fabric in his fingers. "Is this one of your—"

"Yep, it's from our new line of bulletproof clothing for Monster Wear." Mindy nodded and set a shirt beside Zoey, who was so focused she didn't even budge. "We are working on creating an even lighter, more breathable fabric at our manufacturing plant in Sweden. This is one of our new prototypes. It's been field-tested and I recommend we all start wearing them."

Though he completely understood Mindy's reason for giving them new gear, it made their position seem even more vulnerable. He gave her a nod of thanks and threw the shirt over his arm.

Mindy frowned. "It's important that we all remain as protected as we can. It would look ridiculous if one of us got shot when our family specializes in tactical gear and security and we can't even keep ourselves safe."

He knew she wasn't just concerned about business. Mindy was scared.

Jarrod patted her leg, but Mindy straightened her back, putting on a show of resolve—something Chad knew all too much about.

Poorly masked fear slithered around the room. There was no way Chad could sit there, waiting and watching, biding time until they found the answers they were looking for.

"Is there a gym in this house anywhere?" he asked, thinking about taking a run in order to work off some of his excess nervous energy.

Mindy pointed toward the stairs. "Downstairs. It's on the west end of the hall. I took a peek in there, looks nice."

"Cool," he said. He took Shaye's hand and led her

toward the stairs. Shaye didn't protest and instead seemed relieved that he was helping her to escape.

At the bottom of the stairs, to their right, was the hallway that led to the panic room where they were keeping the hostages. From where they stood, he could make out the sounds of Trevor's voice coming out from behind the room's open door. He was saying something about having plenty of time on his hands.

Trevor's words were false. The one thing they didn't seem to have much of was time. With each passing second, they were moving closer and closer to being found, attacked and perhaps even killed.

Yes, he definitely needed to get in a run. Maybe it would help him get his head right. Being pessimistic at a time like this was the last thing that anyone needed. Over the years he'd had it drilled into him that one thing was true above all others—what he thought, and therefore believed, always became reality.

*They would come through this fine. Everything would be fine,* he tried to tell himself, but the sounds of his inner voice sounded just as false as Trevor's words.

The gym was bigger than he had anticipated, and it appeared as though the owners had every piece of equipment he could imagine. As nice and as fancy as this place looked, in reality he probably only knew how to use about five of the pieces. He'd grown accustomed to makeshift gyms, products of war zones. More than once he had resorted to lifting jugs filled with sand and running on cart paths in order to get in a workout. In fact, he probably spent more time working out in those kinds of conditions than he had in a place like this.

As he flipped on the lights, the place was filled with

brightness, thanks to the mirrors that lined the walls. It was purely a gym-rat thing to want to stand there and watch yourself get all sweaty. Or maybe it wasn't gym-rat, but rather a narcissistic thing. He understood the need to know whether or not a person was using the proper techniques, but really…it was too much. He preferred sand and grit any day.

Shaye walked by him and he could hear her suck in a long breath. "Wow, I thought the gym at the palace was nice, but this is a whole different level."

"So you work out a lot?" If he didn't have to work out for his job, he wasn't sure that he would work out as much as he did. It was so much easier to eat Cheetos and watch HGTV

He closed the door behind them, locking it so he didn't have to worry about any unwanted guests.

She looked at him with the raise of an eyebrow. "What do you think?"

No, he had totally just walked into that one. That was stupid. He made a show of looking her up and down, assessing her, even though he knew that she was perfect. He had spent more than his fair share of time watching her curves as she walked, and the graceful way her body moved. By most standards, she might have been a little bit on the heavy side, but a person's weight was ever-changing, so to base attraction on such a fickle thing was tasteless and shallow. All that really mattered was that she felt happy with the woman she was—there was nothing more attractive than confidence.

He put down the shirt Mindy had given him and walked over to Shaye. They were safe here. At least, one of them was.

A fire rippled up from deep in his belly as Shaye gave him a playful smile.

"You know, in order for me to get a really good idea of what I think, I'm going to need to give you a closer inspection," he said, putting his hands on her waist.

She gave him a look of surprise, like she hadn't been expecting him to play along. "The last time I checked, looking was done with your eyes not with your hands." She stepped back, giving him a cheeky grin.

"Then let's pretend I'm blind," he teased, reaching out for her again.

She gave a belly laugh, and looked down at his extended hands before stepping into his grasp. "I think it's only fair if I get to give you a good once-over, as well," she said in a soft voice, as she ran her hands down the muscles of his chest.

He had wanted to get in a good and sweaty workout, but he hadn't been expecting anything like this—not even in his wildest dreams.

She traced her finger down the line of his shirt. "I hear the best kind of workouts are the ones that you do without a shirt," she said in a serious-sounding voice.

"Is that right?" he asked, but the last thing he wanted to do was argue.

His breath caught in his throat as her fingers drifted over his naked skin, tracing the fine hairs on his chest and his nipples. He had wanted her to touch him like this since...well, forever.

She leaned into him and ran her lips over the places her fingers had caressed. Her hot breath made goose bumps rise on his skin. Yes. He wanted this. He wanted her. He wanted it all.

He reached up and pushed her hair back from her

face so he could watch her as she kissed him. She glanced up at him as she pulled his nipple into her mouth and traced her teeth against it, making it spark to life with this little taste of agony.

As she kissed him, his body responded, pressing almost painfully against the harsh fabric of his tac pants. He throbbed as she moved to his other nipple and pushed his shirt from his shoulders.

Her fingers trailed downward, finding the waist of his pants, but she stopped there and let her fingers linger.

It had been so long since he had been touched the way that she was touching him that he was forced to look away, at the awful mirrors. But they were no help. Instead, surrounding him was her—everywhere and from every angle. He was forced to shut his eyes, but that too only intensified the sensations of her lips on his skin.

SHAYE LOOKED UP at him as he gently stepped back from her grasp. What was happening? Didn't he like what she was doing to him?

Licking the flavor of his sweat from her lips, she smiled. Though she wasn't sure she wanted to know the answer—out of fear that he was overthinking everything that was happening between them—she asked, "What's wrong?" She paused for a moment. "Is it okay that I'm kissing you?"

He took her hands in his. As she stood upright, he used their entwined hands to move a piece of hair from her face—it was almost as though he feared letting her go even for a second, and that little gesture softened the blow of his retreat.

"It's more than okay," he said, sounding breathless. "I love that you are kissing me."

"Then why do you want me to stop?" she asked, the hurt flecking her voice.

"Oh, I don't. I just..." He glanced down and then his cheeks reddened.

"Oh," she said, checking her giggle before it could escape her. She didn't want him to think she was laughing at him, not at all... If anything, she was thrilled that she could elicit such a strong response. "We can take things a bit slower."

He ran his hand over the back of his neck. "Yeah, I'm sorry... You just caught me a bit off-guard. I was expecting a run," he said, motioning in the direction of the treadmills.

"We can still use the treadmill if you want." She gave him a toying glance.

Had he really brought her down here just to work out? The way he had sounded in the kitchen with her, he'd been so playful and charming, it hadn't occurred to her that it had been anything other than a ploy for them to be alone. Had it just been wishful thinking on her part?

Ever since they had shared the kiss, she had been envisioning something more with him, and then chastising herself. But standing here, now, her body aching for him to draw nearer to her again, she didn't want to overthink it. She just wanted him to kiss her as she had kissed him, to make him beg her for release...and sate her every desire.

If hellfire was going to rain down on them, the least she could do was take each day as it came—and that meant finally listening to the desire that careened through her, awakening every part of her body. This was their moment. Alone. Together. And it was their time to give in to their needs.

There was no going back. Body and soul, she was ready to give herself to him.

She moved closer to him, wrapping her arms around his neck as he pulled her against his awakened body.

"I want you, Shaye. I've wanted you for so long," he whispered, closing his eyes and dropping his head to hers so their foreheads touched. "You are the reason I look forward to waking up each morning. And when you came here, to me... I've never been happier."

She was shocked to hear him speak so candidly. Chad had never opened up like this to her before. Her already softened heart melted completely.

*Yes. This.*

She leaned up and kissed him, taking in the dill flavor of his lips.

"Mmm, pickles," she said, without taking her lips from his.

"I was thinking the same thing," he said with a laugh. "I could eat you up."

"Here's hoping," she said, pulling out of his arms and moving coyly away from him. She started to jog, beckoning him to the chase. "But I'm not an easy girl to have. If you want me, you have to catch me first."

He threw his head back in a laugh, giving her a moment to put distance between them before he gave chase.

He looked at her with hunger in his eyes, and she was certain that the moment he caught her, there would be no time for second thoughts or removal of nonvital clothes. She loved that primal yearning.

For a moment, she was the master and he was her plaything...but that control wouldn't last for long.

She stepped behind a big black machine with long armlike attachments. Moving fast, she stripped off her pants, exposing her lacy purple-and-black panties, and she threw them into the middle of the room. "How badly do you want me?"

He grumbled, the sound nearly a growl as he stepped toward her. As he reached her pants, he stopped and removed his shirt and dropped it on top.

His muscles...oh, his muscles. He had a faint line of blond hair that ran over his pecks and down past his navel, then disappeared beneath the waistband of his pants. His skin was tan, but markedly lighter than hers—his was closer to the color of honey. She licked her lips at the thought of his salty kiss and the sweet flavor of his nipples as she had sucked them into her mouth.

She darted down the aisle, moving three rows back. He grumbled again, the sound more fervent with desire. Pulling off her plum-colored top, she threw it away from the machine, and as she moved her warm skin brushed against the cold black metal, making her gasp.

Until now, she hadn't realized how electrified her senses had become after being charged by his touch... and his kiss.

He stopped moving as she stepped out from behind the machine in only her bra and panties. She covered her body with one arm and raised her other hand to her lips, making a sexy pose.

Even from a few feet away, she could hear him suck in his breath.

*Good. Exactly the reaction I wanted.*

"Shaye... My... You..." he said, stumbling over his words. "You are so freaking beautiful."

She smiled over at him, sliding behind the last machine—the treadmill—that sat nearest the wall. He moved slowly toward her, like she was a spooked filly and any moment she could bolt. But as he neared, she only stepped back until she was nearly touching the mirrored wall behind her.

He reached up, tracing the edge of her bra with the littlest bit of his fingertip. Her skin flamed as he barely grazed her skin. Her body quaked as he took her fullness into the cup of his hand and he kissed her. He pressed against her, bumping her warm, nearly naked body up against the cold mirror. She gasped at the chill and the fire of his touch and the power of his kiss.

He reached down and touched her over the thin fabric of her panties, running circles over the fabric with his fingers until she nearly couldn't stand.

"Please..." It was all she could think...or say.

He scooped her up and she wrapped her legs around him. Opening up only his zipper, he pushed aside her panties and teased himself into her, slowly at first. As she opened to him, he drove deeper and deeper inside her.

They moved together, finding a natural rhythm. The mirror on the wall behind her bumped as they made love and the sound only made her more turned-on. This was their symphony, the cadence of their union.

Though she wasn't ready, her body betrayed her with a quiver. She exploded around him, collapsing against his body as she gave into the all-powerful ecstasy of their love.

# Chapter Fifteen

She lay on the treadmill, looking up at him. Her face was covered in a thin sheen of sweat and she was breathing hard.

"I didn't know my body could do that," she said, tracing her fingers over the dark hair a few inches below her belly button.

He sat up on his elbow beside her. "I'm glad we can explore new worlds together," he said, leaning down and kissing the skin of her breast.

Three times. It was a new record for him pleasing a woman, but he wasn't about to admit that to her. As he looked down on her beautiful, naked body, he considered going for number four, but his body ached in all the wrong ways.

If he was going to have her again, he would need time to recover and likely so would she. Besides, some things were even better the second time—or the fourth.

He stood up, his knees and hips spent from their adventure. Holding out his hand, he helped her to standing and she staggered a bit.

"I'm not going to lie," she said "I'm glad to get off the belt." She turned to look at herself in the mirror.

Her back and down her round butt was speckled with the waffle pattern of the treadmill's belt.

"Oh, babe, I'm sorry." He ran his hand down the texture of her back.

She gave him a wide smile. "Don't worry, I'm not. Besides, that was exactly the workout that I needed."

He laughed, the sound reverberating throughout the mirrored room.

"And," she said, pointing at the mirror behind him, "I had one heck of a view. When I get my own house, I'm going to have to look in to a room just like this."

"But at least with a couch," he said, pointing down at his knees. They were angry and raw thanks to the nonstick floor that ran throughout the room.

"Oh, you think you would be invited to my house?" she teased.

"Well, I doubt that anyone can please you like I do," he said, more than aware that what they had just done was the best sexual experience in his entire life. He could happily live and die between her thighs.

She gave him a satisfied smile. "You know, if we had a bit more time I would kiss those knees for you, but I think it may lead to number four. I'm not sure my body could take any more. I fear that I would never be able to walk again."

"I would be more than happy to carry you around like the princess you are," he said, giving her buns a little squeeze that made her squeal.

She turned away from him and grabbed her panties and bra, then started to get dressed. "As tempting as that is, I think we probably need to check in with your family and see if anyone has found out anything about the baby yet. I'm worried about him."

And just like that, the lust-filled spell that had come over him disappeared and he was swept back into the gaping maw of reality.

As she slipped on the shirt that Mindy had given her, she looked over at him. "It's going to be okay, Chad. I know you're worried, too."

She must have seen the concern wash over him. "I just want to go back to a normal *life*—stop hiding out. You know what I mean?"

Though they had just spent the last hours making love in several positions, his words seemed to feel almost as intimate. He hadn't really *talked* in a long time.

She picked up his clothes and walked over to him. "Lift up your arms," she said, slipping on the tac T-shirt as she spoke. "I know this may sound cynical, but this—all *this* upheaval is life. It may not be for everyone, but it's ours. And as crazy and manic as it is, for me it's easy to lose sight of what is important and the things that really matter. But one thing I've come to love about you is that you always put the focus on your family and your group."

She must have meant *love* in the platonic sense, but as she spoke, he tried to not overanalyze.

"We try, but we have our issues."

"What family doesn't?" She gave him a look that made it clear she was talking about her own.

She picked up his pants and helped him to step into them. It felt strange, her helping him dress, but at the same time, he loved it—the closeness. There was a sense of intimacy in her actions that made his heart burn in his chest. Whether she meant platonic or not, he loved her with a ferocity he had never known before.

He reached down and zipped his pants, but as he did

his hand brushed against hers. He entwined his fingers with hers and pulled her hands behind his back, and then he took her in his arms. "Shaye," he said, taking in the soft sweet scent of sweat wafting up from her hair. "I want you to know... I care for my family, and I always will be there for them. But you are even more important to me."

She pulled him tighter and buried her face in his chest, and though she said nothing he could feel that she felt the same.

"Shaye, I—"

There was a knock on the door. Stopping him just as he was about to say the one word he feared above all others—love.

*Son of a...*

She pulled herself from his arms, almost as if she feared that someone would see them. His arms had never been emptier.

"What's up?" he asked, sounding annoyed even to his own ears. He grabbed his flannel and slipped it on over his T-shirt as he walked toward the door.

The place where Shaye had buried her face was still warm.

"I need a break," Trevor said, his voice sounding worn and ragged as he spoke.

Chad rushed to the door and flung it open. Trevor's eyes were dark, and as tired as he had sounded, he looked a thousand times worse. His hair was disheveled and there was a line of white, dried sweat around the neck of his dark shirt.

"What's up?" he asked.

Trevor motioned for them to follow him. They rushed down the hall toward the panic room. The door stood open, and as they approached, he recognized the two men who had followed them in the Suburban. The man nearest to him, the one with red hair, looked to be asleep with his chin pressed down against his chest while the other man, who had a wide nose and prognathic mouth, sneered at them as they walked in. He was missing his two front teeth, and the gums that had once held them were swollen and bruised. The room stank of dirty bodies and bile, and the stench assaulted his senses.

"Not surprised you can't handle us," the man slurred at Trevor. "They told me that your clan was nothing but a bunch of pansies." He spat a mouthful of blood on the floor.

Shaye sucked in a breath behind Chad, drawing his attention. Taking her gently by the arm, he walked out of the room as he gave Trevor a look of warning.

She was tough and had seen worse, but she didn't need to get wrapped up in what could be a bloody interrogation. He glanced back at the redheaded man. He couldn't tell whether he was dead or alive.

His thoughts moved to Trish. Seeing pictures of her lying dead on the warehouse floor. She looked at peace as the life had leaked out of her body and poured on the concrete. A lump formed in his throat.

There was so much death in his life. Around every turn, someone died. And it wasn't just him, but everyone in his family. It was like anyone who came into their lives was doomed to a rapid and violent death.

Shaye was watching him, and as she blinked, his thoughts flashed to her lying on the floor instead of Trish.

He wasn't sure if it was some kind of premonition

or just his own fears that put the image in his mind, but he couldn't risk it. He wouldn't be able to live with himself if he lost the woman he loved.

It was better if she got the hell out of this wretched place. It would break him to be apart from her, but for her own well-being he had to do what was right. He loved her. And loving someone meant putting their needs before his own.

Trevor gently closed the door behind them as Chad took Shaye into the hall and out of the room.

As much as he loved her, and because he loved her, this had to be done.

"Shaye—" he began.

"Don't worry about that," she said, interrupting him. "I have seen worse."

This wasn't about what she had and hadn't experienced in her life. This was about what he didn't want her to ever experience again.

"Shaye," he said, looking down at the place on her arm where he was touching her. He stared at the dark hair on her arms. It was the same shade as that on her head but a touch lighter than what he had just seen in the gym—hair he would probably never see again. "I think you should go back to your father."

"What?" she sounded flabbergasted, and she pulled her arm from his grasp and took two large steps away from him. "After what we just did, I..." She threw her hands up in the air. "You are being ridiculous."

Though he was sure that he appeared that way, he knew he wasn't. It was ripping out his heart to say the words he had to say to her. Undoubtedly, when she left, his entire being would shrivel away to nothing, but he had to protect her in the only way he knew how—by pushing her away.

If she stayed here, it was really only a matter of time until she got hurt...or killed.

He could feel time and their enemies pressing down on him, and loving her meant putting her before anything and everyone else, even himself.

"Your father sent a man to get you because he knows how close you are to getting hurt because of me."

"And you think this, what you are saying to me right now, doesn't hurt?"

"I'm trying to do what's best." He jabbed his finger toward the closed door behind him. "These men are just two of hundreds who want to kill me...my family. No doubt, there are teams of people looking for these guys or working for the same people. You and I both know that no matter where I go, or what I do, my shelf life is going to be limited."

"That's a lie and you know it. We are safe here." But as she spoke there was a certain amount of acknowledgment in her tone that told him that she knew he was right.

"Go home, Shaye. Your father and his army are far more capable of keeping you safe right now."

"My father... I would rather die here then spend another second with that man. I wrote him off. He's dead to me." She pressed her back against the wall and he could see tears in her eyes. "He wants to kill..." She paused, unable to continue.

It pained him to make her feel like this, but he loved her. He loved her with his entire being. He had to do what needed to be done.

At least that is what he had to tell himself to get through this.

Once she was gone, he could break down, but for now he had to be tough. He had to get her to go—even if that meant lying to her. This was for her own good.

"Shaye, you know I think you are amazing. And I had one hell of a good time in the gym. But while we were together...well, I realized that I don't think we're relationship material." The lie burned like acid on his tongue.

Her hand came out of nowhere as she slapped him. As badly as his face stung, the burn wasn't nearly as bad as the scorch in his soul. No matter how much she hated him, he hated himself more.

Anger flashed in her eyes. "I can't believe that you are doing this to me. Kash told me you just keep women around for a booty call. I didn't believe him, but now I know, you really are that kind of man."

# Chapter Sixteen

That was it, she didn't understand men. At all. Ever.

He had used her and then thrown her out of his house. What kind of man did such a thing?

*Easy. Chad Martin.*

If STEALTH had a cruelty division, he would be their captain. And she would be his jester.

She had been so stupid for coming here.

As she raced away from him, Shaye tried to control her tears. She was so mad. Mad at him for what he had said and done, and mad at herself for her tears. She bit her lip, drawing blood, as she tried to keep her emotions in check.

He couldn't see her cry.

He couldn't see how much he had hurt her.

If he did, he would know that she loved him. And she absolutely could not, under any circumstances, love that man.

Hate, loathe and despise, yes...but love...

And yet, as she rounded the corner to ascend the stairs, she wanted to look back at him. To look at his face one more time to see if he had really meant what he had said to her.

As he had spoken, he had looked like a broken man,

his head down low and his back hunched. His eyes had been dark and his face haggard, a stark contrast to just moments before when he had been looking down on her face, their eyes connecting as their bodies explored the edges of overwhelming ecstasy.

He had shifted so suddenly, so unexpectedly.

She had to have missed something, something that triggered his words.

But even if she understood why, it wouldn't make the blow any easier to take.

*Screw him.*

She took the stairs two at a time. As she turned the corner toward the great room, her foot struck the baby's diaper bag that was sitting on the floor. Jarrod must have forgotten to give it to Wyatt.

The baby. The hostages. The attacks.

*Ugh.*

She picked up the bag and took a long series of breaths, part of her hoping to hear Chad's footsteps on the stairs as he chased after her, but there was nothing.

She didn't need him in her life, anyway.

But even as the thought floated through her mind, she knew it was a lie. She loved Chad. She was furious with him, but damn it, she loved him.

*No. No. You don't,* she reminded herself.

Running the back of her hand over her cheeks, checking to make sure that nothing would give her away, she entered the room where Zoey was still puttering away. Jarrod and Mindy were sitting on the couch with each other, holding hands as they looked at something on their phones.

They didn't even look up as she came into the room

and made her way toward the front door. But as she pulled the door open, Zoey finally seemed to notice her.

"What are you doing?" Zoey asked, her voice raspy from not being used.

"We forgot to give Wyatt the diaper bag. I think they're going to need it for Peanut," she said, lifting the bag like it was evidence.

Zoey sighed. "Just leave it by the couch. I'll just text him to stop by when he can and pick it up. We're on lockdown. And I'm starting to get reports of possible members of Gray Wolves arriving at the airport."

She didn't care what happened to her if she left this ranch. Staying here was out of the question. "The baby's formula, diapers, everything—they're going to need them," she said, some of her strength leeching from her as she repeated the feeble excuse to leave. Instead of continuing to argue, she dropped the bag onto the floor.

Zoey looked up at her and when their eyes met, Shaye looked away, fearing that Zoey would be able to see all the hurt she was feeling.

"What happened?" Zoey asked, putting down her tablet and getting up off the couch. "Where's Chad?" She sounded concerned.

"He's fine, just downstairs with Trevor. They're working on getting answers." As she spoke, the image of the man with no teeth popped into her mind. Even with teeth the man would have been terrifying, but without them he looked like something out of a horror movie…like the man standing in the shadows holding the butcher knife.

A chill ran down her spine.

In her world, every shadow held danger—even the shadows in which she was standing.

"I'll just run this over. No one knows my rental car," Shaye continued, pulling open the door and stepping out onto the porch.

The cold made her nostrils burn as she took in a deep breath. The subtle pain was refreshing—physical pain was always easier to handle than the emotional kind.

"Shaye, stop. If you go, I can't let you come back." Zoey gave her a pained expression, like she really didn't want her to leave. "You could lead our enemies straight to us. We can't risk it."

The change in Zoey's attitude toward her didn't fail to register. How could things with Zoey have shifted so dramatically?

What was up with this family? Why did everything with them have to be so complicated?

But then, who was she to complain about complicated?

"I know." As she spoke, Shaye closed the door behind her, blocking out all that was the Martins.

Digging her keys out of her pocket, she let the tears finally fall. They blurred her vision as she walked down the steps and out to the driveway, where her rental car waited.

She had no idea where she would go—all she knew was that she had to get out of here.

She couldn't stand spending one more second this close to Chad. Even from here, she could feel the pull, the inexplicable magnetism that made her want to go running to him—they could yell and scream, curse and flail, but maybe if she went back, they could make this right. He could explain to her why he had attacked her with the one weapon he knew would hurt her the most.

Yes, Chad was the worst kind of man.

Angrily, she wiped away the tears. She hit Unlock on her car fob and opened the door.

As she moved to step into the car, a hand grabbed her from behind. A scream rippled through the air, but it was cut short by a hand over her mouth. "Shut up," a man growled in her ear. "If you want to live, you need to shut the hell up."

She tried to pull at the man's hands, to uncover her mouth and catch a glimpse of whoever was holding her, but as she scratched at his skin his grip on her only tightened. She dug her fingernails into his flesh until she could feel the skin give way and a wet, sticky blood ooze over her fingers.

"You little bitch," he said, his voice flecked with what sounded like a Turkish accent. "You're lucky your father wants you alive, or you would already be dead." He leaned in and took a long sniff of her hair, making her squirm with disgust.

She struggled harder, her body flailing in the man's grip, and as she moved to kick, another set of hands grabbed her ankles. The men held her so tightly that even though she tried to struggle, she could barely move.

They lifted her into the back of her car, and as they moved, she silently prayed that someone in the house had heard her scream. A dark-haired man climbed into the back of her car. He had a long goatee, and his face was the color of someone who spent hours in the sun. He pulled out some rope and tied her ankles, then, with a tight yank, he wrenched her arms behind her back and hog-tied her. They slapped a piece of black tape over her mouth. She tried to bite at it and push at it with her tongue, but it was stuck firmly to her skin.

Her heart raced in her chest. They weren't sent her to kill her...but that didn't mean they couldn't beat her. And what about her friends? They were inside, seemingly totally unaware of what was happening out here.

There had been men posted around the house, keeping guard for the family, but where were they now?

And how had these men found her? No one knew where she and the Martins were hiding except Wyatt. Had he told someone where they could be found?

If she saw her father again, she was going to kill him herself for getting her into this situation.

Her hatred for the man who had fathered her roiled in her, threatening to make her explode. Until now, she hadn't thought it possible to hate someone as much as she hated him.

If Chad got hurt because of her father...

A sob rattled through her, escaping through her nose.

*This couldn't be happening again. He had already killed Raj. He and his men couldn't take Chad, too.*

She rubbed her face on the seat of the car, hoping to peel back a corner of the tape. If she could yell, maybe the Martins would stand a chance. They had done so much for her, taking her in and helping her escape her father...and yet she had repaid their kindnesses by bringing their enemies straight to their doorstep.

She rubbed harder until her skin burned and she was sure that she had rubbed her face raw.

She had been so foolish to walk out, to think that

she could just leave and nothing would happen. Everything she did, every choice she made, everything she was—it was all a curse.

## Chapter Seventeen

He felt like a complete jerk, but he had done the right thing by telling Shaye to leave. He picked up his phone and sent her another text message, hoping she would at least tell him that she had made it to the airport okay.

He had handled the whole thing terribly. But she wouldn't have left him unless she believed that he really didn't care. It was a lie he had to sell. And he had sold it well.

His message failed. Had she blocked him?

She was pissed. Actually, probably more than pissed. If he had been on the receiving end, he would have hated her.

That was it—she hated him.

And she had every right.

But he had to know she was at least safe.

He turned to Trevor. "I'm going to check on her."

Trevor nodded, then crossed his arms over his chest as he leaned against the wall outside the panic room. "Yeah, you probably should. You really hurt her, man."

He was more than aware. Not for the first time, he wished Trish was here. She would have told him what he should do.

And as he thought of Trish, he realized he was almost completely alone. Everyone he was capable of opening up to, everyone he could talk about his darkest secrets with, was gone.

"I screwed up." He had meant it with the best of intentions, but it was hard to live with the results.

"Nah," Trevor said, "you were right in wanting to get her out of here. The Gray Wolves are coming—maybe not right now, but they are coming…and they want us dead. You had to say what you had to say." He gave him a tired, drawn nod.

He was glad he had Trevor to talk to, and that his brother understood where he was coming from without a long, drawn-out conversation, but his approval did little to assuage the guilt he was feeling.

He hated lying.

He hated acting like the man Kash had made him out to be.

And, more than anything, he hated that he had to watch her be hurt and then walk away—and he was the cause of her pain.

Even if he couldn't be the man in her life, or show her how much he loved her, he still needed to make sure she was okay. Though it seemed like the only way to get her to leave, he shouldn't have pushed her away like he had.

*Damn it.*

"I know you said you needed a break, but—"

"Go get her, make it right." Trevor waved him off. "Since she and the baby showed up you've started to get back to being yourself… And seriously, I love you, bro, but I don't think I can stand you sitting on the couch and eating Cheetos anymore."

"I do love Cheetos," he said with a laugh.

"And yet, even if I was blind, I could see that you love her more. Now, go get her." Trevor threw him his car keys and he stuffed them in his pocket.

Chad's heart lightened incrementally as he bounded up the stairs and, not bothering to even acknowledge his working family, ran out the door.

Shaye's rental car was still in the driveway, but Shaye was nowhere to be seen. Where had she gone? Had she gotten someone to pick her up?

Knowing her, she was probably hoofing it out of this place and just about ready to hitchhike to anywhere but here.

*No. She wasn't that careless.*

But she had been in a hurry to get out of there.

He took out his phone and tried to call her, but the call didn't go through. *Stupid goddamn thing.*

He looked out on the porch, hoping to spot one of the guards that his sister had posted there, but they were gone. If he remembered correctly, Zoey had assigned men to the perimeter of their new enclosure and yet, he couldn't see a single guard. Lesson number one was always have a visible presence in scenarios like this one. He walked to the far side of the deck, where he would have stood if he had been tasked with acting as the family's sentinel.

There was a set of footprints in the snow from a man's boots.

On the railing, near the footprints, was a tiny speck of blood.

"Zoey!" he yelled, charging back toward the door in a mad dash to raise the alarm. "Zoey!" He pulled open the front door, making sure to close and lock it behind himself. "Did Shaye tell you where she was going?"

Zoey looked up from her tablet, looking somewhat annoyed that he had dared to pull her away from her work.

"You need to shut that stupid thing. I think we've got company," he said, pointing toward the front window, where someone had pulled the drapes closed.

"Huh? What?" Jarrod asked, getting to his feet. "What are you talking about?"

"How many men did you post outside?" Chad asked.

"Twenty-two. But there should be more on the way. If there was anything going on outside, I'm sure one of them would have reported something by now." Zoey set her tablet on the coffee table in front of her, but she kept looking back at the screen. "It's not like anyone could get the drop on us with that many feet on the ground."

"Not just anyone could, but a well-orchestrated group might be able to—a group like the Gray Wolves," Chad countered. "We know they've started to arrive, you've said as much. There's blood on our front porch and I don't see guards anywhere. And now Shaye…" His voice cracked, betraying his terror and panic. "Shaye is missing. I have to find her."

If something had happened to her because of what he had said, and if the Gray Wolves were behind it, he was going to personally kill every single man in their organization with his bare hands. And when he found Bayural, he would rip off his head and feed it to the crows.

He seethed with rage at the mere thought of Shaye being in harm's way.

She had to be okay. Maybe she had caught an Uber… Maybe the guard who was supposed to be on the porch had gotten a bloody nose or was taking a pee or something. Maybe he was just jumping to the worst-case scenario without cause.

And yet, he couldn't help the panic that rattled through him like he was an empty can without Shaye here.

He had to get her back.

But first he had to keep his wits about him. Shaye was fine. She was probably taking a walk. Maybe she was even thinking about how she was going to come inside and ream him out—she had every right.

Yeah, that was it. Shaye was just gearing up for a fight with him. Nothing more.

He let out a long exhale, attempting to quell his medley of negative thoughts.

Jarrod charged toward the window and barely pulled back the curtain to look outside. "She only beat you upstairs by a few minutes. She couldn't have gotten far," Jarrod said, taking in the steadily darkening world outside. "Zoey, can you pull up the cameras, see where she went?"

Zoey clicked to the cameras that were stationed in and around the house. Her screen turned black.

*What in the actual hell?*

He walked over, closer to the tablet, hoping he was just seeing things wrong or that he wasn't understanding something correctly.

But as Zoey clicked, the screen stayed black. She started hitting buttons faster and faster in a manic race for answers.

Jarrod turned away from the window and walked toward Mindy, who was still sitting on the couch.

Mindy looked up at him, a terrified look on her face.

Jarrod put his hand on her shoulder as though he had the ability to calm her fears with just a touch.

Chad wished he had that kind of relationship with Shaye. Instead he had used her anger to manipulate her—even if he had thought it was for the greater good, he had made a mistake. He didn't deserve her. And once he found her, he would tell her exactly that and then drop down to his knees and kiss her feet and beg her forgiveness.

And he would tell her that he loved her.

Not that she would probably want to hear anything of the sort from him. She had to hate him right now.

"What is it, Zoey? What's going on?" Jarrod asked, almost as if Mindy had given him the strength to ask the question that everyone feared the answer to.

"Either there's something wrong with our connection or someone hacked our surveillance system," Zoey said, her voice strained and low. "I don't know how they could have done either. I built those firewalls myself, but something is wrong."

If she was panicking, then he should have been losing his freaking mind. And yet, Chad paused. He couldn't circle that drain. He had to take control.

"Zoey, work on getting those systems back up and running," he said. "In the meantime, Jarrod and the rest of the family will get suited up. We'll take post and make sure that no one enters the compound. I have to find Shaye."

"You can't go anywhere," Jarrod protested. "If we are under attack, you can't leave. The second you walk out those doors, you are going to have a target on your back."

"Well, then you'd better pull the trigger one sec-

ond faster." He pulled out the Glock he always wore
strapped to his ankle and made his way to the door.

He'd already gone out into the hot zone once and no
one had fired on him. Maybe he'd been lucky, or maybe
something else was going on. He had to be ready for
whatever was going to come his way.

He slowly opened the front door. A man stood outside, an automatic weapon at rest in his hands and
blood smeared down the side of his face. He wore a
STEALTH jacket, marking him as one of their guards.
He opened his mouth to talk and stepped forward, but
he stumbled and fell into the house. His eyes rolled
back in his head as he hit the floor with a loud thump.
The gun dropped on the floor beside him with a clat-
ter as the synthetic stock struck wood.

Grabbing him by the collar, Chad dragged him far
enough inside that he could close the door. He took one
more look outside but he couldn't see anyone.

"Hey, are you okay?" he asked, rolling the man over
and checking his vitals.

There was a fast, erratic thumping under Chad's fingertips. The man was alive, but he was in pain.

Chad opened up his jacket. The guard was wearing
a thick Kevlar vest—one of the older, standard-issue
vests that some in their team still preferred in case of
close-range impact.

At center mass were two copper slugs embedded
in the fabric. He opened the jacket wider, but it stuck
slightly as he pulled at the left side. There, he found a
puddle of sticky blood. At the corner of his vest, near
his armpit, the man had taken a hit.

The shock and sudden loss of blood must have sent

him to the floor. He would be okay, as long as they got him some help.

He started to tend to the wound, staunching the bleeding as he yelled for someone to call for EMS. It would take twenty minutes for them to arrive, but the man would need more help than he could provide. Looking up, Zoey was already on the phone as he spoke. The world was whirling around him, fast and slow at the same time. He watched the man's chest rise and fall, but the voices around him all seemed to be muffled and all the words were being spoken at the same time, so nothing anyone said seemed to be audible.

"Hector," Zoey said, her voice finally breaking through the fog in Chad's head. "What happened?"

The man blinked, like he, too, was pulled back by her voice. "Gray Wolves. They ambushed us..." His voice was thin as he struggled to remain conscious.

"How many men do we have left?" Zoey asked.

Hector shook his head. "Lost radio contact—nothing is working. No phones. Nothing." Hector wheezed, the sound wet and rattling.

Chad wouldn't have been surprised if the man's lung had collapsed in his chest. They had to get him help.

"They must have bumped an electromagnetic pulse." Zoey balled her hands into tight fists. "The goddamn bastards. It's probably why everything stopped working."

Though he should have cared about the electromagnetic pulse that rendered their tech outside the Faraday-style walls of the house virtually dead, all he could think about was Shaye. "Did you see her? Is she okay?"

"Huh?" Hector asked, his eyes ablaze with pain.

"Shaye, did you see her leave?"

The man looked away from him, like he couldn't handle the shame. "She…"

"She what?" Chad's blood turned to thick syrup in his veins. He could have died from panic in those nanoseconds while he waited for Hector's answer.

"She was taken by the man who shot me." Hector coughed, blood spatter flecking his lips as he rolled on his uninjured side. "She is probably already dead. In the car." He pointed feebly toward the door.

*No*, his mind screamed. *No. She wasn't dead. The man was wrong. She was alive. He could feel her.*

"Her car?" Chad shot up to his feet.

Hector nodded.

He hadn't seen her when he had gone outside. There had been no movement. No sound. No sign of life.

He had nearly forgotten, but he was still holding his gun. It trembled in his hand as he looked down at the cold, black steel of its barrel. He wasn't sure if he was trembling out of terror or rage, or perhaps it could have even been merely adrenaline, but he had to get control. If he was going to walk out there—into what could have very well have been a shooting gallery— he was going to need every one of his faculties. He stuffed his handgun back into his ankle holster, clicking it in place.

He kneeled down by Hector and picked up the man's assault rifle. He checked the clip—it was nearly full. He grabbed the unused, full magazine clipped to Hector's utility belt.

Those bastards were going to pay.

Zoey touched his arm as he stood. "Find her, Chad. Find the woman you love. Save her if you can. We've got your back." She pulled her gun from her holster and stood up, every bit the badass he had always known his sister to be.

Trevor came up from the basement carrying assault rifles, always prepared, and he gave one to Jarrod. "You're not going out there alone—Martins stick together." He slammed a magazine into his gun and jacked a round into the chamber.

Together, they were unstoppable.

No matter how many Gray Wolves were out there, he and his family held the higher ground. If they were careful and did this right, they could pick off their enemies like they were prairie dogs.

Even Mindy, who normally stayed well out of the fray, took a gun. "I'll cover you guys." She moved beside the door.

He and Trevor got into formation, readying themselves to charge the door and make their way outside.

The odds were not in their favor to make it out of this.

Trevor gave him a grave look that told him that he knew what was at risk and was more than willing to do what needed to be done. Protection was a hard business, but there was nothing better than going out in a blaze of glory and honor.

If giving his life for hers was what he had to do, Chad would gladly make the sacrifice.

He gave Trevor a small nod. They would have to move fast but smooth. The old adage "slow is smooth, smooth is fast" came to mind.

Walking out into a possible active-shooter event was ballsy, and if Shaye wasn't out there, he wouldn't have risked it. Going outside and into the field of fire was setting them up for an ambush. But he had to do what needed to be done and be dynamic.

"Do you have a smoke grenade?" he asked, pointing at Trevor's utility belt.

Trevor answered with a wicked smile and pulled out the canister. There were two more on his belt and he tossed one to Chad, who stuffed it in his pocket. Trevor pulled the pin and chucked the smoke grenade out the door, letting the can land with a clang and roll. It exploded in a burst of light and green smoke.

*Perfect.*

He charged out the door and toward the car, using the smoke for coverage in the uncleared area.

He could hear the cracking and whizzing of shots fired and bullets striking the ground near him. But he didn't fire back.

*No.*

They needed all of the anonymity that the smoke could provide. If he shot recklessly now, they would only help their enemies pinpoint his location in the smoke. It was better to play the shadow.

Though the car was about twenty yards from the front door, it seemed like it was miles away. There was another barrage of shooting, but instead of instilling fear in him, it was like all of his senses came to life. He could smell the acrid smoke of the obscurant, and hear the crunch of the gravel and snow under his feet as he took steps toward the woman he loved. A bit of saliva collected in his mouth and he swallowed it back. Everything had to be under control. He gripped the gun tighter as he carefully held his ready position and stalked deeper into the smoke.

*She was alive. She had to be alive.* He repeated the

words over and over to himself, trying to control his only real fear.

Trevor moved one step behind him, readying for anyone who approached from their nine or at their six. He could think of no better person to have at his side.

A bullet ripped through the air right in front of his face, so close that he could nearly make out the vortex the bullet had created in the smoke as it pierced the veil. He stopped for a moment, collecting himself. That single shot, two inches to the left, could've been the end of him.

He shook away the thought. Now wasn't the time to think about what-ifs. He would have plenty of time afterward.

Though it was not even above freezing outside, a tiny bit of sweat rolled down from his hairline over his temple, and he wiped it away.

He couldn't let the situation get out of hand, or get to him. He had spent thousands of hours training for this, but the only other operation that had felt like this was the day that Trish had died. The thought unnerved him.

*No. Don't go there.*

He took another step, calm and deliberate and in control. He was the master of his fate. And Shaye's life depended on him.

He moved forward until the magenta car came into view. Shaye was nowhere in sight. His stomach dropped. What if she wasn't out here? What if they had put themselves in danger for nothing?

*Control.* He had to remain controlled, deliberate.

He reached down and opened the driver-side door. Thankfully it was unlocked. Glancing inside, he could see Shaye lying in the back seat. She was hog-tied and there was black Gorilla tape over her mouth, its edges rolled slightly and her face reddened like she had been trying to rub off the tape.

*That was his girl. Always the fighter.*

As he looked in on her, she opened her eyes. He could see relief as she looked up.

"I'm here, babe. I've got you—you're safe now." He left the driver-side door open, hoping it would provide him an extra layer of protection from any rounds coming his way.

He motioned for Trevor to take cover in the car, as he stepped to the back door and opened it up. She tried to sit up, but the way she had been tied stopped any major movement.

Whoever had tied her up like this, whoever had done this to her, would pay. He pulled out a knife and cut the ropes at her wrists and ankles in two swift motions. She sat up and ripped the tape from her face with a tiny, pained squeak.

Aside from where the rope and tape had rubbed her skin raw, she looked no worse for the wear. At least whoever had taken her hadn't seemed to have done any physical harm. The simple courtesy may have just saved these men from dying a slow and painful death, but if Chad had his way they would still die.

"Mother hummer," she said, rubbing the place where the tape had taken off part of her skin. But she didn't let the pain slow her down. Instead, she looked at him. "I need a gun."

He handed her his handgun out of his ankle holster. "How many men are out there—do you know?"

"I just saw two, and it sounded like they were working for my father."

He frowned. They had come to believe that these men were all sent here by Bayural, and part of the Gray Wolves. Was her father somehow involved? Was he missing some vital clue? He felt like something was staring him right in the face, but yet he couldn't figure out what it was. And what did the woman and the child have to do with it all?

"But they were Gray Wolves, yes?" he asked.

She shrugged, making sure that there was a round in the chamber of the gun as she moved to step out of the car.

The wind kicked up and the smoke that hung in the air from the grenade started to dissipate. From where he stood, Chad could make out the outline of a man about ten yards to his right. He aimed at the man's center mass and fired twice. No hesitation, no regret.

The rounds struck and the man touched his chest where the bullet had entered as though surprised a bullet had found him. Shockingly, the man smiled. When he didn't drop to his knees, Chad realized he must have been wearing a vest.

*Son of a...*

Whoever was out there, they definitely weren't rookies. Their enemies knew what they were about. And this was one fight that would be hard-won. He pulled off another shot, this time taking an extra moment to carefully aim at the man's head.

His shot rang true. This time the man dropped.

*One down. Who knew how many to go.*

First things first—they needed better coverage than this car could provide.

He pulled the smoke grenade out from his pocket and threw it in the direction of the house. It popped and a new cloud erupted into the air, providing them with a much-needed screen.

"Trevor, watch our six," Chad ordered.

Trevor answered with a simple nod. They moved together in a staggered line toward the safety the house and their family could provide.

It seemed even longer going back. The gunfire pinged around them, but thankfully the rounds seemed to be behind them as they moved. One lucky shot would be all it would take for them to ruin all of Chad's hopes and dreams.

He couldn't let Shaye get hurt. But at the same time, he couldn't simply put his arm over her and escort her through the smoke like she was some kind of victim. Shaye was never a victim. She had been through more than her fair share of crap in her life, but she would always be a strong, capable survivor. She was unflappable.

In fact, maybe if everything worked out, he could start training her for a role in STEALTH. They could always use another skilled team member.

As he spotted the front of the steps leading up toward the house, the gunfire around them exploded with a new wave of intensity.

Shaye squeaked from behind him, the noise almost like the one she had made when she had ripped the tape off her mouth. He stopped and turned. His gaze dropped to the ground near his feet. Shaye was down, clutching her abdomen with one hand and holding the gun with the other. She aimed to their right and started firing wildly, forcing Chad and Trevor to drop to the ground beside her.

"Are you okay?" he asked, reaching over to her and

rolling her slightly so he could see what she was covering with her hands.

She looked up at him with wide eyes and a pained and terrified expression. Blood was seeping through her fingers as they were clamped to her belly.

*Damn. Damn. Damn. He had done this to her. If only he would have kept his damn mouth shut...not pushed her away.*

"You're going to be okay. Let me look at it," he ordered.

They only had a minute or so and then the smoke around them would start to thin and they would be at their enemy's mercy. He had to work fast to get her into the safety of the house or they would all be dead.

Trevor crawled to them. "We have to go!"

He didn't need to state the obvious.

Shaye wouldn't move her hands, so instead of forcing her to do anything she didn't feel comfortable doing, he leaned in. "I'm going to lift you, okay?"

She gave him a small nod.

Wrapping his arms around her, he lifted her up and got to his feet. She bit back a breath and he could feel her tense in his arms. Trevor covered them, sending out a spray of gunfire toward their enemies as they rushed up the steps and into the house, Mindy slamming the door behind them.

He would never forgive himself if she died. Hell, he was never going to forgive himself, period.

He ran to the couch and gently laid down Shaye. "She was hit," he said, his words sounding strangled.

"Watch out," Zoey said, moving to help her. She touched Shaye's hands, giving her a soft look. "It's going to be okay, Shaye. We have everything we need to keep you alive."

Shaye nodded, but there was fear in her eyes. When she looked at him, he wanted to tell her that he was sorry. That he had been wrong. That he'd been stupid. And yet, all he could do was smile at her.

"Shaye, no matter what happens, I want you to know I love you," he said, taking her hand.

Her eyes brimmed with tears. "I love you, too."

If he had the chance, he would spend the rest of his life apologizing, but for now all he could do was pray that she would come out of this alive.

*Chapter Eighteen*

There was a ping and crackle of glass as a bullet struck the front bay window. Shaye turned to look. Mindy stood beside the door, keeping guard. The window beside her had a circular hit, and a conical smattering of cracks where the round had hit—but not penetrated—what must have been bulletproof glass.

Zoey had done well picking this place.

It was strange for Shaye to be thinking about such things at a time like this, when she knew she had taken a bullet to the gut and was likely going to die a slow and painful death. Time had seemed to slow down. Every second was one she got to spend with the man holding her hand and standing at her side—the man who had told her that he loved her.

There were many things she had thought Chad would say to her when he had looked down on her, but confessing his love was the furthest thing from her mind. He had taken her by surprise, but she was glad he had said his piece.

If she was only going to live a few more hours or days, she wanted to spend her last moments with him. If that wasn't love, she didn't know what was.

Zoey gave her a soft, supplicating smile. "You're

going to be okay, but I need to take a look at what you got going on here. Okay?"

She nodded, wanting to close her eyes and save herself the horror of seeing the hole in her belly and the blood dripping down her skin. It was already touch-and-go whether or not she would go into shock. But if she was going to go out, she was going to go out knowing what was in store for her.

Zoey lifted her black T-shirt gently, the fabric tugging on her skin as she pulled it up. Blood oozed from her stomach and as Zoey dabbed away the blood, a swollen black bruise was already rising on her skin. As Zoey inspected the wound, she smiled. "It's a flesh wound." Zoey looked up at her, her smile widening. "I bet you're glad you both took a break and put on the bulletproof gear."

Shaye inspected the wound. As she touched the bruised skin around the angry red circular mark, she winced with pain, but Zoey was right. She pulled the skin back a bit—there were definitely some lacerations, and she was going to be sore for a week or so, but she was going to be fine.

The bastards had failed to take her down.

She looked up at the normally calm and emotionally repressed Chad. Tears were streaming unchecked down his face. Though she didn't know whether they were from fear or relief, she didn't care. She was simply grateful that he was here, in her life, and they were together.

There was another ping and crackle as a second bullet struck the front window.

She pulled down her shirt and took in a pained breath as she moved to sitting. There was no way she could run around and fight without being in agony, but she wasn't going to be some broken woman that the Martins would have to treat like an invalid. She had to do her part to fight their enemies—enemies that she may well have brought to their gate. But first she needed to be there for the man who was here for her.

She got to her feet, wrapping her arms around Chad. "It's all okay. I'm fine," she said, gently hugging him. "Don't cry."

He rubbed the back of his hand over his cheeks, wiping away his tears even as others took their place. "I'm so sorry, Shaye. I shouldn't have—"

She silenced him with a finger to his lips. "I shouldn't have run off. If you love me like you say you do, make me a promise?"

He nodded.

"Please don't hurt me. I've already been hurt enough."

His tears moved faster and harder down his cheeks as he leaned in and took her lips with his, a promise sealed. It didn't matter to her that they were standing in front of his family or that there were active gunmen outside. In this short moment, all that mattered was he was giving her the world.

"Yes," he said, his breath against her lips. "But only if you make me a promise in return."

She nodded, no idea what he was going to ask of her, and it made her unexpectedly nervous.

"Shaye, if we get out of this alive, and it doesn't have to be right away or anything, but I want you to marry me. Sound like a plan?"

She couldn't help but laugh. "That is one a heck of a way to ask a girl to marry you. *Sound like a plan*," she said in a deep, mocking voice.

"I know it's not much of a way to ask a princess for her hand, but you get what you see with me. I'm going to love you until the sun doesn't rise in the sky. No matter what comes, or doesn't come, I'm going to fight for you." He wrapped his arm tighter around her waist, drawing her closer against him.

She could have swooned in his arms, and for a moment the pain that was wracking her body disappeared.

"First, I'm far from a princess. And second, you and your proposal are absolutely perfect. I wouldn't change you for the world," she said, putting her hand on his chest just over his heart, which was beating wildly. "I want you with all your imperfections. I like to think our imperfections are what make us suited for each other."

"So we have a plan?" he asked with joy in his voice as the tears on his cheeks finally began to slow.

"Yes. A thousand times or a thousand ways or in a thousand languages, yes." The air left her lungs as he took her lips with his. The kiss was powerful and unrelenting as his tongue moved against her bottom lip. She met it with her own, tasting the bitterness of fear mixed with the sweetness of safety.

She, without a single regret or second thought, whole-heartedly and without reservation, loved this man.

Trevor cleared his throat, pulling them both back to attention.

As wonderful as this was, and though she wanted to spend the rest of her life kissing those lips and feeling the warmth of his breath on her skin, their fight was far from over.

She pulled back from his arms, her body protesting the loss of his touch.

Her gun was sitting on the floor, its grip covered with her bloody fingerprints. Picking up the weapon, she knew exactly what she had to do.

"Get ready," she said, looking over her shoulder at the rest of the group and the wounded man that was resting on the other couch. "This is about to get crazy."

She moved toward the door, ready to take down all the men outside, but Chad gently took her by the arm, stopping her in midstride. "Soon-to-be Mrs. Martin, where do you think you're going?"

She nudged her chin in the direction of the door. "I'm about to go kill some dudes," she said, but even as the words came out she felt silly. This wasn't her. She was resilient and strong, but she had already fallen victim to their enemies once.

Chad gave her a serious look and shook his head. "I have absolutely no doubt that you could go out there and screw some people up, but we have to be smart about this. We can't go out guns blazing—you can see how well that worked the last time," he said, motioning to her stomach. "And no matter what, I'm not going to put you in a position in which you could get hurt. No way, no matter how badass you think you are."

Her back softened and she lowered the gun in her hands slightly. As she opened her mouth to speak, there was a low hum and then a familiar *thump, thump, thump.* The sound reminded her of a dog thumping its leg against the floor as it gave itself a good scratch.

She knew that sound, but she couldn't quite put her finger on what was making it.

Zoey rushed toward the window and looked up at the sky. A bullet pinged against the glass. "There's a helicopter."

Shaye ran over, hoping against all hope that it wasn't red and embellished with the Algerian flag.

*No. He wouldn't have come this far for her. He would send men, but he would never come himself.*

A blue helicopter moved straight down, landing on the lawn near the driveway. She didn't recognize the man sitting behind the pilot, but her father sat on the other side of the stranger and beside him was the woman from the video—the woman who had dropped off the baby on their doorstep.

Holy shit... They were all working together.

The baby. Little Peanut. The woman had used a child to manipulate and slow them down. Who would have ever thought of using a child in such a brutal, compassionless way?

*Those bastards.*

Her father looked in Shaye's direction and their eyes met.

*What was he doing here?*

She was tempted to be relieved that her father was here. Perhaps she could negotiate some sort of treaty with him for both her and the Martins' safety. And yet she knew that her father would never go for such a thing. He was only there to snatch her and enslave her once again. No matter where she went, or whom she married, she would always be her father's slave. The only way she was going to get out from underneath his thumb would be either her death or his, and she preferred the latter.

"Who's that?" she asked, pointing at the man with her father.

Zoey glared at the man as Chad put his hand on Shaye's lower back and peered out the window.

"That is Fenrisulfr Bayural, the leader of the Gray Wolves." Chad's voice was thick with loathing. "He is the man responsible for Trish's death. I see he's made new allies."

A wave of sickness came over her as she stared at her father, the woman and Chad's enemy together. The leader of the Gray Wolves gave a malicious laugh, no doubt chuckling about how close they were to annihilating the people she loved... And maybe even her.

She stared out at Bayural. He had a wide face and an even wider nose and he reminded her a bit of a Turkish Benecio del Toro. He had the squished expression of a man who was on the verge of seeing his dreams come to fruition. Though there was little physical resemblance between him and her father—the same look of power and malice in their eyes that made them nearly twins.

Zoey hurried from the window and grabbed a house phone Shaye hadn't even noticed. It clinked against its cradle as Zoey lifted it and tapped on the numbers. She looked at them and then walked toward the kitchen.

"What is she doing?" Shaye asked, terrified at the prospect of losing more capable hands, hands that could make the difference in a firefight between life and death.

Chad shrugged. "I have no idea."

"What are we gonna do?" she said, lowering the gun until it brushed against the tops of her thighs. As she looked at Chad, she could tell that he was champing at the bit to get his hands on the man responsible for Trish's death. And yet, it wasn't feasible to leave the building. It was the only place they were guaranteed safety.

The man stepped out of the helicopter and readjusted the tie at his neck, almost as if he was going to business meeting and not here to put an end to an entire family. Her father and the woman remained in the chopper. Her father was no doubt hesitant to get his hands dirtied by coming within a foot of an active shooting situation.

She could make out the sounds of Zoey shouting what sounded like coordinates from within the kitchen.

But why?

Trevor stood beside Chad. "What do you think he's doing here?" he asked, motioning toward Bayural.

Chad shook his head. "Bayural has been chasing us for nearly a year. No doubt he knows he has us cornered and now he wants to watch the execution for himself. And Shaye's father... Well, he probably wants his daughter back." He reached down and took the gun from Shaye's hands. "But we're not going down without a fight."

She was glad to be free of the weight of the thing, but its absence made her feel vulnerable.

Zoey jogged out of the kitchen, the phone still in her hand. "Don't do anything. And get down!"

As she said the words, there was an ear-piercing boom from the skies above. And then a high-pitched whistle.

The world shuddered around them, and the roar of an explosion echoed through the room. She threw her arms over her head as she hit the floor. She heard the crash of glass and the scream of steel warping and bending against its will from the explosive power that had struck it.

No doubt, anyone outside the house and near the helicopter had been wiped out.

She dared to look out from underneath her arms. Chad was lying on the floor beside her, staring at her like a watchful partner. "You okay? How is your stomach? And your head?" He reached over and touched her temple, seemingly worried about the percussive force from the blast.

"I'm fine," she said, feeling like a broken record in her constant reassurance of her tenuous welfare.

The dust began to settle around them, coating Chad's dark hair with fine white powder.

After a moment, he got up and brushed himself off and offered her his hand. They walked to the window— the glass was missing and was lying on the floor, still in one piece but shattered. A fighter jet twisted in the skies overhead, celebrating their victory.

The rest of the family moved beside them as they looked out at the dusty scene in front of them. They held their guns at the ready, a show of power if she had ever seen one.

"Thank goodness for friends in high places," Zoey said, pointing at the sky with a satisfied smile.

"Who did you call?" Chad asked.

Zoey gave them a wide smile. "You're not the only one with an amazing fiancée. Sabrina has made a hell of a lot of friends in high places within the Pentagon. And as it turns out, the US government hated Bayural almost as much as we did. They were more than happy to use the coordinates we provided so they could take out such a high-value target."

Chad wrapped his arms around Shaye's body, pulling her into his embrace like he was her shield.

Shaye choked back the lump that had formed in her throat the moment she had seen her father. Where the helicopter had been, there was nothing more than a shallow pit. Scraps of burned metal and shrapnel littered the ground.

The cars that had been parked in the driveway were warped and blackened. The hood of her rental sat on the ground almost a hundred feet behind the car's body.

"I hope you got the insurance," Chad said, motioning toward her car.

She was glad he had said nothing of her father. She never wanted to talk or think about that despicable man again.

She couldn't help the dry laugh that escaped her. "I'll write them a check."

The family around her broke into stressed laughter as they watched for any signs of movement outside, but the world around them remained as still as a grave.

# *Epilogue*

The next day, snow had fallen on the ground, covering the mess that her father and Bayural had left in their stead. Though Shaye knew she should harbor some sort of grief for her late father, she felt only relief.

In fact, she had never been happier, especially when they left the cabin where her father had tracked them down.

Shaye sat on the couch, the sound of Christmas songs filling the air. Currently it was one of her lesser favorites—"Santa Claus Is Comin' to Town." It was nice, but she had always loved "Silent Night," even more so in the last few hours when all was calm and all was bright.

There was a knock on the front door. Chad walked over and opened it. Standing on the other side were Wyatt and Gwen, who was carrying the baby.

Thank goodness Chad had the foresight to make sure the little one remained safe. She couldn't even bear to imagine what would have happened if they had kept the baby and put him in harm's way.

She already felt guilty enough as it was.

"Merry Christmas," Wyatt said, reaching beside the door and picking up a wreath he had propped against the door frame. He handed it over to Chad as they made their way inside. "We know you probably haven't even thought about the holidays with everything going on, but we wanted to invite you all over to celebrate with us at Dunrovin in the next few weeks."

"And we'd like all of you," Gwen added, looking over at Shaye, "and your significant others." She sent her a smile. "I hear that congratulations are in order."

Shaye blushed. "Yes, I'm going to use my mother's ring. The one her mother gave her."

"That's perfect," Gwen said, her smile growing impossibly larger.

"I'm having it resized but I'll have to show it to you when I get it back—it should be here before Christmas. It's beautiful. It's a Harry Winston with a platinum band and a diamond at its center."

"I'm sure it's breathtaking," Gwen said, readjusting the baby high on her hip. "And I take it that you will be coming for Christmas then?"

"We'd love to," Chad said, looking around at his brothers and Zoey as they nodded in agreement.

"Anything we can bring?" Trevor asked.

"Just yourselves, and that ring," Gwen said, giving her a private wink. "Mrs. Fitzgerald always goes over the top. Be prepared for lots of bows and wrapping paper. Oh, and that tree, at night when the light hits the gold…" Gwen sighed as the baby squirmed in her arms.

Shaye walked over and lifted back the hood on the baby's coat—a coat he hadn't had when they had given the boy to Wyatt. He smiled, but tucked his body in the safety of Gwen's body. "What a happy boy. Thank you so much for taking him," Shaye said, making funny faces at the baby, who giggled as she made googly eyes.

"It was our pleasure," Gwen said, walking into the living room and setting down a brand-new diaper bag on the floor.

"Oh, hey…we have a diaper bag the woman dropped off." Shaye snapped her fingers as she remembered the boy's diaper bag.

As she went to grab it, Wyatt turned to Chad. "About the men you'd been keeping as hostages—we have locked them up and charged them with obstruction of justice, attempted homicide and a litany of other things. They shouldn't be seeing anything but cell bars for the rest of their lives."

Shaye let out a breath she hadn't known she was holding. Glancing back at the family, she took in the sight of them all together—one unit, one powerful force.

"And as for the event that occurred at the cabin last night," Wyatt continued, "news sources are calling it a gas explosion. It was lucky you all weren't there," he said, giving them all a look that spoke of his lie—a lie he provided in order to protect his family. "However, there were some out-of-towners who were killed… looks like it was a hideout of some sort for a terrorist group out of Turkey. Who knew, am I right?" Wyatt looked over at her and gave her an apologetic nod. "And there were also reports that there was a foreign dignitary, a guy from Algeria, on site. They are saying that he was involved in some manner of corruption."

"I have to say, it's always a positive when corrupt officials are taken care of," Zoey said, giving him a salty smile. "Thank you, Wyatt. I know this wasn't an easy mess to clean up—or an easy choice to make to help us."

"After you filled me in on the truth, making the choice to help my extended family wasn't hard at all— it was the right thing to do. However, what *was* messy was trying to explain away a military jet flyover." He smirked. "We even got reports that there were UFOs or bombs. There was all kind of crazy talk." He waved it off.

Shaye grabbed the bag that sat at the top of the stairs and took it into the living room. Opening it up, she pulled out its contents. "We have some diapers, a few clothes and an empty bottle." She turned over the diaper bag and dumped everything out so they could take a quick inventory.

However, as she gripped the bag, her fingers pressed against something hard and lumpy on the bottom of the bag. She let go to reveal a patch. It blended almost seamlessly with the bag, but as Shaye picked and pulled at the stitches at its edges, the patch gave way. She pulled off the patch and there, sitting on the bottom of the bag, was a small black plastic thing that looked a bit like a thumb drive. "What is this?"

Zoey walked over and took it out of her hand. She lifted it up, squinting as she tried to read something that was inscribed on the plastic. "Holy…they used our own gear against us. Bayural was one son of a…" Zoey looked at the baby and stopped before swearing. "This is one of our GPS trackers. We have them implanted in the guns that we sell to terrorist groups. It's how we were supposed to find the Gray Wolves. Not the other way around." She paused. "Those bastards used the baby like a goddamn Trojan Horse. And that goddamn woman…she never deserved to be a mother. At least he has us now, and a family who will love him." Zoey's voice cracked with emotion.

Zoey was right. Some people didn't deserve to have children. Children were meant to be loved, cherished and protected—not thrown into the middle of a war zone.

Shaye shook her head as she stared at the tracker.

A thought sprang to the front of her mind and she tried hard to control her smile. She hadn't been the one to bring their enemies upon them. She had merely been a part of a giant puzzle. Chad wrapped his arms around her waist and hugged her against his body.

"I told you so," he whispered into her ear. "I told you that none of this was your fault."

She smiled up at him and bumped against him with her butt playfully. "I'm relieved. But has anyone ever told you that no one ever likes to hear 'I told you so'?"

One of his eyebrows shot up. "Well, hello, Ms. Snark."

She giggled. "No, you pronounce it Mrs. Martin."

Chad laughed, the sound throaty and rich. He leaned down and gave her a soft kiss on her neck.

Wyatt cleared his throat. "Speaking of children, the baby was part of the reason we wanted to come here today. If you are okay with it, we were hoping that we could adopt him."

"You want to adopt Peanut?" Chad asked, surprised.

Wyatt nodded. "And actually, we've started calling him Peter for short."

Chad chuckled. "You gave him a *real* name. I like it." He turned to face her. "This sounds like a good idea to me—what do you think?"

Her heart lurched in her chest. Though she wanted

nothing more than to take the baby and give him a home, she wasn't in a position to provide for him as well as Gwen and Wyatt. They were married, had a home, family, stability. So much had happened in her life recently that Shaye held no doubt that she would need time to get herself back in order…even with Chad's help.

She nodded through the pain. "I think it would be best. But I would love to be Peter's auntie, and Chad his uncle."

Chad walked over and put his hand in hers. He lifted their entwined hands and gave hers a soft, loving kiss. He must have known how hard the choice was, and from the pained but happy expression on his features, he was feeling the same.

But they had to do what was best for the baby.

Love was sacrifice, and true love was agony.

It was agony that had brought them together. Agony and grief had cemented their friendship, which then became something so wonderful that for years to come, each time she looked over at him, he would take her breath away.

\* \* \* \* \*

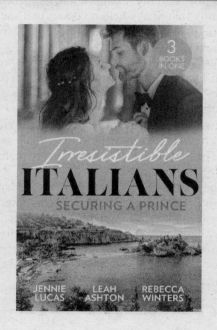

# MILLS & BOON
## MODERN
# Power and Passion

Prepare to be swept off your feet by sophisticated, sexy and seductive heroes, in some of the world's most glamourous and romantic locations, where power and passion collide.

# MILLS & BOON

## THE HEART OF ROMANCE

---

## A ROMANCE FOR EVERY READER

---

**MODERN**

Prepare to be swept off your feet by sophisticated, sexy and seductive heroes, in some of the world's most glamourous and romantic locations, where power and passion collide.

**HISTORICAL**

Escape with historical heroes from time gone by. Whether your passion is for wicked Regency Rakes, muscled Vikings or rugged Highlanders, awak the romance of the past.

**MEDICAL**

Set your pulse racing with dedicated, delectable doctors in the high-pressure world of medicine, where emotions run high and passion, comfort a love are the best medicine.

*True Love*

Celebrate true love with tender stories of heartfelt romance, from the rush of falling in love to the joy a new baby can bring, and a focus on th emotional heart of a relationship.

*Desire*

Indulge in secrets and scandal, intense drama and plenty of sizzling hot action with powerful and passionate heroes who have it all: wealth, statu good looks…everything but the right woman.

**HEROES**

Experience all the excitement of a gripping thriller, with an intense romance at its heart. Resourceful, true-to-life women and strong, fearless face danger and desire - a killer combination!

---

To see which titles are coming soon, please visit

**millsandboon.co.uk/nextmonth**

# JOIN US ON SOCIAL MEDIA!

Stay up to date with our latest releases, author news and gossip, special offers and discounts, and all the behind-the-scenes action from Mills & Boon...

 @millsandboon

 @millsandboonuk

 facebook.com/millsandboon

 @millsandboonuk

*It might just be true love...*

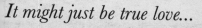

# MILLS & BOON
*Desire*

Indulge in secrets and scandal, intense drama and plenty of sizzling hot action with powerful and passionate heroes who have it all: wealth, status, good looks…everything but the right woman.

# GET YOUR ROMANCE FIX!

Get the latest romance news,
exclusive author interviews, story
extracts and much more!